Crown of Thorns

SIGMUND

CROWN
OF
THORNS

A
NICK BARRETT
MYSTERY

BROUWER

Tyndale House Publishers, Inc.
CAROL STREAM, ILLINOIS

Visit Tyndale's exciting Web site at www.tyndale.com

TYNDALE is a registered trademark of Tyndale House Publishers, Inc.

Tyndale's quill logo is a trademark of Tyndale House Publishers, Inc.

Learn more about Sigmund Brouwer at www.coolreading.com

Crown of Thorns

Scripture quotations are taken from the *Holy Bible,* King James Version.

Edited by Curtis H. C. Lundgren

Designed by Joseph Sapulich

ISBN-13: 978-1-4143-0888-3
ISBN-10: 1-4143-0888-4

Printed in the United States of America

11 10 09 08 07 06 05
9   8   7   6   5   4   3   2   1

To Cindy
my true love

✛

Blessed are the poor in spirit:
for theirs is the kingdom
of heaven.

Blessed are they that mourn:
for they shall be comforted.

Blessed are the meek: for they
shall inherit the earth.

Blessed are they which do
hunger and thirst after
righteousness: for they shall
be filled.

Blessed are the merciful: for
they shall obtain mercy.

Blessed are the pure in heart:
for they shall see God.

Blessed are the peacemakers:
for they shall be called the
children of God.

Blessed are they which are
persecuted for righteousness'
sake: for theirs is the kingdom
of heaven.

Blessed are ye, when men shall
revile you, and persecute you,
and shall say all manner of evil
against you falsely, for my sake.

Rejoice, and be exceeding glad:
for great is your reward in
heaven . . .

Matthew 5:3-12,
KING JAMES VERSION

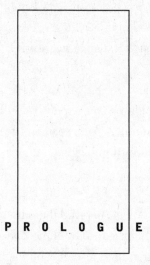

P R O L O G U E

With her feet barely touching the ground, Angel sat on a weather-faded granite headstone in the corner of the cemetery. A ghostly white full moon—so appropriate for the nearby activity—was bright enough to cast crisp tiny shadows in the lettering of some of the newly engraved headstones beside her.

Two large black men, cajoled from a bar just before closing time, were shoveling aside the heavy soft dirt of a Charleston graveyard.

"This gives me the creepie-crawlies, I ain't afraid to tell you." The man on the left paused, fully sober now. His sleeves were rolled up and, in daylight, Angel would have seen rough prison tattoos beneath a sheen of sweat on his powerful fore-arms. "I couldn't hardly dare walk through here in daylight, let alone—"

"Keep digging, man," his partner replied. He pointed his shovel at the coffin beside them. "You don't want to go how this one did. Messing with Grammie Zora is a quick one-way trip into the ground. She ain't the queen of voodoo for nothing."

The first speaker shivered, although the night was warm. "Wonder how it was the spell got 'im."

"I don't know. I don't wanna know. And if you was wise, you wouldn't wanna know either. Could be some spells rub off from one person to the next. And Grammie Zora, she casts a powerful spell. Which is the plain reason I'm digging and not asking questions."

"I'm diggin'. I'm diggin'."

From her nearby vantage point, Angel surveyed them in silence, well aware of the potency of their fears. Grammie Zora did indeed have great power. An hour earlier, just after midnight, Angel had visited one of Grammie's longtime clients, a mortician who showed up at least once every six months to request a curse be placed on his competition. On the mortician's doorstep, Angel had delivered Grammie's request, and the mortician had not hesitated to load an empty coffin into his hearse and drive through the dark city streets to pick up a sheet-wrapped body lying in the unkempt grass behind Grammie Zora's house.

"There won't be no questions about this," Angel had promised the mortician, who had immediately begun to tremble at the sight of the eerily still recipient of one of Grammie's blackest spells. It wasn't the still body that gave him fear; he earned his family's bread by dealing with dead bodies. It was Grammie Zora's power over the supernatural, shown so plainly in this world by her effect on this victim.

Angel had watched the mortician nervously rub one hand against the other and had continued to speak quietly. *"Grammie Zora's already on a bus going far away,"* she had told him, *"just in*

case police ever want to ask any questions. And she'll be gone a
while. But Grammie Zora said there won't be no questions. You can
bet on that. Grammie Zora says she'll place some blessings on those
who help, but those who don't, they might just end up wrapped in a
sheet just like this. And besides, Grammie Zora says no one is going
to come looking for this body because she promises no one is going
to report this dead person missing because it was all part of the
spell and you don't want to mess with that kind of power."

She'd helped him lift the wrapped body into the cheap coffin,
and the mortician had taken the coffin to a nearby cemetery, one
that held countless bodies of the poor and the black, bodies cared
about only by other poor and black. Those in power, the rich and
the white, gave this corner of Charleston little attention and even
if they did, it was a place that the mortician knew held such sloppy
administration records that no one would ever know that this new
plot hadn't been registered. As Angel had told the mortician in her
matter-of-fact and mature-beyond-her-years voice, the best place
to hide a marble was in a bagful of other marbles.

If Grammie Zora's power had worked on the mortician
through Angel, then this same power had in turn worked on the
gravediggers through the mortician. Even though he'd picked
them up at their favorite bar on a payday night. Even though the
furtive burial meant they'd been forced to use shovels to dig
instead of a backhoe.

So it was that Angel now supervised the two gravediggers,
the mortician and his hearse long gone.

At 5 A.M., the gravediggers finished the hole. Not as deep as
it should have been, but with daylight approaching, deep enough.
The men lowered the coffin without ceremony and began to pile
dirt on the coffin.

"Never knew dirt could be so loud," one said to the other, as the clumps echoed on the top of the coffin. "It's enough to wake up the dead."

"The dead don't wake." The reply was so quick and savage that the first gravedigger understood his partner's unspoken words. *Finish the job, man, and don't look back.*

Just before dawn, they were on their knees, carefully replacing the sod. The buried body was now safely hidden among all the others gone to their eternal sleep. When the gravediggers stood, Angel pushed herself off the headstone that had served as her chair during her patient vigil. Hands on her hips, she faced them, a small girl almost twelve years old.

"Grammie Zora thanks you for this," Angel said. "Someday, when you need a favor, all you need to do is ask. If she ain't back yet from where she's gone, don't worry none. Just ask me. I'll make sure she gets the message. She'll treat you fine. I can promise you that. Just fine."

Angel paused. "Unless, of course, you tell anyone about this night. Then there will be a couple of others burying you, same way you buried this one. You understand that, don't you?"

"Yes ma'am," they both said as if they were speaking to Grammie Zora herself. One, unaware of the irony of pitting one faith against another, made the feeble effort of crossing himself as he'd seen priests do on television. "Yes ma'am, indeed."

C H A P T E R

1

As a child, I knew well the greatest tragedy of the Larrabee
family, for many around me were happy to openly speculate on
its delicious horror. This was the tale of the thunder-filled night
that young Timothy Larrabee delivered a potion of death to his
grandmother.

Indeed, most of Charleston's proper families are haunted by
the tales of eccentricity and madness and scandal and deviances
of previous generations, tales flaunted with proud defiance in the
way that the once rich will cling to ancient and fading silks even
as they are reduced to begging. These tales circulate among the
other proper families, so that all of us among the self-crowned
aristocracy of fourth-, fifth-, and sixth-generation Charlestonians
each know the shrouded heritage of the others.

The legacy of the Larrabee family was no different, as its
members could count among their ancestors the regular assort-
ment of rogues and idiots, ranging from pirates and slave traders to

cowards and heroes of the war of Northern aggression, imposed upon the South by Lincoln.

But it was Timothy Larrabee who achieved the most notoriety among all the scandals in the two-hundred-year recorded history of the Larrabee family. This story was not even a generation old at the time of my childhood, so it was treated as recent gossip, and it was not difficult for me to imagine how it happened.

He was only ten the night it occurred, slender and constantly aware of his grooming in clothing and heritage, and had already learned to carry himself with great elegance and to speak with perfect clarity, as if constantly and consciously rehearsing a style of delivering future edicts that would be firmly obeyed once he took official reign of the Larrabee dynasty—even though the dynasty had dwindled to his grandmother, himself, and the vastly reduced fortune that had once bolstered their family name. It was with this great elegance that he stepped into the bedroom of Agnes Larrabee that night, in a mansion two streets over from the similar mansion that would become my childhood prison, and roughly a decade before I was born.

I have been told it was his habit to wear a tailored, freshly pressed double-breasted black suit, and that he greased his hair back Gatsby-style to add maturity to his precocious appearance. As on all other evenings, he approached his grandmother's poster bed where she sat waiting in a white dressing gown, propped against a half dozen pillows. Timothy Larrabee looked like a tiny adult as he crossed the hardwood floor and Persian throw rug, balancing in his white-gloved hands a polished silver tray with shortbread biscuits and a gold-rimmed china cup filled with densely sweetened Earl Grey tea. The sweetness of the hot tea, the delivery of the tray, and the manner in which Timothy was

dressed to perform his task were part of a nightly ritual that
Agnes demanded in the Larrabee household. Timothy Larrabee
did not see it as a burden, for young as he was, Timothy Larrabee
had been well taught to respect ritual and tradition and all the
power they would bestow upon him in adulthood.

On this evening, as on all others, Timothy Larrabee had
taken the tray in the kitchen from Samson Elias, the lifelong
family servant who prepared it nightly. This was the same
servant subsequently accused of stealing from the Larrabee
family a seventeenth-century miniature portrait of King Charles
I, father of the namesake of Charleston. This was the same
servant accused of the murder of Agnes Larrabee, convicted
and sentenced to execution despite his advanced age.

Because on this night, the sweetness of the tea in the gold-
rimmed china cup disguised the taste of enough rat poison to kill a
horse. Among the unkind whispers that followed her death was the
observation that the dosage was so strong simply because Samson
Elias knew well that Agnes Larrabee had the meanness of temper-
ament and constitution that would have survived any less.

Sheet lightning cracked the darkness of the rains that
pounded the bedroom window as Timothy Larrabee glided
forward with his tray and waited for his grandmother's approval
of his manners and presentation before setting the tray on a
nightstand. With those white-gloved hands, he passed her the
gold-rimmed cup that would deliver death.

Perhaps as Agnes Larrabee took that first gulp of cooling
tea, she did taste some of the bitterness of the poison. But a well-
bred Charlestonian simply does not spew as lesser creatures
might. So it was that Agnes Larrabee swallowed her death potion
with as much dignity as she could manage, and within minutes

died beneath a down-filled duvet, clutching the gold crucifix on the chain around her neck and calling out the name of Jesus, her cries of agony lost in the crashing thunder and the rain that poured upon her mansion.

It has been commonly maintained that Timothy's downward spiral into juvenile delinquency and subsequent years in federal prison resulted from the terrible combination of innocently delivering the instrument of his grandmother's death and then watching her die in such a horrible manner.

Yet I now know that what I believed about Timothy Larrabee as I grew up in Charleston was only a small part of the whole truth.

For the childhood that broke him held other stories.

Far more secret.

And far worse.

CHAPTER

2

Nearly five decades after Agnes Larrabee's murder by poisoning, two friends who owned an antique shop on King Street presented me with a request: Meet with a young girl from a part of Charleston known for bodies occasionally being found in alleys, and ask her how and why she possessed the nearly four-hundred-year-old painting stolen by Samson Elias on that thunder-filled night when Agnes Larrabee died in her bed.

It was summer, and I had recently returned to Charleston after years of self-imposed exile. My job as an instructor of astronomy at a community college in New Mexico meant I had a few months to myself, which gave me too many hours to fill each day, and enough income that I didn't need to work.

My daily routine held little excitement. At seven-thirty, I would leave the Doubletree Suites that overlooked the market and walk to my morning breakfast at the Sweetwater Café on Market Street. From there I would make the short walk to King,

turn left, and visit those two friends at an antique shop a few
blocks south toward Broad. I would not outstay my daily
welcome, however, and I made sure I departed for the South
Carolina Archives on Meeting Street well before my friends
began to fidget with impatience. In a chair in the corner of the
archives, I would indulge my interest in local history, reading
until my vision began to blur. At that point—although I knew
I would get nothing but an exasperated sigh from my attorney—
I would leave the archives to call from my cell phone and inquire
about the lack of progress in our ongoing court battle for my part
of the family fortune, which pitted me against my half brother,
Pendleton. Then would come my daily workout in the hotel
fitness center and another evening alone in my hotel room after
a solitary dinner at one of the restaurants in the market area.

One of the dangers of enduring long idle hours is that friends
think you won't mind doing them a favor that requires little more
than time. Another is the accuracy of their guess, as well as the
eagerness with which you will tend to accept such a request. And
a third hazard, among all the other seductions that come with idle
hours, is that the sense of purpose that comes from such a request
will lead you to go to extraordinary and senseless efforts to fulfill it.

Because of this, when my friends asked me to find out more
about the resurfaced painting, I agreed.

With no premonition of how such a simple request would
change the direction of my life.

✠

I had arrived inside the emergency room at St. George's Hospital
just before a cabdriver and his two passengers. The sliding-glass

doors closed with a whoosh behind them as I settled into a chair in the waiting room near the entrance. The air-conditioning was a welcome relief to the high humidity outside.

It was noon, Saturday. At this time of day, the waiting area to the emergency room had no late-night drunks or midnight stabbings to cause confusion. A sitcom played on the television set mounted from the ceiling in the corner. A security guard in an olive uniform stood at bored inattention near the reception area.

"I don't like this, you making me come inside to collect my fare," the cabdriver said. His voice carried clearly in the quiet as I listened nearby, unnoticed by him or his two passengers. "For me, time is money. I should already be picking up my next ride."

Short and broad and easily within range of retirement, he wore gray work pants and a sweater of matching color, although the sweater had likely once been white. The sweater stretched tight on his belly, and greasy hair hung in strings below his ball cap.

"I told you, my hands are full. As soon as I can give Maddie to someone, I'll pay."

I knew this was Angel from the information my friends had given me. She had skin of light cocoa, wide green eyes, a ball cap of her own, and short dark hair that she might have scissored herself. Maybe eleven or twelve years old, she seemed far too frail in a pair of baggy overalls that looked like Salvation Army castoffs, but there was the toughness of endured hunger in her skinny face.

Maddie probably wasn't even two years old. She was riding Angel's hip and clinging hard to Angel's thin upper body, her face showing the sheen of fever, her eyes closed tight against unuttered pain.

Unaware of how closely I was listening, the cabbie snarled. "I'm telling you again, time's money."

Guys who play it tough with preadolescent girls don't impress me. From where I sat, I could smell the mixture of rancid sweat and stale Old Spice on his gray sweater. "I'll take her while you dig out the roll you showed me before," he said, "unless you want me to go back out there and start the meter again."

Angel wrinkled her nose. I could only guess that she had gotten wind of the cabbie's body odor too. Her eyes fell on me, sitting close by. I tend toward blue jeans and black golf shirts on the theory that, at my height, darker colors hide a least ten pounds of extra weight. Today was no different. I hadn't bothered to shave in a few days, and the beginnings of my dark beard had traces of gray. I'm not sure mine was the kind of face to inspire instant trust. Nor did I think any white man past thirty years of age would have seemed like much of a choice to a girl of her age and background. Compared to the cabbie, however, I had showered and my clothes were freshly laundered, so I probably looked like a better bet to her than he did.

"Mister?" she said, pulling Maddie loose from her hip and handing her across to me.

I accepted the child.

✣

My two elderly friends in the antique shop had also given me Angel's address southeast of the Citadel. In terms of distance it wasn't that far from the mansions of lower Charleston; but in this city geographical proximity means nothing, for each different district is merely like one clear hard-shelled bubble touch-

ing another. Where I grew up, we were instructed not to use
the wrong fork; in Angel's neighborhood, barely two miles away,
children were taught not to play with discarded hypodermic
needles.

I drive an older Jeep Wrangler—faded black, well dented,
with a roll bar under a canvas roof—and less than a half hour
before arriving at the emergency room, I'd parked it just down
from the house where Angel lived, ready to walk up and knock on
the door with an excuse to ask her about the Van Dyck painting.

Before I could swing out of the Jeep, however, a taxi had
passed me and stopped alongside the other vehicles parked in
front of the house. The house had faced decades of heat and
storms. It leaned. Old yellow paint blistered on the wood siding,
and most of the railing spindles on the front porch were broken
or missing.

Had I arrived five minutes later, I would have missed my
chance. She would have been gone already. Had I arrived five
minutes earlier, she may well have pressed me into taxi service.

Before the taxi had settled on its springs to a total stop,
Angel had stepped onto the front porch holding a small child,
probably her baby sister. She'd marched to the cab, stood outside,
and shown a roll of bills. Only then had the shaking of the
cabbie's head changed to nodding as he agreed to let her inside.

When they drove away, I followed. According to my friends,
this young girl possessed the painting, easily worth fifty thousand
dollars. If she was going somewhere else to sell it, my friends
would want to know. But the cab had not gone to another antique
shop or a pawnshop. Instead, it had made a long, circuitous trip
here to the hospital. Anticipating Angel's destination, I'd raced
into the parking lot, parked my Jeep, and, hurrying in a way that

made it difficult to conceal my limp, arrived at the entrance just before Angel struggled to leave the cab with her sister.

Her baby sister, of course, was Angel's urgent mission.

Although I wasn't aware of it at the time, by accepting the child in the emergency room that Saturday, she also became my mission.

✠

Maddie didn't open her eyes as she settled into my arms. Her blue-black skin and tightly curled hair were much darker than Angel's; I doubted her eyes would contain any green that reflected some white parentage. The baby whimpered slightly as I cradled her. She was hot, too hot.

"Fare's twenty-four eighty," the cabbie said, "and most people tip five bucks on a fare like that, so make it an even thirty and we're square." His eyes bore down on her, but she returned the gaze until he had to turn away.

Then Angel dug into her front pocket. She came up with a roll held together with a rubber band.

"All ones," she told the cabbie, tossing it at him. "See ya later."

She took Maddie from me again and marched toward the reception area.

He fanned through the roll. I, like him, saw the bright colors of Monopoly money, wrapped in a one-dollar bill.

"Hey!" He caught up to Angel and grabbed her by the right upper arm. I began to stand in her defense, but Angel spun quickly and kicked him in the shin, a remarkable move for someone holding a baby.

I sat but didn't relax, wondering if he would try anything else.

The cabbie took a step backward. His eyes bulged with anger as he let go, and I believed if there had been no witnesses, he would have grabbed the girl by the throat.

"I don't have any cash," Angel said calmly. "I was going to give you a watch or something so you wouldn't feel cheated, but not after how you treated us. See, I got your name and taxi-license number from inside the cab."

She shifted her little sister to the other side of her hip to free her right hand, proof to me that she'd been using her sister as a delaying tactic earlier when she'd handed her to me, a subtle choreography that was impressive for someone her age. Angel reached into a front pocket again. She spoke to the cabbie as she flipped out a cell phone. "Harry Sherman. Four-zero-zero-five-two. I also got the complaint number memorized. You took me the long way, plus you smoked even though the sign said it was a no-smoking cab and even though I asked you not to three times because my sister is sick. And I saw that half-empty bottle of vodka rolling around under your front seat. How's all that gonna sound when I call in?"

She began to punch numbers on the cell-phone pad, difficult as this task was while she held her sister.

"People get thrown in jail for skipping out on a fare," Harry said. "Especially from your part of town."

"I had to get my sister to the hospital. She's hurting bad." Angel held the phone out so he could hear it ringing.

"And I got to put gas in my cab," he answered, trying his tough-guy look on her again.

A tinny voice reached out from the phone.

"Yeah," Angel said as she pressed the cell phone to her face. "I'm with one of your drivers. I'm just twelve, but he's drunk and saying stuff to me that's making me scared, like maybe he thinks I'm way older or something. He—"

"Alright, alright," Harry said, hands up and backing away. "You ain't worth the grief. Hang up and we're even."

It probably made Harry's decision easier that the large security guard had raised his head and swiveled it in our direction, like a fat bear suddenly aware of honey. Harry seemed like the type who preferred to avoid confrontations where he couldn't be a bully.

Angel snapped the cell phone shut, no triumph showing on her face.

As Harry marched out with as much dignity as he could, Angel turned to me. She studied me for twenty seconds. In a way I found her intensity amusing; in another way, unsettling. I wondered about the type of life she had lived that made her seem so much older than her years.

"Mister, want to call anywhere in the world cheap? Cell phone's yours for thirty bucks. Soon's they fix Maddie, I got to get home somehow."

I hesitated.

"Twenty bucks," she said.

I leaned over and reached for my wallet. I didn't need the phone, but she needed the money. I was here because I intended to talk to her when I could, and I'd return the phone then. With what I wanted to ask her, it wouldn't hurt to establish some trust.

"Don't shut it off or replace the battery," she warned me when our transaction was complete. "The way cell phones work, it might need a security code when you power it up again."

"Have the code?"

"Nope," she said. With that, she made a resolute turn toward the admitting nurse.

No code. Happy to give it to me regardless of where I called. The phone was recently stolen then, and only usable until the former owner reported it missing. On a hunch, I hit the redial button and listened. I didn't get the complaint department of the taxi company but an automated message notifying that service to this cell phone had been cut off and the caller should call a toll-free number for details.

I grinned at the girl's cool audacity.

As I set the cell phone down beside me, the luminous face of the phone went blank. Dead battery.

I grinned again.

✢

Five minutes later, the large security guard stepped in to stop Angel's calm, repetitious questions. I'd been listening too, but with admiration, not the irritation that showed on the guard's face. Each time the nurse explained why they couldn't help Angel's sister unless she had proof of insurance or her mother showed up, Angel responded by asking for a doctor. Each time the nurse requested that Angel take Maddie off the counter, Angel responded by asking for a doctor.

The security guard hitched his pants, stepped to the admitting desk, and interrupted Angel as she began to explain for the thirtieth time that her sister needed a doctor. He winked at the admitting nurse, a pale blonde whose dark eyeliner gave her a Bambi look.

"Missy," he said gruffly to Angel, "I think we've heard enough from you."

I guessed him to be over six feet and heavy in a soft way. If he expected his size and uniform to intimidate Angel because he usually intimidated adults, he was wrong this time. Which by now didn't surprise me.

"What's your name, mister?" Angel asked as she set Maddie on the counter. The nurse had no choice but to accept the silent little parcel.

"I'll ask the questions here," he said.

Angel squinted and read his name tag. "Well, Mr. John Nesbitt, like I was telling this lady here, my sister is real sick. Someone's got to help her. Me and Maddie ain't leaving until I get a doctor to fix her up. It's that simple."

"Doctors take money," John said. "So do big fancy buildings like this hospital, filled with modern machines and expensive medicine."

"Don't talk to me like I'm stupid," Angel said. "Not only have I got my own computer, but I get paid to fix them and I'm sure I've forgotten more things about running hardware and software than you could learn in the rest of your life."

John smiled for the benefit of the admitting nurse. Maybe he'd decided it would look better if he played the role of a patient, indulgent father figure.

"Well, missy—" big smile again—"then you understand that you need to show us a way the doctors can get paid. Maybe your dad—"

"Ain't got no daddy. Or Mama. It's just me and Grammie Zora and Maddie. And Grammie Zora is visiting someone out of town right now. Which is why I'm here. Maddie needs help real bad. Don't any of you understand?"

John maintained his indulgent smile, playing to the admitting nurse. "If what you're saying is that you don't have a way to pay St. George's Hospital, that's alright. The Charleston University Hospital is set up to help people like you. We'll make arrangements to send you there and—"

"People like me? You mean poor people? Or mochachinos?"

"Mochachinos?" Nesbitt echoed.

"Half white, half chocolate, just the way Grammie says she loves me. Is that the kind of people like me you mean?" She glared at John Nesbitt, daring him to answer in a way that might offend her more.

"What I mean," he said, his face turning red, "is that programs are in place to help anyone who needs it in the way that you appear to need it at this moment."

"Can't wait that long," Angel said. "My sister's so sick she can't hold down water. Her cough is getting worse and worse. And feel her forehead. It was hot yesterday and now it's hotter today. Which is why I brought her in." No anger. No desperation. Just persistence, like dripping water. "She needs a doctor. How much can it cost this big hospital for someone to look at her for five minutes and fix her up so I can take her home?"

John squatted so he could look Angel in the eyes. Like he'd read somewhere that getting down to a child's level improved communication. "If you don't listen to me," he said, "I'll have to do something about this. You don't want that to happen, do you?"

"What? Are you going to beat me up? A big man like you against a girl like me?"

"Um, no." New wrinkles across his placid face showed that John realized he'd made another mistake, promising a threat he couldn't deliver. Worse, Angel seemed smart enough to know it.

"Well, that's what it's going to take," she said, crossing her arms. "I'm not going no place until a doctor looks at my sister. She's all I've got and I'm all she's got. And right now she needs help bad."

There were a half dozen other people in the waiting room who had found this exchange far more interesting than watching the sitcom on the television or worrying about the ailments that had brought them in for help. From their chairs near the admitting nurse, they intently watched the confrontation. Some snickered at Angel's refusal to move, which didn't help John and how he looked in front of the Bambi nurse, who was fighting to hide a smile herself. Maybe he decided he couldn't intimidate Angel, but he could at least move her to a place where she wouldn't have an audience hanging on her every word.

Still squatting, he reached for the girl's shoulders, keeping his knees apart to steady himself. Yet another mistake.

✛

Her name was Retha Herndon, and later she would tell me about that morning, describing how from the moment she pulled the squeaky door shut and reversed Junior's rusting gray 1978 Chevrolet truck down the red-clay drive from the trailer toward the gravel road that led out of the compound, she began praying hard to Jesus.

Retha figured if there was any time she deserved to have her prayers answered, this might be it. It had been months since she had wasted Jesus' time with selfish prayers, like asking him to help her not be overweight. No, Retha was accustomed to it now when people gave her compliments by saying she was "pretty in the face," knowing exactly what that implied. Besides,

everyone knew it was murder keeping the weight off after
having a baby.

More recently, she had also stopped asking Jesus to inspire
Shepherd Isaiah to let her and Junior move out of Elder Mason's
trailer into one of their own somewhere on the compound. It was
bad enough living with Junior's father in such close quarters,
especially since Junior's father—his own father! —did not tolerate being addressed by anything less than Elder Mason, even in
the dreadfully stifling privacy of the mobile home they were
forced to share with him.

Retha's own parents had joined the church six years earlier
when Shepherd Isaiah founded it. Unlike her older brother, who
had been eighteen then and old enough to choose not to stay with
the family, Retha at thirteen had had no choice but to move along
with her parents, and had lived in another mobile home in the
compound. When Mason Anderson Junior had showed interest
in her just after her sixteenth birthday, she was glad to escape her
own household to be married a few months later, especially since
it seemed like such a privilege at the time to become part of
Elder Mason's family, as Elder Mason was one of Shepherd
Isaiah's twelve Elders of the Chosen.

Not only that, but Elder Mason seemed so confident and
assured. When it wasn't Sunday, he wore snakeskin cowboy
boots, jeans, a denim shirt, and a John Deere ball cap. Take away
his beard and he looked like one of those cowboys in cigarette ads
in the old *Reader's Digest* magazines she'd once found hidden in
her mother's underwear drawer. Before she'd gotten to know
him, Retha had had a secret crush on Elder Mason.

The privilege of living with Elder Mason had lost its luster,
however, when Retha learned that the man of God kept hidden

the fact that he had a worse temper than Retha's own father had, and an iron will to go with it. After she learned exactly how stubborn and mean-tempered he was, Retha had also stopped praying for Jesus to give Junior enough backbone to stand up to Elder Mason, partly because it didn't seem Jesus had been listening, and mainly because now Retha believed if only so many prayers could be answered, she intended to bank them for Billy Lee, her little boy.

She was glad she'd kept some prayers back because if ever she needed them, it was the morning she decided to flee.

✛

In the emergency room, Angel did not hesitate.

As John Nesbitt's hands made light contact with Angel, she swung her right foot hard, centering the impact between his open knees, finding her target with the precision and concentrated focus of a field-goal kicker. Had she been bigger or had he been smaller, the force of it might have lifted him off the ground.

His stunned disbelief lasted during the moments it took his nerve endings to route the shock waves of pain up his spine and into his brain. About the time it took for his eyes to pop wide and for his mouth to form a silent gasp. This brief mercy of delayed reaction disintegrated in an agony that sent him backward into a fetal position, his speech lost in blubbering and choked howls.

Angel jumped on top of him. She wrapped her legs around his neck in a scissors hold, clutching his hair in one hand like a bareback rider grabbing the horse's mane.

I knew from universal male sympathy that John Nesbitt was beyond caring, hardly aware of the pressure her legs exerted against his windpipe. Hardly aware that Angel had pulled a pen out of his shirt pocket and pressed it against the skin of his closed left eye. Hardly aware as Angel looked up at the circle of adults around them to speak in her calm, persistent voice.

"Now is my baby sister going to get a doctor or does this guy go blind?"

C H A P T E R

3

There was a woman I'd met in the spring in Charleston who had
returned to Chicago where she worked as a doctor; we had begun a
relationship of long-distance phone calls. Aside from that, I'd gone
to great pains to ensure that my adult life had been relatively quiet
and settled and alone. I had done a good job of avoiding the messes
and complications that come with committed care about the lives
of others. I was, without doubt, an expert at solitude.

Although I would admit to this as one of many of my character flaws, I wasn't prepared to change it. I knew that part of the
allure of the Chicago woman was the distance barrier to further
intimacy. My biggest commitment was the phone calls, and as she
was a physician, her hectic schedule made that sufficiently difficult.

Even my friendship with the two dear old ladies in the
antique shop reflected my need to avoid closeness; our age difference provided a distance that ensured safety, and if that difference wasn't enough, I knew they were rich enough and mannered

enough and Charlestonian enough that they would never involve me in any personal problems that had potential for embarrassment or vulnerability.

Perhaps, however, God had decided that it was time for me to pay the price for all my previous selfish and complacent solitude, and wanted to show me that living meant involvement with life. Perhaps Angel was truly an angel he had sent to knock me off my comfortable fence and into the fray of pain and joy and sorrow and hope and despair that I was trying to pretend did not exist in lives around me.

For it was Angel who would bring Retha Herndon into my life too. With all of the other events that followed.

✛

Praying fast and hard in a whisper that wouldn't disturb her eighteen-month-old son in the blanket she'd wrapped around him, Retha strapped him into the passenger-side seat, leaving only his dry, unnaturally white face exposed. She knew Billy Lee should be in the backseat, but up front was where she could keep a close eye on his labored breathing. She was so scared he might die that she didn't know what to do if his breathing finally stopped except panic more.

Retha began her prayer, as the dappled shadows of the trees danced across the hood of her slow-moving truck, by asking Jesus to find a way to keep Elder Mason at his town appointment longer than usual, and to let Junior, who was out in his swamp boat fellowshiping with two friends, hook some bass early so they wouldn't get bored and come home in the next couple hours. Retha figured the fishing part wouldn't be hard for Jesus to manage; after all, hadn't he told Peter to throw his net over the other side of the boat and then filled it with fish, when Peter thought one more throw would be a waste of time? And that was hardly a miracle compared to another time when Jesus needed money fast and didn't have to look farther than the next fish, which had a coin in its mouth. In other words, Retha told herself, of anybody, Jesus knew fish.

Retha's plea for Jesus to keep Junior in the bass boat most of the day only took to the end of the drive, where the truck broke out of an archway of trees into sunshine that bounced harshly off all the industrial sheeting of the walls of the other mobile homes scattered between Retha and the church at the front of the compound. But in that short distance to the compound's main road, Retha realized that the few lessons in driving that Junior had given her during their brief courtship were nearly inadequate for the journey ahead, especially as she intended to keep praying.

Junior never disagreed when Shepherd Isaiah or Elder Mason discussed that part in Ephesians six where wives are supposed to obey their husbands. Elder Mason insisted that meant Junior's position was unquestioned head of the household, and it was Retha's duty to stay at home and pop children. "Pop children" was Elder Mason's expression, not hers; Retha knew from ten hours of labor with Billy Lee that it was a lot more difficult than a quick pop. Although as husband Junior was supposed to be head of the household, Elder Mason made all the decisions, including the mandate that Retha ought not leave the compound unless accompanied by Junior. Which meant that Retha needed to ask Jesus to forgive her for stealing the spare key and for driving the truck when it was against her husband's will and against Elder Mason's will and definitely against Shepherd Isaiah's will.

On top of this request for forgiveness, Retha also needed to ask Jesus to look over her and little Billy Lee on the twenty miles ahead into Charleston, especially on the highway and when they got to town where traffic was bad.

Desperately as she needed to pray, she found it difficult to drive at the same time. She feared Jesus might get mad at her if she didn't keep her eyes closed when she prayed, and if he was mad, maybe he wouldn't give her any help at all.

Once on the road that wound through the extensive acreage of the compound, she tried alternating between watching the truck's uncertain progress and shutting her eyes briefly, praying in quick bursts while her eyes were closed, but that had nearly put her off the road into one of the other mobile homes, which would have been a disaster. Imagine what people would say, and how angry Elder Mason would be at that, because as one of the Chosen, he was supposed to be nearly as perfect as Shepherd Isaiah. So halfway to the compound gates at the end of the road, Retha began squinting hard, with her eyes almost closed, trying to concentrate on driving and praying at the same time. But that reminded her too much of the times in church when she'd peeked during the half-hour prayers that nearly suffocated her and had been whipped later for her sin, getting extra licks for the audacity to ask her own daddy how he could have known she was peeking when his eyes were supposed to be closed too. Squinting felt so much like the sin of peeking in church that Retha gave up on it by the time she reached the parking lot of the church. Retha also decided that since she hadn't been able to fool her daddy, it only followed she had no chance at all of fooling Jesus, since both her daddy and Shepherd Isaiah insisted that Jesus was there to watch every sin.

Then came the compound gate. She knew that the remote
opener on Junior's sun visor was operational, but during the eternity it took for the gate to swing open, she worried that someone
from the church would run out and ask questions. So Retha
prayed the entire time she waited, then eased out onto the main
gravel road that led away from the church.

At twenty-five miles an hour, with the tires of the Chevrolet
truck throwing rocks into the low ditch beside the flat, straight
road and with dust coming up through the leaky floorboards,
choking out any smell of the heavy, dark swamp water nearby,
Retha finally settled on closing just one eye, asking Jesus to
understand and forgive her if she was praying wrong, and explaining to him how she didn't have time to pull over to pray properly
every mile or two.

With that problem resolved—she hoped—Retha got on to
her next prayers.

She asked Jesus to keep the road clear of police since not
only didn't she have a driver's license, but she'd covered the
truck's license plate with red mud she'd made by watering a small
patch of the flower bed and mixing it with her bare hands. She
didn't want the truck identified by anyone at the hospital. If she
made it that far.

Lastly, Retha began to pray that for what she was attempting
to do, Jesus wouldn't send little Billy Lee to hell if he died.

That's when Shepherd Isaiah passed her in his large, new
black Cadillac Escalade sport utility vehicle. The wide tires
sprayed stones into her windshield, and instinctively she stopped.
He fishtailed farther up the road, slowing until he could spin his
rear tires hard and swing the Escalade around to face her truck.

Then slowly, he drove toward her.

When he was close enough for his eyes to meet hers through his bug-splashed windshield, Retha discovered the driver was not Shepherd Isaiah but his brother, Elder Jeremiah Sullivan. Same dark hair as Shepherd Isaiah. Same dark beard. Same square face. But six years younger, six inches taller, and one hundred pounds heavier. At nearly thirty years old, a man in his physical prime. A man who worshiped Shepherd Isaiah, and as his bodyguard and one of the Chosen, a man who was prepared to die for him.

Elder Jeremiah put a massive arm out the open driver's window and pointed her back toward the compound.

I had recently learned many truths about my own boyhood, and it
had been a journey of sorrow, sweetened by a measure of joy in
discovering my mother was not, as I'd been long led to believe,
a tramp and runaway thief who had abandoned her only son.

Because of her, I had been born into the Barrett family with
their disapproval. But my mother's marriage to a Barrett had
been tragically cut short when David Barrett died in military
action just months before my birth. My mother had been pregnant when David had already been in service far too long to allow
a claim that he might truly be my father. While Charleston's high
society is riddled with such scandals, my mother's real sin—in
their eyes—was the fact that she, like Angel, had been tainted by
a birthplace too far north of Broad Street.

Broad runs east and west across the lower part of Charleston's
peninsula, a clear line of division in societal terms. Each time I
cross Broad, I think of Hadrian's Wall in northern Britain—still

impressive after nearly two thousand years of decay—built early in the first millennium by the Romans not only to repel the barbarians, but also to remind them constantly that the Romans ruled the southern provinces. Because Broad Street is not lined with stones piled ten feet thick and twenty feet high by the Romans, the aristocracy of Charleston relies instead on the price of their real estate to keep out the barbarians. Given the choice, however, I'm certain the aristocrats would prefer the protection of the Roman wall and sentries armed with shield and spear, for there is nothing to stop tourists and lesser Charlestonians from the irritating habit of freely entering the neighborhoods to gawk at their mansions.

King Street is the one-way arrow that points the invading tourists into the hallowed southern end of Charleston's peninsula. Below Broad Street, King is appropriately quiet, adorned with the mansions and other historically preserved homes. North of Broad the first portion of King, lined with antique shops, serves as a buffer zone between wealth and poverty. The patches of cobblestone and uneven sidewalks serve notice that it is not just another commercial strip for the type of tourist content to stand in line for hours at Disney World. As an added deterrent, the shops farther up King are suitably upscale, a common ground for the aristocracy and upper-class tourists. Yet barely a mile or so to the north, especially on the other side of Highway 17 toward the area where Angel lived, King widens and degenerates so badly that tattoos and cheap beer are actually available in various neon-signed establishments.

Because the pureness of my link to the aristocracy was contaminated by my mother's bloodline, I often felt the subtle disapproval of those around me as I grew up south of Broad. Because of it, my suspicion of them was and is habitually returned.

Much as I feel a stranger among those south of Broad, I have a weakness for the antique shops on King just north of Broad. My mother is to blame. Here, when I was a young boy, she would walk with me from antique shop to antique shop where we played a game, pretending we had enough wealth to purchase various objects of beauty but declined out of decency for those who could not afford a badly varnished writing desk worth as much as a new automobile. During those all too brief years of an idyllic childhood, my mother often told me that she enjoyed being among antiques because they brought to life the history of Charleston that she loved with great passion. Through those events that had led me to the truth about her, I now wonder if part of that fascination resulted because of her sad wish to live among the other Barretts without facing the subtle scorn constantly directed at her.

Either way, walking along that ancient and narrow portion of King, past the various antique shops toward small restaurants and boutiques, always brings me a sense of peace, for it gives back my mother and her scent and her smile and the warmth of her hand on mine. In my memories, it never rains on the cobblestones of King Street.

My two friends own one of the shops here. Spinster twins and institutions in Charleston, they have a keen sense of the happenings of the elite. Gossip provides them with the knowledge of which blue bloods are anxious to pay off loans or taxes by dumping exquisite furniture at bargain prices; it's often remarked that their appearance in one of the mansions south of Broad means the repossession crews or moving vans will be seen soon after.

Glennifer and Elaine Beloise had been proprietors long

before my mother and I made our treks and had always been kind and attentive when we visited and browsed among their antiques. They weren't concerned about mother's background, respecting her passion and knowledge of antiques. Often they invited us to remain with them for tea, something I know had given my mother great pleasure. Early upon my return to Charleston after my years of exile, I had visited them again, asking for help in my search for the truth about my mother and events of my child-hood. Despite all the time that had passed, they recognized me immediately and despite the events that had driven me away, extended their previous kindness and respect.

Now, by learning what I could about Angel and the antique painting stolen decades earlier from Agnes Larrabee, I hoped to show my gratitude to them for what I had learned about my mother and for the small kindnesses that had meant so much to her during my childhood years.

✛

A bell tinkled as I entered the shop just past two o'clock on that same Saturday.

Other antique dealers on King specialized in Civil War artifacts or jewelry or art or knickknacks; Glennifer and Elaine were the experts on furniture. They cared little about the presentation of their desks and chairs and mirrors. Their under-standing of value was so acute, and their prices so high, that only those with the knowledge and income to appreciate these antiques became their clients. Pricing the furniture with hand-written white tags and displaying it haphazardly would not deter those clients. On the other hand, the crammed discount warehouse feel of the shop effectively turned back bored window-shopping tourists who would otherwise simply waste time with foolish questions.

As usual, I was alone among all the antiques as I made my way past full-length mirrors and fine straight-backed chairs. Glennifer and Elaine preferred to spend their time in the back office, sharing a large desk always piled with papers and magazines. Whenever the bell tinkled, they sent out Willy, a tiny and effeminate man who habitually clutched a handkerchief to his nose, sniffing the cologne he soaked it in.

Willy emerged from the back in his dark pants, vest, and bow tie, rolled his eyes upon seeing it was no one more important than I, pointed past himself to the back of the shop, and ran his hands over his slicked-back hair to ensure it was still immaculately in place.

Unlike Willy, Glennifer and Elaine smiled upon my arrival. They wore their hair up in gray piles, their faces were collapsed by age, their cheeks and jowls wrinkled like fine netting. But their smiles brought light to their dark eyes. As always, each wore a black dress, neck to toe. The only way I could distinguish one from the other was by their voices. Glennifer secretly smoked, and her throat rasped because of it.

"Nicholas!" each exclaimed.

I proceeded forward, and as was my custom, leaned over and kissed each extended left hand, sad that age had made their bones so delicate, their skin as light as tracing paper. As was their custom, each pretended great delight at my exaggerated display of Southern charm.

"Tea?" Glennifer offered, the harshness of her raspy voice countered by the softness of her Southern drawl.

"Only if it's guest tea," I said. "I'm not interested in what you serve yourselves when you think no one will notice."

"Laney!" Glennifer gasped to Elaine, hand at her throat. I knew them well enough to understand this was deliberate melodrama, a mockery of Southern manners and something they enjoyed using occasionally as a way to amuse me. "He can't possibly know."

I hid my smile and pointed at a nearby antique wardrobe. "Know that you line the bottom of that with a towel to soak up drippings from the used tea bags you clip to a string inside to dry for future use?"

"Glenny!" Elaine gasped theatrically in return, drawing from me the smile. "He does know!"

She frowned slightly. "Nicholas, how *do* you know?"

"Blame Willy," I said. Willy hadn't told me, but I faced the disdain of his rolled eyeballs each time I entered the antique shop, and I didn't mind the chance to seek petty revenge.

"Oh, that Willy," Glennifer said. "Tomorrow, I swear. His last day."

"You'll never be rid of me," his voice drifted in from the front. "Certainly you've learned by now that a vent lets me hear everything you say back there. I know too many secrets about you. And no, I didn't tell your friend Nicky about the tea bags. But I will tell him about the chewing tobacco."

"Chewing tobacco?" I asked.

Glennifer turned to me, apparently unwilling to discuss the vent or the chewing tobacco. "I believe we were discussing tea. From a new tea bag. Happy?"

In reply, I pulled out a gold Rolex watch and dropped it on their desk.

"Not only happy," I said, "but rich. Look at what that kid Angel gave me for helping her out today in the emergency room at St. George's."

✛

It had taken less than a minute for another olive-uniformed security guard to appear after Angel had taken her hostage on the floor. Unlike John Nesbitt, this one had the body of a serious, steroid-injected weight lifter. His face reflected his steroid use, mountainous with purple pimples. The buzz cut of his dyed-platinum hair hinted at aggression, and a large gold earring proved to the world that he did not need to conform to its mundane rules.

Upon his strutting arrival, the guard's first move was to scoop Maddie off the desk of the admitting nurse.

Everyone else in the waiting room had formed an outer ring around the fallen John Nesbitt. I slipped between people to get to the center.

Angel stared up at me from the floor. With John Nesbitt's neck trapped between her thighs, his head looked like a watermelon in her lap. Against his already flushed face, a darker red splotch grew from the pressure of the pen jammed into the skin beneath his eye.

I spoke to Angel. "I think I can help. You want everyone out of here so we can talk?"

She nodded.

I turned to the security guard holding Maddie. "Why don't you give me the little girl and clear everyone else out of here?"

"I've got this under control. As soon as she lets go of our man, she gets her baby sister back."

"Let me get this straight," I said. "She's got him hostage, so you've got her sister hostage."

"We do what it takes to protect our own." He said it proudly, as if everyone knew security guards had their own soldier's code.

I stepped close. "Give me the baby. Clear the room."

Buzz-cut smirked. "Look, dude, you don't understand who you're dealing with. You do what *we* say."

I grabbed his earring, yanked, and tossed it on the floor. I relieved him of Maddie as he screamed and clutched at his ear.

After the first few moments of shock, he raised his other fist, still squealing with outrage.

"Don't," I said. "Not worth it."

"I'm going to kill you," he said, teeth bared. Blood dripped down the hand he held to his ear.

"How's it going to play on the news tonight? Big strong security guard gets taken by unarmed girl. Other guard tackles man holding sick baby."

His jaw dropped as he tried to think it through. "Give the baby to someone else," he said. "I'm ready for you, man."

"Don't," I said.

"Think you're safe, hiding behind a baby?" He reached for me.

Which I'd been expecting. It was a simple, fast move, spinning sideways out of his reach, grabbing his pinkie and pinning it back almost against his wrist.

"Go," I said. He stood on his tiptoes in agony. "Take the others down the hall and give us some privacy."

✛

I held Maddie and sat beside Angel and the security guard who was still fighting for air. I left enough space between us that she wouldn't feel threatened.

"I like that pinkie move," she said. "Maybe you can teach it to me. Where I live, that would be good to have."

"It's easy enough," I said. "I can teach it."

"What's your name, mister?"

"Nick."

"Angel Starr. I'd shake, but this ain't the best time to be real polite."

I nodded. "And this is Maddie, right?"

The little girl cradled in my arm clutched one of my fingers. She still hadn't opened her eyes.

"Maddie," Angel said. John Nesbitt's head lay in her lap, his mouth gasping like a fish. "She's seventeen months old. She needs help."

"Come on, man," John Nesbitt croaked for my benefit. "Enough chitchat. Get her off me."

Angel squeezed her legs around his neck hard enough to shut him up. John Nesbitt's eyeballs began to roll upward, showing a frightening percentage of white.

"Might want to ease up," I said. "If he dies, he'll make a lousy hostage."

"Oh," Angel said, looking down on the top of John Nesbitt's head. She opened her legs slightly, and John gulped for air.

"Maybe let go of the hair, too. I'm thinking you've done enough damage."

"What about Maddie?" Angel said, refusing to unclench her fist's grip on his hair.

"A doctor will look after her. I'll make sure of that."

"Lots of men lie."

"I'm sorry you understand that already. But I'm going to make sure your sister can stay in the hospital as long as it takes for her to get better."

"What about how much this rent-a-cop said it will cost?"

John Nesbitt squirmed. Angel tightened her hold again.

"I'll pay," I said.

"Why?"

"I can afford it."

"I don't know if I believe you," Angel said. "See, my problem is this. Once I let go of this guy, I got nothing. Maybe you're just making a promise so I'll let go."

"How long were you thinking of holding him?"

"I want a doctor to look at my sister. Until then, I'm keeping this pen close enough to bust his eyeball."

"No," I said.

"No," John Nesbitt groaned.

"No? You saying I can't do it?" Angel pressed harder with the pen, almost breaking the skin of his tightly closed eye.

John Nesbitt cried out.

"Sure you can do it," I said. "But it would be a dumb move. Pop his eyeball, then no one gives your sister help. And thing is, I gave you my word that doctors will help. Your end of the deal is that you trust me. That's the way friends work."

"Friends?" Angel said. "I don't know you."

"But we're kind of the same."

A squint of suspicion. "How?"

"Maybe someday I'll have a chance to tell you where my mother grew up. Close to where you live."

Her squint of suspicion deepened. "Who told you where I live?"

"The cabbie talked about your part of town," I said, hoping it was a good enough recovery.

"That don't make us friends," she said, relaxing her face somewhat, but not the grip of her legs around the security guard's neck. "There's plenty of people there I gotta watch out for."

People, I assumed by the coldness and distance of her voice, which included me. I needed a way to bring her back.

I set Maddie on the floor between my legs and leaned forward and began to roll up the bottom of my pant leg. Angel watched silently, curious. She saw my black dress sock, stretching up my calf. My hands obstructed my view of what I did next, but it was a movement like someone fumbling blindly with shoelaces. I pulled off the lower half of my leg. With the shoe still on the foot.

"Cool," Angel said.

I was hoping she'd see it that way. She seemed like a girl who would not impress easily, and a false half leg was my best and only trick. An unlikely positive resulting from the car accident that had nearly killed me when I was eighteen.

I held up my prosthesis. "What if you keep this until a doctor looks at Maddie? I mean, someone gives you half his leg when he makes a promise, it's got to be a serious promise, right?"

Angel giggled, for a moment like the little girl she was. "Right."

I set my prosthesis on the floor and slid it to Angel. "Nurse?" I called to the woman at admitting. "You'll make sure a doctor examines this girl's sister? I'll cover everything."

"But . . ."

From my wallet, I took out a credit card. I flipped it across the space onto the desk, grateful it landed neatly.

"Nicholas Barrett," the nurse read off the credit card. "As in *the* Barretts?"

I nodded. A wing of the hospital was named after my family.

The nurse shrugged. "I'll still need a driver's license and I'll have to pre-authorize."

Pre-authorize. Which was a good indication of what my family name was worth without any assets to back it. I tossed my license onto the desk. The Bambi nurse studied it and studied my face to make sure it was a match.

"New Mexico?" She frowned. "Back here to visit?"

"Long story," I said, glad the nurse didn't appear to be a subscriber to the *Charleston Post and Courier.* A few months back I'd been front-page news for a couple days, then day by day faded farther and farther back into the local section, then, mercifully, disappeared.

"Really long story," Angel added. She grinned at my surprise, giving John's head a quick yank to let him know she was still paying attention to him, too. "Grammie said the only way I'll find a way out of our neighborhood is if I get educated. I read the newspaper every day, front to back. I remember your picture. Is all that stuff about your mama and those other people true?"

"What was there was accurate." Charleston journalists seemed to possess a substantial part of the Southern sense of honor; they were more than a cut above the vultures who clawed their way to positions at a national level. "But not all of it made the papers."

"Nick Barrett," Angel repeated. She stared at my face for several moments. "Nick Barrett."

As if coming to a decision, Angel dropped her pen, released her grip on John Nesbitt's hair, and stood. John Nesbitt rolled over onto his stomach. He pushed to his knees and crawled away from Angel with a final backward glance to make sure she wasn't going to attack him again.

Angel crossed the small space to stand in front of me and gravely presented my prosthesis to me.

"Maybe someday you can tell me more," Angel said. She picked up Maddie and held her close, smiling as she cradled her sister. "About your leg. And your mama. I don't forget anything I read. She *did* come from my part of town."

Seeing that smile transform the beautiful cocoa skin of Angel's face, once again I felt guilt that I was here simply because I had been following her, because I wanted something from her.

"Hey," she said, as if it had just hit her, "maybe you can help me with something else. That way I can pay you back for this doctor stuff."

"Not necessary," I said. "I actually intend to spend my half brother's inheritance. That makes me happy because he hates to let go of it."

"No, I want to pay you back." she said. "At home, I got this weird old painting. With Maddie getting sick, I knew I needed some money. So yesterday I showed it to a couple of old bags on King . . ."

She paused, studying my face again. I kept it deliberately blank. Felt guilt in doing so.

". . . anyway, I know it's worth something because it got them excited, but they wouldn't make a deal. I'll bet because they think I'm too much of a kid. But you could get plenty for it. I mean, being respectable and all."

"Not many people have called me respectable," I said, my guilt compounded at her eagerness to involve me with the antique that I was pursuing without her knowledge. "You can tell me about it after the doctor looks at Maddie. Deal?"

"Deal," she said.

She reached into her other front pocket. "I kind of ripped you off with that cell phone. Maybe this will make up for it."

That's when I received the gold Rolex.

✥

As a kettle on a hot plate brought water to boil for tea, I explained to Glennifer and Elaine what had happened in the hospital. For obvious reasons, I neglected to mention Angel's reference to the "old bags" on King. Nor did I feel it necessary to include my bullying of the buzz-cut security guard. I'd felt shame and regret as it happened.

Halfway through my explanation, Glennifer had poured the water in a pot for the tea to steep. When I finished speaking, Elaine examined the Rolex through her reading glasses.

"It's a fake," Elaine pronounced. She took the glasses off the bridge of her nose and wrapped them in a soft cloth and set them on the desk before speaking again. "The seconds go *tick-tick-tick* instead of sweeping smoothly. To me, that says she undoubtedly did steal the King Charles I portrait."

"She's a scamp and a scoundrel," I agreed.

"So you like her," Glennifer sniffed.

I grinned and shrugged. "I like both of you, too. Same reason."

"Very amusing, Nicholas," Glennifer said. She poured my tea. "By the way, look closely at your cup."

I had it halfway to my mouth. It was gold-rimmed with a pattern on the china that meant nothing to me. I admitted as much, holding the cup without taking a sip.

"It's from a set from the Larrabee estate," Glennifer said. "Given the circumstances, I thought you might find this appropriate. Perhaps that cup was the one that held the poison that killed Agnes."

"Delightful." I set the cup down, tea untouched.

"We handled her estate," Elaine said. "She didn't have a life insurance policy. Didn't believe in it."

"Just like everyone else around her, she didn't believe she would die is more like it," Glennifer added. "Poor Timothy. Sent north to that school with barely more than the proceeds from the sale of the house and its contents to provide for him. Virtually abandoned to the world, with only his miserable memories to comfort him. Is it any wonder that he became a juvenile delinquent?"

Her accent made it seem like she had graced us with the dispensation of her opinion. When either of them spoke, it seemed like they were making a parody of *Gone With the Wind*. But they had been here in the South almost since it had been written.

"All of the estate except for the miniature portrait of King Charles," I said. "Yesterday you could have had that, too, for the twenty grand she asked. You said it would go for fifty at an auction."

"Nicholas, 'twenty grand' is a gauche expression. Here, we deal in thousands, not *grand* or *k* or *large*." There was a twinkle in Glennifer's eyes.

Elaine chimed in. "Nor do we handle stolen merchandise."

"Nor," I said with another grin, "do you call the police on little girls who show up with stolen merchandise. Instead, you talk Willy into following her home from the shop that afternoon to bring back her address. If word gets out you've gone soft . . ."

"Soft? Never!" From up front, Willy joined in with his high-pitched voice. I could picture him at the front window, his hands behind his back, staring at the passersby on King Street. "I'll testify to that. Not only did I have to walk forever, I ruined my shoes in the rain following that girl back to her horrible neighborhood. Some of the people were so dreadful in appearance that I feared for my life. They stared at me like I was fresh prey to hungry jackals."

I refrained from commenting that in Angel's neighborhood, the sight of a bow tie like Willy's was as rare as city maintenance crews working on the streets.

Willy continued from up front. "And Nicky, don't forget to ask them about the chewing tobacco."

"Chewing tobacco," I repeated, looking back and forth from Glennifer to Elaine.

"You said Angel requested that you help her sell the painting," Elaine prompted. "That means you can tell us more about it now? We are very curious, as you well know, to find out who had it before this young girl found it. To have it resurface after all these years . . ."

"They're going to hold the baby in the hospital at least one night, maybe more," I said. "I stayed at the hospital long enough to find out they think it's pneumonia. Angel asked if I would come back later to talk about it, after the doctors have finished their fussing. I agreed that would be fine, and dutifully returned here to report my progress."

"You are a wonderful young man," Elaine said with coquettish breathlessness, returning to the melodrama that gave me the sense they were allowing me into a private game that they had played since girlhood.

"Yes, always the charmer, aren't you, Nicholas?" Glennifer played along, arching an eyebrow against the imposing wrinkles of her forehead, a valiant effort to rearrange skin aged almost eight decades. "Women of any age are helpless against you."

"Always the charmer." I said it in the spirit of our little game but felt a deadness in saying it. I would be going back into Angel's life under false pretenses, using her vulnerability as a weapon against her. "Now tell me about this chewing tobacco."

"Pigs will fly first," Elaine said quite firmly. "Now drink your tea."

C H A P T E R

5

In the early 1600s Italian artists began to paint in a showy, extravagant form that became known as baroque. They painted large-scale works of dynamic subjects—realistic and emotionally intense, using colors and sharp contrasts of light and shadow to heighten the theatrical presentation of their subject matter— often famous historical events, or magnificent altarpieces to demonstrate church beliefs clearly and directly.

One of the most famous baroque artists was Peter Paul Rubens, who lived in Flanders and obtained many commissions from public and private patrons throughout Europe. Like Caravaggio, one of the original baroque artists, Rubens conveyed drama by placing moving figures diagonally throughout the composition, using strongly contrasting areas of light and shadow, and painting with broken, agitated brushstrokes that emphasized dramatic, exciting action.

Because he was in such demand, Rubens operated a large

studio in Antwerp. Among the crowd of apprentices and assistants was a talented young man named Anton Van Dyck, who made a decision not to compete with his master in the area of historical paintings. Van Dyck left his secure job for Italy, to perfect the art of court portraiture. Events led him to England, where he worked for King Charles I, the hapless king who battled Parliament politically and militarily until his execution for treason in 1649. While alive and in power, however, Charles I had a fondness for portraits, and Van Dyck was canny enough to adorn the king in lavish costumes and elongate the figure and hands of the king to present him in a more flattering light. Altogether, Van Dyck did some four hundred portraits, most of them large.

But one, a miniature portrait of Charles I, was with a passenger on the *Carolina*, a ship that arrived into what is now the Charleston Harbor in April 1670, long after Charles II had been invited back to the throne by Parliament. These early Charlestonians were determined to re-create the cosmopolitan, pleasure-filled world of Charles II's Restoration England, for Charles II—unlike his father—loved women and drink and horse racing and gambling. In his honor, these newly landed immigrants named their peninsula Charles Town.

As for the miniature portrait of the stern and politically suicidal father of Charles II, it disappeared and resurfaced many times over the next 150 years, until finally becoming, as part of the winnings in a high-stakes poker game, an official heirloom of the Larrabee family.

It disappeared one more time, the night that Agnes Larrabee died some sixteen years after the end of World War II, then like a cork in an ocean storm, resurfaced yet again, this time in the hands of that twelve-year-old girl from a bad part of town.

✛

Retha Herndon remained trapped inside a rough wooden shed on dirt, alongside a rusting lawn mower, a bundled length of garden hose, and a can of gasoline. Evening shadows now made the interior darker than it had been all afternoon, ever since Elder Jeremiah had stopped her and forced her to drive back home, his large truck filling her rearview mirror, its front grill only inches from her rear bumper.

Just before padlocking her into the shed, Elder Jeremiah had set a dog bowl half-filled with water on the packed dirt inside the shed. For the first hour Retha had refused to drink from it, knowing the bowl sent a message that he wanted her to fully understand. But with humidity and heat inside the shed twice what it was outside, she'd finally succumbed, first flicking out the dead flies floating on top. It was past seven now; the dog bowl had been empty for at least three hours, and Retha licked her lips constantly, futile as that relief was to a thirst that was almost enough to make her groan in anguish.

Retha was nauseous from the gasoline fumes. At least she hoped that was the reason. She didn't want to bring another baby into her life.

Her face was swollen and smeared with blood. Not because Elder Mason had beaten her after arriving at to the shed later in the afternoon; no, he would wait to do that when Junior was nearby to watch and learn. Her blood was smeared where she'd slapped at the mosquitoes that had been attacking her in a frenzy all afternoon.

Retha's fingers were bloody, too, raw from pulling at the door hinges. It wasn't that she wanted to escape for herself. It was that Billy Lee was in the trailer. Sometimes Elder Mason cut the air-conditioning because he said it was a waste of good money. If he'd shut if off during the afternoon and if the trailer was now too hot with Billy Lee as sick as he was . . .

Retha tried not to think about it. She was frantic to know that Billy Lee was still all right, and useless as it was to claw at the hinges, it was the only thing she could do to try to reach him.

Much as Retha dreaded explaining to Junior why she'd been locked in the shed, she hoped he would get back soon from fishing. She had to know how Billy Lee was doing. She had to get to the trailer to hold Billy Lee.

And there was the new Wal-Mart doll.

She had to get back into the trailer to hide it before Elder Mason happened upon it under a pile of Billy Lee's clothing. Elder Mason hated a mess, and first he'd yell about Retha not folding those clothes and not putting them up on a shelf. Then he'd ask questions about the doll and explode about wastefulness. After that, Retha knew, he'd begin shouting about giving any boy a doll, let alone his grandson who was supposed to grow up to hunt deer and fish for bass and maybe be one of the Chosen, unlike Junior who had no guts or real strength. Worst of all, after knowing she'd tried to escape with Billy Lee, Elder Mason might actually figure out why she'd bought the doll. Elder Mason was not a stupid man.

Buying the doll at Wal-Mart the day before had been part of Retha's plan. Pushing a cart down the aisles was about the only time she had to herself, because Junior just sat in the truck waiting for her to finish the list he gave her.

At the cash register, Retha did her best to hold back sniffles. She was in the ten-items-or-less lane, stuck behind a man in a baseball hat whose cart was half full. Not that Retha was going to criticize him for having more than ten items. Things like that always happened to Retha, and she accepted them meekly, the way the Bible said. Besides, she didn't trust her voice to speak, not when she was thinking about her plan.

In her own cart, with Billy Lee sitting lethargically in front of her, Retha had put a big package of toilet paper along with the dog food she'd been sent in to buy for Elder Mason's hounds. She'd picked up the toilet paper because she knew it would take a big bag to wrap it and that would give her the best chance to hide the doll.

When it was her turn, the woman behind the till gave her the standard greeting, and then grinned at the size of the doll in Retha's arms. "I've seen a few of those go through," the woman said. Her name tag read "Candy," but she looked anything but. "That one's almost as big as your own boy. The doll looks healthier than your boy, though. Girl, has he seen a doctor?"

"Running a bit of a fever," Retha said and put her cash down. Junior didn't know about the money she made sewing for neighbors in the compound. It was against Shepherd Isaiah's rules for women to keep any money, but most of the wives found a way to hide some from their husbands, if only to be part of the tiny black market within the compound.

"Yeah," Candy continued, either unaware of Retha's red eyes or uncaring. "Tell you what, these dolls look like the real thing."

The real thing. Which was why Retha was buying it. But she wouldn't have to if Billy Lee weren't so sick. That brought more tears.

Of course, Candy couldn't understand Retha's renewed

tears at that comment. So Candy shook her head slightly and concentrated on the keypad. Candy didn't know the reason that Retha was going to such efforts to sneak the doll into the trailer.

"I need the doll on a separate receipt," Retha finally blurted, scared to trust her voice.

"I just scanned it in," Candy complained. "With the other stuff."

Normally, Retha wouldn't have put up a fuss, but this was too important. The Elders reviewed all purchases because it all came from the church treasury and there were rules about what was deemed necessary and what was deemed luxury. A doll was definitely luxury, and more than that, Retha had another pressing reason to keep its purchase hidden.

"I need the doll on a separate receipt," Retha repeated, amazed at the hint of anger growing inside her.

Candy caught her tone and went through the hassle of obeying, which, strangely enough to Retha, also gave her a sense of satisfaction.

As for sneaking the doll into the trailer, that part had been no problem either. As Retha had anticipated, Junior maintained his habit of ignoring the packages that Retha bought. He always let her throw them into the back of the truck from her shopping cart, and when they got to the trailer, he always went inside to watch the auto-racing channel on satellite while she unloaded the truck with one arm, holding Billy Lee in the other.

So the first part of Retha's plan had worked; the doll was there and waiting for part two.

Except all of it had failed when she'd been caught escaping in Junior's truck and then been dragged into the shed by Elder Jeremiah. Thinking about Billy Lee alone in the trailer, Retha wanted to cry but was afraid if that dam burst, the tears might never stop.

All she could do now was wait for Junior to return.

Retha kept slapping mosquitoes as the dusk became night.

✛

Angel sat by Maddie's hospital bed, stroking her sister's forehead.

"How are you doing?" I asked, pulling up a chair. The room was a private one, and the bill was to be sent directly to my half brother. I was looking forward to hearing him moan at how I chose to squander a tiny part of our shared inheritance.

"I'm doing good." Angel turned her green eyes toward me. "Except . . ."

"Except?"

"I'm tired of explaining to people about my mama and daddy. You ain't gonna ask the questions everyone else been asking, right?"

I was curious, but this was an effective warning. I shook my head no.

"And you ain't gonna look down your nose at me cause I'm mochachino or because my daddy ran out when I was a baby or because Mama met another man who was black not white and was gonna have Maddie with him, except she died when Maddie was born and that other daddy run off, too?"

So she did want me to know.

"Angel, it doesn't matter to me where a person comes from. Only the direction he or she chooses to go."

"Alright then," she said, relaxing some.

"Maddie's doing better?"

My heart broke to see the little girl in a hospital bed in the children's ward. She was on an IV drip. Asleep. Breathing evenly. The sheen of sweat no longer clinging to her forehead.

"Maddie's doing better. They figure it might be a couple of days here. You still gonna pay the hospital like you promised?"

I nodded.

"What if you can't find the man that told Grammie Zora he'd buy that painting? Or if you can't find no one else to buy it and it happens I won't be able to pay you back?"

"I'll pay no matter what happens with the painting." I tried to hide the extent of my interest and asked casually, "Painting look good?"

"Doesn't seem like a real painting. Too small. Smaller than a computer screen. And the guy on it is dressed funny."

"Interesting," I said.

"Who would think that someone would pay twenty thousand dollars for it." She watched my face, probably to gauge my reaction to that astronomical figure.

I whistled, feeling guilty about playing dumb. This explained why she'd marched into the antique shop with such confidence and refused to sell it to Glennifer and Elaine for any less. "Twenty thousand! Some man promised your grammie that much for it?"

"About two months ago. Except she said no to him that night. Yesterday, though, I called her. See, she's at her sister's out of town and that's okay 'cause my friend Camellia stays with me at night. When I told Grammie yesterday that Maddie was sick and I needed to take her to the hospital, Grammie Zora changed her mind. She said it'd be a good idea to sell that painting after all. So all we got to do is find that man who was going to buy it."

I nodded, encouraging her to continue.

"Camellia's got a brother named Leroy," she said, "and Leroy's friend Bingo knows where the man is, but if I ask Bingo, and if Leroy and Bingo get any idea the kind of money they could get for the painting, they'll steal it from me. Leroy and Bingo steal plenty. Bingo's got a car, and Leroy hangs with Bingo 'cause Bingo's got wheels. That cell phone I gave you? That Rolex? They're the ones who stole 'em."

"They gave you the phone and watch?"

Angel shook her head at my stupidity. "I didn't say they *gave* them to me."

"Oh."

"And that's another reason I need to stay away from them. Leroy, he's okay. But Bingo, he gives me the creeps. He ain't said nothing, but I think he knows where some of their stuff goes. When he's at Leroy's, what me and Camellia do is rock his car until the alarm goes off. Him and Leroy go running out from the house, and then we steal any stuff they got hidden under Leroy's bed. Bingo would love to find a way to prove to Leroy it's me and Camellia. 'Course if he tries anything on me . . . ." Angel paused and grinned. "See, they stole a TASER–"

"TASER?"

"Stun gun. From a cop car. Only now they can't find it, if you know what I mean."

I nodded again. This girl had turned a ballpoint pen into a terrifying weapon. The thought of her with a police-issue stun gun . . .

"Don't look at me like that." Angel stuck her chin forward in defiance but spoke quietly so as not to wake Maddie. "She's all I got. And I'm all she's got. I'll do whatever it takes to protect Maddie."

"Kind of figured that," I said, "from the way you took the guard hostage."

"If I could have sold Grammie Zora's dusty old painting to those bags on King yesterday, I wouldn't have needed to. But they acted so strange, I was afraid to take it anywhere else to sell, so I went straight home."

She glared at me as if it were my fault. "And not only that, some weird little guy followed me, so now I really want to make sure I keep it safe."

I nodded noncommittally, my guilt compounding at the knowledge I concealed from her.

"I figure my best chance is if you can help me find the man who wanted to buy it from Grammie Zora. I ain't bringing the painting out in public again."

I cleared my throat. "It is your grammie's to sell, right?"

"What, you think Grammie Zora stole it?"

"Not her."

"Now you're saying I stole it." Angel straightened her back and shoulders in a perfect picture of indignation.

"I need to be sure. I don't want to spend time in prison for trying to sell stolen property."

"So you *are* saying I stole it."

I smiled. Her indignation was so perfect I knew it wasn't real. "Where did you get the cell phone you sold me this morning?"

"That's different. I didn't know you then."

"You lied to the cabbie. You stole the cell phone from Leroy and Bingo, along with that fake Rolex . . ."

"Fake! Couldn't be."

"Nice try."

She grinned. "So it's fake, it's still worth something. Don't forget how happy you were to take a stolen cell phone and fake Rolex off a helpless little girl like me."

Helpless, I thought. *Sure.* "Did you steal the painting?"

"There you go again. Any dog that ever tried fighting you for a bone would lose, I bet. "

"What I already learned about you today shows you don't mind bending the truth and that sometimes things stick to your fingers. So did you steal the painting?"

She grinned. Her teeth were a beautiful white. Someone had shown her dental hygiene and cared enough to make sure Angel made it a habit. "Sometimes things stick to my fingers, huh? Like it isn't my fault. Sticks to my fingers." Angel held a hand up in front of her and wiggled her fingers. "Look, sticky. So sticky I can't help bringing all that stuff home."

She frowned as suddenly as she had grinned. "Don't think Bingo will believe that if he sees I got some of his stuff, do you?"

"So the painting didn't stick to your fingers? It belongs to your grammie?"

"All you rich people always talk this proper? Biting off each word so clean?"

"Don't change the subject. The painting isn't stolen, right? That's what I need to know before I help you out."

"Grammie Zora had it before I was born." Angel pointed at the top of her left cheekbone. I saw a small triangular scar beneath her eye. "Happened when I was playing with it when I was five. I was running with it and fell on the corner of the frame."

I didn't know if I was prepared to believe her, but there was no point in disagreeing until I found out otherwise. "It wasn't stolen and your Grammie Zora had it a long time then," I said. "Suddenly some man shows up and wants to buy it. How was it this man knew she had it?"

"Grammie Zora had him fetched."

"She sent for him, but when he came over, she didn't want to sell it to him. That doesn't make sense."

"I said she had him fetched. I didn't say she had him fetched to sell it to him. But then when he was there, he asked to buy it off her."

I asked the obvious, feeling like a Keystone Cop. "Why did she have him fetched then?"

Her eyes shifted away from mine slightly. She blinked before answering. "Don't know."

Interesting, I thought. I chose not to pursue it. "How did he know she had it?"

"He saw it on the wall in our living room, I guess. While they were talking. Must have decided he wanted it."

"Know who he was?"

"Only to see him again. White skin, white hair. Talks like you, so he must be rich, too, especially to pay all that for a stupid old painting. He leaned on a cane but walked like he didn't need it. Old. Older than you. Acted like he owned the world. After Grammie Zora had him fetched, someone drove him up in a big black Cadillac with dark windows—not the car Cadillac but a soovey one—and waited in the truck the whole time the guy talked with Grammie in our house."

"What's his name?"

"Don't know. Bingo can tell you where to look."

"Bingo?"

"I already told you it was Bingo that Grammie sent to fetch the man. And I already told you I don't want to ask Bingo anything. 'Cause he'll ask me why I want to know. Like I said, in case you weren't listening to that part either, if he thinks I got something worth something . . ."

"So you want me to ask Bingo where he went to fetch the white-haired man. Why not just call your grammie at her sister's and ask her?"

She shook her head again and sighed at my lack of intelligence. "Grammie Zora just told me it was okay to sell it. She didn't tell me it was okay to sell it to the man she didn't want to get it in the first place. What Grammie don't know won't hurt her. When she gets back, it will be sold and gone. She don't have to know who bought it. Weren't you listening when I told you I'll do what it takes to help Maddie?"

"I do recall."

She stared at me and let the silence build. I was the one to break it with yet another question. "So I just go ask Bingo where to find this white man who showed up in a black Cadillac SUV with dark windows?"

"Exactly. But without Bingo knowing it was me that sent you. Remember that part. Him and Leroy, they hang out at the Velvets for Gents on Saturday nights. They'll be there right now. I'll tell you what his car looks like, so it won't be no problem to find them. They sit in the car waiting to sell stuff that they stole. That's what they always do at night. Me and Camellia know, 'cause we follow them sometimes and watch people buy stuff off them there."

"You want me to ask Bingo tonight."

"Before he gets into a bar and drunk enough to fight." She spoke matter-of-factly, like it never occurred to her that there were places and lives where this was out of the ordinary. "Any next day Bingo could be dead, especially any next day after a Saturday night. It's never too soon to ask Bingo something, believe me on that."

There was a simple flaw in her request.

"From what you've told me," I said, "I see no reason why Bingo would bother telling me how to step off a pier and drown."

"I wrote up a note for you to give Bingo," Angel said. She flashed me that wonderful rogue smile as she pulled a folded envelope from her back pocket. "Once you get him to read it, he'll answer anything you ask. I licked this envelope shut and you gotta make sure this envelope ain't open when you give it to him. You can't read it first, because if it's open when it gets to him, he ain't gonna be afraid of what's inside. And be careful with the envelope. It's got needles inside. You sit on it, you'll jab your rear."

"Anything else?" I said, amused.

"Yeah. Bingo's a bully. That's why he gets drunk before he fights, and mostly he loses. Much as he pushes me and Camellia around, he'll be scared of someone as big as you. He's like a dog that barks but won't ever bite as long as you don't turn your back and run."

She searched my face to see if I understood. My expression must not have reassured her. "What I mean," she said, "is that when he pulls a knife, you can't let him know you're scared."

"I don't like knives," I said. "I don't like holes in my skin either."

"I was afraid of that," Angel answered. She stared at the wall in thought before turning back to me. "Then just go ahead and tell him the envelope is from Grammie Zora."

"How's that going to help?"

"If you can get him to open the envelope first, he'll swallow that knife before he dares to cut you open." She searched my face again.

"Really," she said. "Trust me."

CHAPTER

6

I spun my Jeep to turn into the parking lot of the Velvets for Gents nightclub to search for Bingo and Leroy.

A late afternoon thundershower had passed through a few hours earlier, cleansing the air of dust and humidity. The uneven pavement held puddles that gleamed beneath the streetlights.

I cruised slowly, looking for Bingo's Chevette. The throb of dance music reached me from the Velvets for Gents. It was the bar to visit if you were college-aged and armed with knife or gun. It was also the place not to enter if you were over thirty, had a short haircut, and preferred not to learn the sensation of being stabbed or shot. I really hoped Bingo and Leroy would be in his car as Angel had promised.

I didn't bother locking the Jeep; I often simply put my keys under the floor mat. Locking it was unnecessary, for I never left anything of value inside. When the top was up, if someone wanted to unlock the door, all they'd have to do is slash the upper canvas or the plastic windows with a knife. And this was the place that most passersby would be suitably prepared to do so.

Knife. I thought of Angel's warning about Bingo.

I wanted to step back inside the Jeep and drive away. But the hook had been set the moment Glennifer and Elaine told me about a little girl who walked into their shop with a baby sister riding her hip, and a seventeenth-century painting stolen the night Agnes Larrabee died. Much as that had hooked me, I still might have been able to wriggle free, but then I'd met Angel and watched her fight for her baby sister. I was not going to quit on this.

So I began to search among the cars for a jacked-up red Chevette with mag wheels and black-tinted windows. I found it within a minute, in a dark corner of the lot beneath a streetlight with a broken bulb. Heavy metal music seeped out of the Chevette. As did cigarette smoke.

I knocked on the window, amused at the vanity of youth. A Chevette was all he'd been able to afford, but by adding the mags and tinted windows, it was obvious he was determined to show the world that he was cool.

The window cracked slightly. More smoke rose to my nostrils. The music went silent, and a beam from a powerful flashlight inside blinded me.

"I need to speak to Bingo," I said, stepping aside from the beam.

"Ain't seen you before." The beam followed my face and remained directly in my eyes. "Who sent you and what are you buying?"

"Put the flashlight away," I said, my irritation now slightly stronger than my considerable anxiety.

"You buying?" The beam stayed on my face. I refused to put

up my hands to shield myself. "Show me the money and I'll show you what you want."

A giggle came from the other side of the Chevette. " 'Show me the money.' Man, can't you think of anything better?"

"Leroy, this dude's so old he'll think that was hip."

"Put the flashlight away," I said. "I want to talk to Bingo."

He responded with a vernacular reply that, boiled down to more polite language, instructed me to leave. The window rolled up again. The beam shut off. The music resumed.

I waited until the spots left my eyes. I stepped forward and knocked on the window again.

Nothing. Not even a flashlight beam back on my face. My irritation grew to an unreasonable anger.

I walked back to my Jeep. I drove it, headlights off, until it was directly behind the jacked-up Chevette. I shut the motor off and turned on my headlights. I clicked them to high beam so the light shone directly into the Chevette. I saw two silhouettes in motion in the front seat, turning to look back.

I stepped out of the Jeep again. I walked to the back of the Chevette, leaned on the bumper, and began to rock it hard, remembering the ploy Angel used when she wanted to pull Bingo out onto the street from Camellia's house.

As I'd guessed, the doors were locked. Which meant the car alarm had been set.

Within seconds the alarm began to scream shrilly into the night. An alarm that would attract any police nearby. To a car that undoubtedly held stolen electronics in the backseat or trunk.

I returned to my Jeep, leaned against the fender, and watched and waited.

The doors on each side opened. Standing squarely in the

high beams of my headlights, the kid on the driver's side cursed
at me as he frantically put a key in the driver's side lock and
turned it to shut off the alarm. If he was Bingo, he was, as Angel
had promised, a good six inches shorter than I was. He wore a
loose-fitting sweatshirt, and his shaggy blond hair brushed against
his shoulders. Light bounced off his shiny face.

The passenger was dressed the same, but he was larger,
broader, and much more mellow. Leroy. The skin of his hands
and neck and face was black and seemed to absorb the headlights. He simply leaned against the passenger side and waited
and watched, arm half raised to give his eyes some shade from
the headlights.

When the alarm stopped shrieking, Bingo pulled out a
switchblade.

He advanced upon me, squinting against my headlights.

✛

Retha faced bright light, too.

When she heard the clicking of the lock outside the shed,
she prayed hard that it was Junior, not Elder Mason again. Or
worse, Shepherd Isaiah. Or worst of all, Shepherd Isaiah with
Elder Jeremiah.

Retha held her breath as the door opened, lifting a hand
streaked with dried blood to shield her eyes against the glare of
a flashlight aimed directly into her face.

"What's this Elder Mason said about you driving away this
morning?" Junior had learned to always refer to his father as Elder
Mason, just so he wouldn't slip up in front of him. Junior's voice
had a thick drawl. No beer on his breath like his other bass-fishing

friends. That was one good thing about Junior. He never sinned by drinking beer. "He ain't happy, I can tell you that," he said.

"How's Billy Lee?" Retha shifted to get the light out of her eyes. "How is he?"

"Fine as far as I know. Didn't hear nothing from his bedroom. He must be sleeping."

"Air-conditioning on?" Retha found it hard to speak, her mouth was so dry.

"Yeah. It's always on when Elder Mason's by himself in there. Tell me about this driving you did. What got into your head, trying to leave without signing out? Didn't you know the gates are under video all the time?"

"I want to see Billy Lee." Retha struggled from a sitting position onto her knees. She tried to stand. Junior pushed her down. Not roughly, but firmly.

"Elder Mason just sent me out to give you a whipping. Not to let you out. I told you, he's some kind of mad." Junior set the flashlight on the ground, shining up. He was twenty. The light showed his slight figure, his dirty blue jeans and T-shirt, the piti-ful red mustache, his shaggy red hair. Retha could smell the fish bait on his fingers.

"Whip me fast then," Retha said. "I got to be with Billy Lee. Ain't you worried about him being as sick as he is?"

"Elder Mason says he's sick 'cause you have the devil in you."

"I don't, Junior. I pray to Jesus all the time. Now whip me fast and let me have Billy Lee."

"I ain't gonna whip you. You know I can't stomach that. But if Elder Mason asks, tell him I did. I just brought you something to eat. But don't tell him that."

"I need to hold Billy Lee."

"Not just yet. Elder Mason's got to give us the say-so."

Retha bowed her head. "Junior, can't you and me live our own lives? Ain't that somewheres in the Bible?"

"So's honor your father and mother that your lives may be long in the land that the Lord gives you. Elder Mason's still my Daddy and a widower and—"

"And when he says jump, you say 'how high' and 'when do you want me to land.' Our boy's sick and we need to get him to a doctor."

"Is that where you was headed today?"

Retha didn't answer.

"I'm gonna pretend I didn't hear nothing about a doctor. Praying will bring about the healing. We just need stronger faith."

"I want to run away from the Glory Church, Junior. I swear I do. Take me somewhere else. Please."

Junior crouched down. Fear lit his eyes. "Don't say that. Ever. If Shepherd Isaiah hears it . . ."

Retha held back a sob. From conversations she'd overheard between Shepherd Isaiah and Elder Mason, she knew too much about the Chosen of the church. Far too much. "I just want Billy Lee to be fine. He's our only boy and he needs more than prayer."

"And don't let Elder Mason hear you say that either!" Junior's voice was a harsh, terrified whisper. "He can't have his authority questioned by the ones that live under his own roof." He took a deep breath. "I don't even want to think of what kind of example he'd make of us in front of all the others. . . ."

Junior stopped. He shoved a sandwich at Retha. "Now eat what I brought."

Retha was too thirsty to think of food. "I want to hold Billy Lee."

"I'll tell Elder Mason I whipped you good and you begged forgiveness. Then maybe he'll let you come in."

"I want to hold Billy Lee. Help me take him to a doctor."

"What if we ask Shepherd Isaiah for a Glory Session? That'll drive away the devil. You'll see."

"No Glory Session. It didn't work for the others."

"Because they didn't believe enough."

"Junior, no Glory Session. I couldn't bear it."

Junior stood quickly. He stopped in the doorway. "I'll get back as soon as I can. Remember, if Elder Mason asks, you tell him I whipped you good."

"Junior!" But she spoke to a closing door.

In the dark, the mosquitoes continued to descend on her face and ears and the bare skin of her arms.

C H A P T E R

7

A mile to the south on Queen Street, tourists dined in restaurants where a slab of fish that would fit on my palm might cost them twenty-five bucks. Here, a crack addict might kill to steal anything of the same value. As Bingo moved toward me, the throbbing of the music floated through the parking lot, like a movie score to a fight scene.

But I didn't want the fight.

Holding his knife in front of him in his right hand, Bingo wanted to play it tough, wanted to play it like a cat leisurely moving in on a cornered mouse. What ruined his act were my headlights. He had to keep his left hand, palm out, in front of his face to shield his eyes.

"Car alarm was a stupid move, man," he said. "It's slice-and-dice time."

"Get him good," Leroy said.

I was glad that Leroy wasn't smart enough to use the flashlight to blind me as Bingo advanced. If he had been, I would have lost what advantage I had with the headlights in Bingo's eyes. But the flashlight was still in the Chevette. I held my position.

"This is for you," I told Bingo. From my back pocket, I threw the envelope from Angel down at his feet.

He was far too streetwise to let it distract him. He continued to advance. "I don't know what your game was, but the new one is called bleed-until-you-die."

I saw more of his face as his movement brought him toward me. Lumpy, with his lips forming a tight sneer. He was barely old enough to have a driver's license. Young enough, then, to have delusions of immortality. Especially when he had a knife and I didn't. "Open it," I said. "It's from Grammie Zora."

Angel had been right about everything else. But her talisman didn't work. Bingo didn't even flinch at hearing Grammie Zora's name. He moved closer, until the gap between us was less than three steps. He spit. "Grammie Zora don't need yuppie messengers like you."

Really, Angel's words echoed in my mind, *trust me.* She'd find this funny.

Despite the heat, I'd worn a leather jacket. I pulled it off. Slowly, because Bingo was moving slowly. He didn't want to fight. He wanted to see how badly I'd scare. I held the elbow of each sleeve in each hand and let the body of the jacket hang loose in front of my legs.

Attackers rarely expect anything but fear from their intended victims. So I stepped toward Bingo, ready if he slashed at me to pull the sleeves apart hard and quickly. It would bring the jacket up to tangle his knife hand. Once wrapped in leather, the blade would do no damage. He'd have to let go, but if he didn't, he'd be an easy target for a knee to his groin.

At my move toward him, Bingo hesitated, moved back slightly.

That told me enough. He'd be willing to listen, but I needed to get his attention fast.

"Get Leroy to open the envelope," I said. "He's got a flashlight. Or he can use my headlights. He'll see what's inside. Then we don't have to take this any further."

I hadn't opened the envelope. In retrospect, that was stupid. But Angel had an air of knowing exactly what she was doing. I really believed her—that once Bingo read her note, he'd talk.

"You undercover?" Bingo's voice was suddenly an octave higher. "Because all the stuff in that car is ours. We barter, man. Pick stuff up at garage sales, bring it here. Sometimes people buy. Sometimes people sell. We're like a pawnshop on wheels. That's all, man."

"Leroy," I said with a tired voice, hiding the adrenaline that flowed in me, "just grab the envelope before your friend gets hurt."

Bingo didn't call him off. Leroy slouched forward. The features of his face were surprisingly delicate. Big as he was, I would have been surprised if he was any older than fourteen.

As he neared, Bingo kicked him the envelope without taking his eyes off me.

Leroy retreated to the passenger side of the car again. He opened the envelope slowly, pulled out a note and read it. Then he looked inside the envelope again.

"Drop the knife," he said in a high, urgent voice. "Tell him whatever he wants!"

"I ain't dropping this knife. I'm gonna shred him," Bingo said. Not much bluster left in his voice.

"That was in her note." Leroy was obviously agitated. "Grammie Zora says tell him whatever he asks. Or else."

"Else what?" Bingo tried to make it a snarl.

Standing on the other side of the Chevette, Leroy dug into the envelope and pulled out the contents. He held his fingers high for Bingo to see. Three sewing needles tied together with black thread.

"You know what this is," Leroy said. "Grammie Zora's note says she'll hex you if you don't obey."

Bingo had obviously grown up in Leroy's neighborhood. He knew what the needles were. A suffering root.

Just like I now knew Grammie Zora was a voodoo doctor.

Bingo dropped the switchblade at his feet.

⁜

Some of the descendants of the early slaves from Africa are known as the Gullah. They have their own dialect and are known by tourists primarily for the basket-weaving skills that women have passed down from generation to generation.

In the early 1920s, about ten miles upstream from Charleston on the Cooper River, there was a small collection of houses where many of the Gullah lived, as they still do today, although the tin-roofed cabins and leaning outhouse have long since been replaced.

Among those people was a blacksmith named Jethro Hammer. Because of his trade, he was a well-muscled man. He was also handsome and considerate, and popular among the women. He was married, however, and deeply in love with his wife, Mae. They were childless, and Mae worried that this factor would eventually drive Jethro away. That, combined with the attention given to him by other women, was enough to fuel an unfounded jealousy that led to nothing short of a Shakespearean tragedy.

Mae went to a voodoo doctor and had her husband hexed. The voodoo doctor used a suffering root—three brand-new sewing needles tied together with black thread. In Mae's presence, he empowered the suffering root with a ceremony in a graveyard just after midnight on a full moon. The next morning, Mae hid the three needles in her husband's front pocket and sent him to work with a lunch of ham with mustard on homemade bread.

Before noon arrived, however, Mae was overcome with remorse. She rushed to Jethro where he stood at his anvil with tongs, hammering red-hot iron into shape. She begged him to go for a walk along the river, where she confessed that she'd placed a curse upon him that would certainly bring him death before the next full moon.

She showed him the suffering root that she'd hidden upon him, and repeated again and again, "I've killed you, I've killed you."

He was just as convinced as she was that his death was certain.

At that point, Mae told Jethro that she never wanted to be separated from him. She begged for him to kill her, because that was the only way they could remain together. She told him she would wait for him by the river's edge on the other side of death, where they would live together forever with no fear or pain or poverty.

Jethro later told the judge that he believed he was going to die anyway, and he didn't want his beloved Mae left alone in the world. So with one big, powerful arm, he held her gently and with his other hand pinched her nostrils tightly. He was holding her lifeless body, rocking back and forth and weeping, when the police came to arrest him.

In jail, he patiently waited for the hex to bring him the death that would take him to her. He waited until the next full moon, fully expecting to die any day.

The hex itself failed. It was the hangman's noose that finally sent him beyond, three months later.

✠

"That's all you want? How to find the white-haired dude? The man Grammie Zora had me get for her? I can tell you that easy. She showed me his picture and—"

"She had a photo of him?"

Bingo nodded. He sat on the hood of his car, Leroy beside him. "Black-and-white head-and-shoulders picture. Like it had been taken with a zoom lens. She took it out of an envelope. I remembered that because I saw the name on the envelope."

"The name of the white-haired man?"

"No. The name of the detective agency. Mixson. So right away I was curious—like what does Grammie Zora have to do with a detective agency and what's this about? But I didn't ask. A person don't mess with Grammie Zora."

"And the white-haired man?"

"Grammie Zora told me where I'd find him, and she told me not to take any black friends with me. Said she was asking me because I was white and this was a place only white folk should go."

I'd shut down the headlights of the Jeep. The darkness was a comfortable blanket. I'd grown so accustomed to the music of the Velvets for Gents that it was no more distracting than crickets in the countryside.

"You went," I said. "Alone. That night. Just as soon as she asked."

"You kidding, man? This was Grammie Zora speaking."

"Did she tell you why she wanted you to find this man for her?"

"Smoke, man," Bingo said to Leroy.

Leroy had quick movements, almost sparrowlike, a strange contrast to his size. I guessed that Bingo used the age difference to be his leader. Leroy reached up the sleeve of his sweatshirt, took out a pack. He pulled a cigarette halfway out, extended it to Bingo. Bingo took it and spoke to me without looking in Leroy's direction.

"No, I didn't ask Grammie Zora why she wanted him. Like right now I ain't asking why she don't bother to explain all this to you herself. That's a mysterious woman with mysterious powers. I keep clear of her. That man I found for her, he was just as scared, once I delivered the message she wanted me to deliver."

Leroy flicked a lighter. Bingo half turned and sucked at the flame through his cigarette. Leroy drew on his own cigarette. Two glowing buds faced me in the darkness of the parking lot.

"I heard that doctors take the lungs of smokers at an autopsy and bounce them off the floor," I said. "Weird, huh?"

Leroy flicked his cigarette onto the pavement. Bingo laughed and inhaled deeply.

"Grammie Zora's message . . ." I prompted.

"Grammie Zora told me the man might not want to follow

me back. She said all I'd have to do is tell him one thing, and he'd listen, no matter what he was doing when I called on him. She was right. That woman's got the power."

"What was the message?"

" 'Crown of thorns. I know what you are doing. Crown of thorns.' "

"Crown of thorns?" I repeated.

"Yeah. I found the place easy. It was a church, Glory God something. I had to go through a gate. Imagine that. A church with a security gate. Some guy guarding it with a shotgun. I told him who I wanted to see. He took me went inside and the white-haired man was sitting there with two men so big that bears would run from them. I wanted to git. But I was more scared of Grammie Zora and what she'd say if I came back alone. So I looked past the two big men with the beards and told the white-haired man what Grammie Zora told me to tell him, exactly word for word. He wasn't interested in listening to me."

" 'Crown of thorns. I know what you are doing. Crown of thorns.' " I made sure I repeated exactly what Bingo had just said.

"Yup. That made all of them real quiet. And the white-haired man told his friends it was okay, he'd go. So all of them followed me into town in a big black Escalade, right behind me all the way. What I'd give for one of those if I could afford the gas."

"This church, you remember how to get there?"

Bingo nodded. "But Grammie Zora's note didn't say anything about taking you there. I don't want to go back. And I never want to see them again. One was bigger than the other, way bigger. He stared at me so hard it was like his eyes could kill me." Bingo gave me directions.

I thanked him. "You're a smart kid," I said. "How many

more Saturdays you think you can park here until it's a cop who shows up instead of buyers?"

"What else am I gonna do? Flip burgers for a couple bucks an hour? At least I'm not peddling drugs and hurting kids that way."

I thought of his neighborhood. All the things in his background that had likely brought him to this place. I didn't have a short answer that wouldn't make me sound like a tired, self-righteous WASP born south of Broad. And the long answer? That involved more than I wanted to give.

I didn't answer at all. I began to climb into my Jeep.

"Hey," Bingo said. "It's only because I'm scared of Grammie Zora that I'm gonna tell you something else."

I waited, door open to my Jeep.

"You never asked me for the white-haired guy's name," Bingo said. "That was something weird, too. Grammie Zora told me to call him by his name in case 'crown of thorns' didn't get his attention."

"And?"

"Don't know what the big deal was." Bingo said it casually, unaware of the electrical current of shock it would put through me. "It's not like I ever heard of him before. The white-haired dude's name is Timothy Larrabee."

C H A P T E R

8

"Nick? Sorry to wake you but . . ."

Seven in the morning. The voice in my ear was coming from Chicago. An hour earlier than Charleston. That meant Amelia Layton had called me in the hotel either at the end or beginning of a shift.

"Hey," I said, my voice a little thick. "Had to get up anyway to answer the phone."

It was a pitiful old joke, but it was the best I could do, coming out of a restless sleep.

"How are you?" she asked.

"The usual. Facing down juvenile delinquents armed with switchblades."

"Must have been a long drawn-out fight." She kept her voice light, assuming I'd been joking. "We haven't talked in a few days."

"I knew you were running twelve-hour shifts." Me, making the apology for her so that it wouldn't put her in a position of making excuses. A few months earlier, we'd spent a half hour a day on the telephone. Lately, the phone calls had been a day or two apart. I got her answering machine more often than I reached her. I even wondered if she'd met someone else. So I retreated, the defense I'd used all my life.

She laughed, keeping her voice in that same light tone. "Sorry. We've been short-staffed."

"I know." I sat in bed and stretched. "So how's—" I stopped, because she'd begun talking at the same time, with the same question.

"—the weather?" we each finished.

"I've got a few days off coming up," she said.

"Lucky you. I know you need the break. More kayaking on the lake?"

I'd invited her to visit a couple of times already, and each time she'd had an excuse to decline. Good reasons. But I didn't want her to know how anxious I was to see her again. And I was afraid the next reason she gave me might be poor enough that I'd have to acknowledge her interest in me was less intense than I hoped.

"I don't know," she said. "It's so crowded with boaters that things on the water have been a little crazy. I have a four-day stretch away from the hospital, almost like a vacation. I'd hate to waste it dodging Budweiser maniacs on Jet Skis."

Was she hinting at a visit to Charleston? My pride didn't allow me to ask. Because if she refused yet again . . .

"I've been thinking of kayaking around here," I said, steering the conversation away from her time off work. "Great thing is, doesn't matter if you have one leg or two."

"Take it seriously enough," she said, "and you'd get pretty

good at it. How many other sports could you compete against the other athletes at an equal level, huh?"

There it was. The roller coaster of my emotions. I clung to every word she spoke on the phone. Wanting our calls to be longer. Yet, a few weeks earlier she'd asked if I ever intended to pursue a Ph.D. in astronomy. Which I'd silently interpreted as a question about my ambition in life. Here, despite the surface of that statement about kayaking—or so I interpreted—she was once again exhorting me to be more ambitious. Go into the world and compete. Or was my subconscious working hard to generate resentment as a way to console myself in case she'd lost real interest in our relationship?

"Hey," I said, wanting another subject change, "let me tell you about my trip to the emergency room yesterday."

"Nick!" Real concern. Which lifted me again. I pictured her as she'd been during our walks here in Charleston. Her soft hair blowing against my face as she leaned into me in the park along the river.

"Nothing like that." I described Angel and all the events, minus the meeting with Bingo in the parking lot.

"She sounds interesting, this Angel."

"I get the sense she's very, very sharp," I said. "She knows what she wants and figures out the best way to get it."

"Aren't you concerned about her living by herself? Shouldn't you get someone to check on her?"

I grinned. "The doctor in you goes straight to the problem, doesn't it?"

Before she could reply, there was a knock on my door.

"Hang on," I said. "Room service just arrived."

I threw on a robe to sign for my coffee and bagels and newspaper, as ordered the night before. It was lazy, very lazy. But since I expected my half brother to pay for it once he lost the court case and had to cover my legal expenses, I didn't mind the luxury.

Instead of returning to my bed where I'd answered the phone, I sat on the couch and picked up the extension. I took a small gulp of coffee. "Where were we?" I asked. "Right. Sending someone to check on Angel. I don't think I need to. Seems every-thing is fine. The doctors are looking after her sister. Her grand-mother is coming back. And she gets help from the neighbors."

"Nick, she's a twelve-year-old. On her own. I know that part of town."

Like me, Amelia had been raised south of Broad. Like me, she'd fled Charleston. Except she had not returned.

"Well . . ."

"Honestly, Nick." It was an admonishment. "I don't care if her grandmother's flying back this afternoon on the Concorde. What kind of family situation is that when the grandmother is willing to leave in the first place?"

"Well . . ."

"I hope you do something about it. Find the social services people. Let them know. They'll step in."

"Good idea," I said. I wasn't going to argue.

"By the sound of your voice, you're not going to." So Amelia did want to argue.

"People live their lives. I can't just step in and—"

"That's right," she said. "You have your precious little world, and you don't want anyone to enter."

Where had that come from?

"Well . . ."

"Look," she said. "Got to go. Call me when you have time.

I know it's busy there, what with the archives and your equally precious time with Glennifer and Elaine."

But she didn't hang up.

I started laughing. With relief, hoping I understood correctly her sudden shift of mood. "Please tell me," I said, "that you're as worried about me liking you as I am about you liking me."

"Well . . ." The defensiveness had left her voice. "You haven't asked lately for me to come visit, and now when I told you I had four days off . . ."

Maybe she and I shared the same roller coaster. Which would be wonderful. Maybe her roller coaster was the reason for the vague unease I couldn't shake.

"Amelia," I said, "Since you have four days off and since Charleston has an airport what would you think about—"

"Hang on," she said. "Stupid pager." Ten seconds later, she was on the phone again. "Nick, I am so sorry. Emergency back at the hospital."

"No problem," I said. A familiar ache filled me. "I understand. Call me when you can."

This time, she did hang up.

I set the phone down. I opened the drapes of the hotel room. I watched the sky get brighter as I drank my coffee. I read the newspaper. Twice.

When the coffee was gone, I showered, dressed in a suit and tie, and left the hotel room.

⁜

In my childhood I'd been to many Sunday services. Based on that, I guessed this service was nearing its end. A one-hour sermon had been preached on carrying the burden of the cross of Jesus. Followed by a half-hour prayer that had just finished. Next would come the passing of the collection plate. Then a final hymn.

Instead, Isaiah Sullivan stepped out from behind the pulpit, armed with neither Bible nor hymnal.

"Last night, the voice of the Lord came to me and said we have a sinner in our midst." He spoke in a quiet voice that verged on sadness. "And by his command, I have no choice but to call this sinner forth to confess before God and man."

He stopped and let a heavy tension fall upon his congregation. Despite his quiet voice, Shepherd Isaiah was an imposing old-style preacher. He was rawboned and big, with a thatch of hair that was unnaturally dark compared to the wrinkles around his eyes. He had a square head and wore a beard that made him look vaguely like photos of Abraham Lincoln. I decided he was in his midthirties, but definitely not softening as middle age approached. He had removed his black jacket during the passion of his sermon. The sleeves of his starched white shirt were rolled up to his elbows, showing corded muscle and a tattoo that I couldn't see clearly enough from where I sat to make out any details.

"This sinner . . ." he continued gently, ". . . this sinner has been seen in discourse with an unmarried man not her husband. Among the heathens. And this woman partook in the evils of alcohol. Were it not for the arrival of her husband to save her from the fires of hell, God only knows how much further she would have willingly gone with Satan."

I was impressed at the sincerity of his sorrow.

"It is with pain that I call her forth," he continued. "Betty Crenshaw. A jezebel who must be punished now. In front of her husband. In front of this congregation. And in front of God himself."

"No!" came a cry in the silence that followed. A burly, bearded man had risen, taking his much smaller wife by the arm.

"No!" She cried again, trying to pull away from her husband.

"I wish it could be any other way," came the voice from the pulpit. Suddenly his voice rose as if directing holy anger at an unseen opponent. "Yet Satan must be banished! This very morning!"

The man with the heavy black beard pulled his wife up the aisle toward the pulpit. She struggled against him, her feet sliding uselessly along the waxed wooden floor, as if she were a child being dragged firmly by her father.

And as the man and wife approached the steps leading to the pulpit, a giant of a man rose from the front pew. It brought from the congregation the merest of sounds, as if each member had drawn in a quick breath.

This giant man, I would learn later, was Elder Jeremiah. The preacher's blood brother. Holding a small wooden paddle in his right hand.

"Let the Holy Chastisement begin!" Shepherd Isaiah called out to the congregation. "Let our Lord be served!"

✛

My first steps to belief in a God behind this universe began through my background as an astronomer.

This might surprise those who think that science is "truth" and God is "faith." A hundred years ago, yes, it did look like our universe had no place for God. But quantum physics succeeded in replacing much of the cherished truths of classic nuclear physics and in bringing new mysteries: light was both a particle and wave; matter could flicker in and out of existence. Experimental work on Einstein's theories brought as many questions as answers. And in the last century, mainstream biologists began to see major flaws in the predictions of Darwin.

Just past the middle of the twentieth century, astronomy brought to science the first hint of a staggering concept: the universe had a beginning. Much as atheist astronomers tried to prove otherwise, evidence accumulated until it was nearly impossible to deny the big bang theory. With that, the Genesis view of a universe suddenly had substance—science and Genesis agreed there was a day before which time did not exist, this universe was created from a point of nothingness, and the direction of the growth of the universe had been predetermined by something outside the law of nature.

Then came something more astounding, given that the foundation of science for the previous five hundred years had been built on the notion that this was a naturalistic universe, that all events could be explained by previous events, that our existence on this planet resulted from chance. Some astronomers and physicists began to examine in whole all the inarguable scientific data that related to the constants in physics—gravity, weak nuclear forces, strong nuclear forces, electromagnetism—that were necessary for the creation of life. They discovered that if any one of these and others of the dozens upon dozens of necessary constants in this universe were changed by a fraction of a fraction, Earth and life upon it would not exist.

The mathematical odds of this happening by chance, these scientists knew, were roughly similar to someone winning the

SIGMUND BROUWER

lottery each week for fifty weeks in a row. The science of mathe-
matics says that if the probability is less than one in ten followed
by fifty zeroes, it is essentially impossible or beyond reason. Like
winning the lottery that many consecutive times. Common sense
also tells us at this point there is no other conclusion that to win
in such a way, the lottery must be rigged. So, too, this universe.

Rigged. Beyond reason to expect that all of the astonishing
coincidences in physics factors would be as they are.

Because of this, some respected scientists were willing to
argue and theorize that the mathematical probability for the
universe to exist in a way that makes life possible cannot be
reasonably expected to be accounted for by randomness. Some
scientists were willing to go further and argue that data shows
that the end goal of the universe is exactly the same goal as
claimed in Genesis: to produce human life. In effect, after five
hundred years of denying a creator, twenty-first-century science
was opening the door to the existence of God again.

For me, the platform of the evidence of science meant I
only needed to take small step of faith to believe this universe was
designed by an incomprehensible power beyond the natural. But
as I well knew and well know, there is a big difference between
the relatively simple choice of acknowledging God's existence and
the much more difficult choice of trying to reach for him. Or
attempting to understand who he is, what he expects from us, and
how we should relate to him.

Questions of the soul and of God, of course, do not belong
within the realm of science. Neither do they belong to politics,
but the sad state of wars and terrorism fought in his name shows
that the answers to these questions can be debated endlessly and
murderously.

Even within peaceful societies, God's image can be distorted
ferociously.

Especially with men like Shepherd Isaiah Sullivan claiming
to speak on God's behalf.

✛

Including the lengthy sermon, it had taken two hours of church
service to reach the moment of Holy Chastisement. Two hours of
watching and listening to Shepherd Isaiah when I was simply
curious to find Timothy Larrabee among the congregation.

I had arrived just before the service began and crunched
across rocks through a parking lot filled with pickup trucks. At
first—except for the gated entrance to a gravel parking lot—this
could have been no different from any other small country
church on a hot summer Sunday in the South. On the outside,
this was a beautiful white building built a hundred years earlier—
a small and simple building with a small and simple steeple, the
background of tall oaks making it a perfect picture for nostalgic
postcards. Among the trees in the background were mobile
homes—all identical—as if the church guarded the entrance to a
large trailer park.

The building's interior reflected a peaceful tradition,
perhaps because it had been here long before the mobile homes.
The church had stained-glass windows. Dark, beech-stained pews
with hymnals tucked in the back of each. Ceiling fans. An organ
at the front. Scuffed, worn, hardwood flooring.

At first glance the congregation of about two hundred also
seemed straight from a Norman Rockwell painting. Until a closer
look showed that things were off just enough to verge on eerie.

The women in the congregation were dressed identically, each in a long gray dress. Each wore her hair hanging straight and unstyled beneath a gray scarf. No makeup. This blandness, and the lack of animation in their faces, took away any individuality as effectively as if each was wearing a veil. All of the men wore black suits. Most were bearded. And there were no children seated with the congregation. On my way inside I'd seen the women herding them into classrooms at the back of the small church, while the men stood just inside the front entrance engaged in hushed conversations.

It wasn't until I'd taken my seat that I noticed how much I was marked as a stranger because of my navy blue suit. And as I'd looked around, I'd noticed many looking back at me. Not the women. They stared straight ahead. But the men.

Shepherd Isaiah's eyes had fallen on me many times during the service. I felt as obvious as a porcupine on a dance floor. I wondered if he followed Charlestonian society closely enough to absorb the newspaper articles that had appeared months earlier about my family and me. Disappearance, murder, embezzlement, abandonment, and high society—the past that was a millstone around my neck. I told myself, however, it was unlikely he would remember my face from the articles.

Still, I was uncomfortable here. Not from the heat, but from a sixth sense I could not articulate. Or push aside.

And then came the Holy Chastisement.

✟

The prechurch preparation had been part of Retha's plan. The hardest part had been going through Billy Lee's clothes in his

bedroom at the end of the trailer, knowing what she was going to
do with those clothes, a knowledge that weighed all the more
heavily because Billy Lee was so close she could reach out and
touch his perfect but weakened little body. She was glad the hum
and clatter of the air conditioner drowned out her sniffles as she
decided what would be the best outfit to select. If Elder Mason
or Junior happened to wake early and walk in . . .

As Retha had gone through Billy Lee's clothing, each tiny
shirt, each tiny pair of pants, brought her vivid memories. There
was a blue Nike T-shirt and matching Nike ball cap that had fit
him perfectly, and he'd been wearing it the first day he walked
across the kitchen without falling. The red shorts that showed his
chubby legs and let her kiss the backs of his calves until he
giggled. And the cowboy shirt she'd bought Billy Lee for Christ-
mas, knowing at the time it was too big, but Wal-Mart had put it
on special. What made it saddest for her was the knowledge that
if things went wrong, she might never see him grow into it.

What she finally decided on was the ugly starched dress shirt
and black pants that Junior's grandmother had given them for
Billy Lee to wear to church. Retha would be happy to see those
clothes go. Billy Lee had always fought against them, crying up a
storm because of the rough, uncomfortable material. Because of
that, Retha hated these pants and shirt as much as Billy Lee did,
and hated it worse that she couldn't explain to Billy Lee how
there wasn't much choice when it came to pleasing Junior's
grandmother, who would watch every Sunday morning to see
what Billy Lee wore.

The next hardest part had been dressing the Wal-Mart doll
in those hated clothes. Her tears had been so bad that Retha
could hardly see what she was doing as she pulled the pants over

the doll's legs and the shirt down over its head. All she kept thinking was it should be Billy Lee she was dressing, that if he weren't
sick, today would be like every other day when she could lean
down and breathe in Billy Lee's baby smell, rub her face against
the soft skin of his little man belly, letting him grab her hair with
those tiny, perfect fingers, listening to him giggle as she tickled
him with her nose.

She got through dressing the doll simply because she had no
other choice.

After sneaking outside to hide the doll, she had gone back
into the trailer to make breakfast for Elder Mason and Junior.

✛

A Holy Chastisement.

Retha first thought Shepherd Isaiah had meant to call her
forward as the sinner and jezebel. Until he'd called Betty
Crenshaw. Which meant that Elder Mason had convinced Shepherd Isaiah not to let it be known that one of the Chosen had
been unable to control a family member. When Betty Crenshaw
was dragged to the front, Retha turned her head away from the
spectacle. Halfway up the steps, Betty's husband pinned her arms
to her sides and forced her to crouch.

There'd been whispers that Betty was going astray. Not that
Retha cared. Many of the women who whispered against her
were hypocrites anyway. Like those who found a way to cut their
hair although Shepherd Isaiah instructed that his interpretation
of Paul's New Testament words made it clear that scissors should
never destroy a woman's crowning glory. These were the women
who got around that firm rule by covering their heads with layer

after layer of hair spray until the strands were so brittle that they could break their hair by hand.

"We beseech thee!" Shepherd Isaiah roared, now fully converted from gentle man of God to a man of godly wrath. "Forgive us of our sins!"

He nodded at Elder Jeremiah. Elder Jeremiah brought his paddle down on Betty Crenshaw's rump.

Retha dug into her purse. Watches, like any other jewelry for women, were not permitted by Shepherd Isaiah. She'd hidden a cheap plastic watch among the diapers and baby food packed into her purse. She found it by feel, brought it near the top of her purse, and glanced at it.

It was time. This was when Doreen was supposed to arrive. At the end of the service. With people milling around the church and different trucks moving through the parking lot. With the gate open as it was every Sunday morning—Junior had once explained to Retha that Shepherd Isaiah wouldn't be eligible to apply for tax exemption as a religious organization unless the church appeared open for public attendance.

But in making her plans—calling Doreen and speaking in a whisper on the telephone early this morning—Retha had not expected a Holy Chastisement.

Worse, during a Holy Chastisement, Shepherd Isaiah expected the voyeurlike fascination shared by nearly everyone in the congregation and would notice immediately those who did not remain in attendance.

"Junior!" she hissed to her husband. "I need to go to the ladies' room."

"Now?"

"It's a woman's thing," Retha said. He never questioned her

on woman's things. He was terrified by the mysteries of the female body.

"Hurry," he said.

In a way, the Holy Chastisement was a blessing. All eyes and ears—except for Shepherd Isaiah, who noticed one of his sheep leave the flock—were on the spectacle before the pulpit. Retha slipped out, leaving her purse behind. She'd chosen a spot near the back of the church for this very reason, glad that Elder Mason sat at the front with the rest of the Elders.

"We beseech thee! We beseech thee! We beseech thee!" Shepherd Isaiah's voice followed her as he called again and again and then added the name of Jesus, using the drawn-out syllables as an incantation.

In the hallway, Retha hurried past the ladies' room to the nursery. Where, among all the other young children playing under the care of three teenage girls, Billy Lee was wrapped in a blanket and lying in a corner, almost comatose.

Retha nodded at the girls. "Time to feed my boy," she said. "And I left the bottles out in the truck."

Retha lifted Billy Lee. His dark hair was plastered against his forehead. He didn't stir. Billy Lee didn't have much hair, but that didn't bother Retha at all. His fat little face was perfect to her.

None of the girls questioned Retha as she bundled Billy Lee outside into the hallway. She'd been counting on that. If there were other mothers in the nursery, they would have wondered why Retha didn't get the bottles from the truck and bring them in. Much easier than taking a baby out. But all married women were required to sit in the congregation during worship services.

Holding Billy Lee, Retha half ran to the back door of the church building.

That's where Doreen, her sister-in-law had promised to be waiting to take Billy Lee.

✠

I can't say I noticed Retha leave. I did not know her then. Among all the other women in gray in the church, she would have been invisible to me that morning. And my head was bowed to allow me to stare at the floor as Elder Jeremiah brought his paddle down again and again and again on the helpless woman at the front.

I could not escape Shepherd Isaiah's voice. Nor the shiver that came with the sensation that he was speaking profanely.

"We beseech thee! We beseech thee! We beseech thee!" Now filled with godly wrath, he kept a hypnotic cadence.

Out of the two hundred or so adults in the congregation, half were calling out loud amens. Most of them were men, but a few were apparently spiteful women. The woman at the front sobbed, a noise audible only between the mighty thumps of the paddle when Shepherd Isaiah drew breath to call upon the name of Jesus.

"We beseech thee! Banish Satan this morning! Make this woman pure again that she may behold thy face!"

I kept my head bowed, feeling shame that as a temporary member of this congregation, I was part of this woman's humiliation.

✠

Retha stood in the sun behind the church.

Doreen had not arrived! Maybe Doreen's long-haul trucking husband—Retha's older brother who had not moved into the

compound when her parents decided to join the church—had
returned and she hadn't been able to get away.

Retha strained to hear a truck engine, praying Doreen was
only late, although Retha had made her promise to get there at
the exact time. Above Retha's frantic whispered prayer, only the
high-pitched wail of cicadas in the July heat broke the silence.

What was she going to do? Billy Lee needed a doctor.

She thought of that man in the black Jeep who'd stepped
toward the church as Junior pulled up in the truck. He wasn't
part of this church; Retha knew that. People didn't become part
of the church without a swearing-in ceremony, pledging alle-
giance to Shepherd Isaiah and Jesus. But people sometimes
stopped in by accident. Or out of curiosity.

Retha knew time was slipping away. Betty seemed the type
to break easy. Once the Holy Chastisement ended and Betty
begged forgiveness, she would be baptized again into the presence of God. Then a final hymn.

Retha carried Billy Lee toward the side of the building
where Junior's truck and the Jeep were parked. She told herself it
was to look for Doreen and be ready to get the doll out of Junior's
truck. But Retha knew she was fooling herself. If Doreen was
going to be here, she would have already arrived.

As she walked, she prayed to Jesus again. Retha was careful
to thank Jesus first that Billy Lee was still breathing. She also
thanked Jesus for getting her this far in her plan, although
Doreen hadn't showed up when she promised.

"And dear Jesus," Retha said, eyes closed tight, unaware that
she'd gone from a whisper to full voice. "I pray that you keep a
close watch over Billy Lee. I pray that you let a good doctor take
care of him and that he gets better real soon and doesn't die."

Retha thought over what she had to pray next. Thought about the Elders and what she'd heard whispered about them. She couldn't help herself when she began to cry. "Dear Jesus," she said, tasting the salt of her tears as she found courage to continue. "I pray that if something bad happens to me, someday you will find a way to let Billy Lee know how much I love him—and that I always will."

A sob escaped Retha as she bent her head to kiss Billy Lee's forehead. A tear fell on his tiny nose—the nose that she often stared at for minutes at a time, marveling at its perfection. She wiped the tear away with a fingertip, forcing herself to look directly at Billy Lee's sweet face so she would never forget what might be her last time with him.

At that moment, her resolve nearly failed. Holding him so close to her breast, it was like she was cradling him to feed him. Biting her lower lip and sniffling back her tears, she held him to her face.

"Good-bye, Billy Lee," she said. "No one will ever love you more than me."

She found the courage and opened the unlocked passenger of the Jeep. She set Billy Lee on the floor and covered his face with the edges of the blanket so that he wouldn't have to stare at the sun.

Then Retha heard the final hymn, "Amazing Grace," begin inside the church. Betty had confessed her sins, and now the congregation was singing on her behalf.

Amazing grace! how sweet the sound—
That saved a wretch like me . . .

Retha forced herself to close the door to the Jeep. She still

had things to do if she was ever going to hold Billy Lee again, and
only three verses left to get it done.

✛

As I spoke to Shepherd Isaiah following the service, I had no idea
then that my short conversation would cause yet another death as
part of the Larrabee legacy.

"I have clients who send me looking for antiques," I explained
in answer to his question about my reason for attending his service.
This was not a lie, of course. Glennifer and Elaine would find it
amusing, though, that I had referred to them as clients. "As you
might guess, given the history of this state, antiques can be found
anywhere in the low country. Pieces of your stained-glass windows,
for example, could have been done by the great craftsman Louis
Comfort Tiffany. I was curious enough to want to see them first-
hand, and it was a good excuse to attend this church on such a fine
Sunday morning."

Had Shepherd Isaiah stood any closer, his bearded chin
would have bumped my forehead, such was his size. He looked
more imposing now that he again wore his black suit jacket. More
frightening was the man directly behind him, Elder Jeremiah.
Taller and heavier and staring at me with unblinking focus. I
understood why Bingo had been so intimidated.

Moments before, Shepherd Isaiah had concluded the
service with a prayer, walked down the aisle to organ music, and
positioned himself at the back of the church to shake hands with
every person leaving. It felt like an inspection.

"Antiques," Shepherd Isaiah echoed. It did not matter to
him that the line of men and women behind me had come to a

complete stop as he continued our conversation. "Hidden treasure. Finding value in what others regard as useless. Son, that sounds like an interesting business."

He had a deep radio voice and an interesting drawl and a unique choice of words. Like he'd been born backwoods but had worked at losing it by keeping some of that cadence out of his voice and speaking formally. The effect was of a bad actor playing a part in a bad movie portraying the South a hundred years earlier.

"Yes sir," I said. I thought of this conversation reaching Timothy Larrabee. "Although I believe it would be unfair to offer far less than what a piece is worth." I tried to look past him for an older man with white hair and a cane. Timothy Larrabee.

He spoke again. "And our stained-glass windows?"

"Beautiful," I said, shifting my weight from my real foot to my plastic foot. "But I doubt they're Tiffany's craftsmanship. However, I am always willing to broker an antiques deal. For anyone at anytime."

"Sounds like we work a similar trade. I'm always willing to broker souls on behalf of Jesus. For anyone at anytime. And it isn't that different from the antique business. After all, Jesus looks for the hidden treasure within you, and no matter what your sin, finds value in what others regard as useless. I wish you the best."

"Actually, I had a more specific reason for attending this service than just examining the stained-glass windows. I'm here to see if Timothy Larrabee is still interested in a painting he recently attempted to purchase. If you could be kind enough to point him out to me . . ."

There it was. My purpose for this visit. Out in the open. Of course, I did not know then the truth behind the painting or I would have been more careful. Much more careful.

"Brother Larrabee?" Shepherd Isaiah's tone sharpened. Elder Jeremiah behind him actually took a half step closer to me. "How did you know he was a member of this congregation?"

"Timothy and I grew up in the same neighborhood. My name is Nicholas Barrett."

"That, sir, is an answer, but not to my question."

"Nor have you helped me find Timothy Larrabee."

"I'll let him know you were looking for him."

"I'm at the Doubletree in Charleston."

"I'll inform him of that. Please do not use this church and our service of God as a method of convenience again. While we are open to new members, our degree of commitment to Jesus excludes many, if not most, from taking up his cross the way he demands of his followers."

He turned from me. Deliberately. And that was it. Elder Jeremiah folded his big arms and stared directly into my eyes, challenging me to do anything else but move away.

I moved away, out of the church and into the sunshine. I opened the door to get into my Jeep and saw the note on the front seat.

And a baby boy in a blanket on the floor on the passenger side.

C H A P T E R

9

Without warning, from behind me two hands gripped the tops of my shoulders.

"Don't turn," a voice said, close into my ear. "Tell me who this is."

I was standing in front of the candy machine in the waiting room of the emergency room at St. George's Hospital, and until the hands had grabbed my shoulders, I'd been trying to decide between a chocolate or granola bar. Half an hour earlier, I had brought the baby from my Jeep to the admitting desk. A nurse had taken the boy away. Once I heard more about the baby boy, I intended to go up to the children's ward to see if Angel was there with Maddie.

"Think back," the voice continued. "Think a long ways back."

I tried to spin. Those powerful hands kept me in place.

"After all these years, you still haven't learned to listen, have you?" the voice said.

"And after all these years, you still haven't learned any manners. Good thing you could throw a football well enough to get us into the state finals."

"I'm impressed, Nick." The hands dropped. "It's been a long time since you caught enough of those balls to get us there."

I turned to face Jubil Smith.

He was a picture ready for a Gap ad aimed at the Volvo market—khaki shirt, khaki pants, crisply ironed. He wore the blackest sunglasses I had ever seen. Round, John Lennon glasses. Black as the lenses were, they were almost lost against the luster of the man's dark skin. Tight-cropped hair with tinges of gray. Equally tight goatee, with gray forming an oval within the oval of hair around his chin. Flat-bellied. Big shouldered. I guessed Jubil still went to the gym plenty, as he'd done in high school.

Jubil's hand was extended. I shook it in greeting.

He took off his dark glasses. "One day I get a call telling me you're coming back to Charleston a married man and you want to celebrate," he said. "This was back before a person couldn't punch in the numbers but actually spun a dial on the telephone to make a call. So I wait the next day, to hear from you. Nothing. Same thing, the day after. And the day after. Finally ended up throwing out that bottle of champagne. I must have misunderstood. Didn't think you meant you'd be coming back to Charleston by the time cell phones would be invented. And still you don't call. I had to read the papers to learn what I could."

"Never dreamed you'd still be in Charleston," I said. "Thought you spent a couple years in the big time."

He smiled. "Not long enough to retire rich. Back then the NFL didn't pay like it does now. Especially to backup quarterbacks. It's only been the last couple years they decided a black man was intelligent enough to belong in the pocket as a starter."

There was enough truth in what he said and what it implied that I didn't comment. Then I thought of where we were standing. The emergency room.

"You alright?" I asked.

"Why do you ask?"

I gestured around us. "Thinking maybe you brought someone here. Hoping it's not too serious."

He nodded in understanding. "No, wasn't anything medical that brought me down here."

"That's good to hear." I left the obvious question unasked.

He answered it immediately. "It was curiosity. Your name came up at the station, and I thought I'd come down myself instead of sending some rookie. I've got to ask you about the baby you brought in."

Station. I mentally blinked until it made sense. *Medical station.*

"Doctor is a long way from pro football," I said. "Congratulations. I'm glad to hear the little boy will be in good hands."

"I'm not a doctor, Nick. I'm a cop."

⟊

Angel didn't return to the hospital until after my conversation with Jubil. She was at her secret place. Much later, when she came to trust me, I would learn about it and picture it with a smile.

She arrived at the secret place later than she had promised Camellia that afternoon, burdened by four white plastic grocery

bags that sagged from the weight of canned food. It was a
boarded-up shed beneath a freeway bridge that crossed over railroad tracks and a street lined with sagging commercial buildings.
Two blocks from the row of houses where Angel lived, the shed,
an old outbuilding once used to hold coal, leaned against the
rear of a liquor store which was wedged between the street and
the tracks. Barely larger than a doghouse, the shed was almost
completely hidden from the tracks by willows and assorted weeds
that grew to the height of Angel's head.

The interior was cluttered by discarded store shelves, but
mostly clean of coal dust because of the rain that had been leak-
ing through the shed roof over the years. Angel had moved in
wooden crates to serve as chairs and shared her secret place with
only one person: her best friend Camellia, two years older at fourteen, who lived down the street from Angel. While neither could
explain why, they had come to depend on daily meetings at the
secret place. In their world it was their only refuge; nowhere
else could they step out of their shells of toughness and try their
hidden voices with no self-consciousness or fear.

Above the shed, the overpass rumbled with late-afternoon
rush of traffic. Semi-truck trailers banged and clanked as they
crossed; tires of lighter vehicles slapped the lines of tar on the
concrete. Angel set down her bags and gave the triple-knock-
pause-triple-knock code.

"Hey, girl," Camellia called out in response. "Where you
been?"

"Just you open up," Angel said. "I had to walk back from
the hospital 'cause I didn't want to spend none on a taxi. Then
I stopped to buy you some stuff."

Camellia pushed aside a loose vertical plank. Crouched in

the opening and looking up, she gave Angel a broad grin. Rays of sunlight, coming low from beneath the overpass, shone off the ebony of her face. "Hey! What'd you get?"

"What's it look like?" Angel said. The heavy plastic bags snagged against weeds as she lifted them toward Camellia. "I'm going back to the hospital, so I want you to take them home. Maybe put half in my kitchen and take the rest for you."

Angel followed the groceries inside. She sat on a crate and brushed dirt off her shoulders, leaning forward to keep her head from hitting the interior of the roof. Cracks of light fell between the old planks above her, striping her face with shadows.

Camellia lifted cans and squinted to read the labels in the uncertain light of the shed. "Peaches! Pineapple! And look, sugar ham! This must've cost forty dollars."

"Forty-five. And before you say you can't take some, just you remember that you gave me that electric stun gun you stole off Leroy. And I still got fifty-five. Had to save the rest so when Maddie is feeling good, I can take her back home by taxi."

"The rest? You rob a bank?"

Angel shook her head. "You remember yesterday me taking Maddie to the hospital?"

"I do."

"This man named Nick, after I busted up one of the security guards, he said he'd help and he did. When no one was looking, he gave me a hundred dollars."

"Whoa, girl. You busted up a security guard?"

Angel recounted the events. She did it deadpan, which she knew was the way to make Camellia laugh hardest. Camellia listened with her hand covering her mouth, muffling her giggles.

"He gave me his leg," Angel added. "But I gave it back."

"Child," Camellia said in the best imitation of her mother's voice, "you been smoking some of Herman's weed?"

Herman was Camellia's mother's boyfriend, and the biggest reason Camellia needed the secret place to get out of the house.

Angel frowned. "You know we promised each other not to do stuff like that."

"A man's leg? Girl, he can't just take off his leg."

Angel again explained, and this time Camellia covered her mouth in mock disbelief, her eyes wide and white in the dimness of the shed.

"You had some kind of day yesterday," Camellia said. "Them doctors gonna be able to fix Maddie?"

"A day, maybe two, and I can take her home." Angel looked earnestly at her older friend. "You remember, though, what you promised."

"Be your best friend forever."

"The other thing."

Camellia frowned. "Nothing's gonna happen to you."

"This man Nick," Angel said, "I got him chasing that white-haired man. Stuff's gonna happen now. If any of it falls back on me . . ."

"Nothing's gonna happen to you, Angel. If it does, get the cops."

"Be too late then. And say it wasn't—I can't let them find out about Grammie Zora and what she done. You know I can't. Just promise if something happens to me, you'll look after Maddie. Don't let anyone take her away."

"Nothing's gonna happen to you."

"You weren't there the night Grammie Zora had to leave."

"What's that mean?"

"Can't tell you, except that—"

"Grammie Zora's gone and won't be back for a while. How many more times you gonna tell me that?"

"As many as it takes. But you'd better believe you don't want to know about it."

"Nothing's gonna happen to you." Camellia sounded less certain.

"Just tell me if anything goes wrong and I'm gone, you'll make sure to look after Maddie. Promise?"

✛

"From what I understand, you told the admitting nurse nothing more than the boy is sick and you are trying to help out the family. Not where you found the boy. Not where the boy lives. Not the boy's family name."

We sat near the window of the hospital cafeteria, Jubil and I, at a table for four. He was leaning back in his chair, face tilted to the sun, hands cupped around a mug of coffee. Relaxed.

"Chitchat on old times finished?" I said to Jubil. "It was just getting interesting, how you've worked your way up the force. Where's your notebook?"

"Note to self," Jubil said, keeping an even smile, "witness suddenly hostile and defensive."

"Add impressed," I said. "You went from social to interrogation without missing a beat. To me, the implication is that I've got something to hide and you'd like me to say something important without realizing we're suddenly on the record."

"Do you? Have something to hide?"

"Again, that implication. I brought the boy in on behalf of the boy's mother."

"But you didn't give them the mother's name," Jubil said. "Didn't you expect warning bells to go off?"

"Since I'm now talking to a cop, not a friend, let me tell you that—"

"Detective first class," Jubil interrupted. "Not just a cop. In case you haven't noticed, I'm a muckety-muck. Uniform is not required."

"Since I'm now talking to a detective first class, let me tell you that—"

"Relax, Nick. My questions are standard procedure. Someone brings a baby to the hospital under these conditions, we get a call immediately. Like I said, I decided to handle it myself because I know you."

"Makes it easier to tell if the witness is hiding anything when you think you know him?"

"Next time I'll buy you decaf. The Nick I remember wasn't this high-strung."

I leaned back myself and sighed. "Sorry. Driving to the hospital with the baby beside me, I guessed the police would get involved. I had myself all worked up to spend time in jail to protect the mother. And frankly, if I'm headed there, I wish it was some rookie I didn't know taking me in instead of you."

Now Jubil leaned forward.

"There was a note on the seat," I said. "From the mother. It requested that I do whatever I could to ensure the baby reached a doctor. That's all I'm going to tell you. Not where I was when the baby was placed in my Jeep. Not what else the note said."

"Because . . ."

"I think I was the mother's only hope. Police get involved in this, she may never see her baby again."

SIGMUND BROUWER

"Because . . ."

"I tell you anything else, it will be too much."

The note had been written on the back of a Wal-Mart receipt with a single purchase. *Take my Billy Lee to St. George's Hospital please. These people here won't let me. If you could bring him back when he's better, I'll pay you what I can. I love my baby boy.* The mother had signed her name, *Retha.* She'd circled her phone number beneath. *PS You gotta call before you bring him back. I can't even let my husband know the boy is gone. I think I can fool him for a couple days.*

Taking the baby to a private doctor's office had not seemed like an option. Not on a Sunday afternoon when private practices were closed. Not when the baby boy was so listless I wondered if he might die soon. So it was back to the emergency room. Twice in two days.

"Nick, this is serious business. Anyone else but me is going to look at the facts and accuse you of kidnapping. They're going to say you got scared the boy was so sick he might die."

"If that were true, I'd have brought in a doctor long before he got this sick."

"Not if you'd stolen the baby. And you know that's one of the first things any cop would suspect. We live in a sad world, Nick. Kids disappear all the time and some bad stuff happens to them." He rubbed his face. "Help me out here, Nick. I already know you're footing the bill for another sick kid. Coincidence is one thing, but . . ."

"It's not coincidence."

"No?"

I allowed myself a smile, thinking that if I learned anything about Timothy Larrabee that needed police intervention, the first person to hear about it would be Jubil. For now though, this was my game, and I wanted to keep it that way. It was, I suppose, a way of protecting Angel. "Not coincidence. The first sick kid led to the next. I'll tell you more when I can. So I'm going to ask you the same question."

"Same question?"

"Help me out here, Jubil."

"*Me* help *you*."

"Let me take the boy back to his mother when he's better."

"If he doesn't get better? And what kind of family are you taking him home to? From the sounds of it, maybe the kid is better off with social services."

"The boy deserves to grow up with his mother."

Jubil stared at me. I believed I could read his mind. He was thinking about my motivation. We'd been close in high school. He knew part of my past, the years I'd spent with no real family. He knew I understood too well the bewilderment and pain an abandoned child would face as he grew old enough to comprehend what had happened. If police involvement separated Billy Lee from his mother . . .

"I can't do it, Nick," he finally said. "The call came in to the station. I went out. A report's due."

I knew from where I'd found the baby that Retha belonged to Shepherd Isaiah's church. But I doubted it was a church. In a church husbands did not allow their wives to be beaten publicly. In a church mothers were not prevented from getting their babies medical attention. That was closer to the realm of cults. There were a lot of implications behind the note on the back of the Wal-Mart receipt. If I could get Retha out of her situation, I would. And bringing in the police—at least immediately—didn't seem like the best solution for her and the baby.

"Help me out, Jubil," I repeated.

"You're thinking of your own mother, aren't you? Wishing that someone had stepped in to rescue her like you're trying to rescue this boy's mother."

"Psychobabble." Although it wasn't. I'd sent her away in a moment of anger when I was a boy. And she'd never come back. It had taken me until recently to learn why. But that didn't change the deep-down scars I'd carried for decades. "Help me out, Jubil. Delay your report a day or two. I'll see if I can get the mother to come in and explain everything."

"I wish it was anyone else asking but the person who stepped out of his car with a tire iron the night we won a football game by forty points."

Four linebackers had backed him up to the wall of the high school after that game, bitter at a lop-sided loss inflicted by Jubil, four linebackers whose fathers believed staunchly in the value of the Confederate flag and saw no value in a throwing arm—no matter how powerful or accurate—if that throwing arm was black. None of those four saw my approach, nor had I intended to give warning, not with a tire iron in my hand and rage in my heart, for the words I heard them utter to Jubil were words no boy or man should have to endure. The first I hit across the thigh, and he dropped with a shriek. The second fell when Jubil took advantage of the distraction and kicked him in the stomach. And the other two decided we were serious enough to choose discretion over valor and ran, leaving their fallen companions to crawl away from our anger.

"I only asked for help," I said. "I didn't say you owed me."

"Like I'd forget," he answered. He rubbed his face, pausing to massage his goatee. "You got a couple of days. Wednesday afternoon. Then I file a report and bring in the social services people."

Jubil stared at me long and hard. "I'm going to leave you my cell number. Call anytime from anywhere if you change your mind or if you need help. Just remember, I'm doing this on a gut feeling. We're talking a career breaker here. It turns out you're not telling the truth—the little of it that you gave me—I'm suspended, or worse, discharged."

He put on his sunglasses as he stood to leave. He turned his face down toward me, his eyes hidden. "If you've lied to me, our past means nothing. I will take you down in whatever way I can."

C H A P T E R

10

Retha Herndon stood in the cramped kitchen of the trailer, trying to pull together something presentable from leftovers of cold fried chicken, adding collard greens and cabbage cooked in pork fat. Whatever she had hoped—or feared—might happen in the trailer after sending Billy Lee away with a stranger, it wasn't a houseful of guests, especially the ones waiting in the living room.

Her nerves were frayed enough anyway from worrying all afternoon if she'd be able to get Junior to believe it was Billy Lee in bed, not a doll. Now she had ten more to fool—including Shepherd Isaiah and Elder Jeremiah and Elder Mason—all of them pushed together in front of the television, some of them sitting on lawn chairs that Junior had hauled in without bothering to wipe the dirt off the legs.

"What's the holdup?" Junior pushed his way beside her, almost knocking over the bowl of potatoes she'd boiled earlier in the day to slice and fry for the evening meal.

Nervous about their important guests, Junior had changed from T-shirt and jeans back into his Sunday-go-to-meeting suit. He was nearly a foot taller than she, with the strong nose and jutting cheek-bones he'd inherited from his father, the red hair, with some red in a beard he never trimmed. He'd begun the beard when they married—something encouraged at the Glory Church because all the heroes of the Bible had beards—but since his growth was sparse, the hair hung from his cheeks and chin in thin dirty clumps that would sometimes get in Retha's mouth when he forced kisses upon her.

"Honey," he said, placing a hand on her shoulder, "you got to hurry it up. Those folks are burning with holy heat to get started on why they came."

"I told you already," Retha answered. "Billy Lee is sleeping quiet. I think he's over the worst of it. Seems to me it would do more harm than good to have him taken up in front of all these strangers."

"And tell Shepherd Isaiah that in front of everyone else?" Junior took her face in his hands and looked her directly in the eyes. Junior was careful to use his tall body to block his actions from anyone who might glance into the kitchen from the living room. He hissed in her ear. "It better not get out that you been trying all week to get that boy to a doctor. If Shepherd Isaiah hears you ain't got the faith, we're in more trouble than I care to think about." He let go of her face. "Besides, say Billy Lee is better, it won't hurt none to have him prayed over by the Good Shepherd himself."

Queasy already with the smell of boiled cabbage filling her nostrils, Retha nearly threw up from dread at the reminder. She didn't dare tell Junior about the doll, but it seemed that as soon as the food was served, she wouldn't have much choice.

It had been Retha's prayer that she could keep the baby doll
unnoticed until she got a phone call from the man in the black
Jeep, that he would take Billy Lee to a doctor, and Billy Lee
would be better in a few days, and that she would be able to make
the switch later. It was a long shot, but it was her only hope.

Retha had tried to imagine how it would go when she and
Junior arrived home after the church service. The best thing
possible was that he would take her word for it that all their
prayers over the last week had finally worked and that Billy Lee
was on the mend.

She'd told herself there was a good chance Junior wouldn't
bother to look in the bedroom. Junior often joked that he wasn't
interested in a baby until he was old enough to go fishing, or, if it
was a girl, old enough to tend to housework.

Retha had also imagined a worse scenario, that maybe Junior
would want to see Billy Lee. She had set it in her mind that she'd
try to stop him at the doorway so that from a distance—and in the
darkness of the bedroom—the doll under the blanket would be
enough to satisfy Junior. The worst thing she'd imagined was for
Junior to want to hold Billy Lee. It didn't happen much, but
Retha had had years of learning to expect the worst in life. And
here it was.

Now all of them in front of the television wanted to see and
hold Billy Lee. Retha had never figured on Junior going ahead
and asking for Shepherd Isaiah to deliver a Glory Session along
with all the elders and their wives—all intent on proving the
power of God by the healing that would take place from their
prayers. She could hear their voices, a loud hum of babble.

"Whatever you're making, honey, make it fast and make it
good," Junior said, relaxed again and giving her shoulder

another squeeze. "Don't forget maybe you should get out there quick and make sure none of them are run dry on that store-bought lemonade."

"Sure," Retha said. But her mind wasn't on lemonade. It was on what would happen after dinner, when Shepherd Isaiah and his flock started the Glory Session over a doll.

✛

Magnolia's is a fine, fine restaurant on East Bay, a ten-minute walk from my childhood mansion, which was now occupied by my half brother, Pendleton. There are, however, many fine restaurants within walking distance of that three-story monument, so it had not occurred to me that I might run across him at Magnolia's that Sunday evening.

I saw Pendleton before I saw Glennifer and Elaine. He sat alone at a corner table. This surprised me; Pendleton used attractive blondes as ornaments, and this was certainly the restaurant to exhibit yet another.

Ever the Southern gentleman, he winked and waved, as if he and I were not locked in battle over the estate that Lorimar Barrett had left behind upon his death for Pendleton, each of them confident I would never have my share. Until I'd discovered the truth on my first return to Charleston.

Unlike Pendleton, I was not a Southern gentleman. I stared through him, then followed a young hostess to another table, where Glennifer and Elaine had already started on, of course, mint juleps.

I bowed, took and kissed each of their hands, and sat, too conscious that my back was turned to Pendleton.

"What a delight, Nicholas," Glennifer said. "I believe this is our first social occasion together."

It was a step forward in our fledgling friendship, for as often as I had seen them, it was always at the antique shop. This was, in a way, like moving a work relationship out of the office and to a more personal level.

"I'll mind my manners," I promised.

"With Pendleton approaching?" Elaine looked past my shoulders and smiled. "This should be interesting."

When he reached our table, Pendleton bowed deeply and introduced himself to Glennifer and Elaine. He wore a hand-tailored suit and a silk tie, accentuating his handsome face and well-toned physique. His hair was cut immaculately, and I knew he went for weekly manicures. In all, a wonderful presentation to the world. He'd recovered well from a gunshot wound in the spring, suffering as little permanent damage as his wife's reputation among the aristocracy had. She'd fired the pistol, and her self-defense claim had stood; now she was on her way to becoming a leading mayoral candidate.

"Nick," he said, "we should talk. As in you and I. Not through our lawyers. I'm tired of leaving messages at your hotel."

The interior of the restaurant was suitably dim, and his face was in shadow.

I sipped from a glass of ice water. "Business, politics, religion, and the inequities of the college football playoff system," I said. "None of these should be discussed at the dinner table. As well-bred as you claim to be as often as possible, you of all people should know this, Pendleton."

He smiled. "But the rule doesn't apply, as I'm not part of your dinner table."

"Nor will you be."

Pendleton spoke to Glennifer and Elaine. "He's like a caged tiger, isn't he? All that prowling, restless anger. It must be exciting to spend time with him, wondering when any of it might be unleashed."

"Strange," Glennifer said, "how one brother might be angry when the other has tried to take away his name, his life, and his rightful inheritance."

"His wife, too," Elaine added, speaking to Glennifer as if Pendleton did not exist. "Don't forget how Pendleton took away his wife."

"Good-bye, Pendleton," I said. I'd saved his life as he lay bleeding from the gunshot wound; I didn't owe him anything, least of all courtesy.

"I think I can work out a deal with the IRS," Pendleton answered me. "They're not quite so confident about seizing everything now that you're in the picture."

A few months earlier, during the college spring break, I'd returned to Charleston and learned the truth about my mother's disappearance. It was then I'd discovered Pendleton's role in the car accident that had resulted in the loss of my leg. The role he'd played in the annulment of my marriage to the woman he'd wanted badly since childhood. And how he had kept from me the secret that we shared an inheritance. Now it was about to be trimmed considerably by the IRS because of his tax-fraud actions. By proving paternity, however, I would be able to claim my share before the penalties. According to my lawyer, the outcome was not in doubt. I would not lose in court. With me on one side and the IRS on the other, Pendleton would be left with nothing.

"Good-bye, Pendleton," I said again. Considering what I

knew about Pendleton and the history between us, I was impressed that I could remain this civil. "Please."

"If you sign off on a reduced penalty to the IRS," he said. "we will have plenty to share. I'll give you the house. You could move in tomorrow. Your half of what's left of the trust fund will still be enough to retire on. I won't dispute this any longer. You're only punishing yourself by trying to punish me."

I sipped my ice water again.

"You don't need revenge," he said. "You've won."

"Good-bye," I repeated.

"Please," he said. His habitual smirk disappeared as he paused. "The divorce is final. My daughter won't speak to me. I'm a laughingstock in Charleston. There is nothing here for me. I want to leave and try to begin somewhere else." His face had lost all animation. "You may not believe me. But I'm sorry for what I did. I'm asking you to forgive me."

I could think of no immediate reply to this.

Pendleton studied my eyes briefly. "That was difficult for me to say. I hope you can appreciate that."

He then turned and left without further comment. I twisted and watched him go. When he reached his table, he dropped some bills for a tip and departed the restaurant, his magnificent shoulders squared.

✛

"Juh-hee!-ze-huss, Juh-hee!-ze-huss, Juh-hee!-ze-huss," Shepherd Isaiah Sullivan began in the living room of the Herndon trailer, drawing out the Holy Name in his hypnotic manner. Shepherd Isaiah had dreams of television syndication for himself and the

Glory Church of the Lamb of Jesus, first across the deep South and then north to the heathens. To accomplish this, Shepherd Isaiah knew he needed more than the sizable amount of cash his church had accumulated over the last years. He needed a trademark, something to set himself apart from his competition. Accordingly, he had spent hours experimenting on different ways to emphasize the different syllables of the Holy Name. Years earlier, Shepherd Isaiah had also begun to cultivate a trademark look, and, happily aware that his tallness and Lincoln-like appearance gave him a spooky aura, he emphasized it by wearing dark clothing and a full beard. His approach had proven effective, at least within the Glory Church of the Lamb of Jesus.

He prayed loudly now, repeatedly calling upon the name of Jesus. "We beseech thee and thy Holy Spirit to come among us here . . ."

Retha was on her knees on the orange shag carpet at Shepherd Isaiah's feet. Some of the others, standing above her with hands joined in a tight circle, trembled in anticipation of holy ecstasy. Retha, with the doll in her arms hidden by a blanket, trembled in fear that her lie would be discovered. Entering the living room with the doll, her knees ready to buckle, she'd almost found the courage to confess, despite her terror of Shepherd Isaiah setting Elder Jeremiah loose on her. But when some of the elders and their wives had immediately begun to moan in fervor as a prelude to the Glory Session, she'd been unable to blurt out the truth. So she was committed to the entire Glory Session, devoting her own prayers to self-preservation as the other prayers rained down upon her.

"We beseech thee! Look kindly upon us, for we are the true followers who obey all thy commands. Cursed be those who bring false teachings to the sheep. Blessed be those who rely only on thy goodness and glory and truth for all their needs. Blessed be those who let thy will be done."

Retha knew Shepherd Isaiah was directing this portion of the prayer at her. Early in her marriage, Retha had made the mistake of allowing a makeup person in a department store to talk her into a free makeover. It had been simple curiosity. While Retha had been astounded at the results, she had not broken church law by purchasing any lipstick or eyeliner or blush. Yet one of the other sheep in Shepherd Isaiah's flock had seen her in front of the makeup mirror—her sin had resulted in a reputation that she must be closely watched, a calling forward for public repentance at the next church service, and a private beating at home from Elder Mason, who, like Shepherd Isaiah, taught the part of Scripture that admonished true believers to remember that a spared rod resulted in a spoiled child.

"We beseech thee! Look kindly upon us, for we are the true followers who obey all thy commands."

The repetition was deliberate to remind his listeners that in the Glory Church of the Lamb of Jesus, everyone understood that whatever happened was God's will and purpose. Sickness was brought upon those who had sinned. Health was restored only after repeated pleas for forgiveness to God through the Lamb of Jesus, and then only if God so chose, and all miracles as such then brought glory to his name; last year one member had succumbed to appendicitis, another to unhealed broken ribs that had eventually punctured a lung; these two were deemed by the rest as not having believed enough.

Shepherd Isaiah began to pant as he continued to cry out, raising and dropping his voice like a roller coaster to bring his

Followers on a ride with him. "We beseech thee! We beseech thee! We beseech thee!"

The others began to join in, gripping hands and rocking back and forth, catching Shepherd Isaiah's zeal as they cried out to God and Jesus and the Holy Spirit. Despite the lack of danger in a Glory Session, done right it was almost as gratifying as a snake-handling—activities that required a fervor that would crest and fall, crest and fall, leaving Shepherd Isaiah's sheep exhausted and drained and satisfied.

Shepherd Isaiah allowed his sheep to rock and moan for another fifteen minutes, letting the Glory Session build as he blended his voice in with theirs. When he sensed the time was right, he cried out above them, penetrating their trance with his deep baritone.

"We beseech thee! Rid this child of the demons of sickness! "We beseech thee! We beseech thee! We beseech thee! Forgive the sins that have placed him at the gates of hell!"

At the delicious words *demons* and *hell,* the Glory Session catapulted itself to a higher level.

"Lay on the hands, Good Shepherd!" the followers begged Shepherd Isaiah. "Lay on the healing hands!"

Retha cowered at their feet. Had it been Billy Lee in her arms, her baby would have been shrieking at the storm of prayers around it.

Shepherd Isaiah smiled with calm detachment as the others swayed like trees before a hurricane. He knew the followers were truly lost in their consecration and rhythmic rapture when they called him the name that gave him the secret pleasure of power.

"Good Shepherd! Good Shepherd! Good Shepherd!" The cries of affirmation rolled over him.

"We beseech thee! We beseech thee! We beseech thee!" he responded. "We beseech thee! We beseech thee! We beseech thee!"

"Lay on the hands! Lay on the hands! Lay on the hands!"

Shepherd Isaiah reached down for the baby in the blanket of the arms of the young woman at his feet.

Retha could not help her own impulse. She pulled the doll in tighter to herself.

Shocked by the defiance, Shepherd Isaiah almost lost his rhythmic chant. The others, crying aloud and rocking with their eyes closed, failed to notice, and Shepherd Isaiah was able to get himself together.

"We beseech thee! We beseech thee! We beseech thee!" he said. "Bring this sinner close to thee! Anoint her with thy our goodness and mercy. We beseech thee! We beseech thee! We beseech thee!"

He reached again. Retha protected the doll by curling over it.

This time, as Shepherd Isaiah made his awkward and determined grab for the baby, he did lose his cadence. Enough that it brought a few of the followers back from the brink of bliss. Their voices dropped as they opened their eyes to see Shepherd Isaiah pulling at Retha in an attempt to straighten her. The remaining followers, including Junior, picked up on the disturbance, and they too opened their eyes to become witnesses.

Shepherd Isaiah, furious that one of his followers would deny his will, fought for the baby as if it were a football. Retha screamed and fought back, so filled with terror at the consequences of her deceit that she was blind to how much worse she was making it.

Elder Jeremiah stood from the couch and waited for instructions from Shepherd Isaiah. But this was not a time for anyone's authority but the Shepherd's, and he shook his head. Elder Jeremiah sat back down but remained extremely watchful.

The followers stopped swaying and their voices dropped to silence.

"Anoint this baby," Shepherd Isaiah shouted. "We beseech thee! We beseech thee! We beseech thee!"

To Shepherd Isaiah, possession of the baby had become possession of leadership. He was not going to allow this girl child to thwart him in front of the elders of the Glory Church of the Lamb of Jesus. "The Lord orders you to let it go!"

In the confusion and tumble of flesh, Retha clawed to hold the blanket and protect its contents from Shepherd Isaiah's hands. She stopped her own screaming as she saved strength to maintain her tenacity. Their tug-of-war continued in total silence until Shepherd Isaiah finally found a handhold and pulled hard in triumph.

With a muffled pop, the doll's leg separated from the rest of the body and slipped loose from its pants leg. Shepherd Isaiah fell backward, clutching the leg in his hand. He threw it away from him in an impulse of horror.

At the glimpse of the tiny bare leg and the perfectly formed foot tumbling into the screen of the television, three of the women screamed before they realized it was plastic. Junior fainted outright; with the others mesmerized at the dismembered baby, he fell unnoticed at the back of the crowd and hit his head on the armrest of the couch.

As for Retha, she was so relieved that the Glory Session had ended, she began to giggle in hysterics.

✛

"I'm sorry you had to be part of that," I said to Glennifer and
Elaine after Pendleton's departure. "It's embarrassing."

"Nicholas." Glennifer reached across the table and patted
my hand. I blinked. Aside from what was demanded by formal
manners, this was the first time she had touched me. "We're your
friends."

I nodded. I was wearing a dark dinner jacket. I reached inside
and pulled out an eight-by-ten manila envelope, folded lengthwise
to fit inside. "Perhaps you'll find this far more interesting."

Glennifer reached for it, her hand trembling only slightly. I'd
seen her in the antique shop, writing shaky lines on paper. I knew
the effort it cost her to fool me with this attempt at steadiness.

"I got this from Angel after I asked her to look around her
house for it," I told them as Glennifer pulled out the contents.
"She gave it to me at the hospital just before I came here."

There wasn't much for them to examine, and I was already
familiar with the contents. A recent photo of Timothy Larrabee.
Two sheets of information on him. And a letter from a local
private investigator, Kellie Mixson.

Glennifer and Elaine each donned glasses to study the
papers in the dim light of the candles. While they did that, I
waved away the waiter. We could order later.

"Nicholas?" Elaine said after each woman finished studying
the papers.

"Angel's grandmother paid an investigator to search for
Timothy Larrabee. When I asked Angel why, she said she didn't
know."

"This says that until 1992, Timothy Larrabee spent fifteen of the previous twenty-five years in prison. Repeated offenses for stock swindles, grand theft auto, even assault—" Glennifer picked up the sheet and reread the information—"yet now he's an elder at the Glory Church of the Lamb of Jesus."

"Yes. I went there this morning looking for him."

"I've heard about that church," Elaine said. "They insist that faith in God is all they need. Didn't some child die there because of lack of medical attention?"

"That was a few years ago. Appendicitis. There were also newspaper clippings about the church in the report. But I wouldn't call it a church. As you just read, as a condition of joining, members give power of attorney to the church leader, all property is held as a commune, all wages and salary earned by members go to the church, and in return, the church takes care of all their needs."

"And Timothy Larrabee belongs there?" Glennifer said. "Strange, for someone who has no compunction about stealing cars or hitting people with tire irons."

"That must have been before his conversion," I said dryly. I looked over at our waiter, hovering just out of earshot. He quivered with anxiety. "Shall we order?"

We did. I preferred the crab cakes at Magnolia's, and Glennifer and Elaine ordered steaks, which I found an amusing choice for women who appeared so frail. I wisely kept the opinion to myself, for they weren't frail and would have had no hesitation impressing that upon me.

Then, as Glennifer and Elaine continued to sip their mint juleps, I told them about Bingo, minus the switchblade attack. I told them about visiting the church. I told them about not finding Timothy Larrabee, but finding the baby abandoned in my Jeep.

About Jubil's deadline that gave me only two days to get the baby back to the mother.

At first, they gasped in their whimsical Southern way. As I got further into the story, however, they became so absorbed that the gasps grew less in volume, until they each sat completely still.

"And this baby?" Elaine asked softly. "How is he doing?"

"Better, I think. He had a stomach virus and was desperately dehydrated. From what the doctors indicate, he needs at least a couple days in the hospital."

"You can't take him back to his mother then, not before social services takes him, if I understand right about your friend Jubil's deadline. If you could, do you want that baby back in the church where they refuse to allow doctors?"

"No," I said. "But I can bring his mother to him, something I am quite determined to accomplish."

Dinner arrived before I could say more. Not that I might have said what was on my mind. I had once believed that my own mother had run away from me. Because I knew so well the sense of abandonment, I was not prepared to turn my back on this baby. Alone, who out there in the world would console him? Without help, he was just one more tragedy in a world filled with despair. One of the uncounted many to struggle briefly before sliding beneath the surface to disappear into the blackness. Yet could my involvement make a difference against the wailing and grief that afflict life?

Perhaps Glennifer and Elaine sensed the intensity of my private grief. They turned the conversation to the food, and after a suitable time, back to Angel and her grandmother.

"Why would Angel's grandmother search for Timothy Larrabee?" Glennifer said.

"And how could she know that he was in the lowland area?" Elaine added. "*We* hadn't heard a whisper about his return."

"Shocking," I agreed. "If you haven't heard, then it really hasn't happened."

"Nicholas," Glennifer said in a warning tone, "you know we've spoken to you about your penchant for sarcasm. And remember your admonishment to Pendleton. This was meant to be a civilized dinner."

"Yes ma'am."

"Your apparent contrition fools no one," Elaine said. "Now tell us more. When you met Angel today, didn't she ask you if the Bingo character had directed you to the man who would purchase her painting?"

"I told her that I went to the church and couldn't find him," I said. "I told her that I left my address for him to contact me."

"This young woman seems very determined for you to find the man, doesn't she?"

I nodded. "Whether or not Angel's family legitimately owns the painting now, think about how much selling it would mean to her."

"But not to her grandmother? Don't you expect this Zora to return soon?"

"Angel's done a good job of ducking that question," I said. "And believe me, I would like to meet Grammie Zora."

"A voodoo woman," Glennifer said. "So exciting. I'd certainly like to know how a woman like her came into possession of the Larrabees' Van Dyck. Especially if she got it legally as Angel claims."

"Laney," Glennifer said, "it's simple. There's got to be some connection between her and Timothy Larrabee."

Elaine looked at Glennifer. "After all these years. What could it be?"

"Crown of thorns," I threw out. "The phrase seemed to hold some kind of power over Larrabee. Grammie Zora told Bingo once he heard it, he would follow."

Glennifer frowned. "Say that again."

"Crown of thorns."

Her frown deepened. "You neglected to tell us that earlier, Nicholas."

I realized I had, but it wasn't deliberate. There had been a lot to tell.

"Crown of thorns," Elaine said to Glennifer. "Are you thinking what I'm thinking?"

"I believe I am," Glennifer answered. "After all, when Agnes Larrabee was a child, it wasn't that long after the Larrabee family was forced to free its slaves."

Now it was my turn to be puzzled.

"A dark part of our collective past, Nicholas," Glennifer said. She pushed away her plate, with very little of the food eaten. "Laney and I are old enough to know more of it than most of your generation. Many of our generation pretend today that our families had no part of slavery. But it's there, something we cannot deny. Far worse are some of the actions in our history. Branding of slaves is not easy to forget, much as we would prefer to."

"Yes," Elaine finished for her. "Back when the Larrabee family held a plantation, they, like many other owners, branded their slaves. It sticks out in my memory because of what I heard the brand was."

"They were a religious family," Glennifer said. "So they branded their slaves to belong to Jesus. With the mark of a small crown of thorns."

CHAPTER

11

The next day, I found Pastor Samuel in the office of the Mount Carmel African Methodist Episcopal Church. He sat in an old recliner. He was asleep, with his glasses on his forehead and an open Bible across his lap. He snored softly.

I sat on a chair nearby.

The office was decorated simply. On the wall hung some family photos. The bookshelves held commentaries on the Bible. His desk was clear of paper. The phone on it was a rotary dial.

Samuel was close to retirement. The pants that would have fit him snugly when he was young and muscular now hung loose on him, supported by suspenders. The bald top of his head divided curly white fringes on each side. When he was awake, with his thick glasses in place, his eyes seemed like bulging eggs. But they were eyes that were always kind and compassionate.

Here, I thought as I watched him, *is a man at peace with himself and with his world.* The Bible, for him, was a source of inspiration, meditation, and meaning. If a man like this were to be held up to the world as an example of Christianity, the world would find little to mock and much to admire in those who strive to follow Jesus and his teachings. Yet men and women like him were rarely leaders in a public sense, and rarely wanted to be, just as Jesus himself focused on the heavenly kingdom and refused to get dragged into the politics of his day. And many of those eager for the limelight were anything but the representatives of Christ they claimed to be. So it is that too many outside of faith have misconceptions of what faith should be and no understanding of how faith in the Christ makes for a life of peace and purpose and hope.

I knew Samuel and his wife, Etta, because my mother had once been a member of Mount Carmel. Months ago, during my first return to Charleston, they'd been the ones to help me discover some of the facts of my childhood. I'd visited their home once since coming back again, and it had been over a week since I'd stopped by the church.

Eventually, Samuel realized he was not alone, and the rhythm of his snoring ceased. He dug his knuckles into his eyes and slid his glasses down onto his nose. He levered his recliner upright and swallowed a few times. "I've started sleeping earlier and earlier in the day," he said, blinking recognition at my presence. "Just little naps, you understand."

"I understand."

"Good to see you again. Etta and I enjoy your company."

"I wish this were a social call," I said. "But I'm here to ask if you can help me find someone, anyone, who was part of the Larrabee household."

It was sad that I didn't have to explain I meant someone

black who had been a servant for the wealthy. Samuel had been a pastor for decades. He knew the black community as well as anyone. I wouldn't be here if I was looking for someone white.

He straightened more. "Agnes Larrabee? The one poisoned?"

I nodded.

"That was forty-some years ago."

I nodded again.

He grinned, showing surprisingly white teeth. "And you figure I'm ancient enough to remember."

"*Sharp* enough to remember," I corrected. "The newspaper archives don't mention much about her household."

"Sharp enough, huh? Any more sugar you intend to pour in my tea?"

My turn to grin. "Only if necessary."

"I suppose that's enough," he said, "because you came to the right place. As a matter of fact, one of the members of my congregation did work in the Larrabee household. A woman by the name of Evelyn Palmer."

✢

Retha woke with her face pressed against hard-packed dirt. For her first few moments of consciousness, she didn't move, couldn't move. Pain paralyzed her limbs as surely as if she had been tightly wrapped and bound with red-hot wire.

With returning consciousness came the memories: Shepherd Isaiah's tender regret at her sin, which had slowly built into holy rage against Satan and thundering calls of damnation against human deceit. The angry babble of the elders, giving full voice and approval to the castigating rage of their leader. Their questions, slamming her like physical blows. Her refusal to answer those questions and tell them where the baby was. The slamming of the door as they departed to leave her alone with Elder Mason. Junior, standing sullenly beside Elder Mason, recovered from his fall but cut badly where his head had slammed into the wooden edge of the couch's armrest. The trail of blood that trickled from Junior's scalp into his eyebrow, and from his eyebrow onto his cheekbone, and from there into his wispy beard and his mouth as he watched Elder Mason shout at her. The first punch into her stomach as she backed away from Elder Mason. His fury at the humiliation he had suffered in front of the other elders, and the flurry of kicks and blows as she dropped to her knees to cover herself. Junior protesting weakly but not stepping between her and Elder Mason's rage. And dimly, the darkness of the night and the feel of wet grass as Elder Mason pushed Junior aside to drag her out of the house and back to the toolshed.

All of these memories returned with her first moan. She rolled over, crying in pain as fresh bruises pressed onto the hardpan dirt. Then she realized she couldn't see.

It brought a dry half-scream that was hardly able to leave her broken body. She brought her hands to her eyes. It felt as if they were covered with scabs. She touched her eyes gingerly, surprised there was no pain, then discovered that blood and dirt had caked them over, and she almost sobbed with relief.

She tried to spit on her fingers, but her mouth was swollen and cracked and entirely without moisture. So she had to pick at her eyelids until she was finally able to flutter them open.

Morning was outside the shed, sunlight easily able to penetrate because Junior had built the shed to his usual sloppy standards. Retha saw on the ground, among the scattered tools and beside a rusted lawn mower, the dog-food bowl filled with water again.

She tried to stand but could not.

Last night's voices screamed at her. *"Tell us, child, where is Billy Lee? Satan, let go of this child! Child, let go of Satan! We beseech thee! We beseech thee! We beseech thee! Cast out this child's sins! We beseech thee! We beseech thee! We beseech thee! Loosen her tongue and spare this child from the eternal brimstone fires of hell! Child, where is Billy Lee?"*

Retha's mouth tasted of the copper of blood.

She dragged herself to the bowl of water. Once again, dead flies floated on the surface. She tried to pick them out, but the movement of her arms hurt too much and she wanted the water too badly to have the patience. She struggled to sitting position, leaned against the wall of the shed, and drank the water through her teeth, gagging as one dead fly slipped through. She set the bowl down and rested for a while from that effort.

Something felt strange to her. At first, with all the other sensations, she could not decide what it was. Her legs and arms were covered with chigger bites from hours on the dirt. She burned with aching bruises, and any deep breath brought another stab of fire into her chest. Her tongue was still swollen with thirst, and pushed against a broken tooth.

Why then this strange inner contentment? Then Retha understood.

She was free.

The night before, as the anger and shouting and condemnation thundered louder and louder around her, her determination rose to match it. She clearly remembered telling herself that she did not want Billy Lee brought back into a life where Jesus would hold him prisoner as surely as Jesus and all his rules had held her prisoner all her life.

Now, beaten and outcast for defying them all in a way that made their forgiveness impossible, Retha was finally free, even though all she had now was a bowl of water and the certainty that Shepherd Isaiah would return to the shed and that her own husband would not protect her from him.

In her newfound peace, Retha was able to think clearly. She knew what it would take for Billy Lee to escape Jesus.

A lie. She would tell the lie, knowing it might send her soul to hell. Because she didn't want Billy Lee to know the Jesus that she knew.

✛

Twenty minutes later she heard a man's heavy approach, his breathing as he fumbled with the key, the click of the opening lock.

By then, Retha was ready. Disconnected from the itching of chigger bites and her screaming nerve endings. Calm and ready.

Shepherd Isaiah pushed the door open and entered. Elder Jeremiah followed, his shadow blocking the sun. Although blinded by the light on either side of Elder Jeremiah, Retha recognized a leather belt folded in loops in his right hand.

"Have you repented?" Shepherd Isaiah asked. His voice was almost sweet. "Will you now tell us where the boy is?"

"Woman, do it!" Elder Mason shouted from outside the shed.

"That is enough," Shepherd Isaiah spoke to Elder Mason. "She is a child of God."

"The baby's dead," Retha said. The night before, her

defense had been silence. Now it would be a lie. "I buried him out in the woods."

"If that's true, woman, why did Elder Jeremiah catch you in that truck on Saturday?" Elder Mason again. "Did you find a way to take Billy Lee away somewhere?"

"Elder Jeremiah," Shepherd Isaiah said quietly, "Elder Mason forgets his place. I am the one to ask questions."

Elder Jeremiah backed out of the shed. There was a thud and a muffled groan. Elder Jeremiah returned.

"Now, my child, speak to me." Shepherd Isaiah's voice caressed Retha.

"I told you. My baby boy is dead. The Lord's will. You said no doctors because we would abide by the Lord's will. And now Billy Lee's dead. That was the Lord's will. I was too afraid to tell you, so I put a doll in his bed."

"Then where did you bury him? I have to give that boy a Christian funeral or hellfire will lick at his soul forever."

"Can't say where I buried him. I don't remember where I was, I was grieving so bad."

"Elder Jeremiah, it is with sadness that I ask for your help." Elder Jeremiah loomed over her. He raised the belt in his right hand.

"Can't say? Or won't?" Shepherd Isaiah said. "This is disturbing me greatly, this here disobedience. I'm giving you one last chance to purge Satan from your body and speak truth. Where'd you bury the boy?"

"Can't say." It revolted Retha, thinking she'd once looked up to this man.

"Satan begone!" Shepherd Isaiah commanded. "Leave this child of God." He nodded to Elder Jeremiah.

The belt came down once.

"This pains me, my child. Please cleanse yourself with obedience to me and God's holy Word."

Retha clenched her jaw.

Shepherd Isaiah sighed and nodded to Elder Jeremiah.

Free, Retha told herself as she waited for the belt to descend again. *Finally free.*

✛

"Evelyn," Samuel said to the shriveled woman in room 309 of the Bethany House extended care facility of Mount Pleasant, "this is my friend Nicholas Barrett. I hope you don't mind that he joins us for this visit?"

"Any visit is just fine with me. Especially by a man that looks so fine," Evelyn answered. "He looks real fine. Don't bother me none to have you two good-looking men nearby. Sit by my bed all morning if you want."

I was surprised at the robust voice coming from such a withered body. The woman wore a shiny dark wig, slightly askew. One eye was patched with a white bandage. Her other eye gleamed as she looked from Pastor Samuel to me.

"Now, Pastor," she said, "you bring some grape juice and cheese and crackers like I asked last week? Seems we could have ourselves a real party."

"Evelyn," Samuel said with theatrical despair, "you should know I searched high and low but couldn't find any wine of a quality deserving of you."

Evelyn laughed. Her dentures slipped and she gagged slightly. With a quick pop of the heel of her hand, she knocked her teeth back in place. "You do beat all, Pastor Samuel."

"All this talk about parties aside, how are you?" Samuel asked quietly. "You know I'm serious about that question. Especially after the operation on your eye."

"Mostly lonely," she said. "Nobody from my family comes to visit, and the lady in the other bed, she sleeps most of the time. Won't wake up no matter what I say to her. I can't read magazines because my other eye went so bad on close-up stuff all of a sudden. Seems like when one part goes bad, the others are sure to follow."

The dividing curtain of the room had been pulled back. I glanced at the other bed. This woman was older than Evelyn and asleep, her head barely peeking over the sheets.

"Other eye gone bad for reading," Samuel repeated. "What does your doctor say about it?"

"He says sometimes that might happen when it tries to compensate for the eye that had the operation. He says I shouldn't worry; it will come around. I say, let him try seeing out of only one eye and have it go bad, and maybe he'll know about worrying. Yesterday, my eye was fine. Today it's not."

To confirm her complaint, Evelyn reached for her eyeglasses from her bedside table. She put them on and stared at Samuel. The frame was plain brown plastic, the lenses thick and square. She blinked her good eye, and to me, it seemed she was peering at us through a magnifying glass.

"Just like now," Evelyn said, holding up her hand in front of her eyes. "It's like seeing my hand underwater. Can't hardly make out my fingernails. It's almost as bad as being blind. Sure I can see people and their faces without my glasses, but reading, that's impossible."

Evelyn turned her head, looking around the room. "I puts these on, and things gets bad. I takes 'em off, and my eye works the way it always did without 'em."

"You want I should talk to the doctor about this?" Samuel asked. "Sometimes they get busy and don't listen. If he hears it from the two of us, it might make him pay attention."

"That'd be good. Real good. And while you're talking to him, there's a few other things he ain't listening to real close. I been trying to tell him about my intestinal problems. Like I said, one thing goes bad, and the rest is sure to follow."

Evelyn began to go into great detail about her gastronomical difficulties. With her single large eye looming from behind the eyeglasses, the askew wig, and the animation on Evelyn's face as she spoke about her last four days of intestinal activities with a fondness normally reserved to the departure of close friends, I found it difficult to listen with the seriousness that Samuel was able to maintain.

I bit my lip to keep a straight face and looked elsewhere, nodding sympathetically in rhythm to the cadence of Evelyn's voice. In the other bed, the woman's face twitched occasionally. I began to wonder if she was really sleeping or keeping up the pretense to avoid conversation with Evelyn.

When Evelyn finished, Samuel cautiously cleared his throat. "It sounds serious," he said. "I'll certainly let your doctor know what I can. Now, before we go, can Nick ask you a few questions?"

"But there's more," Evelyn said. "I've got a bunion that hurts even when I'm laying in bed. I swear, it's the size of a pumpkin. Pull up the sheet and take a look. Or if you want, you can run your fingers acrost it. I swear, you'll never feel another that's bigger. Then you'll know why it causes me such suffering."

"Well . . ." Samuel said. He sighed. "Why don't you tell me about it instead?"

"Glad to, Pastor. See, the problem is I can't reach down like I used to when I was younger. Was fun, then, peeling some of the dead skin off it myself. Like layers off an onion. You think that's where they got the name *bunion*? 'Cause it's like an onion? Fact is, that bunion makes my eyes water when I step on it wrong. . . ."

As Evelyn launched herself into further description of her foot ailments, I caught the woman in the other bed with one eye half open. She snapped it shut when she noticed me looking at her. I also noticed a pair of eyeglasses on the other bedside table. Plain brown plastic frames. Lenses thick and square. I slid my chair to the other bed. I leaned close to the other woman's head.

"Ma'am," I said in a low voice, "you have blurry vision, too, but afraid to talk about it?"

In the background, Evelyn's voice rose and fell.

The other woman nodded, still refusing to open her eyes.

"Maybe I can help." I stood from the chair. I took the other woman's eyeglasses in my hand. "Evelyn," I said, cutting her off in the middle of the description of a particularly difficult ingrown nail. "Try these."

Evelyn took the first pair off her head and replaced them with the eyeglasses I extended. She blinked once or twice with her good eye, then clapped her hands with glee.

"That's it!" she said. "That's it! The Lord done give me back my eye and we didn't even pray for it."

She clapped her hands again. "And that ain't been the only miracle in my life. There's been plenty others. While I was birthing my first child, it seemed like the bleeding would never stop . . ."

I set the other eyeglasses on the bedside table of the other woman. "These are yours," I whispered. "My guess is someone switched them by accident when they were cleaning the room."

"Bless you," she whispered. "Now maybe you can ask her your questions so she'll talk about anything but her ailments."

"I'll do my best, ma'am."

C H A P T E R

12

When I finally did ask, Evelyn's face lost all animation. She stared at me as if I were the ghost of Agnes Larrabee.

"Agnes Larrabee," Evelyn repeated in a whisper. "Agnes Larrabee."

She lost herself in memory, and when she spoke again, her voice seemed to come from a deep quiet place inside her. "Believe me, there was plenty about that family that no one on the outside knew."

As Evelyn spoke, she stared straight ahead. She had folded her hands on her lap. Stillness fell upon her body as her memories sent her backward into time.

She described the Larrabee mansion on East Bay where it overlooked the harbor. It was square, a pastel yellow with two-story columns and a long, narrow front porch, with vines climbing its railings. The wicker porch furniture never held anyone on hot summer evenings.

I knew the exterior well. I remembered it because of how my mother had once described the history of the house to me. A century and a half earlier, a shipbuilder had designed it for his fiancée in England. He sent for her after its completion, but she died during the journey across the Atlantic, and he'd sold it without spending a single night in any one of its ten magnificent bedrooms.

As a child, after my mother was gone, I had made a habit of finding a quiet place at the base of one of the massive pillars of the suspension bridge over the Cooper River. The shortest walk to my place of retreat took me up East Bay, so I passed it almost daily, each time remembering how my mother described the different generations that had occupied the house since the shipbuilder lost his true love at sea, each time feeling renewed sorrow at my mother's absence.

But I knew nothing of the Larrabee mansion's interior.

This, too, Evelyn described in a quiet voice that contrasted so strangely to the coarse manner she'd exhibited during the first part of our meeting. Perhaps the first voice she needed to prove she wasn't afraid of old age and death.

If so, perhaps she spoke in her new quiet voice so as not to disturb the dust that had settled on her memories, recollections that would only remind her of how far past youth she'd traveled, and how little time remained until her own once vigorous body would become dust, with all those memories winking into the darkness of eternity at her passing.

Evelyn described the furniture permanently draped in cloths to protect the fabrics against the sun, and she spoke of the furnishings and paintings slowly disappearing from each room as Agnes Larrabee desperately leveraged them against bill collectors. First, the upper rooms farthest away from center of the house. And slowly, like cancer, the ravaging of more and more of the interior rooms.

Evelyn told me about the great expanses of hardwood floor in empty rooms. Of dull walls broken only by brightly colored squares where the artwork had protected the paint beneath from the grime of dust and the bleaching of the sun.

She spoke of the massive table in the kitchen where servants prepared the meals. For though the furniture departed from the mansion, Agnes could not bear the prospect of altering a royal lifestyle that had always included the service of maids and cooks and gardeners.

Evelyn lingered in her description of the kitchen itself and of the dining room and the exquisite cutlery and dishes and plates, for Evelyn had been a kitchenmaid.

And finally, Evelyn described the night that she stood frozen in the dining room, hearing every word clearly as Agnes Larrabee directed a stream of hatred at Celia Harrison in the kitchen, only hours before Agnes Larrabee drank the death potion given to her on that tea tray by her grandson Timothy. . . .

✛

Celia Harrison was pudgy and short, her black face shiny because she had a habit of wiping her greasy palms against her forehead. She stood in front of Agnes Larrabee, her head bowed.

"It has come to my attention that your daughter has actually consorted publicly with my grandson." Agnes Larrabee spoke in a harsh whisper. She was an angular woman, with nothing graceful about any of her gestures. She stooped as she spoke, like a stick insect reaching for its prey. "I will not tolerate this. Especially in light of your daughter's actions at the hardware store earlier today."

Evelyn had been about to step into the kitchen from the dining room. Agnes had her back to the door, and Celia her eyes to the floor. Neither saw her, so Evelyn moved slowly back into the dining room, where earlier she had been stretching across a mahogany table with wax and a polishing cloth. Evelyn wished she could shut the French doors that connected the kitchen to the dining room, but she was too afraid of being seen. There was nothing predictable or logical about the anger of Agnes Larrabee. At the best of times, working in the mansion was a tightrope act of remaining just visible enough not to be accused of laziness but out of sight enough not to draw the old lady's attention.

"It has been reported to me that your daughter actually led my grandson into the black neighborhood north of Calhoun. On several different occasions in the last month. Do you have any idea their destination?"

"No ma'am. Uh ken ax 'e navuh."

"None of that Gullah nonsense with me. Get those marbles out of your mouth and speak clearly."

"I ken ask de neighbors."

"You ask no neighbors. I want no more attention brought to this. Your daughter is not permitted to chase my Timothy anymore. Furthermore, you will take your daughter tomorrow and apologize to Mr. Aimslick at the hardware store. He tells me that without quick action, the fire in the pile of newspapers would have spread to the rest of his store. And he swears he saw your daughter apply the match."

"Ma'am?"

"You heard me correctly. Your daughter tried burning down

the hardware store today. And she dragged my precious Timothy along with her. Into the shop and away from it. They will not see each other again. Am I understood?"

"Yes ma'am."

"I want you to call Samson to the kitchen. After that, you are dismissed. Permanently. You are no longer in my employ."

"Yes ma'am."

Evelyn remained in the dining room, afraid to come out where she might be noticed. Because of it, when Samson Elias arrived in the kitchen a few minutes later, she overheard that one-sided conversation too.

Samson was an ancient giant. Black as dull coal. Dressed immaculately in a dark tailored suit that did not conceal the bulge of his arms and shoulders.

"Samson, prepare the upstairs room. I will be there shortly with Master Timothy."

"Yes ma'am."

✤

"The Jesus room?" I said to Evelyn.

"Mizz Larrabee just called it the upstairs room. What we servants called it was the Jesus room. 'Cause when Mizz Larrabee took the young master in the room—maybe once every few months—all what we heard was screaming and Mizz Larrabee calling on the name of Jesus. Then the young master, well, he'd never sleep in his own room. 'Cause the next morning, I'd go in to make up his bed, but there'd be nothing to make up. The sheets would be in place, perfect from when I'd made up the bed the day before."

"You think they locked him up in the Jesus room all night?"

"Don't know." Evelyn anticipated my next question. "And I don't know what the screaming was for. The door to the Jesus room was always locked. The only other person ever allowed in there was Samson. With him killed on the 'lectric chair for poisoning Mizz Larrabee, the only other person what knows about the inside of the Jesus room is the young master, and I ain't heard much about his whereabouts 'cept the fact he got into bad ways and found himself in jail someplace. As for what was inside the Jesus room, fact is that night after the police left, Samson went in the Jesus room with a canvas sack and locked it behind him. When he come out, the sack was full and the room was empty. He didn't bother locking it then."

I thought about that for a few moments. "Do you remember the painting of Charles I?"

"The one that was stole and the newspapers went on and on about it and how Samson was the one that stole it?"

"Yes. You think Samson stole it that night?"

"No sir. I knew for sure he did not. I told the police that the young master Timothy took it a month before, but no one wanted to listen to me, 'specially since they was most concerned about the fact the boy accidentally poisoned Mizz Larrabee." Evelyn nodded firmly, as if it were forty years earlier and she was trying to convince a detective at the scene of the crime. "Yes sir. It was Timothy Larrabee that took it. Gave it to Celia Harrison's daughter. I know because I saw him take it from the mansion one day. I followed him outside and watched, 'cause I couldn't figure out why he had need of it. And in the courtyard in the back, he gave it to that girl."

"Celia Harrison's daughter. Who started the fire in the hardware store."

"Just like I said."

"Any idea where Celia Harrison might be?"

"Heaven, I hope. She was a good woman."

"Her daughter?" I asked.

Evelyn shook her head. "Got married. Don't know what name she took along with her husband."

"Crown of thorns," I said. "Does that mean anything to you?"

Evelyn blinked a few times. "I'm trying to remember, but nothing comes to me. If all this is important enough, you might want to ask Richard Freedman. He's still alive. He was just a puppy when he helped the gardener what worked for Mizz Larrabee. Now he's some fancy millionaire, or so I heard. When Mizz Larrabee died, we all went our separate ways."

I reached beneath my chair for my wrapped package. I stood and handed it to Evelyn.

"Thank you very much for your time," I said.

"What's this?" she asked.

"Chocolates," I answered. I'd picked them up on the way over.

She grinned wide, showing the gaps in her teeth. "Love chocolates. 'Specially the chewy ones, 'cause they last longer. Can't bite down on 'em, but I can suck on 'em till the chocolate's gone."

✛

Samuel held my arm as we slowly walked out of the nursing home, down the steps, and along the sidewalk to my Jeep. I held the door open on the passenger side and helped him into the interior.

Charleston was hot again, as it always was in the summer. Inland, however, it was much hotter, and there would be none of the ocean breezes that blessed the peninsula. This was why plantation owners had forsaken their lands during these months to come to town, leaving behind the hell for their slaves. I drove with the air-conditioning off, as I knew he preferred not to have his bones chilled.

Samuel was strangely silent the entire trip. I would glance over at him occasionally, and I saw that his face was troubled. I wondered if I had given him offense. If I had been too aggressive with my questioning of Evelyn. If he thought that had been an abuse of his trust in taking me to her.

When I pulled up to the church, the process was reversed. I helped Samuel from the Jeep, and led him up the sidewalk and into the church. The smell of jasmine was pleasantly cloying, but Samuel's face remained troubled.

Finally, at the top of the steps, with his hand on the open door, the cool darkness of the church beyond, Samuel cleared his throat.

"I've been trying to decide what I can tell you," he said. "It's about this crown of thorns. This is the second time I've heard that mentioned in less than a couple of months. I know something about it, but I don't know that I can pass it on to you in good conscience."

Etta hurried up to us, but he waved her away. She remained just inside the church. She was a large, wide woman, wrapped in a colorful dress.

"You see, Nick," Samuel continued, "some people reach out to me because to them it's like reaching out to God. They want my help getting to our heavenly Father. I tell them they don't need me—they can pray direct to Jesus himself—but I still hear things as they unburden themselves. Confessions and the like. I wish I could tell you more about the crown of thorns, but I heard it in the confidence given to me as a man of God."

"I understand," I said.

"No, you don't. What I heard was horrible. Such a thing should be done to no man, especially in the name of Jesus. I would like it stopped, but telling you anything else would be a violation of a good man's trust in me and in my calling."

Samuel lifted his eyes to mine. He clutched my arm, although he no longer needed support. "I'm going to talk to this man. I'm going to ask him if he'll tell you himself. It's the best I can do. If you see him, you'll learn more."

Samuel looked past me briefly, staring at nothing. "And if you don't," Samuel said, "it means the crown of thorns holds more power over him than the good Lord's justice."

C H A P T E R

13

From the church I drove to East Bay, then headed north to the industrial section along the Cooper, where warehouses had been built decades before for the businesses that leeched off the former naval base upriver. I had the canvas top off the Jeep, and the sour smell of decay and swamplands hit me with the humid hot air that flowed into my face.

I turned off Morrison toward the river and crossed the railroad tracks down a narrow paved road with grass growing between cracks. A quarter mile in, where the road had deteriorated to chunks of asphalt, I drove into a parking lot and stopped in front of a low, flat-roofed building with faded stucco siding. According to the signs, the building held three businesses. I was interested in the one in the center, flanked by an exterminator business on one side and rust-removal specialists on the other.

For protection against the sun, the front windows of the center office were mirrored with the cheap silver lining glued to

the inside of the glass. Bubbles showed where the lining had
begun to separate.

I stepped inside to the rattle of an ancient air conditioner
and tried to breath shallowly against the smell of wet mold that
trickled from it with a stream of cold air into the small front
office. I was five minutes early for my appointment.

"Be right out," a voice called from behind a door that was
closed to the back office.

I studied my surroundings. A dented metal desk served as
the focal point of the room. It held an old rotary-dial phone and a
computer monitor as ancient as the air conditioner and the desk.
Two chairs with fake-leather cushions served as props in front
of the desk; an identical chair sat behind. The walls consisted of
fake-wood paneling, with large, framed photos of jazz greats looking down on me. The floor was covered with scuffed and graying
linoleum.

I looked again at the monitor, at the small circle in the
center of the back of it.

Thirty seconds later, the door opened.

"Nick Barrett?"

I nodded. By her voice, I recognized her as the woman I'd
spoken to when I made my appointment.

"Kellie Mixson," she answered.

"Thanks for making time for me on short notice."

Given what little I knew about private investigators—the
real ones who trace people or gather evidence for divorce cases,
not the ones in novels who solve murders—the office and its loca-
tion were no surprise to me. But Kellie Mixson was not what I
had expected in a private investigator. This was not a burly, beer-
bellied man in a seersucker suit that showed sweat stains at the

armpits. I'd been fooled by my stereotype assumption and the unisex first name. When I'd spoken to her on the phone to ask for an appointment with Kellie Mixson, I'd assumed she was the secretary and that the name belonged to a man.

"No need for pleasantries," she said. "I've got plenty to do, and I can't believe you're here on anything but business. Nobody comes by for any other reason."

Kellie Mixson wore a tight, sleeveless vest of dark blue cotton. Normally, I don't think of arms as beautiful. But hers were tanned and well toned and worthy of admiration. As was the rest of her. She was about five years younger than I. I'd begun to notice that by that relatively young age, for most women, personal habits have begun to override any advantage that genetics and youth give them. It was obvious by her appearance that Kellie's personal habits included a lot of discipline and that she had invested time at the gym. Her shoulder-length hair was wavy, with blonde streaks in the brown. What I liked most were her eyes, a hazelnut brown.

I found her appraising my appraisal of her. Her face had an odd beauty; as a Hollywood actress, she could have played a lead but would have been given the roles that required character, not simpering.

"If you're thinking what most men think, don't," she said, moving to her chair behind the desk. "I began as an assistant for my pops, and when a heart attack took him a few years back, I kept on. There are plenty of times it helps to be a woman in this business. And I'm good at what I do, despite the fact that the office I took over reflects his lack of taste and unwillingness to dip into the bank account."

"Office like this makes it easier to hide the fact you spend plenty on technology."

That stopped her halfway to the chair.

"The video lens mounted inside the back of your monitor," I said, pointing at her desk. "I imagine you've got a working computer in your back office with a feed from the video here. I imagine you checked me for visible weapons before leaving your back office. The door looks solid enough to stop an ax. You've got an exit from there, in case the client has obviously bad intentions. Right?"

That earned the first smile. "Right on all counts. At least you're not a nose-picker. I hate nose-pickers, standing around in here so bored they decide to do a search-and-wipe. Then when I come out, first thing they do is offer me a handshake."

"Better to see them pick their noses than march in with a baseball bat."

She smiled again. It seemed like a rare privilege and I enjoyed it as such. "Yeah. Every once in a while they come in spoiling for a fight. The ones married to clients of divorce cases. I always recognize them because of the video clips that show them cheating on their spouses. That's when I let them believe I'm the secretary here."

"Like when I called," I said.

"Wasn't hard to fool you, was it? Few guys think a PI is going to be a woman."

"I'm sorry," I said. "At least it didn't take a high-rent office to impress me that you know what you're doing."

Her smile faded. "And most guys work a different angle when they try to impress me. Drop salary figures maybe, or let me know they live south of Broad. It did get my attention that you figured out the hidden camera. But if you were really smart, you would have held back, walked out without letting me know that you know about the monitor. Really smart people don't need to let the world know they're really smart."

"And here you said there was no need for pleasantries."

She pointed at a chair behind me and moved to her chair behind the old desk. "Clock's ticking."

I sat. "You found a man named Timothy Larrabee for a client named Zora Starr. I doubt you'll tell me much more than what I read in the report you gave Zora, but I figured it would be worth a shot to ask you about it."

"What would you like to know? Not that I intend to answer."

I had nothing to lose. And, prickly as she was, I liked her way of dealing. I had no place to go, and no hurry to get there. I laid it out for her. "Timothy Larrabee left Charleston as a young boy, drifted into trouble with the law, and seemed to have departed Charleston permanently, keeping a low profile until he joined the Glory Church of the Lamb of Jesus on his return to this area. So how'd Zora know to begin looking for him nearby? And what connects them that she'd be interested to locate him?"

"If you don't know, then Zora refused to tell you herself. Or you have the report without her knowing it. Timothy Larrabee send you?"

"Her granddaughter gave the file to me."

"Tiffany. Fifteen, but acts like she's twenty-five."

"Angel. Twelve years old," I said. "A guardian angel for her little sister Maddie. Did I pass?"

As she stared at me, Kellie steepled her fingers beneath her chin and pressed the tops of her short nails into the soft skin beneath her jaw. "Angel gave it to you because . . ."

"This is how it works?" I said. "I answer all your questions but get nothing from you?"

"This is how it works." No smile. "I keep pumping till the well runs dry. Then I'll send you on your way. The first thing Pops taught me was that clients deserve confidentiality. Unless they break the law. So do you want to tell me about Zora's granddaughter? Or you want to end this now and walk out the door?"

"I hate getting pulled over for speeding by a woman cop," I said, smiling. "Male cop pulls you over, you got an outside chance at just a warning. Woman cop writes the ticket every time. She can't afford to look weak. Really tough people don't have to show the world they're really tough."

Her features remained expressionless, but I saw a return smile touch her eyes. "Alright then. Angel gave you the files. Tell me in a way that I can believe it's not a story. And let me warn you, I've heard enough stories that you'll have to be real good to fool me if you're not telling the truth."

"Want the short version or long version?"

"You're more interesting than most people desperate enough to hire a PI from a low-rent district. And I'm not as busy as I'd like the world to believe. I'll take the long version." She paused. "Over a late breakfast. I doubt I'll have anything I can bill you for. But I'm hungry, so I might as well get a free meal out of it."

✠

What Shepherd Isaiah had never realized was that Retha had brains to go with the unexpected courage that she'd found to remain silent as she endured the beating. Shepherd Isaiah couldn't be blamed for this. Retha hadn't realized it either. Not until Elder Jeremiah had shut the toolshed door on her and

walked out, not until Shepherd Isaiah had whispered through the
closed door as he put the lock in place that he wasn't finished
trying to rid her of Satan's presence in her body.

That's when she firmly decided she was only going to
depend on herself for as long as she lived, not trust anybody but
herself. Which, she also decided, might not be long unless she
took action. Especially since she had to find a way to get Billy Lee
out of the hospital.

Retha heard Shepherd Isaiah's truck roar down the driveway
away from their trailer, and, much to her surprise, assessed her
situation with calmness and clarity.

She had little water.

The temperature was rising in the confines of the shed.

And a husband she had decided to leave because he didn't
love her enough to protect her. In her mind, free from Jesus and
free from the church and free from Shepherd Isaiah and Elder
Mason and Junior, there was nothing left to force her to stay.
Certainly not her own parents, who told her again and again to
follow Shepherd Isaiah.

Strengthening her decision was the knowledge that Billy Lee
needed her to find him once she left the compound.

First, she needed to escape the shed. Retha had no crowbar.
No hammer. Nothing to pry the door off the hinges or pop it
loose from the lock. She looked around the shed. There was the
lawn mower. Some gasoline in a container. Some wrenches lying
loose on the dirt. Junior couldn't be bothered to hang them up.

Retha waited for an idea to hit her. She sure wasn't going to
burn her way out with gasoline, even if she had matches. That left
the lawn mower and the wrenches.

Junior was too lazy to cut the lawn. He left that to her. She was the one who took the blade off and went into town to get it sharpened. So her solution came quickly.

Retha lifted the bottom of her shirt and ripped off a swatch of material. She couldn't work if she couldn't see. She padded the cloth and wiped blood off her face and forehead, clearing her vision. She was surprised at how little pain she felt. She enjoyed her anger, thinking maybe it was the painkiller she needed.

Once the blood stopped dripping into her eyes, Retha turned the lawn mower on its side. This time, pain did strike her. Quick and savage, as if a snake had snapped its fangs into her side. She'd have to go easy on her ribs as she twisted and turned.

Retha fumbled with the wrenches, moving without haste as she found one to fit the nut on the bottom side of the lawn-mower blade. She braced until the nut was loose, then removed it easily with her fingers.

She was grateful that her fingers were still strong. They were the only part of her body that Junior had left untouched. Including her heart and soul.

The lawn-mower blade popped off easily. Here was the crowbar she needed. She levered it between the door and the hinges and pushed hard. The frame splintered at the hinge screws. If Junior hadn't been such a lazy carpenter, he would have used deeper screws into a reinforced frame. Retha would have been a prisoner until Elder Jeremiah was tired of beating her. As it was, she broke the door free easily and limped into humidity and sunshine.

Free.

The trailer was locked. Which meant Elder Mason was gone. He never left it unlocked, despite the relative security of the compound where everyone was supposed to obey him instantly.

And Junior was probably fishing again. He always did that when
he was under stress or afraid.

Retha swung the lawn-mower blade and smashed the
window of the door of the trailer. She reached inside and
unlocked it.

What she needed from the trailer wouldn't take her long to
collect.

Cash. Retha had always kept some aside, dreaming of the
days she'd take Billy Lee to Disney World. Barely over seventy
dollars, and she'd been saving since Billy Lee was born. It was in
a jar at the bottom of the flour bin. Junior never went into the
cooking supplies.

Clothes. Only what she could stuff into Junior's gym bag.
As soon as she could, she'd get herself a new wardrobe. Get rid
of the ugly loose stuff that Junior made her wear.

Finally, makeup. Even when all the church had been mad
at her for daring to try a makeover, she'd held on to the free
samples that she'd been given at the department store. So deep
down, she guessed, this meant she always wanted this day of freedom to arrive.

It had. She'd paid for it with bruises. Blood. Cracked ribs.
And felt like it was a bargain.

Retha stepped outside of the trailer. She'd never go back.
Elder Jeremiah would have to kill her before she returned.

Retha walked across the yard and disappeared into the brush
that led to a swamp trail. Sure, there was a fence around the
entire compound, but she'd find a way under it or over it. Billy
Lee was waiting to be found.

She needed to put some miles between her and the trailer.
And this close, she didn't trust the road where compound neigh-

bors might see her and take her back to Junior and Elder Mason. Much as she feared the swamps, she feared the road more.

As the shadows of the swamps closed on Retha, she found herself smiling.

✣

Kellie Mixson drove an old red BMW. She followed my Jeep to the downtown core of Charleston, into the parking lot right beside the Sweetwater Café. We took a booth that overlooked the street. I was amazed at the type and quantity of food she ordered for breakfast—sausage, eggs, grits, French toast. I could only conclude that her workouts were long and intense.

"What are your fees?" I asked. I'd given this some thought during the drive here.

"Fifteen hundred retainer. Cash. Or I wait until the check clears. It goes against five hundred a day plus expenses. Most files I can clear in three days or less. If it's less, I return the balance."

"Wow."

"Come on," she said. "Don't make me wrong about you. I'd already decided you wouldn't treat me like a little missy or a breakable doll or a bimbo or a challenge to pursue. Otherwise I wouldn't be here for breakfast."

I laughed. "This is all about you, huh?"

"Meaning?" My laughter hadn't eased her immediate resentment.

"It was 'wow' as in 'Zora Starr wow.' I've seen where she lives. She must have wanted to find Timothy Larrabee badly if she came up with that kind of retainer."

Behind us came the clatter of the action of the open grill. I
heard the waitress shout our order to the cook.

"This is all I'm going to tell you about Zora," Kellie said. I
noticed she didn't apologize for her flare of temper. "I didn't ask
her for a retainer. She had a long history with Pops. He'd go to
her when he needed help in her community. He owed her plenty
of favors. That's why she came to me. I didn't charge her a dime
for my work either. She's helped me plenty, too."

"A voodoo woman would know a lot that could help in your
business."

"Yeah, well—" Kellie stopped. "Angel tell you about the
voodoo?"

"Not in so many words. But that's part of the long version."

"Get started," she said.

I began with a description of the Van Dyck portrait of
Charles I that had disappeared from the Larrabee estate. I told
her about Glennifer and Elaine and their request for me to talk to
Angel. I paused for a few moments when our food arrived, then
continued. Without describing Maddie's hospital situation or my
involvement in paying the hospital fees, I explained how Angel
had sent me to Bingo, how Bingo had told me about Zora's detective report, then sent me to the church. How Shepherd Isaiah
had sent me away before I could talk to Larrabee. I didn't think it
was Kellie Mixson's business that I'd found a baby in my Jeep or
that I'd delivered the boy to the hospital, so I kept that to myself,
too. I finished by telling her what I had learned from Evelyn
during my visit earlier in the morning, how it appeared that
Timothy Larrabee had taken the painting and given it to a girl his
age all those years ago.

"So it was Timothy Larrabee who stole the painting from his

161

grandmother," Kellie said when I finished. "He was a born thief. Things haven't changed much."

"Angel gave me the rest of your report. I read his background. Bad checks, grand theft auto. Various assault charges. Looks like when Agnes died and they had to yank the silver spoon from his mouth, he kept trying the easy way."

"He's found it again in the Glory Church of the Lamb of Jesus." Kellie pushed away her plate. It was so clean of food a sparrow wouldn't have bothered to give it a second look. "Do you have any idea of the kind of assets that organization has accumulated?"

"It wasn't in the report."

"I only gave Grammie what she wanted. But I was curious, given that a man like Larrabee was so heavily involved in a religious organization. So I did the usual boring background stuff. Access public information. Call a contact at the IRS. Credit checks."

I nodded.

"Let me put it this way," she continued. "It's a great legal tax dodge. Everyone who joins the church donates all of his or her wages. They work at regular jobs off the church grounds, but all live there in housing provided by the church."

I nodded again, thinking of the mobile homes I'd seen scattered in the trees behind the old church building.

"So if you're a church member, your taxable wages drop so low as to be laughable. You give up all you make, but the church takes care of every need. You've got no worries, because if you lose your job or get sick, everyone else picks up the slack. Now start running numbers from an administrative side. Give or take, there are seventy families in the Glory Church of the Lamb of

Jesus. These people are working the low end of the economic scale, so say the average monthly wage is three thousand dollars per family. That means over two hundred grand a month—virtually tax free—goes into the church treasury. That's cheap land out there, and mobile homes are the most inexpensive type of housing. Buy food in bulk for all the families, disperse some of the money for their other needs, get more tax advantages by home-schooling the kids and use that home-schooling to indoctrinate them so that they remain members of the church when they get old enough to earn wages."

"You sound cynical."

"I *am* cynical. It's about numbers. Compared to revenue, the expenses are nothing. You do the math. Timothy Larrabee has his hand on a yearly purse that, after expenses, gets fatter by close to a million a year, if not more. The church was founded just under ten years ago, started small and grew to its present size about four years ago. Do the math again for the total assets since it was founded. Larrabee is onto something sweet."

"Shepherd Isaiah," I corrected.

She frowned at me.

"Shepherd Isaiah's the pastor of the Glory Church. He's the one sitting on a million a year."

She shook her head. "This was interesting enough that I made it a pet project. Larrabee is the brains behind this. Isaiah Sullivan is the believer. They met in prison nearly fifteen years ago. Larrabee is about fifteen years older; he became a mentor of sorts. From my sources, I understand they formed an effective partnership, each protecting the other against the usual predators you'd expect in a federal prison. You might not know it, but the racial tension in there is incredible. Black gangs against white gangs. Larrabee and Sullivan shared the same cell for three years. That's a lot of time for one man to get to know another, especially if the younger one looks up to the older one like a father. Sullivan was in for involuntary manslaughter. Killed someone outside a bar who tried to fight his younger brother. Saw the error of his ways in prison. Started preaching when he got out. All he needed was a flock. Larrabee helped deliver it. Who knows, maybe they spent all that time in there planning it out. Prison library's got all the information Larrabee would need to help him think through the tax and investment implications. And what a way to come up with a monthly revenue base."

"Isaiah seemed passionate enough in the pulpit," I said. "That would draw a certain type of person to his congregation."

"Passionate? Understatement. And the type of people he draws? Let me put it this way. When you were in the church, did you see any black people?"

I shook my head.

"A hundred and fifty years ago," Kellie said, "some people in the South used the Bible to argue their case for slavery. That's where Isaiah's at. Don't get me started on the use of the Bible as a weapon for white men to hold their power over women and other races."

"Not the Bible's fault how people decide to abuse it."

"I told you not to get me started. Especially about the Glory Church. Although I feel sorry, in a way, for Isaiah Sullivan."

I raised an eyebrow.

"A few years back, before Shepherd Isaiah became media shy, he allowed an interview," she explained. "I'll get you a copy of the magazine article. You'll want to read it. Especially his past. Gives you some insight into how such a man might be formed.

The jury knew about it, too. It became the main reason the prosecutor pushed for manslaughter instead of first- or second-degree murder."

"The overview?" It was pleasant, sipping coffee, listening to her talk.

"Born and raised in the Smoky Mountains. His mother was a coal miner's daughter. His father was unemployed. Both were alcoholic. Both beat Isaiah and Jeremiah routinely. Jeremiah was a lot younger, and Isaiah protected him. When Jeremiah was a baby, his mother would get mad at him for dirtying his diapers. For her, that was enough reason to beat the baby. So Isaiah took responsibility for changing the diapers. And cleaning the house. And cooking. Anything to keep their mother from losing her temper. Father had a worse temper and was so big, the boys knew if they tried to fight back when he whipped them, he'd kill them. When they were teenagers, they ran out and lived in the hills like wild animals, coming into town to steal food from Dumpsters at night. It was on one of those nights that a drunk began to taunt Jeremiah, who was thirteen or fourteen at the time, and dressed in rags and filth and rooting through a Dumpster. Isaiah stepped in, went berserk, like he was fighting the entire cruel world instead of a drunk hardly able to stand. Pounded the man's head into a car bumper until . . . well, you get the picture. They put Isaiah in prison. Jeremiah ran away, lived in the hills until Isaiah was released from prison and found him again."

"How long ago was that?"

"Isaiah and Timothy have been out of prison ten years. Like I said, the church grew slowly at first. Last few years they broke through into the big bucks. A weird partnership, but effective."

"You interested in learning more?" I asked.

She frowned slightly.

"On my tab. I'm fine with your retainer and fee structure. Which is why I asked about it. I'd like you to find the gardener's assistant—Richard Freedman, if Evelyn's memory was correct. And the daughter of Celia Harrison."

The waitress stopped at our table. Kellie accepted a coffee refill, then turned her attention back to me. "Why?"

"Since when do you care why a client wants information?"

"Most of the time someone comes into my office, I know exactly what motivates them. Security issues. Or someone is behind on payments. Or they want to prove a spouse has been cheating. I can't see what's in it for you to find out about Larrabee. And that makes me a little gun-shy."

Why?

I thought of Angel bravely standing up to the taxi driver. I thought of Maddie, clinging to Angel. I thought of a woman who was so desperate to help her child get away from the Glory Church that she had placed him in the vehicle and care of a man she hadn't met. I thought of the demons I carried with me from childhood, and the ones I'd finally driven away.

Private demons.

"Look," I said. "Are in you interested in the retainer or not?"

"That's your answer?"

"That's my answer. Want the retainer?"

"Well," she said after a short hesitation, "you know what they say. Money talks. But I won't do any work until the check clears."

CHAPTER

14

"Jubil."

"Got some news for me? You're down to a day and half."

I spoke as I walked. Despite the heat, after breakfast with Kellie at the Sweetwater, I'd decided to take the short walk to the hospital from King and Market. I wanted time to think. And in general, I tried to walk as much as possible. At least in short stretches, when the pain of my prosthesis pressing against the stump of my leg was bearable. The longer I walked, however, the more noticeable my limp.

"No news." I'd called Jubil's cell phone from mine. I had the plastic pressed to my ear as I dodged tourists wandering in and out of the shops. "Another favor."

Jubil's laughter was tinny. "Must have a bad connection here. Sounded like you were asking for another favor. I'm taking enough heat already about delaying this report. And if the media finds out this one was buried—"

"There's a couple of kids in the Citadel district hawking stolen electronics. I'll bet if you stop them, it'll cut down on your B-and-Es."

"So now you talk like a cop?"

"So now you talk like a Mafia tough guy?"

"Where are these kids? I'll send a patrol car."

"No."

"No? You talk like a cop and you act like my chief."

I dodged a large woman who was trying to push her husband into a used-book store. "I'm asking you to go yourself. Confiscate what they have and give them such a scare they decide what they're doing is not such a good idea."

"You talk like a cop and act like my chief, but your heart bleeds like a social worker. What's next, an imitation of my wife?"

"Jubil, in high school you told me plenty of times how easily your life could have taken a different direction. All I'm saying is, you have a chance to do the same for these kids. Tour them through a penitentiary if that's what it takes for them to decide on a different direction."

"I get it. Kids in that district are black. I'm black. So they'll listen to me."

"Racist," I said. "One's white."

"Oh."

"You're a cop. You have a badge, a gun, and a shiny new car with lights that flash and a siren that makes big noise. More effective than a WASP like me with a boring lecture on why it's bad for kids to steal."

"You made your point. Tell me where to find them."

"That's the easy part," I said.

I told him about Bingo and the bright red Chevette with jacked-up wheels and when and where to find it.

"If that was the easy part, what's the hard part?" Jubil asked when I finished.

"Let me put it this way. Make sure you flash your badge real early in your conversation with him."

"Why's that?"

"The kid's handy with a switchblade."

⊹

Retha had been gone for about an hour when she first heard the hounds. At first, she thought she was hallucinating. The mosquitoes swarmed her in frenzied clouds. She'd wiped her face of their crushed bodies and her warm blood so often that she'd tired of carrying the gym bag and had left it in a hollow log, tucking one tube of lipstick and her cash in a roll inside her back pocket. The torment of the mosquitoes, the constant buzz in her ears, the gagging as she breathed in the husks of their bodies—all of it drove her into near madness.

So when the eerie music of the hounds on a trail reached her, she thought it was simply another sound inside her head. As the chorus grew closer, however, she picked out the individual voices of their baying, and it jolted her back to her surroundings.

It didn't occur to her to be surprised or angry that Shepherd Isaiah had chosen to find her this way. Shepherd Isaiah always said loudly that a man had to do everything possible to protect his property. If that meant running her down like she was a mule busted out of the fence, so be it.

It did occur to Retha that there was only one way to escape the hounds. She knew from listening to endless stories of her own father, and of Elder Mason, and of all his friends. She'd have to take to water.

She was afraid of the dark still pools, the moist mud that would suck at her feet and ankles, the cottonmouths or water moccasins that might rise from the disturbed waters to curl around her thighs and waist.

But her anger at Shepherd Isaiah and Elder Mason and Junior, and her desperation to get to Billy Lee, outweighed her fear.

Without hesitation, she turned toward an opening in the swamp grass. Cypress trees cast serpentine shadows onto the water, but she ignored the ominous signs and waded forward.

It was a small pool, and she crossed it in less than five minutes.

She stepped out, water coursing down her body, long-dead rotted vines clinging to her hips. The hounds wouldn't take long to circle it and pick up her scent on the far side. Retha ran hard, branches crashing against her face, cracked ribs searing her at every jolt.

Then she reached it. A small river, slow current.

She jumped in, startling a pair of sunning turtles into slapping the water beside her and disappearing into a trail of bubbles. If she stayed in the water and moved with the current, the hounds wouldn't find her. And soon enough, she'd find a bridge. The bridge would get her to a road. And tonight, in the dark, she'd follow that road to her new life.

She swam with the current.

✛

"Here she is, my mama before she died," Angel said. "Would you like to see her?"

I was at the opposite side of the hospital room. It was semiprivate, with only two beds. I'd been looking down on Billy Lee. He was sleeping, half covered with bedsheets. He seemed far too tiny for the bed, and far too alone. The sides of the bed were up so that they formed a crib. He wore green hospital pajamas, and that institutionalization bothered me too. I made a note to get him some flannel pajamas with cartoon characters. I still didn't know if I was going to call the woman who had signed her note 'Retha,' or just show up later in the day and offer to drive her here to the hospital.

"See your mother?" I said in answer to Angel's question. "Yes, I would."

I stepped back from Billy Lee and moved across the room to Maddie's bed.

Angel sat cross-legged on top of the sheets of the bed, with a laptop computer between her legs. Maddie, her black skin and black hair a contrast to tan-colored Winnie the Pooh pajamas, was propped against a pillow beside her. Although an IV tube was still hooked up to her matchstick-thin arm, Maddie's eyes were bright and alert. At my entrance into the room, they had been staring at the computer screen. When Maddie noticed my approach, she had clutched Angel and held tight until Angel told her everything was fine.

Angel had plugged the laptop into the nearest outlet. The hard drive whirred as her fingers ran over the keyboard. She tapped the built-in mouse pad a few times, running a DVD program.

As I looked over Angel's shoulder, the screen brightened into life.

"Was easy to do," Angel said. "Ran video from my digital camcorder to my laptop, then made a home movie and burned it on a DVD disc. Now I can take the clips anywhere. At home I've got this projector that hooks up to my laptop. I project it onto a wall, and me and Maddie watch it all the time."

I kept a straight face as I did the mental arithmetic. Laptop, DVD burner, projector, digital camcorder. Not bad for a twelve-year-old in a low-income neighborhood. Bingo, I was sure, had given her a lot of inadvertent help in securing the electronics. Was it my business to step in and lecture her about the morality of stolen property? Or should I remain what I had been all my life? An observer, staying detached with whatever limited participation I grudgingly gave.

"See," Angel said, "I don't want to grow up poor. What I figure is I'm smart enough that I can go places. I just got to learn as much as I can. If I don't know anything about computers, I may as well just get ready to live with cockroaches all my life."

I nodded. There was truth in that. Enough truth that I told myself now was not the time to discourage her aspirations, even if they rode upon what had been stolen from the people who live in the neighborhoods she wanted to claim someday as her own.

"I'm impressed you understand that," I said.

"Mama always told me that," Angel said. "Grammie Zora, too. No drugs for me. No chasing with boys later like the older girls in my neighborhood do. And now with just Maddie and me, it's 'specially important that I listen good. If I don't get out of the neighborhood, then Maddie don't."

Angel pointed at the screen. "There's Mama. That was when

I turned nine. Her and Grammie Zora took me to the water park. Maddie wasn't born, so you won't see her there."

Walking toward me and waving from the computer screen was a slim black woman in a one-piece bathing suit. Holding her hand was the Angel of three years ago, her unmistakable grin wide across her face. She wore a pink bikini and her spindly legs were bowed. Behind them were the giant, gleaming plastic tubes of the water park and running splashing figures of swimmers of all ages. I assumed Grammie Zora was holding the camcorder, because she was nowhere in sight.

Angel adjusted the volume of the laptop. Screams and laughter reached me. As did a low, calm voice from off camera. "Sir, would you kindly hold this for me?"

I assumed the voice belonged to Grammie Zora, because the scene abruptly shifted forty-five degrees, as the camcorder was passed over to the unseen bystander.

The scene straightened again, and Grammie Zora walked into view. She was an elegant woman, hardly what a person might conjure up at the phrase "voodoo woman." She was slender, with a gracefully aged face and neatly cut, short, white hair that contrasted nicely with her jeans and red sweater.

"Here we are on Grace Louise Starr's ninth birthday," Grammie said, speaking straight into the camera. "And we love her more than life itself."

Angel's mother knelt down and hugged Angel. "She's our little angel. And we want to sing her 'Happy Birthday.' "

Angel hit Pause, freezing that moment in time when her mother was alive and hugging her.

"That's my born name," Angel explained with great seriousness. "Grace Louise. But they always called me Angel."

She began the DVD again. The next few minutes of the clip showed Grammie Zora and her mother singing lustily, with Angel looking upward and alternating grins at each of them. When they finished, Angel clapped enthusiastically.

"I love you, Angel," her mother said one more time on the computer screen. She knelt, lifted Angel, and hugged her. Angel squeezed her arms around her mother's neck.

Then the screen went dark.

"I cut the rest of that clip," Angel said, very matter-of-fact. "Photoshop and a Macintosh. Mac's the best. Anyway, the jerk holding the camera started going on about not having all day to stand there and hold it for complete strangers. It kind of ruins the rest of it. So I used Photoshop to get rid of him."

I was touched. Not necessarily at the obvious sentiment on the DVD clip, but at Angel's unawareness of her bravery. When I lost my mother at her age, I was filled with resentment, self-pity and longing. It took me two decades to find my way back, and even after that, when I was prepared to admit it to myself, part of me still clung to the adolescence of suspicion and sorrow that had shaped my psyche and my inclination toward solitude.

"I got plenty more video clips," Angel said. "I put them on a bunch of different DVDs. Instead of watching TV, I show them to Maddie all the time, mainly from the projector at night onto a wall. That way it's closer to life-size, instead of watching it on TV through the DVD. Mama always said TV would rot my mind. So me and Maddie watch the DVDs of Mama and Grammie Zora, and I explain it all to Maddie. I think she knows what I'm saying too, though she don't talk. I want Maddie to understand how Mama would have loved her just as much as Mama loved me. Good thing I got all those DVDs, huh?"

Better thing if you had a mother, I thought. I drew a deep breath and fought a slight quiver of sorrow for Angel that came with it. I wondered if she would think it all right for me to take her for a walk down King this afternoon, the way my mother had sometimes taken me.

"Good thing you have those DVDs," I said.

Angel snapped the laptop closed and set it aside. She jumped off the bed but stood nearby, holding Maddie's hand.

"How's everything else?" I asked. "Is the little boy doing fine?"

Angel nodded. "I watch him close, just like you asked. When's his mama coming to look after him?"

"Good question. I don't have the answer," I said. But I intended to do something about it, one way or another. "How about Maddie?"

"The nurse said that Maddie could go home tomorrow afternoon. That's been a good couple of days. You sure you're going to pay for all this? Or maybe you've already found Timothy Larrabee and we can use what he pays me for the painting."

"Timothy Larrabee." I was startled to hear his name from her.

"I'm not stupid. I read that detective report before I gave it to you."

"You're definitely not stupid."

"From what Bingo told you and from the detective report, you ought to be able to drive up to his front doorstep. You gonna see him this afternoon?"

"I told you already, I went to his church. I left a message for him. When I hear from him, I promise I'll let you know."

Then what was I going to do? Negotiate the sale of something that may or may not have been stolen? I needed to know more, and what little I had already learned simply hinted at what little I knew.

"Do more than let me know. Sell it to him. He offered a bunch of money for it. You tell him it's for sale. Sounds simple to me."

"Angel," I said, "I'd sure like to talk to your Grammie Zora. I have a few questions. You give me her number, and I could call her this afternoon at her sister's. Or is she traveling on her way back to Charleston to help you with Maddie?"

"She's coming back later this week, but you can't talk to her. I don't want her knowing who bought the painting. Remember?"

"I do remember. So maybe you can tell me. It's something Grammie Zora wanted Bingo to pass on to Timothy Larrabee. If I understand the importance of that, it would help when I talk to Mr. Larrabee myself."

Angel shrugged.

I took that as permission to continue. "Crown of thorns," I said. "Does that mean anything to you?"

Angel stared up at the ceiling for long moments. "I don't know if I want to tell you," Angel finally said. "You being white and all. You'd laugh at voodoo."

"Nope. I already know Grammie Zora's a voodoo doctor."

"You do?"

"That suffering root scared Bingo plenty."

She grinned. "Maybe you're not as white as you look."

"Maybe I'd like you to tell me what you can about the crown of thorns."

"Some man came by one night with his son, asking Grammie Zora to lay a curse," Angel said. "It wasn't good. Not at all."

And she described it to me.

✣

Grammie Zora's altar was a dressing table in a room off the kitchen. The doorway from the kitchen was covered with strings of ruby red beads, and the windows of the room were draped with black. Little light reached the warped wooden floors, even during the height of day.

The dressing table was against the back wall; because the floor was uneven, chunks of folded paper beneath the rear legs kept the top of the table level. Grammie Zora kept most of her ritual supplies in the top drawer—red velvet mojo bag, parchment paper, dip pen, and dove's blood bottled as ink for writing out magical intentions on the parchment, scales for weighing ingredients, and pestle and mortar.

The tabletop was covered with red velvet cloth. A white candle stood on the far right side and a black candle on the left. A glass tumbler filled with springwater and witch's salt served as a centerpiece. For a voodoo doctor, this tumbler was the equilibrium point between the white candle's representation of the positive forces and the black candle's representation of the negative.

The entire back side of the altar was lined with incense burners, half filled with sand to keep the heat from damaging the altar cloth. Soot covered the wall directly behind, where years of rising smoke had baked particles into the thick gray paint.

It was to this room that Angel brought the father and son, where incense cloyed the air, swirling above Grammie Zora, where she sat hunched in an armchair.

The son wore greasy mechanic's overalls, a tight cap over dreadlocks. He followed his father with reluctance, a man respectfully dressed in black pants, white shirt, and vest. The father walked with the stoop of a man who had lifted bricks and set them into mortar for an entire adult lifetime. The son moved identically, but his stoop, as Angel would soon discover, came from experiences much different.

Once the middle-aged man and his grown son were in the presence of Grammie Zora, the old woman nodded at Angel, giving the signal for Angel to depart. She did, but once beyond the ruby-bead curtain, stepped to the side to listen to the voices that carried clearly to her.

"Grammie Zora, we needs hep. De boy, he skay'd tel 'e mout' dry up. Sum de dey, de boy so 'f aid 'e foot tie tuh de groun'."

From all her time around Grammie Zora, Angel knew Gullah well enough to understand. *The boy was so scared his mouth was dried up. There were days he was so afraid to move, it was like he had a foot tied to the ground.*

"Please," the son said. "You know I don't want to be here. Talking mumbo jumbo just makes it worse."

"You and me," Grammie Zora said to the father in her deep, quiet voice. "We know the past and our traditions. It's good that the young people are moving on, staying with the world as it goes. There's no harm in talking so's the boy will understand."

The man sighed. "He maybe don't believe. But I do. Just so you know."

"Otherwise you wouldn't be here," Grammie Zora said reasonably. "Why's the boy scared?"

"White folks. They took him. And I heard on different occasions they took two of his cousins too. What I want is you to lay a curse on them white folk, make them suffer the way my boy suffered, but worse."

"You know where these white folks live?"

"Tell her, Son," the father said.

"They said I tell anybody," he replied, "they're coming back to kill me."

"Grammie Zora, she afraid of nobody," the father said.

"But I am," the son replied.

Another sigh from the father. "He come home one night, all wet and shaking. Could hardly talk to tell. But I gave him a little whiskey, and that helped him some. These white folks, they wore masks. Like the KKK. But they weren't KKK, were they, Son?"

"I don't want to say nothing. I'm scared already, you telling the story."

"They wanted to baptize him to Jesus," the father continued. "Said he was a sinner."

"They said," the son finally broke in, his voice high and excited, "they said I was a drug dealer, that my case had gone to court and even if the judge had thrown out the evidence, they would not."

"My boy ain't ever taken drugs," the father said to Grammie Zora. "He was cleared of the charges. Those white men in the masks, they had it wrong."

"They said justice had to be done," the son said. "They said they were going to baptize me to Jesus through water and fire."

"What they did," the father said, "was dunk him in water again and again till he was close to drowning. Then they asked him would he accept Jesus into his heart before he died, otherwise he'd be going to hell for eternity."

"I said yes." The son had begun to cry. "Then came the fire."

"Fire?" Grammie Zora asked.

"There's no way to explain it 'cept to show you," the father replied. "Son, lift your shirt."

Angel could only rely on her ears. She heard a zipper as the son undid the front of his mechanics coveralls. Then rustling, as if the son was lifting off his shirt.

"Turn around, Son," the father said. "Let Grammie Zora see your back. Show her why we want her to lay a curse on those white men."

A long silence followed.

"You'll lay a curse on those white folks?" the father asked.

Grammie Zora, sitting deep in her armchair, waited several heartbeats to answer.

"I believe I can stop this," she said. "Leave it in my hands."

✠

"Angel," I said when she finished telling me the story, "how long after this did Grammie Zora wait to send for Timothy Larrabee?"

"Next day she asked her detective friend to find him," Angel answered. "Then, soon's she had the report, she sent Bingo to fetch him."

I sat parked in my Jeep, with Retha's Wal-Mart receipt in one
hand and my cell phone in the other.

Earlier, I'd taken Angel for a walk around town. It had been
fun to indulge her, and she more than repaid me with her wide-
eyed appreciation of everything new to her.

Now it was five in the afternoon, and the temperature had cooled
to become almost pleasant. It helped that I had parked in the market
area opposite the Doubletree, where the hotel threw shadows on
the bustling of tourists. The top was off my Jeep, and I smelled the
nearby horses. This was the staging area for carriage rides, and I was
close enough to hear the snorts of blindered Clydesdale horses.

I had decided first to call the woman named Retha. My
intention was to ask her if she wanted me to come and get her, as
it didn't seem I would be able to bring Billy Lee back to her. I
wondered if she had been able to keep her secret, that Billy Lee
was no longer in the household.

The cell phone is an amazing tool, a by-product of the wave of technology that has transformed the world in the time since my childhood. It is the same technology that I take as much for granted as the next person; it never occurred to me that something as simple as caller identification on the other end of my call would lead to as much trouble as it did.

So I dialed the number on the Wal-Mart receipt, blithely unaware of yet another chain of events that my bumbling would set in motion.

"Yup," a male voice answered after two rings.

"Hello," I said. "Is Retha there?"

"Nope. And her husband don't take kindly to men callers for her."

The line went dead as the person on the other end of the phone hung up on me.

⊹

"Girl! You look good!" Camellia squealed with delight as she pranced around Angel in tight quarters of their secret place. "What done happen to you?"

Angel grinned. "Fancy hairdresser. And shopping. Today, with that guy I told you about. Nick. The one with a leg he can take off. We went to some fancy shops on King, and he caught me looking in the window at some clothes."

"Girl, you look pretty but your face is sad."

"You know I can't stop thinking about Grammie Zora."

Camellia reached across for Angel's hand. They sat in silence for several minutes.

"There's been other people gone dead," Angel said. "We

both seen that. But it wasn't real because it was other people. Know what I mean?"

With her other hand, Camellia stroked Angel's hair. Camellia was the only person Angel allowed that from.

"What do you think happens to people after they die?" Angel said.

Camellia leaned back again and hugged her knees to herself. "My sister asked me that. I told her we just get put in some dirt and bugs eat everything except our bones, and that's what they use for those skeletons in the doctor's office."

"Yuck," Angel said. "It's bad enough people die. They don't need other people to see their bones."

"I didn't say it was true," Camellia answered. "I said that's what I told my sister. I didn't want to scare her by telling her most people get thrown in hell and burn forever."

"Don't do me no favors," Angel said. "You know I'm always thinking about Grammie Zora. I wished she could see me like this."

"Don't get mad just yet," Camellia said. "Remember how I told you 'bout my grampa, how he used to come round with candies and take me to the park and the zoo sometime?"

"The one that's dead now."

"Him. He took me to church some when I was little. Made me learn about God and Jesus. That God lives in heaven but he's around us all the time, too."

"You can't see him but he's everywhere." Angel rolled her eyes. "And you say it's me smoking Herman's weed?"

"It's what my grampa told me. See, you can talk to God by praying to him and he listens. Or to this guy named Jesus, some dude could walk on water and stuff like that. God sent him so we could learn more about God. Except when Jesus was telling people about God, they got mad at him and killed him and sent him back to God, so now Jesus is in heaven with God and steps in and helps God when there's so many people praying all at once that God cain't listen to 'em all."

"So when you pray, what's God do?"

Camellia sighed. "Mostly nothing, near as I can tell. I ask him all the time to make Herman be nice and it don't work. But it cain't hurt to keep at it because Grampa said God loves you and he's waiting for you in heaven when you die. Sometimes when I'm scared and alone it makes me feel better thinking that."

"Heaven . . ." Angel had a lot of theology to grapple with, and she wanted to be clear on the terms and definitions.

"Angels fly around and Grampa said you're never hungry and you don't got to worry about people hurting you."

"That doesn't sound bad like burning forever in hell."

"Heaven's what's good. Hell is the other part I learned about on television," Camellia said. "After Grampa died, and there was no one to take me to church, I used to watch church on television on Sunday mornings to learn more, but it didn't take long for me to get scared and so I stopped. Folks on television like to yell about going down in this big fire and burning forever with the devil chasing you all the time."

"I don't know about this stuff," Angel said. She carefully stood, remaining stooped to keep from banging her head on the shed's roof.

"Me neither," Camellia said. "But if it's true, heaven means after you're dead, you get to see the people you love when they're dead."

"If they're not burning in hell. Or if *you're* not burning in hell."

"When Grampa was dying," Camellia said, her voice quiet, "he promised he'd be there in heaven waiting for me."

Although Angel was standing, Camellia, still seated, had lapsed into her own little world. "I just hope in heaven Grampa don't smell like moldy clothes no more and that his teeth are fixed so they don't click when he talks."

"I got to go," Angel said. "I don't like to leave Maddie alone at the hospital for too long."

Camellia didn't hear her friend. She was still thinking about her grampa.

"And his nose hairs," Camellia said aloud to herself. "Be nice he didn't have no nose hairs in heaven."

✢

For several minutes after the man at Retha's home had hung up, I sat in the Jeep, one hand on the steering wheel, the other holding my cell phone. I stared, unfocused, through the windshield.

What options did I have if I wanted to continue with the obligation that had been placed on me the moment Retha had put her baby into my Jeep? Help Retha escape the compound? But that was assuming she wanted to. Or that it was possible to drive through the gates, past the church, to find her trailer. Steal the child from the hospital before Jubil's deadline and keep trying to reach Retha? No. Give Jubil Retha's name and let the authorities handle it? No. Walk away? Tempting, but no.

I was in no hurry to get out of the Jeep. I didn't have anything to do except work out, have another quiet dinner alone, and hope I was tired enough to sleep soon after, instead of lying awake wondering what Amelia was doing in Chicago and if she was spending time with someone else.

I tapped the steering wheel, letting thoughts circle. Thinking about what I'd learned from Angel. A vigilante group had been terrorizing young black men. Grammie Zora had promised to stop it. Then had immediately begun her indirect search for Timothy Larrabee. As if she knew without doubt that somehow he was connected. But how did the painting tie this together? How did she know Timothy Larrabee? And what power did she have that he had been so willing to go to her?

Faint music reached me from one of the restaurants on Market Street. Shopkeepers began closing up. Tourists stepped into horse-drawn carriages; other tourists stepped out. All this life happening around me, and I felt on the outside.

Then a familiar red BMW passed me, and the driver found an open spot a few parking meters up the street. I watched the driver, with some admiration of her gracefulness, as she stepped out of the BMW and across the street to the lobby of the Double-tree. She carried an eight-by-ten envelope tucked beneath one of her arms.

Kellie Mixson.

✛

I reached the lobby desk just as Kellie was asking the clerk to accept the envelope for me.

"Kellie," I said.

She turned, smiled, slid the envelope back across the counter, and thanked the clerk for his time. "Nick. Got a minute?"

I pointed toward the lounge. She smiled again and nodded. When we were seated, she ordered a tonic water with lime. I did the same.

She handed me the envelope. "Here's background on the gardener. Except, as Evelyn said, he's no longer a gardener. I'm not sure he'll give you the time of day, but I've included a number where you can reach him."

"Five hundred a day gets fast results."

"Still working on Celia Harrison's daughter."

Our tonic waters arrived. She took a sip, grimaced. "Tastes so bad that I make it last. Used to drink too much alcohol. Loved Coronas. Then when Pops had his heart attack, I cut back, way back. Started working out. Dropped thirty pounds. I love the difference in the way I feel." She took another sip, grimaced again. "What's your excuse for ordering it?"

"It was easier to say 'double that order' than think of something else. I don't want to make any more decisions for the rest of the day."

She laughed and raised her glass in my direction. "Here's to helping the abandoned babies of the world."

I frowned.

"Nick, what do I do for a living? Of course I checked you out. I know a guy on the force, Jubil Smith. He's the first call I made."

I groaned.

"Yeah," she said. "Small town. Pops helped him when Jubil first made the streets. I've kept in touch."

"Trading favors over the years, right?"

"Seems like I do favors for half the town. 'Course, it helps business. Jubil? He told me plenty. I wondered about your limp. Now I know. Tough break but you handle it well."

"Because you didn't see a handicapped sticker on my Jeep."

"Easy now."

"Sorry," I said. "And let me just add that you're not bad at what you do. For a woman, that is."

She laughed again. "Point taken."

I glowered, but couldn't maintain. It was nice to be sitting here with her. No pressure to be someone that I wasn't.

"This Angel," she said. "I know you didn't ask me to look into it but I did. Discovered something you might find interesting."

"Part of my five hundred a day?"

"Freebie. Especially after discovering that you've committed to pay her sister's hospital bills."

"Yeah, yeah. What about Angel?"

Kellie was about to answer when she leaned back in her chair and looked over my shoulder.

I glanced behind me.

A woman approached. She had loose and long dark hair. She wore a silk blouse and silk slacks. A Gucci purse tucked beneath her arm. She was a few years younger than I, and attractive. Other men watched her approach, too, but not with the emotions that I did.

The woman stopped at our table. Smiled. But it was a hesitant smile. "Nick," she said. "Is this a bad time?"

"No, not at all." I answered quickly. I felt a flush of happiness and stood. Awkwardly. "Hello, Amelia. What a nice surprise."

✛

Retha was huddled beneath a bridge, where she'd been waiting for the past hours for the safety of nightfall. Her shoes were gone, long lost in the sucking mud of the swamp. Her legs ached from where Elder Jeremiah's belt had wrapped around the muscles. And she was hungry, ready to faint.

She listened to tires hum overhead as the occasional car or truck crossed the bridge. Each time she was convinced the tires would slow and stop, that Shepherd Isaiah would send Elder Jeremiah out of his black Escalade to jog down the embankment to search beneath the bridge and find her trapped, wet and shivering like a dog nearly drowned.

But his Escalade never stopped.

A few times she had nodded off to sleep, waking herself with cries from her own nightmares. She stooped occasionally to cup her hand in a puddle to slake her thirst with a palm full of dirty water. The river had a high content of salt water, so its slow current was merely an empty promise, one increasingly difficult to ignore as her throat grew more and more parched.

She was surrounded by empty beer cans and shredded cigarette butts. Beneath the bridge seemed to be a gathering place, and Retha knew that once darkness hit, she didn't dare wait much longer.

With the approach of dusk, however, came more mosquitoes. In the swamp, they'd found her as she disturbed the grass and brush. Beneath the bridge, it wasn't until the air began to cool that they could sense the heat of her body. The frenzied clouds attacked her again, and her frantic slaps broke scabs that had formed during the afternoon.

Not once, however, did Retha break down into tears. Not once did she regret the path she had chosen. All of this was better than what she had left behind.

And ahead was Billy Lee.

She knew where she wanted to get during the night, even if it meant ducking into a ditch as each new set of headlights approached.

To the hospital.

Thinking of Billy Lee in her arms again gave her the courage to wait. Without realizing it, she began to hum his favorite lullaby.

✜

"Amelia," I said. "This is Kellie Mixson. She's . . ."

"Doing research for Nick," Kellie said quickly. "I'm a private investigator."

"How nice," Amelia said.

"Kellie," I said. "This is Amelia Layton. She's . . ."

My girlfriend? What exactly was Amelia to me? What was I to her? It seemed Amelia had been trying to keep her distance, but now she was here. I was confused. Happily confused. Unless she'd come down to wrap up some things in Charleston and decided to tell me in person that maybe things weren't going to work out.

". . . a doctor," Amelia filled in, putting an arm around my waist. "I'm in town from Chicago to spend time with Nick. And I'm looking forward to it."

"How wonderful," Kellie said.

They appraised each other.

"We were just finished with our business," Kellie said, standing. "And I've got a lot of work ahead of me. I'm sure you two will enjoy yourselves. It's a romantic town."

"It is," Amelia said. "We will."

Kellie's face was expressionless as she handed me the envelope. "Let me get the drinks, Nick."

"No, that's alright."

"I insist." Still expressionless. Kellie motioned for the waiter. "By the way," she said. "About Angel. Didn't you tell me that she said Grammie Zora was out of town with one of her sisters?"

I nodded.

"Angel's lying to you, Nick," Kellie said. "Grammie Zora has no living sisters."

C H A P T E R

16

Home alone at night didn't bother Angel at all. Usually after she'd fixed Maddie some food, cleaned the dishes, and straightened the house, she let the DVD videos of their mama keep them company.

Tonight was different, of course. Maddie was in the hospital. Angel sat on the couch alone, watching images of her mama move across the white of the wall.

Then came the knock at the door. It was too dark outside, too late for Camellia to come visiting. And Camellia never knocked. Angel had given her a key so she could come over anytime and spend the night if things were too rough down the street. Angel decided to ignore the knock.

It came again.

"I can hear the television," a voice shouted. "I know someone's in there and if the door ain't opened in less than half a minute, I'll bust it down."

Bingo. That was a relief to Angel. That she knew the voice at least.

"Go away," she shouted at the door. As soon as she said it, she knew she'd made a mistake. Now Bingo knew she was inside.

"Let me in so we can talk," Bingo said.

"Go away," Angel said. "I'm getting my dog. My guard dog."

"You ain't got no dog."

Angel didn't answer. She was running into her bedroom.

The house was tiny. The kitchen, with Grammie Zora's voodoo altar in the small room beside it. Two bedrooms off the living room. One for Grammie Zora. One for her and Maddie. Camellia's room had clothes spread all over. Angel's room was neat, the bed made. Camellia might spend half an hour looking for a certain T-shirt only to discover it was under the couch. Angel knew where every possession she owned was stored.

It took her but two seconds to retrieve what she wanted. Small, white, plastic, with an opening for a miniature speaker.

Angel ran back to the door. She set down the plastic object and pushed a button. An angry German shepherd began to bark loudly.

"Go away," Angel said. "I can barely hold him back." Angel grinned at her tactic. Angel pushed the button again to send out more ferocious barks.

When the noise stopped, she heard Bingo's footsteps moving away from the door.

Her triumph was short-lived.

His footsteps returned in a rush, and he crashed into the cheap wood of the door. The doorjamb busted on impact and he skidded inside.

"Got one of those fake-dog intruder alarms, huh?" he said, smiling his twisted, hungry, bully smile down on her. "They haven't stopped me yet."

✛

I met Amelia again in the lobby twenty minutes after Kellie's departure.

"Good to see you," I said. I meant it. I gave her a hug. Enjoyed the smell of her delicate perfume. "Where shall we go for dinner?"

"The bellman, didn't he . . ." Her smile was puzzled.

"He knocked on my door as I was shaving." I gave her another hug. "Thank you so much. I think it's a great-looking suit. And I sure didn't expect it. Thanks."

"Armani. I knew you'd look good in dark blue." She gave me a peck on the cheek and hugged me back. Then she stepped away and smiled. "I was hoping you'd take the hint and wear it tonight." She held her smile in place. "Don't get me wrong. You look good right now."

I was in my usual khakis and one of my many golf shirts. Casual comfort.

"Just that," she continued, "I have this thing for a man in a great suit and . . ."

"Be right back," I said. "I only have two ties. I'll bring them both down and let you decide."

"Actually," she answered, "you'll find a new tie tucked in the jacket pocket of the suit. If you need helping knotting it, just let me know."

✠

Angel backed away from Bingo.

"Go away," she said, trying to hide her fear. "Grammie Zora's on her way back from getting groceries."

Bingo responded by slowly widening his smile as he spoke. "Remember the white-haired guy Grammie Zora sent me to fetch once? One of the big dudes that guarded him at the church is parked on the street waiting for me to get something that belongs to the white-haired guy. That painting." Bingo frowned slightly. "Hey, you look different. Cleaned up."

"You got to get going," Angel said. She wasn't afraid often, but this was one of the times. Her tongue seemed to stick to the top of her mouth. "When Grammie Zora gets back, she's going to mess you up."

"I don't think so," Bingo said. "I know your secret about Grammie Zora. After the dude pays me for getting what he wants from you, I'm going to come back and get you to pay me, too."

"For what?"

"Keeping secret what you're trying to keep secret."

Angel stepped behind the couch.

"Run," Bingo said. "There's nowhere to go."

He turned, and with leisure, shut the door. It popped open again. He dragged a chair over and leaned it into the door.

Angel took advantage of his distraction and darted into her bedroom and locked the door handle. Seconds later, the handle wiggled as Bingo tried to turn it. Angel wished she had a phone in her bedroom. If there was ever a time to call Camellia for help, this was it.

"Hey," he said, "I can break this door down, too. And if I

have to do that, I'm going to put your hind end on the stove top. Won't take long for the heat to learn you to mess with me."

"Leave me alone," Angel said.

"Thirty seconds. Open the door in thirty seconds, or you get the burner."

Bingo chuckled at his brilliance.

"Go ahead, start counting," Angel said. "Once you get past ten, it'll take you all night to figure out how to reach thirty."

The door banged, almost bulged off the hinges. Bingo had punched it.

"Don't make me mad," he said.

That wasn't Angel's intention. She was just stalling for time. From under her bed she grabbed the electric stun gun, first stolen from the police department before she and Camellia had restolen it from Bingo. Camellia knew how it worked—she'd seen Bingo kill a cat with it, which is why she'd made sure Bingo wasn't going to get the chance again—and had shown Angel how to use it, too.

Still, Angel wished it were a real gun. At least she knew that real guns worked. At least she knew she could shoot the gun through the door and kill Bingo that way. She was ready to do that—anybody who'd put a girl on a stove deserved a gut full of bullets.

While it was better than nothing, the trouble with the electric stunner was that Bingo might see it in her hand before she had a chance to jab him, and he'd take it from her.

Bingo wiggled the door handle again, kicking the bottom of the door with his foot. "Don't make me burn you to toast."

"Okay, okay, okay," Angel said. She was ready to take her chances. "I'll let you in. But what you're looking for is in Grammie Zora's desk. Don't you want that instead?"

"Where's her desk?" Bingo's voice relayed suspicion.

"Go into the kitchen and through the beads. You'll find it."

Angel heard scraping noises and grunting.

"There's a sofa against your door," Bingo announced. "You won't be running out on me while I look."

That wasn't what Angel wanted. She figured Bingo was going to hurt her one way or another. What she wanted was something to prove he did the hurting. Maybe later she could trade that secret off against the one he wanted to use against her.

✦

Changing into the suit took five minutes. When I returned to the lobby, Amelia took my arm as we departed.

"Cary Grant," she murmured, "has nothing on you."

"He could only wish to be walking with someone as beautiful as you," I answered gallantly.

She squeezed my arm. Suits weren't my style, but it wasn't much of a sacrifice to make her happy. And much as I disliked the constraints of the tie, I did feel stylish.

I stopped with her on the sidewalk just outside the hotel. We were in the market area, and it was already filling with couples on their way to the nearby restaurants. After a wave of people moved around us like a current, I looked down the street for the valet and my Jeep.

With gentle pressure on my arm, Amelia nudged me forward, steering me across the street in the direction of a late-model black Chrysler Concorde.

"I already talked to the valet," she said. "Told him we didn't need the Jeep. I mean, I've rented this anyway, so we might as well use it."

The smell of new leather greeted me as I opened the passenger door for Amelia. Then realized she wasn't beside me. She was across the car, already getting behind the steering wheel.

"Sorry," she said when I got in and closed my door. "I would have put your name down on the rental agreement as an extra driver, but I didn't have your driver's license number."

"No problem," I said. It was childish of me to feel resentment. She wasn't trying to take control. She was doing her best to make this a fun evening. "I'm going to sit back and relax and enjoy the ride."

Automatic climate control sent cool air into my face as she turned the key in the ignition.

"So," I asked, "where are we going?"

⟡

Behind the door, Angel heard Bingo's footsteps clunk toward the kitchen.

Angel spun and ran to a small closet at the back of her bedroom. She shut herself inside and locked the handle. Then, in the darkness, she reached for the digital camcorder she kept on a shelf in there.

The side wall of her closet was the dividing wall between Angel's room and Grammie Zora's voodoo room. There was a small hole, nearly invisible from the opposite side, especially when Grammie Zora had her altar lit by candles and the rest of the voodoo room in darkness. This spy hole gave Angel a clear view of Grammie Zora's voodoo room.

Angel brought the camcorder up to her eyes and began to video Bingo's actions. He snapped the light switch on and began to pull at the drawers, throwing out the voodoo contents. After all the drawers were empty, he yanked them out completely and checked beneath, in case the painting was taped under one of them. When that didn't bring results, he kicked the wall in frustration.

Bingo ripped the entire room apart, cursing Angel the whole time, unaware that she caught every moment with digital clarity. When he finally decided it wasn't in the room, he ran back to the kitchen.

Angel shut off the camcorder, hid it beneath some sweaters on the shelf in the closet, and waited. Seconds later, she heard another grunt as Bingo yanked the sofa away from the door and a crash as Bingo broke down her bedroom door.

"Where are you, you little puke?" he shouted.

Another second passed, and the door handle to the closet rattled. "You're going to pay for this," Bingo shouted. He wiggled the door handle with impatience. "You better open up now or I'll bust this in, too."

It was the wiggling door handle that inspired Angel.

"Okay," she said. "You can open it now."

She watched the handle. It jiggled again. She jabbed the handle with the prods of the stun gun. A blue arc sizzled at the contact of electricity on metal, almost throwing her onto her back.

On the other side of the door was a shriek. And a thump that shook the floor.

Cautiously, Angel opened the door. She didn't know what to expect. She saw his feet, opened the door wider, saw his legs, opened the door still wider and saw his upper body and his head.

It was like Goliath, down for the count. Bingo was stretched out flat and unmoving.

SIGMUND BROUWER

✛

"Amelia, I imagine you've heard of those who refuse medical treatment because of faith issues."

Our salads had just arrived. She'd offered to make me dinner—she was staying at the house on the lower peninsula that she'd inherited when her father died—and I'd suggested a restaurant, telling her that it would be inconsiderate of me to expect her to put together a meal after her travel time. I wondered if she suspected I was simply afraid of the more intimate setting alone with her at her house.

"Of course," she said. "It's a difficult situation. Why do you ask?"

"There's a church outside of Charleston. Its members are like that. Just wondered what you thought of it."

"In one way, I admire them. Even though some people think belief is a matter of faith and no reasoning, I disagree. I think too often it is just the opposite. An intellectual belief that provides comfort. It takes courage to actually live out what you believe, and these people are doing just that. They say God is in control, so they leave it in his hands. They say the life hereafter is of far more significance than life on earth, and they're prepared to risk death unnecessarily because of it."

"So you approve?"

"You did hear me say 'unnecessarily.' I'm a doctor. I want to use all the skills that God has given me, and all the medical knowledge that God has allowed us to accumulate, to help people regain their health. Take their argument to the extreme. God is in control. His will will be done. Don't operate on me when I have appendicitis because he will decide if I live. Fine.

God is in control. He'll let me live or die and I shouldn't take action. Therefore, I won't support the extension of my life with healthy habits. For that matter, I won't even eat. God will decide my life."

She paused for breath. "Each of us is on this earth for a purpose. We've been given a strong will to live for that reason. My opinion is that medical care is an extension of the care we should provide our bodies in everyday living. Let's do everything humanly possible—within moral boundaries—to keep our health. Then let God decide. Some people make it through heart transplants; some people don't. To me, that's God's will. But when someone keeps their kid from getting leukemia treatments because healing is supposed to be God's will, that someone is actually making the choice for God. A choice to let the kid die."

"Too bad you don't have a strong opinion on this."

She laughed. "Yeah, too bad. What prompted your question?"

I told her about finding the baby the day before, about taking him to the hospital. About the note. About what I'd seen in the Glory Church.

"That makes me so sad," she said.

"Me, too. That little boy—"

"Sad you didn't think I was important enough in your life to call me Sunday night and ask the same questions you are now."

"I thought you were at work."

"After I told you Saturday night I had some days off?"

"But—"

She held up her hand. "Sorry. I overreacted. I shouldn't put you on the spot like this."

"But—"

"No. You don't have to defend yourself. Let's find something else to talk about. How's it going with Pendleton?"

I grabbed the chance to move on. "He tells me he's legitimately regretful. Wants to make a deal that is actually in my favor. He says he wants a chance to start over."

"And?"

"And I don't know if I believe him."

"Don't know if you *can* believe him?" she asked. "Or if you *want* to believe him?"

I took a bite of salad.

She smiled to take the sting out of her words. "See, if you can convince yourself he's running another con on you—"

"Like he's been doing all his life."

"—then you're free of the obligation to forgive. But if he's truly sorry . . ."

I took another bite of salad.

"Back to living your faith," she said. "Is it a philosophy or something more?"

I didn't answer.

"Forgiveness is an act of love," she finished. "And faith without love is nothing."

"You're right." I spoke softly.

"Enough lecturing, huh?" she said, probably trying to ease the tension. "So, how's the weather been?"

The conversation continued from there. Not once did she or I get around to exploring why she'd hung up on me during our last phone conversation. She probably thought it was obvious, given that she'd shown up here in Charleston a day later to be with me.

And I was too afraid to get to the issue because of the answers that might be there.

✠

With Bingo unconscious, Angel wished she could call the police. But that would lead to other questions.

While she wondered what to do, she was tempted to jab Bingo a few more times with the gun. She wanted to see his body jerk with convulsions. But she told herself that would make her a bully just like him. She raised her leg to kick him but held back for the same reason.

Bingo's chest heaved as he took ragged breaths. She tried dragging him away but he was too heavy.

Then she heard another voice. She recognized this one, too. "Hey!" the voice called. It was the giant, the one who'd come to visit Grammie Zora with Timothy Larrabee the night Angel went to the cemetery. "You said you'd only be a minute."

Angel scooped up the stun gun, darted back into her closet, eased the door shut, and locked it. She had never been more frightened in her life. She was glad she hadn't used up all the charge on Bingo. She waited, holding the gun poised, ready to do the same thing to the door handle when it wiggled.

But she didn't have anything to fear from the footsteps that entered her bedroom.

Later, much later, when she finally dared to open the closet door again, Bingo was gone.

✛

"Will we see each other tomorrow?" I asked as Amelia drove me back to the Doubletree.

"I've got a lot of things to do. Wrapping up all the legal stuff with my father's estate."

"I understand," I said. I tried to keep the disappointment out of my voice.

At the hotel, she leaned over and gave me a quick peck on the cheek. I tried to hold her, but after a few moments, she pulled away.

"Good night, Nick," she said.

I waved as she drove away, but I don't think she noticed.

CHAPTER

17

I slept poorly. Each time I woke, the traces of Amelia's perfume that clung to my hair reminded me of how she had eased out of the hug I gave her in the car in front of the hotel.

I made myself some coffee in the hotel room machine. I threw open the curtains and let the early morning sun flood my room. Below me was an elegant courtyard.

I sat near the window and sipped my coffee until eight o'clock, the earliest I felt I could call Richard Freedman. I finished my call and lifted my coffee again. Before I was able to take another sip, the phone rang.

I hoped it was Amelia, calling to say she wanted to see me today.

I was wrong.

✛

In the hotel lobby fifteen minutes later, Timothy Larrabee introduced himself, transferred his cane from his right hand to his left, and then offered me a firm handshake of greeting. His smile seemed to hold genuine warmth. He wore light khaki pants and a crisply ironed light blue shirt. Because it was summer in Charleston, he could have easily blended in with the attorneys and accountants crowd.

"I hope you have a few minutes," he said. "I'd appreciate the opportunity to speak to you about several matters."

"I have a few minutes."

"Excellent." His face was drawn tight, the skin candle-wax smooth. As he spoke, there was unnaturalness to the movement of his cheeks and lips. The result, I guessed, of a face-lift. Still, forewarned and armed with a photo of Timothy Larrabee as a child, I might have had a slight chance of recognizing the man. His face was elfin-shaped. He had a large forehead and narrow cheekbones tapering to a tiny chin. This was a genetic imprint no plastic surgery could remove.

It was his voice, however, that provided him a camouflage that was almost impenetrable. He was in his fifties, and, unlike now, there would have been little television in his childhood to corrupt his native tongue.

"We have a lot in common, Nicholas Barrett." Larrabee spoke softly with cultured tones. This was a man who'd grown up south of Broad, receiving the best that private schooling could offer. "It was in April, wasn't it, that the *Post and Courier* ran a few stories about your search for your mother?"

"April."

Businessmen flowed around us in the lobby, intent on checking out and getting to their next meetings. The tourists would make the next wave.

"I remembered your face when I saw you in our church Sunday, but I couldn't quite place it until Shepherd Isaiah told me about your conversation with him and how to find you here. Quite the tragedy, the events of your childhood."

He smiled sadly. "You probably know, then, that we have childhood tragedy in common. I grew up not far from you. My grandmother was Agnes Larrabee. She was murdered when I was a young boy. Does that sound familiar to you?"

"Yes." I said. "You lived on East Bay. Your grandmother Agnes was poisoned to death by one of her servants."

"Hard to escape the past."

"Indeed."

"I like you. I like the way your face hides so much. We never really escape our childhood, do we? Always hiding, one way or another."

"I doubt this was one of the matters you wished to discuss, Mr. Larrabee."

"Are you always this guarded?" He touched my arm before I could answer. "Please, let's sit. I do know about your leg, and I'm sure it's not comfortable for you to stand for long periods of time. The courtyard . . ."

Larrabee pointed to the same courtyard that I had looked down upon before his call. I followed him through the breakfast area and into the warm morning air. An elaborate fountain was in the center of the courtyard. He took a seat on a bench, and I sat on the opposite end.

"The newspapers had surprisingly little to say about the

events of last April. I had to inquire elsewhere to learn more about you," he began. "My first call was to your half brother, Pendleton." Timothy Larrabee leaned his cane against the front of the bench. He leaned in my direction. "Please have patience with my curiosity. I'll explain shortly."

"It must have been interesting, your conversation with Pendleton."

"There you are again. With that blandness in your face that makes it impossible to decide what you are really thinking. Fascinating."

"Far more fascinating that you now belong to a backwoods cult and wish to purchase a Van Dyck stolen from your family decades ago."

"Hah!" He grinned. "Finally. A reaction. And I'll get to that soon enough, too. In answer to your comment about Pendleton, no, it was not an interesting conversation. He seemed very protective of you. Which surprised me. I had gathered from the newspapers that you two were not the closest of brothers. What little he said was high praise."

That was a surprise to me, too. But curious as I was about Larrabee's reason for visiting, I was determined to play the waiting game.

"To make a long story short," he said. "I really couldn't learn much about you."

"Not much worth learning."

"That's where you are wrong. I thought it would help before I approached you. I wanted to know what was important to you. What you want in life. I find that's the best way to understand someone. Or perhaps the most important way for people to understand themselves."

He lifted his cane and tapped it against the courtyard stones at his feet. He stopped and stared at the water fountain for what was nearly a full minute. "For me," he said softly, "I've come to realize what's most important to me is regaining my heritage."

"By joining the Glory Church?"

He smiled. "Isaiah Sullivan and I met in prison. I will tell you frankly that he is a man of deep faith. Misguided, I believe, but passionately and deeply faithful to the God that he found in prison. He loves the Bible, that man. Finds in it everything he needs."

"And you?"

"My god is wealth. Should you ever meet Shepherd Isaiah again, I would prefer that you keep that statement to yourself, although it would not surprise him. But I won't lie to you. I like what I can make from religion. To me, it's a business. Shepherd Isaiah and I have an arrangement that allows me a certain portion of the church's proceeds. Once I am financially able to maintain the proper Charleston lifestyle, I will leave the Glory Church and resume my rightful place among the elite of Charleston."

"Charming," I said.

"Not my intent. I simply wish for things to be very clear between us. The people of Shepherd Isaiah's flock are very content. They get what they pay for: a belief system that serves their needs. I am a facilitator. Without me, the church would not exist. I get paid for that, one way or another. For me, it is simply very convenient that his flock wants to believe in an invisible God who holds them in judgment for their wrongdoing."

✛

An invisible God who holds them in judgment for their wrongdoing.

My mother was gone from my life well before I reached my teenage years. It was without her continued gentle guidance then, that I formed my opinions about God and religion.

First, I allowed the god of science to fool me. I believed what I had been taught in school. Even if some of the answers were yet to be found, science could explain everything. And so I bought into a naturalistic theory of existence, going as far as reading the classic *Religion and Science* by outspoken atheist Bertrand Russell, who said that before the Copernican Revolution, it was natural to suppose that God's purposes were specifically concerned with Earth, but now—after what science has shown us—it has become an implausible hypothesis. Learning what I did in high school science, I accepted this.

Hiding behind the false god of science, then, it was very easy for me to decide that the God presented by religion was simply Santa Claus on a grand and omniscient scale. After all, I thought, when children are taught that there's an invisible God who sees and knows everything they do and is displeased when they do wrong, it is a very convincing method for ensuring their obedience. And once you get them to believe that, you can keep adding all the rules and regulations that are needed to keep them in place as they grow older.

And as I grew older, with a seed of rebellion against religion growing inside me, all I had to do was learn history to become more bitter in my near hatred of religion.

An invisible God who holds them in judgment for their wrongdoing.

No accident, I thought, that the Catholic church of the Middle Ages denied churchgoers access to the Bible by making sure only Latin versions were available. Keep the priests as go-betweens, and allow only the priests the power of the knowledge of what the Bible contained. In my cynicism, I admired this strategy and its effectiveness but saw it clearly and I decided it would not ensnare me.

Yes, I grew to be an enlightened man of the dawn of the third millennium.

Then I learned more. For as Francis Bacon said, a little science estranges man from God, but a lot brings him back.

Bertrand Russell's famous book was written in the 1930s, before physics and astronomy had pushed science to the frontiers of the truly unknowable. When Russell wrote his book, scientists, including Einstein, believed we lived in a steady-state universe, one that had existed forever. And now? Even atheist physicists and astronomers acknowledge there are questions that cannot be answered, for those answers lie outside of science. More recent science has shown us that the idea of a steady-state universe is as inconceivable as that of a flat earth—the same steady-state universe theory cherished in the centuries following Galileo as evidence that the Genesis account was merely a quaint myth.

As for the God in the sky as omniscient judge of evil actions, it was Martin Luther's great reformation that broke the historical Catholic church's stranglehold on politics. When the abuses of wrongful authority and corruption were stripped away from the Catholic faith, once again the power of the love of Christ and his message to humanity was able to triumph in individual lives.

The radical, civilization-transforming message brought to this world by the man named Jesus was very simple: You do not have to make yourself right to approach God. Rather, approach God and he will make you right.

When I finally understood this, my own life was transformed. The Creator of this universe was not a vengeful judge of my actions. He was a father—as Jesus had said to his students over and over—who ached for me to turn to him and his love, regardless of what burdens of regret and resentment and guilt I carried.

Yet the fight against a legalistic approach to God that Jesus brought to the religious establishment of his day continues and continues and continues, with the oppressors of each new generation using God as a bludgeon against the oppressed. A bludgeon to give the oppressors power, to give the oppressors wealth.

And I was face-to-face with one of those oppressors.

✠

"Since you appear offended that I freely admit the church is a business opportunity for me," Timothy Larrabee said, "let me ask you: Do you have faith in Jesus?"

"Yes." I wasn't prepared at this moment to argue that it was a different faith than Shepherd Isaiah's. But Timothy Larrabee brought the argument to me.

"Because of all my time among the members of the Glory Church," Timothy said, "I am very familiar with the gospel events. You, too, may recall the moment that Jesus answered a Pharisee who wanted to know the greatest commandment. The reply Jesus gave? Let me quote from Matthew chapter 22. 'Thou shalt love the Lord thy God with all thy heart, and with all thy soul, and with all thy mind. This is the first and great commandment. And the second *is* like unto it, Thou shalt love thy neighbour as thyself. On these two commandments hang all the law and the prophets.'"

"Impressive," I said. "The church is rubbing off on you."

He ignored my sarcasm. "Love God and love your neighbor," he said. "As a nonbeliever, I will admit those two commands are frightening, especially with no other clauses to clarify them. It puts an onus on each of you believers as humans to be constantly aware of how to fulfill those commands. They are wide, boundless commands. Impossible to fulfill with anything near perfection."

"I was in the church on Sunday," I said quietly. "I'm not sure how the public beating of a wife with her husband's consent fits within either command, no matter how broadly you might try to stretch either."

"Exactly my point!" Larrabee thumped his cane down for emphasis. "It is a lot simpler to follow a list of don'ts than to decide what to do. In fact, I will tell you candidly that Shepherd Isaiah's church is for those who are terrified—whether they admit it or not—of the vastness of the command of love given by Jesus. The people who are attracted to his church want the rules and regulations that will comfort them, even if there are times they seem too harsh. They want the don'ts, not the dos. They want a shepherd with an iron rod and a map of their lives laid out in front of them. Shepherd Isaiah understands that, much as it grieves him at times to wield the iron rod. He truly cares about his flock."

He drew a breath. "It is his life's goal to be their shepherd. There are those on the outside who disagree with his methods. But those outside a flock are not familiar with the flock. The people who are strong and whole are not part of his flock. But the ones who are weak, he does protect. Oddly enough, despite having no belief and no concern but the pursuit of wealth, I respect him for that passion."

"Nick?" The voice that interrupted us came from Amelia. She stood at the edge of the courtyard. "I couldn't reach you in your room, so I thought I'd come by the hotel."

I stood, happy and surprised that she'd stopped by.

"Just a few more minutes," Timothy Larrabee said. "Please."

I held up a hand to Amelia to indicate five minutes. She nodded and retreated back into the hotel lobby.

"I've spent a lot of your time this morning without getting to the reason for my visit," he said. "But I wanted you to know about me first before I ask what I came to ask. It has to do with my childhood, and with the fact that you came with the offer about the painting."

I nodded. "I understand you are willing to pay twenty thousand dollars for it."

He frowned. "And you know that because . . ."

"Are you willing?"

"Here's the truth," he said, after staring at me for a few more moments. "When I was a boy, I stole the painting from my grandmother. I needed money and she refused to give me an allowance. I now understand the financial circumstances that led to her refusal, and my remorse is that much greater because of it. Now, as you know, the painting has resurfaced. I am willing to purchase it and wish for you to be the middleman as you offered."

"Why not simply purchase it yourself?"

"The person I sold it to forty years ago sought me out and has asked an outrageous price. It is a form of blackmail. She has threatened to go to Shepherd Isaiah's congregation if I don't pay what she requests."

"I would guess most would understand and forgive something you did years and years ago."

"No." Timothy Larrabee shook his head vigorously. "My childhood was more complicated than that. There are other issues that I prefer to leave in the past. I want the painting without the questions it could raise."

He stood and leaned on his cane. From his back pocket he withdrew an envelope.

"Here's ten thousand dollars in cash. That's your broker's fee. I'll pay up to thirty thousand more for it. If you can negotiate to get it for any less, you can keep the difference. Does that sound fair?"

"You're telling me the antique was rightfully hers to sell you."

"Correct."

I did not want a broker's fee, but I took the envelope anyway, knowing Angel could use the money.

"That's not quite all," he said. "Now that you're indirectly in my employ, I have some simple questions for you."

"Which are?"

"Answer my earlier question. Did Grammie Zora send you to me? And what else has she told you?"

I was about to answer, simply because they were simple questions. Then I thought through the implications. He'd chosen to remain hidden among the congregation of the Glory Church for years already, although he professed not to share their fervent beliefs. What he essentially wanted to know was how he'd been found. For all his apparent openness to me, there was something he was hiding.

I handed him back the envelope. "I've decided I would prefer not to be in your employ." I stood.

There was one person who could answer all of this. Grammie Zora.

"You're a fool," he said. "Shepherd Isaiah and his flock are fanatics. Fanatics are dangerous. Financially, I represent those fanatics, and you have something that I want. Therefore, I can be dangerous."

"That was a threat, wasn't it?"

"Oh, yes," he said. "Yes indeed."

I walked away, hoping the weakness of my limp wasn't too obvious.

✚

"What would you think about a carriage ride, Nick? We could pretend not to know anything about the city. After all, if I didn't have my memories here, I would love everything about it."

Amelia placed her hand on mine at the breakfast table, where I joined her immediately after the departure of Timothy Larrabee. I enjoyed the softness of her touch. It was part of the roller coaster. Being with her had begun to feel like a dance— two steps forward, one back. Was this the woman who had pulled herself away from me the evening before?

"How about midafternoon," I said. I really wanted to say yes and go with her now. To succumb to my rush of feelings for her, the sudden gratitude that she'd graced me with her presence and was showing a small degree of physical affection. "There are some things I simply can't get out of this morning."

"I understand," she answered. She withdrew her hand. "I didn't give you notice and . . ."

I took her hand again. "Please. It's not that I don't want to see you. I wish I could change things."

She relaxed and smiled. "You've got my cell number. Call me as soon as you're free today."

18

I believe one of the finest and most underrated locations in
Charleston is along the Ashley River, upstream of the Citadel yet
close enough to hear the bugles from the parade grounds. Here
the egrets appear like ghosts rising out of early morning fog on
the river. Here the city noises diminish enough that the splash
of jumping fish and the croaking of bullfrogs replace the hum of
traffic.

And here I was to meet Richard W. Freedman, who, according to Kellie Mixson, had been a gardener on the Larrabee estate
south of Broad.

The drive was long and circular, cutting through oak-shaded
grounds that would not have been out of place on a country estate.
In parking my Jeep, I passed a Jag convertible, a Mercedes SUV,
and a Lexus sedan. The automobiles matched Freedman's white
mansion and guest house in ostentation.

Freedman was a stockbroker who had moved well beyond

gardening. Kellie's report indicated that Freedman was nearly sixty, but he looked much younger. Forty years earlier, he had been in his teens, a puppy in the Evelyn Palmer's eyes, when he was in the employ of Agnes Larrabee.

He was waiting for me on his front porch, leaning on the railing as I walked up to the house. I noticed that he noticed my limp. He said nothing, however.

Richard Freedman's black face had the angles of an eagle's. He wore rimless glasses and had the white, even teeth that suggested a major investment in orthodontics. He wore black pants and a tan silk shirt with the sleeves casually rolled up to expose a gold Gucci watch on his left arm.

He beckoned me up to the porch. "Glad you're punctual," he said. "I don't have much time and I don't think I can be of much help to you." His voice was surprising high and soft, given that he was not a small effeminate man by any stretch.

"Nice place," I said.

"Yeah, it is." He pointed beyond a short section of reeds at a sailboat on the placid water of the Ashley River. "I love my name. Freedman. Became a family name after the Civil War. I think of it when I stand here and wonder how many of my direct ancestors I would have seen going upriver on barges to the rice plantations. I like to imagine how they would have reacted to knowing that one of them could proudly own a place like this one day."

Freedman turned to me. "I've been able to trace my lineage back to 1805. Amazing, actually, considering how few of our marriages and births were registered and how often families were split when slave owners sold brothers and sisters to different plantations."

I nodded neutrally. Any other response seemed inadequate or inappropriate.

"You're not a Barrett from the Barrett family, are you?"

"I am." I'd introduced myself over the telephone earlier, when I set up the appointment.

"If I brought out my papers, I bet I could find a place or two in time where your great-great-grandfather buggy whipped my great-great-grandfather for stealing a chicken to feed hungry kids, or maybe sold some of my family like livestock." He grinned. "What's your old Jeep worth?"

Before I could answer, he said. "I'll write you a check for it for twenty thousand dollars. That's easily triple what you'd get anywhere else. Interested?"

"No."

"Take it. Buy another Jeep, same old vintage. Pocket the twelve- or thirteen-grand difference. I'm serious now. I'll write you the check this minute. Be a pleasure."

"No."

"See? You've got as much pride as I do."

"Except whatever answer I give you, I'll feel stupid. And whatever answer you get, you'll feel like you've thumbed your nose at those nineteenth-century Barretts. Would you feel better to have me buggy-whipped for stealing a chicken off your property?"

He laughed. "Alright. I am obnoxious. But let me tell you, it feels great. And I'm not as bitter as you might guess. Yeah, there are racial issues. But I was born in an America with enough freedom for me to dream big and reach what I wanted to reach."

"The gainful possession of enough wealth to casually humiliate white strangers."

"Exactly." He laughed again then glanced at his watch. "Ten minutes. In Charleston, you should be late for everything, but tee times are the exception. And I went to a lot of work to force this club to take me in as a member. Drives them nuts when I show up with a couple of black friends." Another grin of triumph. "Love America. Love capitalism."

"Me, too. And I don't golf."

"Smart man. Golf's addictive." Freedman frowned. The small talk was over. "What do you need? You said over the phone it had to do with Agnes Larrabee and the time I spent there as a gardener's assistant. Not many people know about those days. Nor will they, correct?"

"Correct," I said. "It was a lousy way to force you into this meeting."

Over the phone he'd been reluctant. I'd merely asked him how much he might like for his business associates and clients to learn about his days as a gardener for a rich old white woman.

"How'd you find out?" he asked, still frowning.

"Evelyn Palmer mentioned your name. She remembers you as a teenager there."

"Evelyn!" The smile returned. "She was twice my age and every time I walked past her, she would slap my backside and giggle. It was about the only thing I liked about working there. Old Agnes Larrabee was a weird duck. Always spying on us to make sure we weren't lazy. Stingy? She could hear a penny drop from a mile away."

"How about Timothy? Her grandson."

"Timothy . . ." Freedman gave it some thought. "There were those who thought he was snooty, and he had his moments. Can't blame him, knowing what Agnes did all the time."

"What Agnes did?"

"Insisted on perfection. In everything. Like he was going to grow up to rule a country. Poor kid. I'd tell him about sitting at the side of the river fishing with my father, and he'd soak it all up, eyes wide, like he was aching to get out of that prison just once. I think he looked up to me like an older brother, which was ironic because Agnes treated blacks like they were convenient machines. I hated it so much, I almost went to the authorities to report her for child abuse. But I didn't. I kept waiting, because they wouldn't have believed me, a black kid. And before I could work up the courage to do it anyway, she died."

"Child abuse?"

"Timothy had no one to talk to. Except me. Once he told me how they used to punish him. It broke my heart. The only good part about the story is how it made the kid tough. I really remember that, how he told me he finally stopped being so afraid of them."

"You'll tell me now?" I asked.

"Why not? She'd dead. He's gone. It's not like I'll be liable for a slander lawsuit, is it?"

✛

"Please," Timothy said. "Not again. It makes me cry."

Samson led Timothy up the stairwell. His massive right hand engulfed Timothy's wrist and fingers. Samson was prepared to drag Timothy if the little boy's begging became actual physical resistance.

But Timothy was only four. He was still as compliant as a puppy that returns to the master after each whipping, quivering for any signs of affection.

"Please, Mr. Samson. I won't make Grams angry again."

"You done what you done. And it's my duty to follow Mizz Larrabee's orders. You know Mizz Larrabee don't abide with no pets. No animals. And what you was thinking, keeping a mouse in a box . . ."

"Please. No."

Samson tightened his grip as they reached the top of the stairs, always expectant of the day the boy would finally pull away. Instead, Timothy straightened. A tiny soldier stiffening with pride at the approach to a firing squad. But his resolve faltered as Samson took him past the door to the Jesus room.

"Oh, no. No, no, no." Timothy let all of his weight collapse. Terrified as he was, his obedience to disciplinary actions was so ingrained that his only attempt at escape was passive. He did not struggle to escape. Simply closed his eyes as Samson dragged his limp body toward the end of the hallway.

Timothy began to shake with sudden sobbing. As Samson had dragged him up the stairs, Timothy had hoped for the Jesus room. If only it were the Jesus room, it would be just a good whipping. Much as he hated the Jesus room, Timothy preferred it over the balcony.

There was a slight crackle of cartilage in the boy's wrist—all of his weight was strained against the ligament and muscle of his tiny hand in Samson's. Samson merely continued moving down the hallway; meeting the boy's resistance was as simple and mundane a task as dragging a sack of potatoes.

Samson opened the door to the attic stairs with his free hand. He climbed slowly, still dragging Timothy's weight entirely by the boy's hand. Timothy did not kick or try to pull loose. His sobbing and shaking had stopped at the realization that Samson

would not let him go; already Timothy was in his private world
of paralyzed fear.

In the attic, Samson let Timothy slide against the far wall,
where the small boy collapsed, entirely silent, tears wet on his
cheeks.

There was a rope on the floor, below a four-paned window
that opened in a gable set into the roof. The lower left pane was
missing, and the night's soft summer air breezed upon the two of
them.

Samson rolled Timothy over and tied one end of the rope
around Timothy's chest, then snugged the rope tight below Timothy's armpits. The boy whimpered but did not move. Samson
opened a window to the night air. The hinges squeaked. He
decided when he returned at dawn that he would have to come
with a can of oil to take care of the problem.

Beyond the window was a small ledge, more ornamental
than functional. Below the ledge was a sheer drop, three stories
down to the immaculately tended lawn of the mansion.

Samson did not pause to enjoy the view of Charleston at
night, or of the harbor and the lights of the passing ships. He
merely squatted and lifted Timothy by gripping the boy beneath
his armpits. With a smooth, almost effortless motion surprising in
a man of his age, he thrust the boy through the window and onto
the ledge.

"Stand," he commanded.

Timothy was almost catatonic because of his fear of heights.
But self-preservation made him stand.

Samson kept a firm grip on the boy with one arm as he
pushed the free end of the rope through the small hole provided
by the missing pane of glass. With the rope now inside the attic,

coiled at Samson's feet, Samson let go of the boy and closed the window. He took the rope and tied it securely to a hook in one of the inner support beams of the roof. It was a crude but effective safety harness. It would not do for the boy to fall to the ground. That would lead to awkward questions.

"Please," Timothy whispered one last time from his tiny ledge far off the ground.

But it also might have been Samson's imagination, so soft was the plea on that summer breeze. Either way, Samson ignored it.

He locked the window on the inside, even though he knew it wasn't necessary. Heights instilled such terror in the boy that Timothy wouldn't move at all, not even to attempt to open the window that would lead him to the safety of the interior of the attic.

Samson walked away, wrong about one thing.

Timothy did move. A gentle rocking that even Timothy was unaware of during the long hours that he stared sightlessly straight ahead, waiting for dawn when, like the times before, Samson would finally take him back inside.

Just before dawn, something broke inside the boy. All fear. All caring. This was his freedom. The realization that fear was worse than death. Later, he would look back and realize this was the greatest moment of his life.

He untied the rope around his chest, sat on the edge of the balcony, and smiled a cold, cold smile until the sun finally rose and Samson returned to take him back into the attic.

✣

Richard Freedman made an obvious point of checking his watch again after telling me the story.

I didn't want to leave. Not yet. "Evelyn said after Agnes died, you told a few others in the household about a voodoo curse that Timothy . . ."

"A few others. You mean servants. That's what I was. A servant to an old white woman. Now I could buy her out just like that." He snapped his fingers.

"You told a few of the other servants that only a month before her death Timothy had told her she would die."

Freedman spent more time in thought. "Yeah. That's right. It's been years but I can remember the look on his face when he told her that he'd made a deal with the devil and that she would be dead in a month. Weird thing, her dying like that the next night."

"A deal with the devil," I repeated.

"I had been pruning a hedge in the courtyard. On the other side of it, Agnes was outside, sitting on her swinging chair and drinking lemonade. I was taking a break myself and keeping very still, knowing if she knew I was nearby and not sweating hard, she'd threaten to fire me. When Timothy came by with a little girl, I heard every word. Two reasons I remember it so clear. One was because I hated how she treated the little girl. Like because she was black, she was nothing. Just made me more determined to get my MBA and come back and buy her out. Wish old Agnes was still alive. I'd love to write her a check for her mansion and—"

"Second reason?"

"Her boy. She asked him what he'd been doing north of Calhoun with a common little black girl. He didn't answer right away, so she squeezed his arm hard and he yelped. That's when he laid into her about the deal with the devil. That he'd gone to a voodoo woman and paid her to put a hex on her. Said she was going to be punished for all that she had done to him. Agnes hardly listened before telling that black girl to get and started cussing her like she was a dog."

"The girl went?"

"Of course. But I had nowhere to go. If she saw that I'd been listening in the first place, I was in trouble. So I stayed hidden. That's when it got interesting. You know, now that you've got me remembering, I can almost hear every word again, like I was there right now on the other side of the hedge."

I nodded.

"Timothy told her that he'd given a painting to the voodoo woman. The one with the letters in it. Timothy started laughing hard, saying how if Agnes didn't stop hurting him, maybe that voodoo woman would do more than lay a hex; maybe she'd tell everybody else about the letters. And then Agnes started scream-ing at Timothy that the power of Jesus was far greater than the power of the devil or the power of voodoo, and she dragged the poor boy inside and up to the Jesus room, calling for Samson to join them. From what the others told me later, that night was the loudest that Timothy had ever howled in there."

"Know anything about the letters? Did anyone talk about it later?"

"If there was anything to talk about, it didn't matter when Agnes got poisoned to death, did it?"

"The little girl's name?"

"Don't know."

"Any idea who the voodoo woman was?" I had a good guess. I just wanted it confirmed.

"None. I wasn't into any of that stuff of my ancestors. It was the past I wanted to shake and the future I wanted to chase."

"What about the Jesus room? Any idea what happened in there?"

"Just that whenever Timothy did something wrong, old Agnes hauled him up there with Samson. There'd be yelling and screaming of the name of Jesus. Half an hour later, they'd come back out again, all three of them. Like nothing had happened. Spooky, if you ask me. 'Course, old Agnes and Samson, they might have had something going, if you know what I mean. That was spooky, too. Her thumping the Bible so hard but having that strange connection with that big, strong black man. And he was strong, even in his eighties. They'd been together all their lives, or so I'd heard. And their connection, I don't think it was anything physical. But still strange."

"Strange?"

"Rumors and whispers. Nothing concrete. Except . . ."

"Yes?"

"The letters Timothy threatened her about. When I was behind the hedge and she and Samson were leading Timothy away, Agnes told Samson that the letters were missing, and it was the first time I ever heard him threaten Timothy. He flat out told the boy he'd kill him or the old lady if they didn't get those letters back. They took Timothy upstairs, and like I said, the next night she was dead."

Richard Freedman pantomimed a golf swing. The past was something he wanted to discard. "That enough, my friend? I can't be late." He made another phantom golf swing.

My cell phone rang.

"Perfect timing, huh?" he said, then started walking down the porch, waving me to follow.

I fumbled for my cell. The caller ID on the cell phone display told me who was calling.

"Jubil," I said as I answered, limping as I tried to keep up to Richard Freedman as we walked to our respective vehicles.

"We've got to talk," Jubil said.

I started toward my Jeep, fully five paces behind Freedman. "Now is good."

"I mean we have to talk in person. It's about this Bingo kid you wanted me to scare."

I watched Richard Freedman swing into his Jag convertible.

"Now would be better if we could do it over the phone." I'd promised Amelia to try to get back as soon as possible, and there were still a couple of stops waiting for me.

"Not good enough. Drop whatever you're doing and meet me at the canal just south of the old naval base," Jubil said. "You can't miss us. Look for about a half dozen marked cars."

I stood beside my Jeep. I heard the whine of an electric motor. Freedman might have been cutting it close to his tee time, but that didn't stop him from lowering the convertible top before he started the engine.

"What if I can't?" I said.

"Make it happen," Jubil snapped.

Richard Freedman gave me a wave from his Jag as he left me behind. A free man happy in a free world. Knowing what I did about Charleston's history and the subtle racial issues that simmered civilly from generation to generation, I couldn't blame him for what seemed like an obsessive need to thumb his nose at the white world.

"It's that important?" I asked as I swung the door to my Jeep open. It had a convertible top, too. But Richard Freedman was too far away for me to wave at him.

"No," Jubil said. "That bad."

✛

Retha was still humming Billy Lee's favorite lullaby. It was the only thing that had given her the strength to continue walking all through the night.

She was on the downhill slope of the bridge that curved over the Ashley. To her left, she saw the square buildings of the Citadel, separated from the river by lowland marsh grasses. To her right, the masts of yachts at the marina.

To drivers of Land Rovers and Mercedes and Lincolns, the commuters on their way from the islands into Charleston to fill law and accounting offices, she appeared as just another homeless person, filthy and walking in the erratic manner of someone with no particular destination.

But they were wrong. Just ahead was the hospital.

She didn't know what she would do when she got there. She was too exhausted to think about it. She wouldn't let herself wonder if the man in the Jeep had taken her baby to this hospital as she'd asked in her note. She just told herself he had. It was her only hope. And she just knew that she had to reach Billy Lee. When she did, everything would be all right.

Retha made it only as far as the hospital parking lot. A nurse going into work saw her stumbling progress and caught up with her.

"You alright?" she asked Retha, then opened her mouth in a silent gasp as she saw the welts, bruises, and dried blood.

"Fine, fine," Retha said.

"You poor woman," the nurse said. "Let me help you get to emergency."

"No," Retha said. That wasn't her plan at all. She was nearly delirious with exhaustion and pain. All she wanted to do was get into the hospital and sneak to Billy Lee's room. She had no idea how terrible she looked.

Retha's protests didn't matter. The nurse lifted one of Retha's arms over her own shoulders and helped her toward the sliding doors of the emergency room.

Though she was soon surrounded by a Démerol-induced cloud, Retha had enough sense to understand she must not ask about Billy Lee. Especially in the emergency room. They'd wonder how she knew about him. She yearned for Billy Lee though. She wanted to smell his skin, listen to his gurgling, feel his fingers clutch at her, hold him to her chest.

When the tall orderly began to push her wheelchair to take her to her room on the second floor, Retha was unable to stop herself from blurting out a question.

"Mister, would it be alright if you pushed me down the hall to where the children stay here in the hospital? It always makes me smile to see children. And believe me, I could use a smile right now."

Retha hoped that if the orderly went slow enough, she might be able to see in the rooms and get a glimpse of her little boy.

"Wish I could, lady, but we're short-staffed. I've got to take you straight to your room and hurry straight back."

"I understand," Retha said.

Retha closed her eyes. She didn't open them until he wheeled her into her room. On the other side, asleep in the bed, was another woman, only the top of her head visible above the sheets tucked around her body.

Retha was glad the other woman was asleep. The way Retha felt, aside from how her body felt, was that if someone tried talking to her right now, she'd burst into tears.

She missed Billy Lee badly. And she was all mixed up inside about what to think, being in the same hospital as him. Being that close, which was good. But not knowing anything about him, which was bad. Real bad.

What if he had died?

After the orderly helped her into bed and took away the wheelchair, Retha allowed herself to cry for the first time since her whipping.

Retha waited until her face had dried of its tears. She rolled to the edge of the bed and lowered her slippered feet. She had to see if Billy Lee was fine.

The woman in the other bed remained asleep. She wouldn't know or care what Retha did.

Retha stood and wobbled. She remained standing for several minutes, until the blackness that buzzed around her eyes dissipated. Then, holding the bed, she shuffled along its length. She paused again, waiting for a new cloud of blackness to dissipate. From the edge of the bed, she tottered to the wall, falling into it for support like a child just learning to walk. She used the wall to keep herself upright as she shuffled toward the hospital room door.

Billy Lee. That's all she cared about. Billy Lee. She had to find out if he was fine. She had to hold him.

When she reached the door, the cloud of blackness grew and buzzed and grew, an angry swarm of bees attacking her consciousness. She fell forward onto her chest and face.

✛

I arrived at the canal just as the tow truck began to drive away with a bright red Chevette.

Two marked cars were parked, lights flashing. Jubil stood at his unmarked sedan.

He waved me past the uniformed officers. When I reached him, he pointed at the disappearing tow truck.

"That was the car you told me to look for, Nick. We found it. Correction, a boater found it. Called it in." Jubil wore his dark sunglasses and nothing on his face gave me any indication of his thoughts. "Nick, no skid marks. No brake marks. Just deep foot-steps alongside the tire tracks in the mud off the road. Someone pushed the car in the canal. Didn't fall far. The water barely covered the roof."

He took my elbow. It was a rough grip. He pushed me toward the marked cars.

Then I saw it. On the ground. A dark body bag.

"You also told me to look for a kid named Bingo," he said. "We found him, too."

"Was he driving drunk?"

"I don't like these coincidences, Nick. What do you know about him? Why'd you send me after him?"

"You know the reason."

"No. I know the reason you gave me."

"Anyone tell you that when you play tough cop, it looks like you're sucking on a lemon?" It was a bad attempt at a joke. Wrong place, wrong time. I felt stupid as I said it.

Jubil didn't answer. He yanked me closer to the body bag.

Wordlessly, he unzipped it. In death, Bingo was placid. A wax dummy. Pale, still gleaming wet.

"This the kid you wanted me to find?" Jubil said.

"Yes," I said. Sobered.

"I'm asking you again. What do you know about him? Why'd you send me after him?"

"Jubil, he's a friend of Angel's. The kid in the hospital that I'm trying to help. Can you tell me why you're so upset?"

"He drowned, Nick. He was strapped into his seat belt. The car went into the water. The water rose. It filled his car. No one should have to die that way."

"You're right," I said. Quietly.

"And no, he wasn't drunk. There was a very simple reason he couldn't undo the seat belt."

Jubil zipped up the bag again and straightened. "Whoever did this meant for the kid to drown. Because whoever did this taped the kid's wrists to the steering wheel before rolling down the window and pushing the car into the canal."

CHAPTER

19

Drowning.

Agnes Larrabee was twenty years old in the spring of 1890, the spring that she watched her twin sister sink into the east branch of the Cooper River, just out of reach her flailing, outstretched arms.

Spring was the traditional time of year for their family to visit the remaining holdings of a plantation that had once included forty-two hundred acres, four hundred acres of rice paddies, a colonial mansion, ten cabins and the slave families to fill them.

The drought of the rice industry had waged the first inroads against the Larrabee wealth. That was followed by various hurricanes, poor investments, and one or two fires. But the true beginning of the end of the plantation was marked by the war of Northern aggression. Without the manpower to sustain the land and buildings already ravaged by Union soldiers, the Larrabee family was forced to sell most of their land holdings and invest in businesses within Charleston.

Agnes and her sister arrived into the Larrabee family at the closing of the nineteenth century, barely on the downside of its pinnacle of greatness. Accordingly, their childhood was steeped with the manners and illusion that it had never departed.

Their father, an older man, still remembered his childhood on the plantation. He never wanted his children to forget the family's glory, so he insisted on yearly treks to what remained of the plantation. He preferred spring for their family's annual pilgrimage to the Larrabee shrine—before the summer months, when the unbearable heat rose upward from the lowland planta-tion grounds.

It required nearly a full day's travel with four wagons and teams of horses to transport the family and necessities, which included a dozen servants, the eldest among them able to remem-ber their own childhoods as slaves on the plantation.

Agnes and Mary were judged old enough to be permitted time unescorted as ladies. They took a young servant with them to carry a blanket and a picnic basket heavy with food and the proper dishes and silverware. With the servant following, they lifted their skirts high with one hand to step through the grass that had grown along a path to the river; with the other hand each carried a parasol to shade her delicate skin from the sun.

They did enjoy their picnic in the mild spring weather beneath a perfectly blue sky, speaking lightly of debutante balls and prospective husbands and upcoming travel to Europe. They sat talking long after the final pieces of dessert had been served to them. Perhaps an hour later, they approached the edge of the river, determined to cool their feet. It was a daring move, removing their shoes and stockings and lifting their skirts to wade into the waters, but they felt safe because they knew there were no prying eyes of young men to behold such an indecency. That the servant was a young black man was held of no account.

They giggled and prattled until Mary ventured too far into the water. A snapping turtle startled her and she slipped and fell forward into deeper water. The material of her long dress wrapped around her legs as she thrashed to keep her balance, and this filled her with panic. Her efforts to surface drove her into deeper water. Much as Agnes tried to pull her back to shore, Mary fought with the blind panic that robbed her of all her senses.

As she began to drown, she ripped at her clothing, pulling most of it loose. But it was too late. Her lungs filled with the dark water leached from tannic juices of submerged trees, and all light faded from her life. When her body was recovered, she was found in her knee-to-shoulder undergarments, and her beautiful dress was never recovered.

Although Agnes went through the motions of the life required of a Charlestonian aristocrat, it was said she never truly recovered.

As for the servant who helplessly watched the horror from the edge of the bank, unable to swim or attempt a rescue, he was allowed to remain with the Larrabee family.

His name was Samson Elias. At the time, he was fourteen years old.

✢

I recounted all of this to Glennifer and Elaine in the back room of their antique shop. I'd learned it earlier in the South Carolina

ness of the friendship between Agnes Larrabee and Samson Elias? This was my main reason for the current visit to the antique shop.

"I have a delicate question," I said then, "related to all of this."

"Yes?" Glennifer's delicate fingers hovered above a cup of tea.

I told them about my conversation with Richard Freedman and finished by asking about Samson Elias.

"After all," I said, "he was there the day her sister died. Maybe it created some kind of bond. So maybe they had something to hide from proper society. Maybe Samson killed her because as Timothy grew old enough to understand what was happening, she tried to end it, whatever it was. I mean, this whole thing about the Jesus room seems so spooky."

"Samson Elias," Elaine said.

"Samson Elias," Glennifer repeated.

Neither spoke for long moments.

I leaned back in my chair and waited as one or the other decided what to say. Above their heads, on the wall behind them, was an eight-by-ten photo that showed Glennifer, Elaine, Amelia, and I at White Point Garden the previous spring. Following my mother's funeral, we had gone for a lunch that was celebratory of her spirit, and our time together had lifted our spirits to match the pleasant warm afternoon. In the park after, to my surprise, Glennifer had asked a passing tourist to snap a photo of us with a camera that Elaine carried in her purse. And, to my surprise upon my return to Charleston this summer, I saw it on the wall. I'd not once commented on its presence, but it served as a reminder that our friendship, unlikely as it seemed, continued to grow.

At this moment, too, it served as a reminder of the unsettled emotions I had regarding Amelia and her return to Charleston.

I pushed those thoughts out of my mind, especially with something else tugging for my attention. What was it about the photograph that was significant? I had no time to ponder further.

"Samson and Agnes," Glennifer finally said. "I seriously doubt there was any hanky-panky. Aside from her weakness for alcohol, Agnes was a very stern, strict, conservative Christian."

"Some of the sternest and strictest may be hiding the most outrageous sins," I said.

"We would have heard," Elaine said.

"True." I grinned. "Silly of me to think otherwise."

"However . . ." Glennifer said.

"However?"

"Samson was rumored to be wealthy. Much wealthier than one would expect for someone who had served in a household all his life. Isn't that correct, Laney?"

Elaine nodded. "He was also the one who looked after Agnes in the years that she spent inside the mansion."

"Inside the mansion? I don't understand."

"Nicholas," Elaine said, "there was a spell of several months when Agnes Larrabee stayed in one room inside that mansion of hers. It was a nervous breakdown. That was long ago, just after her son and daughter-in-law died in a tragic fire. And that was only a year after her husband died of a stroke."

"I didn't know about that."

"The nervous breakdown?" Glennifer asked. "The fire? Or that her son died with his wife?"

"All three."

"Some things were very hush-hush," Glennifer said. "And that most definitely isn't common knowledge. I suppose we could have told you earlier, but we were simply interested in the painting."

"I think the story is far more complicated than we ever guessed," I said. "Now I'm trying to find out everything I can about Agnes."

"When she had her nervous breakdown," Elaine said, "she didn't leave the mansion for months. The only person she allowed in her room was Samson Elias."

"As for the rest," Glennifer said, "I apologize. We simply assumed you knew why Agnes had taken in Timothy. He was the only survivor of the fire. Only four or five years old at the time."

"Tough childhood," I said. "First his parents dead, then his grandmother."

"No one was surprised when he ended up in prison," Elaine said. "Sympathetic certainly, but not surprised."

"Let me tell you about my conversation with him earlier," I said.

"Please do," Glennifer said.

I related as much as I could remember, including his surprising admission that he'd stolen the painting himself and was now interesting in purchasing it.

"Very, very interesting, Nicholas. I suppose that ends it for you."

"Ends it?"

"We can legitimately make your young friend an offer for the Van Dyck. That will solve a lot of her family's problems, I would guess."

Elaine nodded in agreement. "We know you have a soft spot for Angel. Perhaps you can help her and her Grammie invest the proceeds of the sale for her future education."

"Perhaps," I said. But I was thinking of Timothy Larrabee's insistent questions. Of Bingo sending me out to the church. Of

Bingo in a body bag. Of the Glory Church and how it forced a
mother to give up her baby to keep him healthy.

"Nicholas, such a dark look."

I forced a smile onto my face. "There remains, however, one
little mystery. It has to do with chewing tobacco."

Glennifer snorted. "Have you seen any pigs flying down
King Street?"

I shook my head.

"That's your answer then."

✛

When Retha reached the room, a young black girl was holding
a sleeping toddler. Retha leaned on the doorway and looked in,
hardly daring to breathe to be this close to Billy Lee.

The girl waved her free hand at Retha, careful not to wake
the child. "Hey," she said, friendly.

"Hey yourself. That your sister?"

The girl nodded. "Maddie. My name's Angel."

"I'm Retha. Can I hold her?"

Angel was standing right beside the bed by then. All she had
to do was lift Maddie into the woman's outstretched arms.

Retha stroked Maddie's hair. She wanted to go over to Billy
Lee's bed but was afraid if someone walked by, they'd know
instantly she was Billy Lee's mother.

"You look pretty hurt," Angel said. "It makes me sad for
you."

"That's a nice thing to say. In one way, I guess am pretty
hurt. And in another, I'm doing just fine." Retha nodded and
smiled, confirming it for herself. "Yup. Just fine." She lifted one

of Maddie's hands. Maddie curled her fingers around Retha's forefinger.

"What happened?" Angel said. "My friend's mama, she looked kind of like you once. Her boyfriend, he done it."

"Get right to the point, don't you, Angel?"

"That mean I'm right?"

"Right enough. I run off."

Angel nodded at the self-evident wisdom of Retha's statement. "I'm glad you got away from him."

Retha began humming Billy Lee's lullaby.

"You got any kids?" Angel asked.

Angel could not know this was a swing moment for Retha. Retha had blindly trusted everyone in her life, and all it had given her was grief and heartache. Less than twenty-four hours ago, she had decided never to trust anyone again. Finally free, here was her first chance to test that vow. Nor could Angel know that something about her own straightforward compassion reached out and touched Retha. Because of that compassion, Retha made her decision.

"I have a baby boy," she said. "And I love him as dearly as you love your sister. If you make me a promise that you'll keep it secret, I'll tell you all about him."

✢

It took Angel nearly an hour to return to Retha, who was in her own room by then.

In Angel's free hand was an orange popsicle. She pushed it toward Retha. "Have it," Angel said. "I remembered you saying how you were so thirsty all the time."

As Retha accepted the popsicle, her hand trembled. "And Billy Lee?"

"What I got is good news and bad news," Angel told her.

"Billy Lee is still sick? He's dying? He's dead?" Retha's words came out in a jumble of panic.

"No, no, no." Angel shook her head to emphasize her denial. "He's healthy. For a baby, he's pretty big and strong-looking. The doctors are impressed that he's getting better so quickly. At first, they figured it might be a week." Angel let a smile touch her face. "Anyway, that's my good news."

"Can't be any bad news after that," Retha said. "My Billy Lee is fine and healthy. That's what matters."

"I don't know," Angel said. "See, tomorrow afternoon? That's when the social services people are coming to take him away to a foster home."

CHAPTER

20

With her hand in mine, Amelia and I stood at the iron railing that
overlooked the convergence of the Ashley and Cooper Rivers.
The shadows were long and the evening was as calm as the
waters. A barge moved slowly upstream, temporarily blocking
our view of Fort Sumter.

East Battery Street was named for the cannons positioned
there to prevent ships from entering the harbor during the Civil
War. Behind us, marking this historic site, were the cannons of
White Point Gardens. Behind the cannons was the park itself,
a buffer for the genteel columned mansions.

Countless times I'd stood here as a boy, hearing in my
mind the whistling cannonballs as the city lay under siege.
During the years my mother was with me, I was enchanted by
the history of the city and deeply loved Charleston. In the years
of solitude that followed, I felt abandoned by her and chose
accordingly to reject all that she stood for, including the sense

of belonging to the tapestry of Charleston. It seemed, however, that my heart was returning to that boyhood sense of wonder and the love I'd buried for this fine city with all its flaws and beauty. Suddenly the prospect of selling the family mansion and leaving Charleston was not a future I wanted.

As if in confirmation, a light breeze suddenly sprang off the waters and caressed my face. It was a romantic delusion, that Charleston was welcoming me back, but I lifted my face to the breeze and smiled.

"Penny for your thoughts," Amelia said.

"Hmmm," I answered. For a moment, I'd forgotten she was beside me. With her voice bringing me back to the present, I returned also to the slight sense of discomfort.

"Penny's not enough, huh." She laughed softly. She squeezed my hand.

And I forced myself to squeeze back. At that moment, I realized I was pretending to have something that wasn't there. I turned to face her squarely. This was also the moment to tell her what was bothering me. We were grown-ups. She would appreciate my honesty far more than she would dislike hearing the truth.

"Well," Amelia said, seeing that she had my full attention again, "shall we wander the streets and find a restaurant worthy of the evening? My treat." She stood on her tiptoes and kissed my cheek. Then stood back and smiled.

She wore a light blue dress that accentuated all of her curves yet suggested grace and hinted at allure. There was a beautiful light to her eyes and a genuine happiness in her hopeful smile. She could have stepped off the cover of *Vogue* into this moment. I hadn't seen such lightness in her being since her father's funeral.

With my heart fluttering—such an odd but accurate way to

describe the feeling I had to see her face—could I truly say what
I needed to say?

"Sounds great," I said, returning her smile. I would find a
different moment. I wanted to enjoy my time with her because
too soon she would be back in Chicago.

She turned, leading me back toward the spot where I had
parked the Jeep. Halfway there, she stopped. "Remember?" she
said. "Here?"

"Here?"

"Glennifer and Elaine sent me the photo I took. Right here.
With the three of you overlooking the water. Remember? We'd
gone for lunch after your mother's funeral. Looking at you as I
took the photo, I knew I wanted a chance to walk alone with you
and hold hands."

⊹

That had been the moment for me, too. The beginning of the
roller coaster of my emotions. Love her? Risk rejection? Or grow
a thick skin and prepare the defenses in case the journey took me
nowhere with her?

The tentative steps along the path of a shared life are so
difficult. A paradox. How can you discover whether you want
to be committed unless you first spend enough time with that
person to be sure about the decision? And spending time with
that person seems to bring an obligation to take further steps
together. Unless the first few occasions together prove to be like
mixing oil and water, there seems no sensible reason to go to the
effort of breaking away from the path, especially if one or the
other seems inclined to continue.

Inertia. Was that the reason she was with me? And how could I find out without plainly asking her? But did I want to risk the wrong answer?

For the unwilling one, without an obvious and compelling reason to stop the journey, it is easier to continue than it is to fight to break free. So the journey continues. And continues. Until the moment of truth, when going further means a vow of commitment. And suddenly the vague sense of unease must be acted upon.

Some, I guess, continue, and it is only when the unease faces the pressure of marriage that something snaps and the commitment is broken in a sudden struggle for the freedom that should have been claimed much, much earlier. Yet at the beginning, when there seems to be promise and hope, should one avoid taking that first step on the path for fear of a messy ending?

I did not know how far Amelia was in the journey we'd begun. I was grateful, however, that Amelia and I had avoided the one thing that can make all of the courtship so much more difficult, for the process of disentangling is far, far worse with the complicating factor of a physical relationship. It is common knowledge that women give of themselves in exchange for love, and that men will give love in exchange for the woman and what she will provide. The currency, however, is not love but the pretense of love, on one side or the other. And intimacy without commitment of love in its true sense creates scarring damage, leaving one with empty pleasures to leach the soul and taking from the other soul a sense of self.

I had not wanted this hollowness for Amelia. Or for myself.

And, given my uncertainties, was grateful we'd avoided it, no matter how tempting.

✢

I thought of all this as Amelia and I stood briefly where I'd absorbed her beauty as she had stepped back to take the photo of Glennifer and Elaine and me.

I thought of all my confusion. The easy way for me was the wrong way. The difficult way was the right way. I decided I would plunge forward with what I needed to say to be honest with her. That the subtle pressures she put on me to better myself in the eyes of the world were pressures that would ultimately destroy our relationship. If she was even interested in going that far. I would ask her about that, too.

The roller coaster.

"Amelia, I . . ."

An image of the photo she'd just mentioned flashed into my mind. The place where I'd seen it last. On the wall behind the desk in Glennifer and Elaine's shop. Across from the chair where they sat prospective clients for both the purchasing and selling of antiques. Where most certainly Angel would have sat, the afternoon she wandered into their shop.

"Yes, Nick?" She wrapped an arm around my waist. It felt good, but I was too distracted to be able to remain here with her.

Because suddenly I knew.

And I knew that I needed to make a different sort of confession. To someone else.

"Could we make a quick detour before dinner?" I asked

Amelia. Her face showed confusion at my erratic subject change.
"It's important."

✛

Angel was at home, and she answered my knock by asking me to
identify myself.

I did. As I waited, I noticed a new lock in place.

Angel swung the door open. "Nick." She didn't invite me in.

I noticed the splintered doorjamb, too. "What happened,
Angel?"

"Nothing."

The set of her face told me I would get nothing out of her
by pursing the question more.

"Your Grammie Zora back yet?" I asked.

"Told you before. Not till the end of the week."

I looked over her head at the interior. A single bulb in a
dusty light fixture lit the narrow front hallway. Along one wall
was a table stacked with mail. Beyond, the parlor. The back wall
was bare and white. Or would have been, without the larger-
than-life-size figure of Angel's mother, standing among flowers
with a much younger Angel holding her hand. The scene was in
full color, covering much of the wall.

Angel caught my glance. "Just running one of my DVDs.
I've got it on Pause."

She still didn't invite me in.

Dusk had begun to settle, but there was still enough light for
her to clearly see the Jeep parked just down the sidewalk. With
Amelia on the passenger side, her hands in her lap. She wasn't
happy that I'd made this a priority.

"Who's that?" Angel said. "She's pretty."

"Amelia."

"You and her shacked up?"

"No."

"Working on it? I mean, you're dressed pretty fancy. Seems strange you'd come here if—" Angel brought her knuckles to her mouth—"It's not Maddie, is it? They said at the hospital she'd be fine. Maybe out tomorrow. So when Maddie fell asleep, I just walked home."

"It's not Maddie."

"Good."

"Angel, I want to talk for a few minutes."

She shrugged. "Alright." Angel stepped outside, swung the front door shut, and sat on the steps. "Don't take it personal, but my friend Camellia has told me stories. I ain't letting any man into my house when I'm alone."

I felt sorrow that the innocence of her childhood had been stolen from her so early. I sat beside her on the steps. We looked out onto the street at the Jeep in the foreground and the crowded, leaning houses beyond on the other side of the street.

"Hot summer nights like this," Angel said, "Mama would sit right here with me and we'd eat watermelon. Spit the seeds too. It was fun. I miss her; I don't mind telling you."

"My mother and I would do the same," I said. "When the fireflies came out, she'd help me chase them down, and we'd keep them in an old pickle jar. It seems to me, though, that there's not as many fireflies now as when I was your age."

"Sad, huh."

"All of it," I said.

"Yeah," she said. "But I don't let the sad get in the way of remembering what was good. That would make the good not so good."

Again, I was struck hard by Angel's unawareness of her bravery. That worsened what I had to say. But unlike the situation with Amelia, I was not going to let cowardice stop me.

"I want us to be friends, Angel." I spoke softly, not wanting any of this conversation to reach the Jeep. "But you need to know something about me before you can decide if you want to be my friend."

Angel pushed away, not rising but increasing the distance between us on the steps. "You the same as that creep that followed me across the playground one day?"

"I'm someone who lied to you at the beginning," I answered. "You see, when I offered to help you and Maddie in the emergency room, I wasn't there by accident. Or because of an accident. Or because I was sick. Or because I knew someone who was sick."

I paused. "You're smart. You would have wondered about that sooner or later. I'm guessing you realized it that afternoon, even before I helped you with the security guard."

No reply.

"Before I tell you why I lied, I really want you to know that everything after that has been honest." I stopped myself, remembering my meeting with Timothy Larrabee and how I hadn't yet told Angel about that. "Everything except for the fact that I've already spoken to Timothy Larrabee. He wants to buy the painting. But so does someone else. So now you know that, too. I'll arrange it if you still want me to."

"Sure."

"That's all that matters to you, isn't it, Angel? Not the fact that I let you believe it was an accident I was there in the emergency room. "

"Maddie's all I got, and I'm all she's got." Angel hunched forward and wrapped her arms around her knees. "Nothing's more important."

It felt strange, having this private conversation with Amelia so near. But I would not have been able to sit through dinner without talking to Angel first. Nor could I have simply bid Amelia good night and left her to come to visit Angel.

"I understand," I said. "I'm not mad or hurt at what you've pretended. And I'm asking you to forgive me for what I pretended. I was trying to help two friends. They don't mean as much to me as Maddie means to you, but they are still important to me."

Angel stared straight ahead. In the growing dusk, a few fireflies began to glow among the weeds at the side of the steps.

"You know who my two friends are, don't you?" I said. "You saw me in a photo with them. In the antique shop. When you tried to sell them the painting."

"They sent someone to follow me home that day. Then they sent you. And you pretended that you were just trying to help me and Maddie. But you wanted something else. People always do."

"Not always. You're helping Maddie without expecting anything back. Your mother loved you simply because she loved you."

"That's different."

"It is. Thank God for that."

"You believe in God."

"Yes."

"I thought believing in God meant you didn't lie and steal

and do mean things. But you don't mind pretending to be helping me when all you want is the painting."

"I'm here to tell you how wrong that was. I want to help you and Maddie. That's become more important to me than the pretending I did when we met."

"I don't believe you."

"Why else would I be here right now?" I asked.

"Because you finally realized I knew who you were."

"Not true," I said.

"So why didn't you tell me this before?"

I fought for a good answer.

"See?" Angel stood up and reached for the knob of the front door. "All along," she said without taking her hand away. "I've been pretending, too. I've been pretending I never did see you in the picture with those two old ladies. I've been pretending that you were like what a father would be. But if you've stopped pretending then I've got to stop. So maybe it's good we each know what the other wants. You want the painting for your old-bag friends and I want what I can get for it."

She opened the door. "Do what it takes to sell the painting. Then you and me can be through with each other." Angel stepped inside. To a lonely house. With the memories of her mother on that big, white, empty wall.

And I stepped down. Past the fireflies in the wisps of weeds. Feeling the loneliness that comes with a deep sense of loss.

✦

I chose 82 Queen for dinner with Amelia, a place where I'd once met her for lunch. Most of our conversation consisted of trading stories of our childhoods. It was an enjoyable evening, but I could not shake the sense that below our stories were other issues we needed to discuss. I knew what it was for me and became afraid again of what it might be for her. Time in her presence was so good that I decided to hold what I needed to say until just before her departure for Chicago.

Our good-night hugs were automatic; again, Amelia gave me a quick peck on the cheek before getting into her car. It hurt me less this time than the night before. I was thinking of Angel sitting quietly on the steps in the darkness among the fireflies.

I made the short drive to the Doubletree. It was nearly eleven o'clock, and the market area had begun to quiet. A valet named Steve took my keys, and I moved slowly through the lobby to the elevators.

I doubted that I would sleep easily, and my prediction was correct. When the phone rang a half hour after I'd crawled into bed, I was still awake, with Angel's sorrow heavy on my mind.

"Sir?"

"Yes?"

"Mr. Barrett, it's Steve. Down here in valet. A woman drove into your Jeep in the parking garage."

"It's a beater. It can wait until morning."

"Sir, she's very upset."

"Okay, I'll be right down."

✣

I didn't make it to the lobby. As I waited for the elevator to arrive, two men approached, then one stood on either side of me. I gave them a polite glance.

The dark suits and the beards set off a pang of alarm inside me. Had I shouted or screamed immediately, I might have been able to prevent what happened next. But fear of ridicule is a strong countering emotion. As I debated what to do, the doors to the elevator opened.

I made my decision. "Sorry," I said. "Forgot something."

I turned back between them to go to my room. Too late. Each grasped an arm and shoved me inside the elevator. As the doors closed, one pushed me up against the wall. The other wrapped wide white adhesive tape around my eyes. The first one punched me in the stomach. I doubled over. Fought the tape going over my mouth without success. Blinded and muted, I had no chance as they bound my wrists with the same tape.

I suppose they had calculated the risks. What were the odds of someone else taking the elevator this late at night? I know what I was hoping for. But the odds ran in their favor.

The door opened. I could only guess it was any other floor but the lobby. I heard the footsteps of one of them leave. Half a second later, he'd returned.

"Come on!" he urged his partner.

I couldn't kick against them with any degree of effectiveness. Not with only one good leg. They dragged me down the hall. In the absolute darkness imposed upon me by the tape, I heard the click of a door opening, then closing.

It wasn't the stairwell. I would have heard the echo of the metal door closing, and the scuffling of their feet on concrete. Instead, the door clicked quietly shut, and my shoes dragged across soft carpet.

They'd used the valet's name to get me to the elevator. Rented a room near the elevator. It told me something I didn't want to know. This had been well planned. As I tensed my body, waiting blind for another blow to my body, I heard a low hissing sound that I could not identify. Plus the breathing of other men.

✛

The water in the bathtub was ice-cold.

Five times they brought me to the point of drowning. Held me beside the tub and shoved my face in the water and held my thrashing body until pinpoints of light stabbed my eyes, the pinpoints of unconsciousness that would force my straining lungs to suck in water instead of air. Five times they brought me up again, gasping for life. Then they hauled me to my feet and brought me into another room. Hands forced me to my knees.

A voice whispered in my ear. "You like them so much? We're gonna treat you like one of them." The voice remained a whisper in the total darkness. A whisper devoid of any characteristics, except whatever I projected into it because of my fear. "Consider this a warning," it continued. "We can find you anywhere, anytime. And next time, you won't be let off so easy. Whatever you're trying to find, let it go."

Fingers grasped my hair and yanked my head back. "Understand?"

I felt something across my throat.

"Understand?" the whisper repeated. "This is a knife. All I have to do is draw it across your throat, and you have a brand-new smile. But tonight, you're going to live. Tonight's a warning. Mind the business that belongs to you. No one else's. Or we'll be back. Don't go to the police. Or we'll be back. Don't tell a single person. Or we'll be back. And it'll be much worse."

Archives, reading the account of a journalist at the turn of the century who had interviewed various family members to give a breathless, if occasionally melodramatic, tone to the newspaper story.

"How very sad," Glennifer said.

"Indeed," Elaine echoed. "That explains it some, doesn't it? I mean, first her sister, then her husband and daughter and son-in-law. Tragic, tragic, tragic."

I sat across from them, looking over a stack of papers that likely had not been moved in weeks. "Explains? Some of it?"

"What Laney means is—and we will absolutely kill you for repeating it—that Agnes, so we heard back then, enjoyed the occasional tipple."

Reading between the lines of Southern grace, I understood that *occasional* meant just the opposite. "In solitude?" I asked. Long and hard tippling at social functions was nothing worthy of hushed whispers. But those who sought solace in alcohol privately were seen as weak.

"In solitude," Elaine answered.

To a list that grew longer as I got to know them, I added something else worthy of admiration about these two women. Earlier, when they told me about Agnes Larrabee, neither mentioned alcohol abuse. It wasn't pertinent to their story, and such gossip would have been malicious. Gossip might have been a staple of their business, but mostly it was a one-way street.

"Poor woman," I said. The pressures she inflicted on Timothy had no doubt been inflicted on her in her own childhood. I thought of the private, lonely life she must have endured as the matriarch of the legacy passed on to her. What if Richard Freedman, as a teenage gardener's assistant, had misread the strange-

Strong arms pushed me over, and with my knees still on the floor, my chest fell into the couch. My face was shoved against fabric. Someone else pulled my shirt out of my pants, exposing the skin of my lower back.

I kicked frantically. Almost gasped with relief when I realized they had no intention of undressing me further.

"It's ready," someone else whispered.

That's when I recognized that the low hissing sound was a propane torch.

CHAPTER

21

"You're late," Jubil said.

"Five minutes," I agreed. Morning had arrived and I was still alive. "I was at the archives."

"First thing in the morning?"

"First thing in the morning. As they opened the doors." Anything to take my mind off the terror of the night before.

"Scholarly research as part of the lifestyle of the rich and infamous," Jubil said as he surveyed the paintings and décor of the Doubletree restaurant. "You do live high."

"Wonderful, isn't it?" I said flatly. "Pendleton's tab."

"Thought he hated you."

"Makes it more fun," I explained. My attorneys had assured me that when Pendleton lost the lawsuit, he would pay their attorney fees as part of the settlement. And part of the attorney fees, they had explained, would include my living expenses here in Charleston. It was a stretch to say that Maddie's hospital expenses were part of it, but I was going to give it a good try. If not, it would come out of the inheritance I was almost certain to gain.

Jubil wrapped his hands around his coffee cup. "Winning popularity contests everywhere, huh?"

I thought of the previous night. Of the attackers leaving the room after cutting through the tape on my wrists. Of sitting there and ripping the tape off my face and mouth, shaking so badly with fear and relief that I didn't care about the extra pain of pulling away hair with the tape. Of walking on wobbly legs to my own room. Of putting on a dry shirt and slowly walking to the twenty-four-hour Harris Teeter for bandages and ointment. Of sitting in the quiet of my own room and wondering what to do.

Popularity contests. Like last night.

"Yeah," I said to Jubil. "People everywhere love me."

"I don't think you caught my drift. I'm not the only one keeping tabs on you." He grinned, drank coffee, and surveyed me for a reaction. I was too tired. "There's a investigative firm on Broad. Discreet. Very discreet. They don't advertise. No sign on the street. It's the place you go when you live south of Broad."

I thought of Kellie Mixson. Chances were this firm wouldn't allow ball caps as part of the dress code.

"Sometimes, unofficially, information gets traded back and forth," Jubil continued. "I have a guy there, helps me out when I need to make inquiries about the blue bloods on your side of town. And sometimes, he comes to me."

"Same deal you have with Kellie Mixson."

He chuckled. "Same deal. I think she's got a personal interest in you, too. I might have laid it on a little thick, the high school football stuff."

"Great. And you did the same for your Broad Street connection?"

"He's not your type. And his interest was a lot different. It was a couple days ago. What's today? Wednesday? Yeah, it was Monday. Guy from the firm buys me lunch, same way you're going to buy me breakfast today. Says he's got questions about someone I know. Says asking me is also like giving me a heads up, 'cause he remembers me talking about my high school football days here, and when the name came up first thing Monday morning, it startled him. Guess what, Nick? The client hired their firm to find out what they could about you. You've been followed the last few days. Everywhere you went."

The waitress dropped off our plates. Fruit plate for Jubil, grits and butter and brown sugar for me. My body wasn't up to a task as difficult as digesting solid food.

Jubil jabbed a slice of cantaloupe with his fork. "I didn't bother asking him who the client was. That's not part of the deal. And he didn't complain much when I didn't give him much on you. 'Course, the whole time I'm thinking there's a lot more going on than I know about from you. Especially when all you have for me is questions, not answers."

He stopped, made a face at a mouthful of grapefruit. "Especially with everything else happening. First, you bring a kid with no mother to the hospital, then clam up about it. And don't think I've forgotten the deadline this afternoon. Then you send me after some punk who shows up dead. You ask me to look into a murder that happened forty years ago. You've got one PI on retainer, and I'd like you to tell me why when I get to that part. Plus, somebody else has another PI putting together a file on you. And there's a voodoo woman I can't track down no matter how hard I try." He grinned. "Finally, a reaction. What nerve did I hit? Got to be the voodoo woman."

I shifted, trying to ignore the searing pain just above my right hipbone.

"Grammie Zora," he said.

I nodded.

"Look, just because I didn't file a report on the hospital baby doesn't mean I twiddled my thumbs. You told me the connection was the other girl, the one with the medical bill you're covering. Pretty simple, getting her name and address. More interesting when I match that to Zora Starr, voodoo legend on the streets. So I spend Monday trying to hook up with Zora, just to get some background, plus I'm curious as to why she's not helping her granddaughter. She's got a good reputation, and leaving the granddaughter alone in the hospital doesn't fit in with that. I ask around the neighborhood. Go to the grocery store. Everyone knows Grammie Zora, but no one remembers seeing her. Angel's been around plenty at the different places. But no Grammie. It's been a month or two, my best guess, since Grammie Zora's been seen. Word's out she did some serious voodoo and is on the run. I'd like to ask a computer geek about it, but if he smells cop, I won't get a thing."

"Send me," I said.

"You're not on my good-person list right now."

Jubil stopped talking and returned to his breakfast. He ate in silence. I watched him in silence. The hum of business conversations filled the breakfast room. Occasionally, the ring of a cell phone interrupted all of it, sending people searching their pockets and purses until they realized it was someone else's phone.

Jubil pushed away his plate. "This afternoon's deadline for the baby? That only applies to the baby. The other official business starts now. I've got an open file on the drowning murder of that kid in the Chevette. Looks like there might be a missing person case with Grammie Zora, only the granddaughter's not reporting it. So we put the baby and the unknown mother aside until afternoon, when I expect you to come in and give me what you got. But starting now, I'm going to ask questions and you're going to give me answers. That was our deal. As for the other official business, starting now, we can do it here over coffee, or you can follow me to the station. Me, I prefer here."

"Here's good for me, too," I answered. "Believe it or not, you were going to be my first call this morning. Something happened last night, and I need help. You decide if you're going to make it official police business."

"My ears are open, pal, but my favor bank is closed."

"Fair enough. But I do have a question."

"No, you don't. My answer bank is closed, too."

"Have you heard anything lately about secret vigilante attacks?" I said. "Like a weird KKK thing?"

"What kind of smokescreen you throwing at me here?"

"Weird, like baptizing and branding weird?"

Jubil squinted at me. "Branding." It wasn't a question. He knew something. "You tell me what kind of branding."

My cell phone rang. I fumbled for it. The caller ID showed it was Kellie's cell.

"Don't answer it," Jubil said. "You tell me what kind of branding. We'll start from there and work backward."

I didn't answer the phone. My voice mail would pick it up.

"I've kept some tape that was used on me last night," I said. "I'm thinking maybe it will be a match to the tape used to keep Bingo's hands on the steering wheel."

"What?"

As calmly as I could, I described the events of the night before. I wanted this in Jubil's hands. The decision what to do. Anything to give me a sense of protection. My calmness was forced; all I could think of was the feeling of helpless terror as they pulled down the top of my pants. I now understood why the others who had been branded kept the violation to themselves. Shame. The fear of the men returning. The fear of the blindness and the drowning and the searing pain of being branded. Jubil let me finish without interrupting.

"We've got a lot more talking to do," he said. By then, most of the area had cleared of businesspeople. Only an older tourist couple remained, the husband reading a copy of *USA Today,* his wife talking as if he weren't.

"I'm ready," I said. "Is it you on one side and me on the other? You know, question and answer, here or at the station, which do I prefer, bad cop routine. Or you going to relax some?"

"I can go easier now. For now, you're a victim. Not a possible perp."

"Comforting," I said. "I feel I'm in good hands."

"The best." He swirled his cold coffee in his cup. "Alright. This branding. Yeah, word on the streets is that some of the blacks acquitted in local cases have been attacked. But no one will come forward, so we haven't been able to do anything about it. This might be a lead. I doubt they were dumb enough to register the room under a real name, but it will be worth a shot."

"I think the connection is with a church," I said. "One just outside of town. The Glory Church of the Lamb of Jesus. But it's not a church. It's a cult. The preacher spent some time in prison. Heard he was involved in gang wars inside."

"Interesting," Jubil said. "Got anything more?"

"I should have told you this before. That kid Bingo? He's the one that sent me out there."

"On what business?" Jubil was intense. "Don't dream of holding back now."

Angel was in the clear on the painting. So I told Jubil about it.

"Good," he said. "Some of it is making sense. Anything else?"

I shook my head. Retha and her boy were still my business. Despite the fact I had no idea where she was.

⁜

Retha was awake when the first crack of sunlight penetrated the window shades of her hospital room. The night before, a nurse had offered her painkillers. Retha had hidden the pills beneath her tongue and pretended to swallow, waiting until the nurse was gone before spitting them out. She wanted a clear head.

Twice during the night, desperate to see her son, Retha had forced her aching body out of bed. Twice she'd made it down the hallway without fainting. Twice she'd seen nurses, lost her courage, and returned to her room.

Billy Lee, a ward of the state?

Sure, when she had him brought to the hospital, she had chosen that as a possibility for him over death. But now that he was alive and she had made her decision to leave Junior and the Glory Church, she could not bear the thought of losing Billy Lee to a total stranger.

When Angel had returned with the news that Billy Lee

would be discharged from the hospital today, it had thrown Retha into a panic. She knew she couldn't pay for Billy Lee's medical expenses, and she certainly could not claim him as her son.

First of all, she'd have to prove she was his mother, and that might involve Junior. Retha definitely did not want Junior to find her or Billy Lee. Because then Shepherd Isaiah would know where they were and would send Elder Jeremiah after them. No, she was free of the Glory Church and intended to stay that way. Second, she was afraid nobody would understand why she had abandoned her baby. And third, she was pretty sure she might get in trouble with the law for it, which was why she'd put mud on the license plates of Junior's truck when she had first tried to bring Billy Lee to the hospital.

Since she couldn't openly claim Billy Lee now, Retha told herself as sunlight began to brighten her hospital room, that left only one option. She'd have to somehow take Billy Lee and escape with him before the state welfare authorities arrived at the hospital.

The straw of hope that Retha had clung to during her sleepless night was the promise that Angel had made. *"I'll help you lady,"* Angel had said when leaving the night before. *"Don't you worry. I stole plenty of things before. A baby should be no problem at all."*

Retha had begun to believe that Angel had forgotten about her promise to help with Billy Lee. It was eight-thirty when she popped into the hospital room.

"Hey," Angel said, grinning from ear to ear. "Sorry it took so long. Had some things to do. You ready?"

Angel set a large paper bag on the bed beside Retha. "Here's some clothes like you asked."

Angel drew the curtain around Retha's bed to let her change in privacy. A minute later, Retha swung her curtain open.

"Looks good," Angel said.

She'd brought sweatpants, a sweatshirt, and a big blonde wig, all taken from her mama's closet. The clothes stretched tight on Retha, and the wig was twisted. Angel motioned for Retha to kneel and straightened the wig.

Retha followed Angel through the door in silence. In the hallway, Retha saw a wheelchair.

"What do you think?" Angel asked. "Will it be good for a getaway?"

✛

Retha sat in the wheelchair. Angel pushed her down the hall of the children's wing. They'd made it down and back once and were about to begin their second trip. With all the bustle of interns and orderlies and nurses and parents, nobody gave them a second glance.

"Anytime now," Angel said. "Really, anytime now."

She was right.

Less than thirty seconds later, a high-pitched scream echoed from the nurse's counter. It drew two other nurses, who began screaming at the sight of cockroaches roiling through papers and out from under the computer keyboard.

"Let's go," Angel said. "We've got to make it fast without looking like we're in a hurry."

Retha nodded.

The screams continued.

Angel guided the wheelchair into a nearby room. Retha

nearly sobbed with joy at the sight of Billy Lee. She picked him up and cradled him.

"Baby, baby," Retha said. "I missed you so bad."

Angel tugged on the edge of Retha's sweatshirt.

"Later," Angel said. "We don't got time for that now."

Billy Lee gurgled.

Angel had a soother ready. She plunked it in Billy Lee's mouth as Retha pulled and placed Billy Lee onto her lap. Angel placed the blanket over Billy Lee.

"Bye, Maddie," Angel said to her sister in the other crib. "Don't worry. I'll be back later."

"Let's go," Angel told Retha. "Those cockroaches won't last forever."

✣

I found Kellie waiting in a booth at the Sweetwater Café at ten-thirty, just as she had promised in the voice mail she left during my conversation with Jubil.

"I didn't hear back from you, but I thought I'd take a chance," she said in sardonic greeting. "Glad you could make it."

"Just finished a meeting," I said. Jubil had grilled me exhaustively. "It was easier to come straight here than call ahead. I figured if I didn't find you here, I'd call."

I didn't add that I had used the time walking here from the Doubletree to call Amelia and postpone until afternoon the midmorning date I had with her at the South Carolina Aquarium. So tempting, just to leave all of this to soak up every possible minute with Amelia.

"You going to sit?" Kellie asked. "Or are you on your way somewhere else?"

I answered by lowering myself into the booth. Again, the searing pain.

"That's a look of constipation," she said.

"It isn't. Trust me."

"Never trust a client. Pop's advice."

"Good advice."

Kellie leaned forward. "So I've got good news and bad news and good news and bad news."

"No different than the rest of my day."

"That woman you wanted me to find. The daughter of Celia Harrison? Good news, I found her. Bad news, she lives in Germany. Married some army guy and they transferred there a few years back. Good news, I tracked her down by telephone and she didn't mind answering my questions. Bad news, it was about an hour-long call. Your expenses jumped some. Plus, because of the time difference, I had to call her about two in the morning. I'm billing you extra for keeping me up late."

"Sure."

"Agreeing implies you have a choice. You don't."

"Sure."

"Ditto." Kellie grinned.

I liked it. I thought of the complications with Amelia. That took some of the pleasure out of enjoying Kellie's smile.

"Celia Harrison's daughter remembers Timothy Larrabee and Agnes?" I asked.

"Want the written report?"

"I imagine you're looking for another free meal. Otherwise you wouldn't have asked to meet here. So order, then talk."

She did.

"Her name is Jasmine," Kellie said. "She was only about nine years old when all this happened, but she remembered it very clearly. And when she told me about it, I understood why. You will, too. I recorded the conversation for you."

Kellie pulled out a microcassette recorder. She clicked the play button and handed it to me.

I lifted it close to my ear and listened to a woman in Germany tell me about events that had happened decades earlier.

✛

"See, what happened was my mama had to bring me over one day, and me and Timmy started talking and playing. You know how kids do when they're too young to understand that income level and skin color are reasons for people to keep apart from each other.

"Except we didn't play all that much—I mean, there was nothing for kids to do around that big old house, and looking back, I feel sorry for how he had to grow up with that mean old lady—and his talk was always pretty serious for a kid his age.

"I can't remember exactly what it was he did that one day, but I teased him, saying if he didn't quit, I'd get Zora to lay a curse on him. He got real quiet and asked what did I mean, so I told him about the voodoo woman what lived in our neighborhood and that opened up a bunch of questions that he asked.

"I explained and after, he said he wanted her to lay a curse on someone, but I said she always needed to be paid, and I thought that was the end of it. 'Cept a couple days later, he gave me this dusty little painting and asked would I take it to Grammie Zora to pay for what he wanted her to do.

"I said sure, I wasn't scared of Grammie Zora. She was old then, but I knew she was only mean if you got on the wrong side of her. So about a day after that, I brung him over to her house and she took us inside in front of her voodoo altar and asked him what did he want.

"He said he wanted his own grandmother hexed. That surprised Grammie Zora and she said she didn't know if she could do that, and Timothy, well, he busted out crying, saying that his grandmother whipped him plenty and he hated her.

"Grammie Zora wouldn't budge though. Said it wasn't right to try to hex his grandmother, just because she was a little heavy with her punishment. That's when all his tears stopped and he grew real still and quiet.

"He said it was worse than that. 'Course, I was right there and listening to all of it with my eyes as wide as you can imagine. She asked him what it was that was worse, and he said he'd show her, right there. Then he looked at me and got real shy. He asked me to leave the room because he had to take off his shirt. So I went out into Grammie Zora's kitchen and a few minutes later, I heard her start into a heavy hex on old lady Agnes. To this day, I wonder what it was.

"And to this day, I don't like Timothy Larrabee much, no matter what was done to him. Because a week or two after, he said I needed to help him. He said I had to start a fire for him. I told him no, was he some kind of crazy. He said if I didn't help him, he'd tell his grandmother that it was me that stole the painting and once he did that, then my mama would lose her job and I'd go to jail.

"So what I did was go into the Aimslick's Hardware with him one morning and drop a lighted match on a pile of newspapers at the front. It started a fire alright, and there was hollering and old man Aimslick stamping on the papers with his feet to put the fire out, and a lot of smoke and confusion. When it was all done, there was Timothy Larrabee, standing out in front on the sidewalk, with a little smile on his face. He didn't tell me why he made me do it, and I didn't want to ask. I didn't have anything to do with that boy after that; you can be sure."

⁜

"Forty years ago," I said after clicking the recorder off. "That's the connection between Timothy Larrabee and Grammie Zora. He was ten. Grammie would have been in her forties then. And now, after all that time, in her eighties, she sends for him."

"Why?" Kellie asked.

"Crown of thorns," I said. "It's only a guess, but things keep coming back to that phrase. Except it's more than a phrase."

"You will explain, right?"

"I'll need three days of fees up front, and I don't get started until the retainer check clears."

"How about instead of a retainer, I don't apply any of my judo expertise to your stupidly grinning face."

"I will explain." I told Kellie about Grammie Zora giving Bingo that phrase to bring Larrabee back to her house. I told her how Glennifer and Elaine had passed on the information about the Larrabee family using it as a brand a century and a half earlier. And although I didn't want to tell her about the humiliation of the torture of the night before, I did have something else for her.

"I learned something interesting about Agnes Larrabee today," I continued. "Her name was mentioned in a letter written by her uncle, Seth Larrabee, to his fiancée, Elizabeth, in England."

I thought of the self-righteousness of the letter, part of a lengthy correspondence between the two. Seth was an older man, answering questions of a girl across the ocean, young enough to be his daughter and obviously marrying him to escape poverty in London. A portion of the letter reverberated in my mind.

> . . . *Elizabeth, regardless of what others might say about them, I have lived my life amongst them, and they are barely better than animals. It is the responsibility of the superior creature to introduce the inferior creature to the sacrament that will lead their souls to God. Because of it, our family maintains the tradition that the northerners tried to take from us. Some would call this tradition harsh, but it is a matter of practicality. The Bible speaks of slaves who must obey their masters. . . .*

"She kept all her letters, even after moving here to become his wife. When Elizabeth died, her son sent the entire collection to the archives, where I spent the first hour this morning after it opened."

"How exciting," Kellie joked. "The archives. Makes my head spin, thinking of the danger involved."

I ignored that. "Keep in mind that forty years ago when she was murdered, Agnes Larrabee was ninety years old. She was born only a few years after the Civil War ended. She was a young girl in the incident that Seth Larrabee describes for Elizabeth in England. While the ownership of slaves was illegal, there were many plantation owners alive who remembered how it was before the Civil War. Some of this generation still felt a moral right to treat their servants merely as slaves who received a daily stipend. It would appear the Larrabee family was no different, as related in the letter written by Agnes's uncle Seth."

"I remember those years well," Kellie said dryly. "I invested in a horsewhip manufacturing company while fools around me invested in some young whippersnapper named Ford and his newfangled contraptions."

"You're off by decades," I answered, "The first Model Ts didn't appear until 1908. By then Agnes was in her thirties."

"Oh," Kellie said.

"Impressed?"

"Very. What did you learn about Agnes?"

"I'll tell you, as long as you keep in mind I'm reading between the lines of the letter. But I imagine it happened like this back in 1877, a decade after the Civil War ended. . . ."

✣

The carriage doors were wide open, but the inside of the barn smelled of horses and human fear. Rain threatened, and the humidity pressed down like the darkness of the day outside.

Agnes stood on one side of her father. Her sister Mary stood on the other. They were seven years old, wearing dresses of starchy material and fanning themselves against the humid heat.

Their father, Ephraim Larrabee, wore his Sunday best and held a Bible open, facing a black man in rolled-up cotton pants. The black man's head was bowed, and he cradled a small child asleep in his arms. His son.

"There is no cause for this," the black man said. "My daddy

and granddaddy bear the mark, and so do I, but we were born into slavery. My boy was born free."

"You are welcome to seek employment elsewhere," Ephraim answered.

"You know I cain't, not in times like these."

"Then you have answered me. As a member of the Larrabee household, are you prepared to commit your son to the Lord God your maker?"

"Please, suh, not like this. Anything but this."

"Turn the child over."

"Suh! Please, no! He ain't no slave. Abe Lincoln saw to that."

"We are all slaves to sin. Be grateful that the Larrabee household is a godly household. The Larrabee mark commits his soul to Jesus, as it did for you and your father and grandfather."

"Suh! This child is no slave!"

"Dare you contradict me?"

"No suh."

"A disobedient servant of this household will be cast out into the world. Turn the child over."

The black man cried quietly as he woke his child. He was further humiliated by the presence of Mary and Agnes, who had been brought into the barn to learn that the power of the Larrabee family had not been diminished by the fall of the Confederacy. For the baptism was not about the baby boy's soul, but about power.

"Seth!" commanded Ephraim Larrabee.

Called forth from where he had been waiting by a stove with full fire, the uncle of Agnes and Mary advanced upon the black man and his child, carrying a slender iron rod heated to a glowing red.

"In the name of the Father and the Son and the Holy Spirit,"

Ephraim Larrabee droned, "so be this act of mercy carried out as a seal of consecration to the Lord God and his Son, Jesus Christ."

The rest of what Ephraim said was drowned out by the wailing of the little boy.

The boy had been branded. With a crown of thorns.

His name was Samson Elias.

C H A P T E R

22

Pastor Samuel was awake when I knocked on the door to his office.

"Good morning, Nicholas. Social or business?"

"I'd like to show you something," I said. "If there was any way of doing it modestly, I would. However . . ."

I unbuckled my pants and rolled the waist down several inches. I peeled back the tape that held gauze in place at the top of my buttock. I held my shirt up as I half turned and let Samuel see the results of what had happened the night before.

He made no comment.

I patted the gauze back in place, pressed the tape against my skin, tucked my shirt in, and rebuckled my pants.

"You've seen that before, haven't you?" I said. "A crown of thorns."

Samuel stood from his recliner and set his Bible on his desk. "That's a difficult question for me to answer."

"I know," I said. "Especially if the answer is yes. Because then you would be violating someone's confidence."

"Nick, I've already done my best to see if it was possible to discuss this matter with you, and the men involved were strongly opposed."

"Could you do this? I'm going to tell you what happened last night. I'll leave the office. Call this person and tell him what I've told you. See if that changes his mind. I just want to know if this is what happened to him."

"I'll call," Samuel answered. "But I can make no promises for what he will allow me to say."

✢

"We did it," Retha said. "We did it!"

Angel was pushing her in her wheelchair down the sidewalk on a street outside the hospital. The sunshine felt so good and Retha was so happy to be back with Billy Lee, she didn't notice her pain anymore.

"We sure did," Angel said. "The next thing we got to do is get you to that hotel down by the river." Angel pointed. Their destination was less than ten blocks away. "You can rest there and decide what you want to do next."

"I don't have much money," Retha said.

"I got some," Angel said. "I want to give it to you and Billy Lee as a present."

"You can't."

"I can. And I will. This guy Nick gave me a bunch to help out me and Maddie, and I guess I can give some of it to you. Should be enough to get you and Billy Lee bus tickets, too."

"Thank you, Jesus," Retha said. "Thank you." She frowned briefly. She'd meant it, thanking Jesus. She had not done it because Junior or anyone else in the church was forcing her to. She felt a lot of joy and it seemed natural to want to share it with Jesus. But that was a direct contradiction to how mad she was at him. Retha wasn't able to think much about it at that moment.

Billy Lee gurgled again, loud enough to be heard from under his blanket on Retha's lap. Retha picked him up and hugged him close, crooning his favorite lullaby.

In her joy in the sunshine, Retha didn't notice a vehicle follow slowly from the hospital parking lot, a new black Cadillac Escalade with smoked dark windows, a recent acquisition of the Glory Church of the Lamb of Jesus, driven at this moment by Elder Jeremiah.

✠

"He wasn't in, Nick," Samuel said, joining me barely a minute after I stepped into the cool and quiet dimness of the sanctuary of the church. "But I expect a call back very soon. I'll be able to hear the phone from here."

"Thank you, Samuel."

We stood only a few feet apart. Ahead, up on the wall behind the pulpit, was a wooden cross.

"Two thousand years," Samuel said, knowing where my focus was directed. "That's a lot of time for his message to become a tool of oppression."

"Oppression," I answered, "is a political term. It sounds strange, coming from you. Didn't Jesus avoid the politics of his day and address his efforts toward the heavenly kingdom?"

"Exactly. But the oppressors don't care. The Bible's like anything else good that God's given us. It can be misused tremendously. It wasn't that long ago that the oppressors used the Bible to argue for slavery. Our Western culture is based on a biblical interpretation to use the environment as we see fit. And plenty use the Bible to argue a woman's place in the world."

"It has given them great power," I agreed, "being able to argue that God is on their side."

"Wrong!" Samuel's voice was so sharp, I snapped my head to look at him. "The Bible gives them no power. They begin with power and use their interpretation of the Bible to enforce it. The powerless aren't in a position to do anything about the interpretation, for they aren't allowed to disagree. That comes with being powerless. Simple as that. It wasn't the slaves who ended slavery. But it wasn't the Bible that kept them as slaves."

His voice gentled. "This is something I've fought all my life, Nick. But it isn't a fight I can fight with the weapons of the oppressors. All I can do is follow the example of Jesus. He didn't call forth the crowds to overturn the corrupt religious establishment or the Roman occupation. No sir. Jesus was always concerned with what we should do to take our place in the heavenly kingdom. Looking back, he had the right priority, for what he preached is still with us, long after the Romans and the corrupt religious establishment he fought have gone. It was simple folks believing and living according to that belief that changed things."

I gestured at my back. "You're telling me I shouldn't stop the men who did this?"

"I'm telling you that stopping them and a hundred like them isn't going to do much good if your own heart isn't right. You can spend your whole life fighting for Jesus, Nick, but in the end it's going to be the love in your life that matters. Read 1 Corinthians chapter 13."

The phone rang from his office.

"Think about your life, Nick. You've taken from God by accepting a faith in his love. But what are you giving of yourself? To anyone?"

Samuel patted me on the shoulder and shuffled toward the ringing of his phone.

✛

From behind bushes that screened the view of his car from Retha and Angel and Billy Lee, Elder Jeremiah accelerated out of an alley and jammed the brakes to stop on the sidewalk, blocking the forward progress of Retha's wheelchair. The bumper of the Escalade narrowly missed the wheelchair as it settled on its springs. Elder Jeremiah was out of the car and in front of the wheelchair before Retha or Angel could react.

With his black suit, pale skin, dark beard and dark hair, he was a tall specter suddenly appeared in sunshine. Retha stared at him in horror, Angel with a clutch of cold fear. Angel told herself the giant had never seen her before. That she knew him but he didn't know her.

Elder Jeremiah took advantage of their temporary paralysis. He scooped Billy Lee from Retha's hands. "You want this baby," he said in a low voice, "you're gonna have to get in the truck and stay with him."

He spun around, taking Billy Lee with him. He vaulted back into the truck behind the steering wheel, then lowered the front passenger window directly in front of the wheelchair.

"Back door's open," he said, leaning across Billy Lee where he'd set him down on the new leather of the front seat. "You've got five seconds to get in or I'm gone with your baby."

"I got to go," Retha said to Angel. "I got to go. I can't leave Billy Lee." She struggled out of her wheelchair.

"Not without me," Angel said. She jumped into the backseat with Retha. Much as she feared the man, Retha and Billy Lee needed help. In her backpack, she had the stun gun. She'd use it when she could.

"Who's this?" Elder Jeremiah demanded as he gunned the Cadillac into a traffic opening. He had tilted his rearview mirror to keep an eye on the two in the backseat.

"Grace Louise," Angel said. She sat on the passenger side, with Retha directly behind Elder Jeremiah. "I'm Retha's friend. You better stop and let us out."

"I'm letting you out at the next light," Elder Jeremiah answered. "This business is none of yours."

"Good," Angel said. "It will give me a chance to scream for police. Plus, I'll have a chance to get your license plate. So maybe you oughta let Retha and the baby go with me."

"Changed my mind." Elder Jeremiah hit the electric locks and engaged the child safety button to prevent them from disengaging the locks. "It's why I got the baby in the front and you in the back. So's you won't try nothing foolish. Including jumping out at the next light."

Retha hadn't said a word. She was just staring down at her lap in total defeat.

"Tracking you was as easy as shining deer," Elder Jeremiah continued. He rarely spoke in the presence of his older brother, content to let him do the talking. So away from him, he talked freely, as if to make up for his voluntary muteness around Shepherd Isaiah. "The fool you gave Billy Lee to called the house looking for you. Elder Mason took his number, and Shepherd Isaiah put a private detective after him, so it didn't take long to put all of this together. Imagine our surprise when we found out that the fool had taken a baby to the hospital. Shepherd Isaiah sent me there to wander around like I had official preacher business and sure enough, there was Billy Lee. I knew you'd get there sooner or later."

They were off Calhoun Street and onto the bridge over the Ashley, heading away from Charleston, retracing the route that Retha had walked in agony two nights earlier.

"All I had to do was wait and watch. Thought you was smart stealing him away, didn't you? Well, it didn't work. I'm bringing you back home to Junior where you belong."

"Mister, if she don't want to go, this is kidnapping," Angel said in the absence of a protest by Retha. She didn't dare use the stun gun while the man was driving. "And I'm her witness. So stop this car and let us out."

"Kidnapping? It's the will of the Lord Jesus that a wife belongs to her husband and the church. She's a lost sheep and I'm taking her back to the flock."

"Retha?" Angel asked, an edge of uncertainty in her voice. "Say something here. Retha?"

✣

"I've got your answers," Samuel said.

He'd found me in the sanctuary, staring at the front of the church, thinking about what he'd said to me.

"He won't let me share his name, but he said it was okay for me to tell you it happened in the same way."

"Thank you," I said. "That's all I needed to know. That it was the same people behind the branding. Someday I hope you'll be able to tell your friend the police have the men who did this. Then he can step forward as a witness and make sure those men are punished."

"Whoever they are, Nick," Samuel said, "stop them. You have the power to do that. Just like it was men and women with power who stopped the oppressors who used God's Word to inflict slavery upon the powerless. But that's the earthly kingdom. Remember to find your place in the heavenly kingdom, too."

✛

I rang the buzzer at the address that Jubil had decided in the end to give me. The house was only four blocks from where Angel lived, no different in weather-beaten boarding and sagging doorframes from the houses on each side.

What was different, however, was a security setup that would rival any half-million-dollar home. I noticed a small video camera with its unblinking round eye focused on the steps that led up to the door. Bold decals proclaimed the eternal vigilance of a local security company. And after about a minute's delay, I heard the sliding of one bolt, then another, then another and another. Finally, the door swung open.

The black man peering downward at me might have been anywhere from his late teens to early thirties. His storklike skinniness matched an angular face that was hidden by dark glasses and a nylon ball cap, with the tight curls of his hair elevating the cap well off his skull so that it seemed to float above his head.

"Guthrie Klingman?" I said.

"Don't bother—" he waved away my handshake—"I don't do social contracts."

"I'm–"

"Nicholas Barrett," he said. Not coldly, but with no smile either. I nodded, surprised he knew.

He read my face correctly.

"If I didn't know your face," he said, "the door would still be closed." He looked both directions, blinking at the light of day. "And I don't talk with the door open either." He pointed inside.

I stepped past him. Behind me, he slid all the bolts back into place.

The windows had been covered on the inside with tinfoil— a poor man's drapery, but very effective for privacy. The front room was dim and smelled of stale cigarettes and cat urine. I understood the source when I noticed a thin Siamese scratching sand in a litter box at the end of the hallway. It darted away, and I saw dozens of cigarette butts in the sand, as if thrown there from the nearby working bench.

The front room had no social amenities at all. Computer monitors and torn-down hard drives were stacked haphazardly. Wires and circuit boards littered a low table in the center. The workbench itself held the skeleton of another computer, its pieces scattered. A half-empty bottle of Mountain Dew stood guard. Other empty bottles littered the floor at his feet.

"Talk," he said. He moved past me and immediately began piecing together the computer.

I was fascinated at the deftness of his thin fingers.

"Talk," he repeated. "I multitask."

"How'd you know who I was?"

"Angel. She's my friend. When she told me about you, did a little prowling. At the door, I matched your face to the one I've seen on your different files. Let me tell you, man, you look third-world on your driver's license. Even I'd be ashamed of something that bad, and look at me."

"Prowling."

"Through the Internet." His fingers kept moving. His words were as rapid as the movement of his fingers. "Don't make me repeat myself. Get on with why you're here. I hate wasting time."

He wanted direct. I could do direct. "Tell me why for the last few months all of Zora's social security checks have gone through your account."

He looked at me, grinning. Swigged on his Mountain Dew. Wiped it away with the back of his hand. "Someone else did some prowling, huh? Old world or new world?"

My face was as blank as I felt.

"Traced the checks backward from the source? Or hacked into the bank records?"

"So you don't deny it." I had no idea how Jubil had learned this.

"Not at all. I'm only telling you this because Angel says she likes you. Angel comes in for computer stuff from me. She gives me the checks. I give her the change in cash. And sometimes I owe her more than the check. She does a little work for me and I pay her fair. Let me tell you, she's a genius with computers. Hardware and software. Not many are intuitive with both. Her? She was maybe eight years old when Grammie Zora sent her to me for her first computer lesson. From day one, that girl knew what she was doing."

"Grammie Zora? Knew what she was doing when she made sure Angel was computer literate?"

His nostrils flared. "Angel, fool. Angel knew what she was doing. Nobody calls Grammie Zora a girl. Let me tell you. You don't want to mess with Grammie. That's why I cash those checks like Angel asks. And I don't ask no other questions. Grammie Zora, she—"

He paused, and for the first time, weighed his words carefully enough so that the pace slowed. "Her spell put a man in the ground. That's what all of us know. And that's why she's gone for a spell. I just want you to know that she could do the same to you."

"For asking about the social security checks."

"No, fool. If you do anything to hurt Angel. And if Grammie Zora don't mess you enough, then I will."

He swigged his Mountain Dew again. "See, all I need to do is go prowling again. Be the virtual virtuoso that I am. You lose your fine credit rating. Maybe even acquire a criminal record. Or better yet, I just make sure the government thinks you're dead. Be years for you to straighten that out. 'Course, I wouldn't ever do that to a friend of Angel's. So as long as she's happy with you, I'm happy with you. That girl, she's like a little sister to me, and I don't want to see her hurt."

"Good," I said. "Then I'm sure you never smoke when she's in here working on computers for you."

"Man . . ."

I'd hit him where it hurt. Like he'd never thought of it until now. "Secondhand smoke," I said. "Look it up online. It's a killer."

✛

Elder Mason waved Elder Jeremiah through the gates, and Elder Jeremiah parked in front of the Glory Church of the Lamb of Jesus and turned the radio music down.

"I thought you was taking me to Junior," Retha said. Until this point, she had not spoken for the half hour it took to drive from Charleston.

Part of the reason for her silence was her sense of total defeat. The other part was the fact that she wouldn't have been heard anyway. After a few minutes of trying to get Angel to end her insistent requests to turn around, Elder Jeremiah had resorted to drowning out Angel by listening to southern gospel at top volume, which had woken Billy Lee and set him to wailing. But in Elder Jeremiah's opinion, the music and the wailing had been better than much more of Angel's persistent arguing.

"I'm bringing Junior to you. Now step out of the car, and I'll give you your baby."

Elder Jeremiah disengaged the child lock and unlocked the back doors with a push of an electric switch. He loved driving Shepherd Isaiah's new Escalade with all its conveniences. Neither of them had ever owned a car newer than fifteen years old, not until the wealth delivered to them by the growing financial strength of the Glory Church of the Lamb of Jesus.

Angel pushed open the door on her side and stepped out of the air-conditioning into the humid heat of midday, wondering if she should have stayed in the truck and tried jabbing him with her stun gun now that the big man had parked. But Retha had chosen to go out Angel's door, directly behind Angel, blocking any chance for her to reach back in.

As soon as Retha shut the door, Elder Jeremiah, still behind the steering wheel, hit the electric locks again. He lowered the front window of the passenger side just enough to be heard.

"You ain't getting Billy Lee," he said, grinning with the triumph of a man who had thought through every action. "I just told you that to get you out of the car. No, I'll hang on to him. That way I know you'll be here for Shepherd Isaiah."

Billy Lee was crying loudly.

"No," Retha cried. "He's hungry. He needs me."

"Get yourself up into the projector room. You just wait there till tonight when I've assembled the flock for a Glory Session of the Holy Rod of Chastisement. Repent and you'll get your boy back."

He grinned, his big teeth gleaming from his beard. "By the way, in case you was thinking of trying to climb the fence and walk far enough down the road to find a phone and call the police, you might want to reconsider. Unless you want to explain to them how it was you abandoned a baby at the hospital in the first place, then stole it away without paying the hospital bills."

He waved at Retha by wiggling his fingertips. Then Elder Jeremiah slid the window up, cutting off Billy Lee's wails to the outside world.

✠

The projector room was in the upper loft of the church, overlooking the pews below. It was barely larger than a bedroom. Here, one of the women used a slide projector so that the words to the hymns could be put on the wall of the church during Sunday services.

Retha, nineteen and still carrying the chubbiness of adolescence, was much bigger than Angel. Yet it was Angel who stretched an arm around Retha's broad back, trying to comfort her.

"They left me my backpack," Angel said. She hadn't seen a good chance yet to use her stun gun hidden inside. "I got a cell phone. I can call for the police."

"No!" Retha lurched forward. "Then Billy Lee will just vanish. You don't know these people. He's getting better now. That's what matters. All I have to do is face the Holy Rod of Chastisement, and everything will be alright."

"The Holy Rod of Chaz . . . Chaz . . . ?" Angel asked.

"Chastisement. Shepherd Isaiah says it's the will of Jesus for sinners to be punished in public. Shepherd Isaiah does it on behalf of Jesus. Frankie Stafford caught his wife kissing a plumber who came to replace their toilet, and he brought her up in front of the church. And Dollie Mae Robins was seen stepping out of a bar by one of the elders. Stuff like that."

"How bad is it?"

Retha had her head in her hands. "What happens is that Shepherd Isaiah prays over you and asks if you're sorry. And the whole church sings hymns. When they're worked up and you're ready to repent, up at the pulpit in front of everybody, Elder Jeremiah whacks you a bunch of times across the backside with a Holy Rod."

"Spanked in front of a bunch of people? You told me you were going to find a way to pay the hospital, even if you had to be a waitress for a hundred years. You ain't done nothing wrong, trying to help Billy Lee."

"Nothing wrong except for disobeying the will of Jesus."

Retha lifted her head. In the shade the yellowed bruises of her face were invisible. She showed her first moments of life since Elder Jeremiah had stopped her in her wheelchair. "Still, I ain't sorry."

"You telling me that Jesus wanted Billy Lee to die?" Angel asked. "That Jesus wanted Junior to whip on you for trying to save Billy Lee?"

"Don't ask me nothing about Jesus," Retha answered. "I'm done thinking on him."

"I'm just getting started," Angel said. She watched swallows dip and swoop in the open air of the clearing. "Mainly because I'm confused."

"Ain't nothing to be confused about," Retha said mournfully. "All I ever got from church is grief."

"Nick and me—this guy I know—he took me for a walk the other day so I asked him about this stuff. What Nick told me was that a person shouldn't get the church and Jesus mixed up," Angel said. " 'Cause sometimes they're two different things. I asked him about it, before him and me had a falling-out."

Retha straightened. She turned to face Angel, whose hand slid off her back.

"Nick told me all I got to do is believe that God made this world and all of us. Said some people get hung up on how God made the world when maybe all we got to do is wonder why. Said if I can believe that God made this world, then all I got to believe is that God wants me to come home to him after I die, which is why God sent Jesus, and all I got to do is believe Jesus came from God and follow what Jesus told us when he was here. So I said to Nick 'what's that?' And Nick told me it was to try to love God as best I could and try to show that love to other people. I told Nick there had to be more to it than that, and he said other people keep trying to build rules around it, but no, Jesus spent his time fighting against people who made too many rules, and no, there weren't much more to it than that. He said love is a special thing, and of all that's in the world, love's the one thing that points us to God."

Angel patted Retha's knee. "I got to tell you, I felt a lot better after Nick explained it that way. I asked him to pray for me, and that was nice, too." Her voice lost some of its confidence. "Makes me sad it turned out him and me ain't gonna be friends."

"Maybe it's nice for you to think about Jesus," Retha said. "But you don't got to face a Glory Session of the Holy Rod of Chastisement to get your baby back."

23

I heard the ring of my cell phone all too clearly above the clattering of feet over wood planks.

"Don't answer it," Amelia said.

She stood beside me at the edge of the pier overlooking the Cooper River. To our left was the entrance to the South Carolina Aquarium. To our right came the clattering, from the steps that led to the ferry that took tourists out to Fort Sumter. Storm clouds were building high over the Atlantic, and the first colder air coming in from the ocean had begun to nip at our faces.

"It could be Jubil," I said. "He might know something about the missing baby."

Twenty minutes earlier he'd called, angry. Wanted to know what kind of stunt I was pulling, yanking the baby out of the hospital as his deadline for me had approached. It had taken a lot of talking to convince him I wasn't the guilty one.

"Just one afternoon. We haven't had any time just to ourselves."

She put her hand lightly on my arm. "If it's Jubil, there's nothing you can do that the police aren't already doing."

I had the cell phone in my hand. "And if there's nothing I can do, it won't hurt to answer and hear any news."

She turned away from me to stare, arms crossed, at the water.

I put the phone to my ear.

"Nick?" Static broke the incoming voice, but I still recognized it as Angel's. "Can you come get me? I need your help. Bad."

"Where are you?"

"At the Glory Church of the Lamb of Jesus. The preacher guy has us up in a room."

"Us?"

"Me and Billy Lee's mother."

"I'll bring police," I said.

"No! They took Billy Lee somewhere. If the police come, Retha might never see him again. But I got a plan. It don't need police. Just go to my place and load up all my computer stuff. Remember how you met Camellia once? She's got a key. She can let you in. Then bring my computer stuff here and drive around the back of the church. I'll be waiting there. Okay?"

A plan? What kind? To do what?

"Angel . . ." I said.

The connection broke. I doubted it was bad reception. My guess was that Angel had ended it, giving me no chance to argue.

"Amelia." I took her hands in mine. "You know I want to spend all day with you. But this little girl. It sounds like she needs help."

"Sure, Nick." Her smile was hesitant.

"Ride with me?" I asked. I did want as much time with Amelia as possible.

"No." She gave me a peck on the cheek to soften her rejection of my offer. "There's a few other things I need to do while I'm in town. Call me on my cell when you get back."

So I went.

Alone.

✠

The gates to the compound were closed. Immediately on the other side, a lean and weathered older man in snakeskin cowboy boots, jeans, a denim shirt, and a John Deere cap, sat smoking a cigarette on the hood of a late-model Ford truck. Minus his graying beard, he could have been the Marlboro Man. His truck was the only vehicle in the church parking lot. Beyond the church were the mobile homes of the compound. I noted again how unusual it was that there were so few trucks or cars parked near them.

Marlboro Man stepped onto the ground.

"Hey!" He moved to the gate, the heels of his cowboy boots crunching on the rocks. He left his cigarette at the side of his mouth, perched lightly on his bottom lip. The set of his face showed permanent mean.

"Hey!" He didn't like the fact I hadn't responded.

I left the Jeep's engine running but moved out into the heat. There was a calmness to the air. The storm was almost upon us.

"Didn't know churches needed security guards," I said.

"What's your business here." Not a question. A demand.

To get inside the church, I thought. *To search for Angel.* But

I used the only plausible excuse I had. "I want to see Timothy Larrabee."

"He expecting you?"

"Tell him it's Nick Barrett."

He grinned at me. Had he been among those last night? I told myself nothing would happen here in daylight. I told myself that Timothy Larrabee wanted the painting, and that would be enough leverage to get me out of trouble if it happened here.

Marlboro Man inhaled deeply from his cigarette and flicked it through the wires of the gate at my feet. He pulled out a cell phone, dialed a number. "Got someone here named Nick Barrett."

He listened. Then snapped his cell phone shut. "Five minutes," he said. He retreated to the hood of his truck and sat on it again, staring at me like a bird of prey.

A few minutes later, a golf cart rolled out from behind one of the mobile homes, with Shepherd Isaiah at the wheel.

Only then did Marlboro Man unlock the gate.

✛

"I trust you're the one who sent out the cops." Shepherd Isaiah wasted no time on small talk. He sat at a desk, a bearded giant beside him, the same one who had stood behind him at the end of the church service. Jeremiah Sullivan, of course, the one mentioned in the article. The younger brother he'd protected throughout boyhood. Now it looked like Jeremiah was returning the favor.

"They found a kid dead," I answered. "A kid who had sent me to you. I told them about that. I didn't tell them what to do with that information." I paused. "But I also told them about the crown of thorns. That makes it much more than a coincidence. I'm sure that's why they decided to visit."

I watched his face as I continued to speak. "It's more than coincidence, isn't it?" My fear remained. But anger was its twin. "Isn't it?" I repeated. Sharply. "And I know I'm not the only one."

"The only one what?"

"I know you know what I mean." The pain of the burn on my lower back was a constant reminder of the actions the night before.

"I fail to understand the purpose of your visit. To look for what the police found? Which was nothing."

I took a half step toward Isaiah. The bearded giant beside him leaned in my direction. It was enough to stop me from approaching closer. But not enough to stop me from talking. "They'll put it together soon enough."

"You came here to tell me that?"

"No, I came here because of a painting. I'd like to speak to Timothy Larrabee about it."

"He's not here. You've wasted your time."

I'd come here to help Angel. Not expecting to meet with Shepherd Isaiah. But while waiting in my Jeep at the gates of the compound, a wildly melodramatic and amateurish notion had occurred to me. I would bait Shepherd Isaiah into admitting something incriminating enough to help Jubil's investigation. As Isaiah spoke, I would hit the send button on the cell phone hidden in my pants pocket. I'd programmed it to dial Jubil's cell. If he were there, he would pick up. If not, his voice mail would get our conversation.

I kept my hands in my pockets, where they'd been since I'd

stepped into his church office. "How much do you know about Nathan Bedford Forrest?"

Isaiah smiled, an even smile that, along with the darkness of his heavy beard, easily hid his thoughts. "Enough."

"He founded an organization," I said. "For political purposes. Helped him get elected. Then the organization got away on him. It became a white supremacist group called the KKK."

"I still see no point to your visit."

"Some people would call your church a cult. If you're not behind the branding, then your church is getting away on you, too."

"As you may recall from our first conversation, I told you that few are willing to pay the price of truly following the Lord Jesus."

"And that includes branding and torturing?"

"I find that remark offensive." Isaiah smiled at Jeremiah. "Brother, please take this man away."

✜

I did get a chance to use my cell phone. But not in the way I had hoped.

It rang just as I settled behind the steering wheel of my Jeep.

"Nicholas. I'm calling you because I'm too cowardly to talk about this in person."

"Hello, Amelia."

"I think I'm leaving early. Tonight. Back to Chicago."

"Amelia . . ."

"I wasn't totally honest with you. I came down because I wanted to see if you and I had what it takes. There's . . ." She hesitated. ". . . there's someone else. He finds me interesting. I haven't done anything with him, but I'm interested, too. He's a doctor."

"Wears the right clothing? Drives the right car?"

"Don't be like that, Nick."

"Amelia . . ." Why couldn't I say anything else?

"My flight leaves at eight o'clock. In a way, I hope you'll be there to stop me. Otherwise . . ."

She hung up.

I set my cell phone on the passenger seat. I wondered how to feel. Without giving it much conscious thought, I reached below me for the keys that I'd hidden under my floor mat.

Still thinking about Amelia, I fished for the keys, coming up empty.

Footsteps approached.

I turned my head. Jeremiah Sullivan held my keys, dangling them from his fingers. "Don't learn too good, do you?" he said. "Baptism and fire wasn't enough. Too bad for you that you're so dumb."

I reached for my cell with my right hand. It was still programmed to dial Jubil's cell.

"No sir," said another voice, from the opposite side of the Jeep. I turned my head to see the Marlboro Man, and the muzzle of a shotgun he propped through my passenger window in my direction. "Hand me that phone. Now."

CHAPTER

24

The sanctuary of the church was so dark that when Jeremiah
Sullivan propelled me forward from a side corridor into the choir
loft at the side of the pulpit, I had little hope that any of the
congregation would notice that my hands were behind my back
or that my mouth was covered with a strip of adhesive.

When he had seated me, he leaned forward and taped my
ankles again.

Briefly, he stood beside me and stared down on the congregation. Dim as it was, I saw Angel and Retha in the front row.
Retha's head was bowed in resignation. Angel sat, arms crossed,
with an almost Buddha-like air of patience. Obviously, they, like
me, had been brought to their places for the great ceremony that
was about to begin.

Jeremiah checked my wrists to make sure I had not somehow loosened the tape. Satisfied that I would be a helpless

observer, he patted my shoulder as if I were his son attending a church service.

"Shepherd Isaiah don't know you're here," he said in a low voice in my ear. "I'm giving you the chance to listen. Listen and repent. That way you'll meet Jesus on the other side."

Then he leaned back and watched his brother begin to speak to the assembled people of the Glory Church of the Lamb of Jesus.

⁜

In the black of night outside the church, the first of the storm hit as a wall of rain that pounded the roof. Lightning appeared in jagged bursts through the small windows, along with the rumble of thunder.

For Shepherd Isaiah, it was a perfect setting for a Glory Session of the Holy Rod of Chastisement.

"We beseech thee! We beseech thee! We beseech thee!" he began from the pulpit. "We call upon thee and thy Holy Spirit to come among us here. . . ."

More bursts of lightning and more deep vibrations of thunder. Shepherd Isaiah hid his satisfaction. The church's sound system had been expensive but well worth it. He wore a lapel microphone that let him walk freely as he spoke. Tonight, with the speakers cranked because of his anticipation of the storm, his voice would easily outweigh the might of the storm, giving his flock the comfort that they could trust his power.

"We beseech thee! We beseech thee! We beseech thee!"

Shepherd Isaiah had perfected his rhythm and cadence, was so familiar with what it took to build excitement among the flock that half the time he didn't bother to put full concentration into what he said from the pulpit. This detachment normally gave him the opportunity to scan the flock as he spoke, allowed him to mark which of his followers needed special attention or future discipline.

"We beseech thee! We beseech thee! We beseech thee! Look kindly upon us, for we are the true followers who obey all thy commands. Cursed be those who bring false teachings to the sheep. Blessed be those who rely only on thy goodness and glory and truth for all their needs. Blessed be those who let thy will be done."

This service was not a sunlit Sunday. Tonight was a special meeting. To set the mood, the church was dark, lit only by candles. Whatever the disadvantage of his reduced vision of the flock, it was amply made up by atmosphere. If Shepherd Isaiah knew anything, it was how to put on a good show. He'd situated the candles so that the pulpit was bathed in the flickering lights, so that his own tall white figure seemed to glow, so that every movement of his hands cast giant shadows of radiating power on the wall behind him. Below, on the steps, where Elder Jeremiah would administer the Holy Rod of Chastisement, it was dark, the darkness that the sinners of his flock deserved.

"We beseech thee! We beseech thee! We beseech thee!" Shepherd Isaiah raised his hands high, knowing the shadows of his arms would appear like angel wings on the wall behind him. He listened hard, trying to gauge the fervor of his followers. "We beseech thee! We beseech thee! We beseech thee! This woman's sins are great! Her need for forgiveness greater!"

Shepherd Isaiah didn't need to bore his flock by reciting Retha's sins of defiance. They all knew through gossip. And the wonderful thing about gossip was how much it distorted things. Shepherd Isaiah had no urge to dispel the wildest of the rumors.

"We beseech thee! We beseech thee! We beseech thee!"

Tonight, for this special assembly, the church was so full that people stood in the aisles at the center and sides. Already the body heat and smell of humid sweat mixed with the aroma of melting wax, filling the church with a primal charge of anticipation. As his followers chanted in unison with Shepherd Isaiah, the echoes rolled and rolled like God's own thunderous voice.

"We beseech thee, Juh-hee!-ze-huss! Forgive this woman for the sins that have placed her at the gates of hell. Where the flames lick and the smell of brimstone scorches the air! Where the groans of sinners cry out to thee for eternity! We beseech thee! We beseech thee! We beseech thee!"

On the heels of his loud cries of damnation, a bolt of lightning struck so close to the church that the report of thunder was an instantaneous crack of exploding cannon fire. In that instant, the entire sanctuary lit up, showing his flock frozen in positions of swaying ecstasy.

"We beseech thee! We beseech thee! We beseech thee!" Shepherd Isaiah took immediate advantage of the added sound effects. "We beseech thee! We beseech thee! We beseech thee!"

Unlike with the sins of the other Glory Sessions, Shepherd Isaiah had a personal stake in the punishment of Retha Herndon. He'd already heard plenty of whispers and blasphemous laughter about the Glory Session of Healing over a doll. Worse, word had gotten out quickly how Retha had run out of the church. It was necessary for the rest of the flock to see—and enjoy—the consequences of that defiance. *Yes sir,* Shepherd Isaiah told himself, *a leader has to be as infallible as Jesus himself.*

"We beseech thee, Juh-hee!-ze-huss! Forgive this woman for the sins that have placed her at the gates of hell." Repetition, Shepherd Isaiah knew, was one of the keys of building and cresting and rebuilding the flocks fervor. "Where the flames lick and the smell of brimstone scorches the air! Where the groans of sinners cry out to thee for eternity! We beseech thee! We beseech thee! We beseech thee!"

Lightning flickered and filled the church with eerie light, thunder hard on its heels, as if the storm had settled above the church, as if God were visiting to help place special punishment. *Oh glory, glory,* Shepherd Isaiah thought, *tonight is going to be special.*

"We beseech thee! We beseech thee! We beseech thee!" He listened hard for what he needed to hear, and finally it came.

"Good Shepherd! Good Shepherd! Lay on the rod!"

Good Shepherd. The crowd was his. And much more quickly than usual.

"Flee, you demons of hell! Flee, you spawn of the devil. Flee from the holy might!" Shepherd Isaiah glanced down at the front row. There were the Elders of the Chosen on both sides, and centered in front of him were Junior and Retha, along with that brat of a girl who had made such a scene when Shepherd Isaiah tried moving her that finally he'd given up and left her there. "We beseech thee! We beseech thee! We beseech thee!"

The flock roared and chanted and swayed and swooned. Lightning strobed the congregation every thirty seconds, thunder drumrolled in tempo with the chanting and shouting. Heat and the smell of frenzied bodies filled more and more of the church.

"We beseech thee! We beseech thee! We beseech thee!"

Shepherd Isaiah wiped the sweat from his face. In front of
him, behind the pulpit was the paddle that he would use as the
Holy Rod of Chastisement. Tonight he would not delegate the
task to Elder Jeremiah. Tonight Shepherd Isaiah intended to take
personal satisfaction to dispel the wrath of God. He stepped to
the side of his pulpit, took the paddle in his right hand, and raised
his arms again. In an instant, every voice in the church stilled.
The silence was eerie, powerful, pregnant. Bathed in the glow
of candles, arms high and almost as white as his robe, Shepherd
Isaiah truly did appear like an avenging angel sent down from on
high with a sword of retribution.

"Bring forth the sinner!" he shouted.

✣

Hours before the service, the Marlboro Man had taken away my
cell phone and marched me into a room at the back of church at
the end of a shotgun. There, Elder Jeremiah had taped my wrists
behind my back, then placed a piece of wide adhesive over my
mouth.

"It was me that drowned the kid in the car," he said. "He
was the only one that knew Grammie Zora had sent for Brother
Larrabee. I sent him back to the girl's house to look for something Brother Larrabee needed. When he couldn't help me
anymore, I gave him a chance to commit his soul to Jesus, and
then I killed him to protect Shepherd Isaiah."

I sucked air through my nostrils hard, as if Elder Jeremiah
were about to drown me, too. If he was telling me this, he wasn't
going to let me leave the church. Ever.

He caressed my face as he spoke to me; it was an eerie

sensation of gentleness coming from such a giant of a man. Especially with the words that came with that caress. "You'll die, too. I promise you that. I will do anything to protect my brother. It's too bad the police know that Bingo brought us to Grammie Zora, but she's not going to talk about it. And neither will you. But first, you'll have a chance to save your soul. Tonight, at the Holy Chastisement, you can learn from the Good Shepherd. Commit your soul to Jesus on your last night on earth."

That's all he said.

He wrapped my ankles, lifted me in his massive arms as if I were a child, and carried me to a small room postered with sheets colored by crayons. A Sunday school room. Then Jeremiah gently laid me on my side, walked out of the room, and left me there to stare at the children's drawings and think about Jesus in the hours before the Holy Chastisement and my execution to follow.

⊹

Another flash of lightning outlined Shepherd Isaiah in his glory. The rain had quieted, and because of it, the thunder boomed more, shaking the church as if God now held it in the palm of his hand.

"Bring forth the sinner!" he repeated. *A man's a fool,* Shepherd Isaiah thought, *to waste a good bolt of lightning.*

Earlier, Shepherd Isaiah had coached two Elders of the Chosen to bring her forward from the front pew at this moment, one on each side to ensure she would not speak as he rebuked her. Her sin was so great, he had explained, that Retha was not to be given the chance to repent but would have to endure her punishment in silence. The truth, which Shepherd Isaiah did not want known, was that he feared what she might say in front of the flock if given the chance. So another elder held the boy, Billy Lee, as hostage to ensure her silence.

Shepherd Isaiah had wondered about the girl who insisted on staying near Retha and decided the brat could witness his wrath, too. Two other elders had been placed on the front pew in case the brat girl tried shouting out. They were instructed to drag her away at the first sign of rebellion. This, Shepherd Isaiah had decided, was the best alternative.

"We shall close the gates of hell," Shepherd Isaiah shouted. "The sinner will not be spared the Holy Rod, and in so doing, she shall be spared an eternity of burning brimstone!"

"Amen!" an enthusiastic follower shouted.

Shepherd Isaiah slowly turned his head toward the source of the noise and stared. This was his show, not to be disturbed unless he wanted it disturbed.

"We beseech thee," Shepherd Isaiah finally said softly, so the flock would remain silent. No further amens burst forth. They had understood his look of stern anger. "Juh-hee!-ze-huss! We beseech thee."

Shepherd Isaiah slowly moved down the steps of the pulpit area. The elders held Retha's arms and guided her forward. Shepherd Isaiah wasn't worried about Retha resisting punishment. Not with her baby held hostage.

"We beseech thee! We beseech thee! We beseech thee!"

Candlelight and more bolts of lightning illuminated Retha clearly as she knelt on one of the steps.

With gravity, Shepherd Isaiah beckoned Junior forward to hold his wife in submission. No need to hurry this. Everyone had been waiting for this moment, and it was good showmanship to drag out the suspense as long as possible. And, with luck, another—

Lightning struck outside. The rain had completely stopped. A boom of thunder hit, then complete silence.

His face now hidden in shadow with the candlelight behind him, Shepherd Isaiah moved toward Junior.

Lightning again, then another rumble of thunder. Candles flickered as if a spirit were moving through the church.

Shepherd Isaiah waited for Junior to position his disobedient wife for punishment. Shepherd Isaiah stood poised to bring the paddle down and punish the woman for disobeying the will of the husband.

As one person, the entire crowd drew in breath.

"We beseech thee! We beseech thee! We beseech thee!" Shepherd Isaiah roared. "In his most Holy Name, I command you to follow his will! We will not spare the Holy Rod of Chastisement."

A crack of lightning flashed so bright that the crowd gasped; then thunder drowned out their awe.

Junior had not made an effort to ready his wife.

"I will strike her!" Shepherd Isaiah commanded. "Strike her in the name of Juh-hee!-ze-huss!"

Junior hesitated.

"I will strike her!" Shepherd Isaiah cried again. Didn't Junior understand the cue? That he must now allow Shepherd Isaiah the chance to bring down the rod? "By the will of Juh-hee!-ze-huss, we must chastise this sinner!"

Junior still hesitated.

"Juh-hee!-ze-huss wants us to punish this wayward sinner! We must do it now. Do it now! Do it now!"

Slowly, so slowly it began as a tremble, Junior began to turn away. Shepherd Isaiah saw that he was about to take his wife with him.

Disobedience! Shepherd Isaiah moved a step down to strike quickly.

Lightning hit, showing clearly for an instant the fury on Shepherd Isaiah's face.

"No," Junior said. Shepherd Isaiah's lapel microphone picked up every word, throwing the softness of his voice all through the church. "I can't do it. I've stood aside too many times. I love her. I can't let it happen again. Ain't Jesus supposed to be about love?"

✣

Angel could see the disbelief on Shepherd Isaiah's face. But only because she was so close to the front. For the rest of the congregation packed in the church, the shadows from the candles behind Shepherd Isaiah put him in black outline.

"Boy! It is the will of the Lord that all sinners be chastised. Do it now or suffer the wrath of God yourself."

"No!" Junior's voice grew stronger. "I've been thinking on it and praying on it. Jesus don't want people hurting other people. She run off and it wasn't until she was gone that I knew how much I loved her. It tore my heart into pieces, thinking it was me could have stopped it from happening. I'm leaving the church and taking her with me."

Jagged light flashed through the church, showing that Junior was pointing his hand at Shepherd Isaiah in anger. "When Retha put our boy in the hospital she disobeyed you," Junior said, "not

Jesus. If she hadn't disobeyed you, our boy would be dead, and it would be you to blame."

Shepherd Isaiah fumbled for the switch of his lapel microphone. The man's words had carried too clearly in the calm that followed the thunder.

"Maybe it's Jesus' will that doctors help us, doctors who care like Jesus did," Junior continued. "Ever think of that?"

Retha had risen, turned to her husband.

More rumbles in the church. Not from thunder. From the congregation.

Shepherd Isaiah frantically gestured to his elders. They moved forward and began to drag Junior to the side. Others hauled Retha into position again.

Shepherd Isaiah lifted the Holy Rod again. "Blasphemer!" His voice carried through the church, drowning out Junior's angry protest. "The sinner shall be punished!"

The elders who had rushed to take Junior away were the same elders who had been guarding Angel. From the beginning, she'd seemed too small to be much of a threat. Because of that, it had never occurred to them that she might have a weapon of any kind or that she'd attempt to use it.

Angel, of course, had taken advantage of this. The stun gun was hidden beneath her loose shirt. And now, unguarded, she scuttled forward in the darkness, unseen to anybody.

"The will of Juh-hee!-ze-huss! shall be done!" Shepherd Isaiah thundered. His voice rumbled through the darkness of the congregation, quelling the mutterings. He raised the Holy Rod of Chastisement as another lightning strike threw his entire arched figure into relief.

"If I am wrong," his voice echoed throughout the church

before the ensuing thunder hit, "let God himself strike me down!"

Another bolt of lightning.

In the total brief blackness that followed, before any eyes could adjust after the flash of light, Angel reached forward with her stun gun.

"I said, let God himself strike me—"

Angel jabbed the prongs of the stun gun solidly into the calf of Shepherd Isaiah's right leg. Just as another bolt of lightning flashed.

He croaked, then convulsed as he fell forward, landing on the steps in front of the pulpit. He twitched twice, moaned into his microphone, then lay completely motionless before the entire congregation in the candlelit church.

Angel fled at a full run.

A woman in the back of the church screamed. Then another. Yet all the screams stopped suddenly when an image flickered on the wall at the front of the church.

Angel had reached the projection room. It had not occurred to any of the adults around her that she could enter it by squeezing through the square hole in the wall that allowed for the projection of light. She'd gone looking for Nick earlier and found his Jeep parked behind the church. With her computer equipment. She'd retrieved it and gotten it ready, hoping for the chance to use it.

And now was the time.

She'd left her computer running, and all it took were a couple of quick mouse movements and a couple of mouse clicks.

Then, up on the entire front wall, where normally the verses to hymns were shown from the church projector, there was

Grammie Zora, sitting in her voodoo room. At first the image was
fuzzy, then became focused as Angel adjusted the projector.

✦

Grammie Zora's voodoo altar was framed by two chairs facing
each other, with the altar centered behind them. All the candles
were lit, and Grammie Zora sat in the chair on the right, allowing
her to view the plastic bead curtains that I knew were just off
camera.

"I'm here," she called out. Her face was in shadow. "Where
you remember the altar from your last visit forty years ago."

The candles in the church flickered, as if her voice had sent
a ripple through the air. Moments later, the person she'd been
speaking to appeared on the wall. Timothy Larrabee. White-
haired, in dark slacks and a dark turtleneck.

"Sit," Grammie Zora commanded. She pointed at the
empty chair.

Larrabee sat. The positioning of the chairs in front of the
altar and the way each faced the other suggested to me that
someone had taken great care to make the arrangement fit in the
viewfinder of the hidden camcorder.

Grammie Zora's voice was low, eerie. "When you last sat
here, I pitied you. Such a sad boy. Because of that, I indulged
your request."

"The curse worked." He laughed, slightly nervous. "She
died."

"The curse had nothing to do with it. I know now you came
here because you wanted it known that your grandmother had
been cursed. I have a witness. From the hardware store. She told

317

me something years later because she needed to confess and had no one else to listen to her. The night your grandmother died, we both know that you—"

"Are we here alone?"

"My granddaughter is asleep in her room. Why does that matter to you? Are you afraid someone might overhear what you have to say to me? or what I have to say to you?"

Larrabee gripped the edges of his chair, sitting straight. "No. Whatever you say is your word against mine. Do you still have that painting? I'll purchase it from you. How does twenty thousand sound?"

"Your word against mine? Are you talking about the past or the present?"

"The present?" Larrabee seemed genuinely puzzled. "What do we have to talk about now? Forty years have passed."

"Let us leave the past for now. But I will use it against you if I must. There is the painting you gave me. I'm sure the police will find it interesting to know why. And, of course, the letters hidden in the frame have their use, too."

"Sell me the painting. You know the price I'm willing to pay."

"So you do fear the past?"

"Name the price."

"Here is my price," she answered. "Make sure what is happening in the present ends. This is my only warning before I go to the police."

Larrabee leaned forward in his chair, showing his profile against the candlelight as sharply as if it had been cut with a knife. "Make sure what ends in the present?"

"The crown of thorns."

"You make no sense, old woman. I showed you the crown

of thorns when I was a boy. My grandmother is no longer alive.
It has already ended."

"Don't play me for the fool. I know about the torture, the
branding. It must end."

Frustration was obvious in Larrabee's voice. "What torture?
What branding?"

"I saw the marks. I remember what they looked like on you.
I've seen them again. On the others. Identical brands. It is
continuing, and it could only be happening because of you. It is
the Larrabee brand. Something that should have ended when our
people were set free."

Silence dragged out before Larrabee replied. He sounded
genuinely confused. "You're telling me that others . . ."

"My people, Timothy Larrabee. Held down, baptized, and
branded with the crown of thorns. Who else can be responsible
but you and your church?"

"Your people?"

"The people of my community. People with black skin. I want
it ended."

"You are speaking to the wrong person."

"Did you come alone? Or once my messenger brought you
the message about the crown of thorns, did others come with
you?"

Larrabee half stood. His intake of breath made his sudden
comprehension was obvious. "I don't believe this." He slumped
back onto the chair, burying his face in his hands. "I don't
believe this."

"So you are not alone," Grammie Zora said. "As I thought."

Larrabee stood, turned, and shouted. "Get in here! We need
to talk!"

Seconds later, the clicking of plastic beads off camera gave away the presence of the person he'd called.

That person spoke. Not to Larrabee. "Jeremiah, you can stay out there. I'll be fine."

The voice was easy to recognize. Shepherd Isaiah.

Larrabee faced the doorway. "It's you, isn't it? The only other living person who knows about my family's horrible past."

Isaiah stepped into the view of the camcorder as he answered. "The laws of the land are godless laws. Too many of God's people suffer injustice, and the godless courts set the guilty free."

"It's you," Larrabee repeated. He remained standing, almost a head shorter than Shepherd Isaiah. Larrabee clenched his fists. "It's you. And the elders. That's where you go on those nights. Your talk about Nathan Bedford and a third wave, it's more than talk. You're nothing more than a vigilante committee."

Isaiah showed no signs of anger. "My chosen ones follow me. I lead them on a path to glory."

"Glory? You hate blacks. I know that. Don't forget, I spent three years with you in a cell. The same three years when you found out about—"

"I don't hate them. I hate that they have gone beyond their rightful place. In the Bible—"

"No. Not here. Not more of your crazed Bible talk." Larrabee did not hide his anger.

Grammie Zora remained a silent spectator.

"Crazed Bible talk." A statement. "The same talk that makes it convenient for you to remain among us? Don't forget, I know how much of the church treasury goes to you. Convenient when that crazed Bible talk lets you take from the flock."

Larrabee refused to back away. "You're no different than I am. The flock really are sheep to you."

"They are my flock. They support my mission."

"A mission you hide from all but the Chosen. The rest—you take their gifts. Like trimming fleece."

"So be it. While sheep do need a shepherd, they also have their purpose."

"No longer," Larrabee said. "When I tell them, this will be over. I'm a lot of things, but I will not be part of—"

Isaiah put a hand on Larrabee's shoulder. Larrabee shoved it away.

Isaiah spoke gently. "Every one of my elders is prepared to swear that you've led them. All any judge needs to see is the scars on your own body. Why else do you think I chose that method? You, too, are a sheep waiting to be fleeced."

Larrabee backed away. He paced the room.

Isaiah spoke with equal softness to Grammie Zora. "You said there was something more you could take to the police. What was the threat you intended to use on this man? What's his secret? I thought the crown of thorns was all of it. He came to you as a boy?"

Grammie Zora didn't raise her head. She remained motionless, her hands folded in her lap.

"Speak to me, old woman."

Larrabee interrupted. "How are you going to stop her from going to the world with what she knows? End your KKK stuff now. I'll remain silent. I'll leave the church, but I will remain silent. As will she."

"I will not let an old black woman prevent me from carrying out God's mission."

"And God's mission is to kill her so that she will never speak again?"

"No!" Isaiah stopped, took control of himself. "No. I swore to God that I would never strike another person dead. Unlike you, my conversion in prison was real. No, I will only promise her that if she talks, someone, sometime, will come back and—"

"Do not make those threats." Larrabee raised his voice. "I agreed to help you build a church, not fund a white supremacist movement."

"You will not stop me. I believe the word as given to me by God. The word that puts us in our rightful place, a place that has been taken from us by the nonbelievers."

"The word that you've twisted for your convenience. End it."

"The word that I believe. You're the one whose soul is damned for using it for your convenience."

Grammie Zora finally spoke. "Enough."

Each turned to her, as if surprised she was still in the room.

Grammie Zora lifted a small pistol from beneath her shawl. She pointed it at the belly of Shepherd Isaiah. "Leave my home now. I have delivered my message. And you will listen."

CHAPTER

25

"There are a lot of things I'd like to ask, Angel."

"Maybe some other time, Nick? I don't feel much like talking right now."

I had knocked on the locked door of the projector room and asked her to let me in. She'd opened the door, then stood beside me, so quiet I could barely hear her above the rumbling of the rain on the roof. I doubt she realized she had reached for my hand.

The vibes inside the church had changed radically. It had begun to rain again, and it fell heavily, underscoring our conversation with that constant noise. But the worst of the storm had passed. The lightning strikes were far more sporadic now, and had lost their dramatic visual effects because the lights were on full power in the church sanctuary.

Below us, people stood in small groups, each group in animated discussion, as if a convention had just broken up. At the

front of the church, Retha now held Billy Lee in her arms. Junior
stood behind them, hugging Retha with one arm and stroking her
hair with his free hand. They seem lost in a little world of
contentment.

Shepherd Isaiah and Timothy Larrabee and Elder Jeremiah
had disappeared sometime during the incredible revelation that
had appeared on the wall at the front of the sanctuary. And when
it ended, the murmurs had begun, stopping when someone hit
the light switch, and beginning again as people slowly stood from
the pews and began to gather in clusters. Before going back to
Retha, Junior had unwrapped the tape from my wrists and ankles
to set me free.

"I can wait on questions," I said to Angel. "I know tomorrow
the police are going to have questions for you, and if you want,
I'll be there with you."

"Yeah," she said. Her voice was dull.

"Let's get your computer equipment together and go,"
I said. As soon as we got out of the church building and into
my Jeep, I'd call Jubil and tell him about it, and he'd send out
uniforms to look for Larrabee and Isaiah and Jeremiah. Jubil
would also want to see what I'd just seen. Tonight, maybe. Or
tomorrow. I just wanted to get out of the compound and back
into the city. The men who had been incriminated in the video
footage were not my worry.

"Yeah," Angel repeated, same dullness. "Get my stuff and
go." I wondered what had taken her to the depths of her obvious
sorrow.

I didn't know what else to say. My questions could wait.
I knew the answers to some of them anyway. When Grammie
Zora had seen the crown of thorns branded on the young man

who'd visited with his father, she would have remembered the
last time she saw it. That was the connection to Timothy
Larrabee. The scars on his back were so similar. So she'd
searched for him through Kellie Mixson and then sent for him.
Maybe she intended to have the scene filmed by Angel, as
enough proof for the authorities to stop the elders of the Glory
Church. Or maybe Angel had done it on her own. That question
was less important to me than my curiosity about the reason
Grammie Zora and Angel had waited so long to make the incriminating evidence public.

Other questions only Timothy Larrabee or Shepherd Isaiah
or Elder Jeremiah could answer, whenever the authorities caught
up to them. It was my guess that during three years of sharing the
same cell, Larrabee and Isaiah would have shared a lot about
their respective pasts. Maybe Isaiah noticed the crown of thorns
on Larrabee, or maybe Larrabee had volunteered it. And Isaiah,
in his twisted theology, had decided that it was time to continue
the Larrabee tradition on a whole new generation. It saddened
me greatly to think that he'd been able to assemble a group of
men who wanted to follow him and his quest for white suprem-
acy. It saddened me more that he'd used the Bible to justify it.

But fanatics were fanatics. Pastor Samuel was right. The
truths of the Bible gave them no power. But it was whatever
power they gained that allowed them to misuse those truths.

And so the innocent suffer.

✠

In the room, I saw how easy it had been for Angel to set up her
projection equipment. Because Isaiah had used a projector

himself, all she'd needed to do was put hers on the table instead of the church's. One cable connected her laptop to her projector.

"You snuck to my Jeep and took it out while I was talking to Shepherd Isaiah earlier, huh." One last effort at conversation.

"This is where he locked me and Retha after he picked us up near the hospital. Except I found my way out." She pointed at the square hole in the wall.

"How do you think he knew where to find you?"

"Nick, I don't want to talk. I just want to get back to Maddie."

"Right," I said. I had to remind myself it wasn't yet nine o'clock. An hour after the flight that had taken Amelia away from me and back to Chicago. It seemed far, far later into the night.

"Please take me home," Angel said. "I'll give you something that I found in the painting. Something I've kept hidden from you. That will make us even."

I met her eyes. "Sure."

"Even," she repeated. "I don't owe you. And you don't owe me. That way Maddie and I can get back to our lives."

She left the other part unspoken.

Without you.

C H A P T E R

26

The next morning I found Pendleton at a marina well south of Charleston. One of the low-rent places, without any yachts. It was early enough that the morning air was still cool. A slight breeze rattled cables against sail masts.

Pendleton had stripped to the waist. He scraped loose paint off the side of a sailboat as old and dilapidated as a dozen others moored to the same dock. He stood at my approach.

"Your attorney said I could find you here," I said.

"What do you think?" Pendleton gestured at the sailboat. "Needs a little work, but when I'm finished, it should be okay." He winced and held out his hands, palms up. "Blisters. I've heard about them. Just didn't know they could hurt this much."

"I've read through the documents," I said, not succumbing to his boyish smile.

"Forty feet." He patted the hull of the sailboat. "I don't need much more than this. I started looking around at one-bedroom apartments in the price range I figured I could afford once all the legal stuff was finished. How depressing. When you think about it, a person doesn't need much more room than a sailboat like this. I told myself that living on the water beats putting up with neighbors. And there's the view. The worst marina in the world is still better than what you'd see from those crowded apartment buildings. So I figure boat living is the way to do it."

"If I understand what I've read," I said, "there's nothing left to dispute in court. Once I sign off on the papers, the deed of the mansion is transferred to my name. I get my portion of the trust fund. The IRS takes from your half."

"Everything you wanted, Nick. You haven't told me what you think about the boat. What I'm going to do is move slowly down the coast. Look for a small town, maybe on the gulf side of Florida. You know, go where the wind takes me. When I find the place that's right, I'll know it. Hook up to services at some marina, find a job. A regular job. Pumping gas, maybe. Some kind of job where I don't have to think, at least until I can find the courage to go beyond that. It'll give me enough to pay for docking fees and groceries. It'll be a simple life, but no one will know me. I'll find out who I really am. Growing up as a Barrett in this town, it's kind of like . . ."

He stopped. Stared at a pelican that floated overhead.

"Just like that," I said. "Everything is over. You're gone."

"Growing up a Barrett in this town is kind of like having an . . . exoskeleton. That's the word I'm looking for. Exoskeleton. Like insects, they have their skeletons on the outside, but it limits their growth. Sure their skeleton is hard and it's great protection, but it's also a prison. Growing up with our money and our name

was like having an exoskeleton squeezing me and keeping me
from growing. I'm breaking loose, Nick."

"What about your wife and daughter?"

"I've left all my tailored suits in the closet. Same with my
shoes. We're pretty close to the same size, Nick. I figured you
wouldn't mind having that kind of wardrobe waiting for you
when you moved in. That doctor friend of yours, she likes the
fancy stuff, doesn't she, Nick? She'll love that fine clothing on
you. And if you don't like it, there's always the Salvation Army.
But I thought I'd give you first chance at it."

"What about your wife and daughter?"

"Ex-wife, Nick. She and I are strangers. Our daughter?
She's not really mine." He caught the look of surprise on my
face. "Oh, biologically, she's mine. But I've been giving this a lot
of thought. I haven't been a father to her. And all the chances
she's given me. I keep remembering her at different times.
When she was little, she'd come running across the room every
time she saw me, as if I'd been gone for a year, even if I'd just
gone to the kitchen to grab a drink. What hurts is remembering
how I'd never stop to pick her up. Still, she kept trying. When
she was in school, again and again, she'd believe me when I'd
tell her that I'd show up for a play or a soccer game, and again
and again, I'd disappoint her. She's seen me do other things,
Nick. Drink too much. Yell at her. Yell at her mother. Worse
than that. I made that girl grow up far too quickly. And for all
practical purposes, without a father."

"So you're running away."

He lost his placid, sad expression as the old Pendleton
returned. "You know, you should grow a white beard and walk
around with one of those shepherd's crooks. That way you'd not

only sound like Moses calling down judgment on sinners but look like him, too."

"Sorry." I meant it.

"I'm not running from Charleston, Nick. I'm running to . . . to . . . to . . ." Pendleton leaned against the hull. "All my life, I've taken the easy way. Leaving here is one of the hardest things I've ever done. You think I don't know what's ahead? Lonely, lonely nights, when every dark hour squeezes your soul like a vise. The same nights I've faced here. I hope I get through it, Nick. I hope I don't end up a bum with a bottle in a bag. That's the easy way out. But the only way to find out if I'm somebody worth anything is to go looking. Break out of this exoskeleton and find out what's really me. And if who I am turns out to be worth anything, then I'll send for my daughter—summers, maybe—and she and I will get to know each other, and then she'll see that she really does have a father worth loving."

"I wish you the best," I said.

"Sounds like you mean that."

"It's the reason I came out here."

"Ship sails this afternoon, Nick. Guess that's one good thing about growing up a Barrett. You learn how to handle a boat."

I hesitated. What I needed to say was not going to come easy for me. "Remember what you asked me in the restaurant?"

"Forgiveness? Didn't think I was going to get it by asking again. Or by waiting. Making sure you got the house and the trust fund that you should have inherited won't make up for all the rest of it, Nick. But at this point, it's all I can do. Lets me leave with the clearest conscience possible."

"What's this sailboat worth?"

"Ten years old. Needed more work than I imagined."

"So someone gave it to you?"

"Broker owed me a favor," Pendleton answered. "Found it for me at next to nothing."

I knew what "next to nothing" was. Ten years old or not, it was still a forty-foot sailboat. Plenty of people didn't make what it cost in a year. I knew it because his attorney had told me. In confidence. Told me about the monthly payments that Pendleton faced.

"Pendleton," I said, "here's how you can make things straight between you and me." I handed him an envelope. "Promise me you won't open this until you've found the marina you told me about. You know, on the gulf side of Florida."

"That's it?"

"That's it. And what you asked me in the restaurant." Funny how difficult it was to even say the word *forgiveness*. This was my brother. I stepped forward and hugged him. "Yes."

"Takes a load off," he said when I stepped back. His eyes met mine. "You can't know how much."

Holding on to hatred is just as big a burden as carrying the sin that caused it. In the envelope was the deed to the sailboat. He owned it free and clear. When he got to where he was going, he'd be truly free.

"You're wrong," I said. "I do know. When you're settled, give me a call. Tell me how you're doing."

✠

I reached lower King Street an hour later. Was grateful to find a parking spot almost immediately.

At the antique shop, Willy stopped me at the front door, just before I stepped out of sunshine, midmorning heat and humidity, and worn-out tourists. He squinted at me suspiciously.

"Yes?" I said.

"I opened that package you had sent here for me. Did you make a mistake and give me something you meant for someone else?"

"Someone else?"

"Yes." His squint deepened. "Like a friend."

"Trust me. It was for you."

"But a first edition of *The Catcher in the Rye.* How did you know I collect?"

"I asked Glennifer and Elaine what would impress you."

"Why?"

"They asked the same question," I said. "I didn't give them the answer. But you, I will."

"And?"

I dropped my voice to a whisper. He stepped forward. "I need a favor."

He stepped away. "What kind of favor?"

I motioned with my hand for him to keep his voice down.

I continued to whisper. "Please," I said, "It's driving me nuts. Tell me what you know about those two and chewing tobacco. I mean, how much worse can it be than reused tea bags?"

⬦

"When Timothy brought the painting to Grammie Zora as a boy," I said, "it also held two letters hidden between the canvas and the frame."

In the office in the back, Glennifer and Elaine had settled down with their tea, for I'd promised them an interesting story.

"Angel gave me the letters," I said. "And they explain a lot."

"The letters Agnes was heard screaming about?" Glennifer asked.

I nodded. "Timothy found them while searching for loose money in her bedroom. As you will see, there was good reason for Agnes to want them back so desperately."

I opened two folded sheets. I was on my way to deliver them to Jubil, but I knew Glennifer and Elaine would want to hear me read them first.

The paper was ancient, the fountain-pen ink faded. One letter in a woman's dainty handwriting. The other in a man's blockish printing, words misspelled. But I could read each plainly. And each told the same story. One was signed by Agnes Larrabee, the other by Samson Elias.

Identical letters of confession.

And the story they related took place over a hundred years earlier, when Agnes and her sister Mary were twenty years old, in a boat on the Cooper River.

For Mary had not drowned by accident as the newspaper reporter believed in 1890.

✛

That day, Mary and Agnes sat at the front of the dingy.

In the center of the dingy, facing the opposite direction, Samson Elias rowed with powerful strokes.

"Faster," Agnes called.

"Faster," Mary mimicked. She had a light branch and tapped his broad, muscular back. "Faster!"

Mary and Agnes had been tippling, as they liked to call it.

They'd tippled all through the picnic, not caring that Samson was able to observe. What did it matter to them, the opinion of a black servant?

As they had become giddy with the wine, they'd begun to comment, giggling softly at first, then more loudly, about the manlike frame of the fourteen-year-old boy. Samson's mother must have been prescient at his birth, for he'd grown like his biblical namesake.

On shore, standing and sweating in the formal clothing he'd worn to serve them their meal properly, Samson had become more uncomfortable at their giggles and comments. But he could not run from them, not without causing trouble for himself and his parents, who needed the income provided by the Larrabee family. His discomfort, plus more wine, had prompted more remarks and giggles from the girls.

Finally, they had commanded Samson to remove his jacket. He did, reluctantly. They walked around him slowly, examining him as if he were an exotic animal. He wore a white shirt with his black pants, held up by suspenders, which they plucked and let go. He bore it stoically, staring straight ahead as sweat drenched his shirt.

"Agnes," Mary said, "shall we see this magnificent creature at work?"

"What do you mean?" Agnes asked archly.

"Why, he can row us across the river. Those big, big muscles of his will be a wonder to behold."

It was a combination of the wine, the sense of power, and the hint of engaging in something taboo that became an elixir of danger that afternoon.

As Samson leaned into the action of rowing, his shirt loosened and worked partway up his back. The waistband of his black

pants folded and unfolded with his rhythmic actions. It showed
a four-inch band of his gleaming black skin.

And the scar. A crown of thorns.

"My, oh my!" Mary giggled. "Agnes, do you see?" She
pointed at the scar.

The memory of watching the baby get branded sobered each
of them. But only a little. Not enough to stop Mary from reaching
forward and touching the scar.

Samson jumped.

"Row harder!" Mary commanded. "You belong to us!" She
touched the scar again.

At this, Samson finally set the oars down. He half turned to
face them. "It ain't right," he said. "What you're doing ain't right."

"Shush," Mary said, still giggling. "What's it any different
than patting one of our horses?"

"Ah was born to a freed man," Samson said with what dignity
he could. "Ah've learned to read and write. Ah ain't no animal."

"You still belong to us," Mary countered, slyly. "Lift your
shirt. Show us that scar again."

"No ma'am."

"You dare disobey!" She said it with mock anger and giggled
again. "Lift your shirt!"

"No ma'am."

Mary stood, prepared to pull the shirt loose herself. She was
not accustomed to having her way thwarted. She lost her balance
and fell. Half drunk, she flailed, but her head hit the side of the
dingy and she splashed into the dark water.

In a flash, Samson leaned over the side. Managed to grasp
her long skirt. But his sudden action tilted the dingy too severely,
and Agnes toppled into the river, too.

"Help!" she screamed.

"Cain't swim!" Samson grunted. He pulled Mary closer. With great effort, he turned her over, barely managing to keep his balance as he remained in the boat. Mary was unconscious, but at least her face was above the water. "Cain't swim!"

"I'm drowning!" Panic and thrashing managed to keep her afloat, but Agnes could feel the weight of her sodden dress pulling her down.

She kicked toward Samson. "Help! Help! Help!"

Samson couldn't let go of Mary to grasp Agnes. Yet Agnes was going to drown, within his reach.

"No!" Agnes shrieked. "No!"

She managed to grab Mary's inert arm and used that to pull herself closer. Had she been thinking clearly, she could have hung on while Samson pulled Mary toward the boat. She could have then transferred her grip to the side of the dinghy and waited as Samson first pulled in Mary, then her.

But alcohol and panic disoriented Agnes. She climbed half out of the water on Mary's body and clutched at Samson's arm. "Pull me in!" she shrieked. "Pull me in!"

She pushed Mary away to get at Samson. Mary slipped out of his hands, and he grabbed Agnes.

Agnes sobbed and sobbed as he struggled to pull her into the dinghy.

And when they turned back to look, Mary was gone.

⊹

"Why the incriminating letters?" Elaine asked.

"All I can give you is a best guess," I said. "Each had a letter of confession from the other. The only way to guarantee that each would hold the secret. If one was exposed, the other would be."

"And for the rest of their lives," Glennifer added, "they were doomed to a servitude to each other. Samson was paid far more than any other servant in his position, because she had no choice."

Which, I believed, explained their odd relationship to each other for the rest of their lives. Neither could escape the other.

But there were unanswered questions. Glennifer spoke some of them out loud. "Were these letters why Samson poisoned her in the end? And why then, after all those years? Was he afraid with the letters missing that it would finally all come to light and that he needed to get rid of the only other witness to the drowning?"

"That's something I doubt we'll ever know," I said.

"My, oh my," Elaine said. "This is all so interesting."

"Interesting, Laney? That's a word we reserve for the excruciating times that someone forces us to listen to their child perform a horrendous rendition of a violin piece. All of this goes far beyond *interesting*. Poor Timothy Larrabee. Poor Samson. And all the others who have been hurt. It goes far beyond interesting."

"Let me remind you of an ancient curse," Elaine said, drawing herself up straight. " 'May you live in interesting times.' I am not insensitive to all the tragedy here. But I think, as that curse indicates, my adjective suffices. To think, it all began when we sent Nick to search for a small painting."

"It *began* with Agnes Larrabee and whatever happened in her life. Poor crazy woman. It *unraveled* when we sent Nick to that young girl's house."

"I think," Elaine countered, "that next Sunday I shall let you win at least one chess game. I always seem to suffer when you hold your bitterness throughout the week."

"And I think I shall make some more tea. Nicholas?"

"No, thank you, Glennifer. I told Jubil I'd meet him at the Sweetwater in half an hour."

"Well, that gives you plenty of time. It's just down the street."

"But a half hour? To walk that short distance?"

"Best excuse I could think of to leave now," I said. "I know you want to discuss your Sunday chess games."

"Satisfied?" Elaine said to Glennifer. "Your quibbling has driven this handsome young man away."

"*My* quibbling?"

I grinned. "I'll be back. I can't imagine life without the two of you."

"Hmmph," they said in unison.

"Go then," Glennifer told me, waving me away. "Before you get sentimental on us."

"Just so you know, I think there's still more to this," I said. Which was why I was meeting with Jubil.

"Really?"

"Give me a day or two."

"Certainly, Nicholas. We'll have tea waiting. Guest tea."

"One last thing."

"Yes?"

"After all that I've gone through to satisfy your questions about the painting," I said, "won't you at least finally tell me about the chewing tobacco?"

Both of them giggled.

C H A P T E R

27

"This explains their motivation," Jubil said after reading the letters.

The table I preferred—at the window—was already taken. So we sat in a booth at the wall, beneath Billy Holiday, who looked down us from a large poster.

"Motivation?"

"Timothy told me about the Jesus room," Jubil said. "The true version. Of course, by then I'd found more than enough leverage on him to get him to talk."

"True version? More than enough leverage?"

"Didn't have much to begin with. The digital video footage that Angel showed in the church shows that he was likely unaware of the vigilante action. Prosecutor would have a tough time nailing him with that. But he was using Isaiah, and Isaiah was using him, and all of them were using the Glory Church.

"For Larrabee, we had to chase the money trail. We've

been busy, Nick. The accounting people have been ripping apart the Glory Church's books. Turns out Larrabee hadn't done anything real fraudulent. At least in the eyes of the law. He paid himself an enormous salary, kept it from the church members. Also diverted funds into real estate investments that were starting to snowball in a big way. Those guys were getting rich. There's enough to prove it was not a charitable or religious organization."

"No surprise."

"Maybe this will surprise you. Through a third party, Timothy Larrabee had already purchased the old Larrabee mansion. He was ready to bolt the church and start his Charleston life all over again."

"In a way," I said, "I feel sorry for him."

"I've been a cop too long to feel sorry for people. I figure people make choices. When they end up in trouble, they should only blame themselves. Not the government. Not their family. Nothing. But . . ." Jubil let out a long breath, looked out on the street, then turned his gaze to me. "I see Timothy Larrabee today and I think of him as a little boy, and I'll admit there were a lot of reasons for him to be messed up."

"The Jesus room."

"What happened in there had nothing to do with Jesus," Jubil said. "Let me tell you what Timothy told me about his last night in the Jesus room."

✣

In his early eighties, Samson Elias was still strong by most standards, and certainly powerful enough to force any struggling ten-

year-old boy into submission, especially Timothy, who spent little
time playing sports.

Impassively, Samson held the boy's hands while the old
woman tied one end of a rope around his ankles. "This is for your
good, Timothy," she said. "Soon you will learn obedience to Jesus.
Since you are unwilling, I will commit your soul to him. Unless
you tell us where the letters are."

She repeated it again and again, while tightening the knot
with considerable expertise. Something in her eyes suggested the
insanity she'd long been fighting to keep from the outer world.
When she was satisfied the knot would hold, she moved to the
other end of the rope. It ran through a pulley that hung from a
center beam of the attic. She pulled it as tight as she could, then
nodded at Samson.

Samson stepped away. He took the rope from her and with
the same impassiveness, slowly pulled tighter and tighter, until
the boy's ankles rose off the ground. He kept pulling until the boy
was upside down, his hands scratching uselessly at the floor.

After struggling until he was exhausted, Timothy finally
ended his screams.

Agnes moved to the blazing logs in the fireplace of the
Jesus room on the third floor of the mansion. A long-handled
piece of iron protruded from the heart of the fire. She pulled
the iron out. An iron with the brand of a crown of thorns. The
end of it glowed red.

"No!" the boy screamed, finding new energy. He squirmed,
trying to jerk the rope loose. Instead, he dangled helplessly. "No!
No! No!"

"Hush," Agnes said, unperturbed by the volume of his
screams. "No one will hear anyway."

⁜

"Four separate scars," Jubil said. "Four little crowns of thorns. From the branding iron that had been used on the Larrabees' slaves during the Civil War. Think of the life that kid had."

"All Timothy had to do was show someone the fresh scars."

"Nick, this was 1961. Before crisis lines were set up. When things in the family were kept in the family. Besides, what boy wants to admit to the world he's been branded like a slave?"

Our waitress stopped by and took our orders. I grimaced at the fact that Jubil only wanted a chef salad. Then I reminded myself there was a reason he had a flat belly and ordered one myself.

"He admitted it to you now," I said.

"I'd done some routine follow-up," Jubil said. "Gave me enough leverage on Larrabee to get him to tell the story. One of my calls was to Celia Harrison's daughter. Remember her, married to a serviceman stationed in Germany?"

I nodded.

"When she heard I was a cop from Charleston, she broke down. Seems she's been waiting a long time to tell her story. Not the one she gave you. But the rest of it. At the hardware store the day she started the fire, she knew why little Timmy did it. He wanted a diversion so he could do some simple shoplifting."

I nodded again. Took my coffee, thought of adding cream, thought of why I needed a chef salad, put the cream back, told myself a few extra calories would make life a lot easier, added the cream.

"She said she never told anyone at the time because she didn't know why he wanted it. Then, when Agnes was dead, it was too late. She was afraid maybe she'd get blamed, because in a

way, she'd helped him. She was a black girl, and here was a rich
old white woman dead."

Jubil sipped his own coffee. Without cream. "It was rat
poison, Nick. Little Timmy shoplifted some rat poison. That's the
leverage I had on him. That's why he told me about the Jesus
room. All of it. More than what Angel learned by listening to him
and Grammie Zora."

"*Samson* didn't poison the old woman; Timothy did?"

"Yes. But he didn't intend to kill her. At least that's his story.
He said he went to Grammie Zora to get a hex put on his grandmother. He stole the poison to make Agnes sick, to prove that the
hex of a voodoo woman was stronger than what she believed in.
After they branded him that night, he was more determined than
ever to poison her. When she died the way she did, right in front
of him, he panicked. In the confusion that night, he slipped the
rat poison into Samson's room, thinking that if Samson got sent to
jail, Samson couldn't hurt him anymore. Poor kid didn't understand a black man killing a white woman would face the death
sentence. And by the time it got that far, little Timmy was in way
too far to turn around and come clean with the truth."

"Just like Celia Harrison's daughter," I said.

"Just like Celia Harrison's daughter. We're going to have
to reopen the case, but I doubt the prosecutor will do anything
with it."

"And Samson," I said, "he was just doing what he was told
in the Jesus room."

"No." Jubil said it sharply. "He had no choice either. He
was her slave. You and me, we're friends. But you're not black.
There's some things you'll never really understand in your gut,
where it matters."

I couldn't argue, so I didn't.

I was glad when the salads arrived. I could concentrate on eating, make it a distraction, let the tension settle. I searched my mind for a subject change and came up with one easily.

"Any word on Grammie Zora?"

"Just what Angel has said again and again. That sometimes Grammie Zora leaves for weeks at a time and doesn't explain where she's going or when she'll be back. Angel said it's voodoo stuff."

"I don't buy that. Zora admitted on the video footage that she doesn't believe in her own voodoo."

"Opium for her people, huh?" There was bitterness in Jubil's tone. " 'Course, that wasn't much different than what Shepherd Isaiah was giving to his flock." Jubil set his fork down. "So you tell me. Why's that different from the faith you have?"

I thought about it for a moment. "I think when you truly follow Jesus, it's not for what you get outright, it's for what you get when you give. And you don't understand it truly until you're there."

"You understand it then. You're there?"

"I've got a long ways to go."

More silence as we ate. It felt like Jubil had been happy to take me away from my questions about Zora. I could be as stubborn as he was. "So," I said, "you're not worried about finding Zora."

"Angel seems fine."

"That wasn't my question. You've got a material witness. Gone."

"If she doesn't come back, I'll have to file a missing person report. And if that happens, the state will move in and Angel and

Maddie will become part of a foster-parent program. In the meantime, Angel seems fine living as she is. Camellia's family is right down the street. I mean, Angel's been fine for the last few months. What does it matter if I leave her where she is? Especially since I'm going to make it a point to stop by two or three times a week. And she has my cell phone number if she needs me quick."

"You sound defensive, Jubil."

"I'm not." Anger. "Let it go."

"In the meantime, what does Angel do for money?"

"I said let it go. She's fine where she is. She'll get a good chunk of change when the painting sells. And for now, we don't need Grammie Zora. When we find Jeremiah Sullivan, he'll face prosecution for murdering Bingo, even if the only thing we have is his confession to you. The tax people are working on getting the goods on Timothy Larrabee. And because Angel had a backup DVD, we'll get enough on Isaiah and his white supremacist group to do some big damage there, too. My only worry is the media's really playing up the torture and branding, and setting a bunch more white idiots out to copycat the Glory Church." He grimaced. "And no apology for that 'white idiot' remark."

"So you're not worried about Angel."

"Nick, one more time: Let it go. She's not your problem anymore. What are you going to do, adopt her? You'd need a wife first, and you chased the best prospect you had out of town."

"Funny."

He turned the conversation away from Angel, and I didn't fight him anymore on it. We finished and moved out to the street.

"Thanks for lunch. See you later. Don't call me. I'll call you.

Good-bye." And he left me alone in front of the Sweetwater. In a hurry to leave me and my questions about Grammie Zora.

✢

I was to move into the Barrett mansion the next day. Tonight would be my last night in the Doubletree. As midnight approached, it was little consolation against a loneliness that was as familiar to me as my own skin.

I did have one certainty in my life. After an adult life of rootlessness, I'd decided not to resist the siren call of Charleston. It was my home. I loved its history, the Old World feel of the lower peninsula and my sense of belonging to it. I would live here in the Barrett mansion, even if my coexistence at times might be one of mutual suspicion with those neighbors south of Broad that I regarded as hoity-toity. But my judgment of them, too, was snobbery of sorts; perhaps in the end I wasn't much different than those who had surrounded me in my childhood.

Earlier, I'd drafted a resignation to the community college in New Mexico. I'd decided my love for astronomy would simply be that of an intense amateur. Later, when I told Elaine and Glennifer about my decision, they made noises about a nearby antique store for sale, one that specialized in Civil War artifacts. After all, I did love history.

I'd met Retha after lunch and spent most of the afternoon with her. At the Sweetwater Café, of course. She'd talked and talked and talked, then surprised me by giving me a gift, a coffee-table book with photos of Charleston. It wasn't that I needed the book; it was the fact that I knew it would have taken a substantial part of her family's cash to pay for it. She and Junior were embarking on a new life, and that cash would have been very helpful.

Jubil and the authorities, of course, were taking care of the aftermath of the dissolution of the Glory Church. But I still had my final questions, and I ran them through my mind as I tried to fall asleep in the quiet darkness of the luxury suite. Strange, how the trappings of wealth did so little to console the soul.

When the phone rang just after 1:00 A.M., I wondered if it was Amelia to tell me she was sorry. And I was vaguely surprised that my heart didn't jump on its roller-coaster ride at the thought.

"Hello." My voice had congealed because I'd spent so many hours in silence. I cleared my throat. "Hello."

"Mr. Nick?"

I blinked. Placed the voice.

"It's Camellia," she said tentatively. "Angel's friend. She sent me running out the back door with Maddie to call for you. It's that big man. He's at her house."

"The police—"

"No. Angel said not the police. Anyone but the police. She said you. Can you come over?"

✢

The front door was slightly ajar and I smelled gasoline. I walked in, carrying a tire iron from the Jeep. The house was dark, but I knew immediately where to find Jeremiah Sullivan. I knew by the sound of Angel's voice.

"I'm not scared no matter what you do," she was saying. "I'm going to heaven."

"You're running out of time. Tell me or I light this match and you'll burn with the house."

"Then you'll never know where it is. And you can ask me for another half hour and I won't tell."

The voices came from the kitchen. I didn't hesitate. I pushed forward through the small living room and rounded the corner, forcing my mind not to think about what I needed to do. It is not something to contemplate—the act of smashing a man's skull. His outline was easy to distinguish, and I roared with primal rage to give myself the courage. The tire iron caught him across the side of the head as he half turned in surprise.

And that was it. He fell hard, scattering chairs on his way down.

"Angel!" I turned on the light.

Elder Jeremiah had remained true to his MO. She was taped to a kitchen chair, arms behind her, legs to the legs of the chair. There was a can of gasoline at her feet. A baseball bat on the floor.

"I tried hitting him," she said, "but he was too strong."

The smell of gasoline was nauseating. He'd splashed it everywhere. Blood trickled from his scalp into a puddle of the gasoline. It didn't mix.

"The police," I said. "We've got to call them."

"No."

"Angel—"

"No. Untie me. I'm going to kill him. I'll make his body go away. I've done it before."

I would not let her kill him. But I would not tell her that. Once I had her out of the house and away from Jeremiah, I would call the police.

I began to rip the tape loose. My hands shook with delayed fear. She didn't complain as I yanked the tape off the bare skin of her wrists.

"Let's go," I said when she stood.

She ignored me and picked up the bat. "I owe you now," she said. "Someday I'll repay you. But go away. I can do the rest."

I took the bat from her hands. "You're not going to kill him."

"If I don't, he'll come back."

"That's what the police are for."

"They'll ask why he came here." She tried to pull the bat loose from my hands. "I can't have that."

I picked her up and began to carry her, fireman-style over my shoulders, with her legs dangling in front of my chest. "I'm going to call Jubil."

She beat at my back and shoulders with her bare hands. She squirmed and wiggled. It was difficult enough for me to carry her in the first place; her resistance made it next to impossible.

Then, in the living room, I heard a *whoosh* behind me and a yellow light flared.

I spun and saw movement and fell backward, with Angel tumbling to the floor.

That's when the baseball bat whistled sideways over my head and into the wall. It had been swung with such force that the bat was stuck in the plaster.

As the attacker pulled it loose, I pushed awkwardly to my feet.

It was Jeremiah Sullivan, aluminum bat raised high again. Fire roared from the kitchen. I never would have believed a man could rise from the blow I'd delivered with the tire iron, let alone had the presence of mind to light a match before pursuing us.

"Angel! Go!" I shouted. She had grabbed his arm.

The bat came around again. Not at Angel, but at me. In the growling light of the fire, his blood was a mask down the side of Jeremiah's face. He swung in silence and I was barely able to dodge backward. Again the bat smashed into the wall. He pulled it loose and advanced again. He was calm and methodical, and it was terrifying.

I didn't speak to Angel. Just pulled her in the direction of the open door behind us.

But Jeremiah stepped sideways and with his massive body, blocked our escape. "You're dead," Jeremiah said. Same terrifying calmness. "Both of you."

I shoved Angel toward the kitchen. "Run." My voice was suddenly hoarse and guttural from the surge of adrenaline that washed through me.

She didn't run. That distracted me.

He'd learned from his first two misses. He did not swing at my head with the next move, a move relatively easy to duck or jump away from. Instead, he grunted and swung the bat sideways at my knees to cripple me. It was a move more difficult to dodge, and once I was crippled, writhing on the floor in agony, it would be a much simpler task to smash my skull.

With two healthy legs, I wouldn't have been able to jump or dive out of the way of that swooshing bat. Jeremiah hit me with a fully extended blow, directly at the knee. Had he been on the other side of me, it would have shattered the side of my knee.

Instead, the force of the swing carried his bat all the way through my leg, an unexpected lack of resistance that jerked him off balance. And my prosthesis popped loose, sliding out from the bottom of my pants leg and across the floor into the wall.

It startled Jeremiah just enough to distract him as badly as his loss of balance.

Angel chose that moment to attack. She jumped onto the baseball bat and wrapped her body around it. He brought his fist down on her back, and she screamed in pain.

With only one leg, I had no stability, nothing for a base to make an effective swing. But I had two good arms.

Jeremiah raised his fist again, staggering at the weight of Angel's body on the bat that she refused to relinquish. His back was toward me, and I leaped feebly upward.

I wrapped my forearms around his neck, squeezing hard against the cartilage of his throat.

He staggered backward, ramming me into the wall. I kept my head forward, and my shoulders took the brunt of the blow.

Jeremiah dropped the bat and clawed over his head, trying to get a grip on my hair. Then he rammed me into the wall again, driving us through the plaster. A support beam hit me square between the shoulder blades, sending agony into my ribs. I almost let go at the audible crack of separating bone.

He reached for my forearms as he staggered forward again, trying to rip them loose from his throat. I clutched harder, amazed at the strength of his fingers on my wrists. But with my body weight pulling me down on his back and his massive hands straining to pull my arms apart from the front, I felt myself slipping.

How much longer before he passed out?

My arms began to slip apart. He grunted with satisfaction and rammed me backward again. I was a rag doll, flopping nearly uselessly, sliding down his back, unable to endure the searing pain of my broken ribs taking another blow. As I slowly lost my grip, I heard the sound of death. My death. He took a ragged gasp for air, a horrible sound of triumph for him. I knew I'd lost.

Yet the next sound was more horrible, a sound clearly heard above the growing roar of the fire. It was the pinging sound of a bat resonating at the impact against bone.

Jeremiah began to topple as he screamed, an unnaturally high-pitched animal cry.

The horrible ping came again as Angel swung at his other knee. "I hate you! I hate you!" she screamed.

He fell sideways, and I had to roll away from him to avoid being crushed.

"I hate you!" Angel screamed. She swung at his head, but with him tumbling, the bat bounced off his shoulder. "I hate you!"

The next blow glanced off his shoulder and into the side of his head. Just enough to daze him. "I hate you!" She brought the bat up again.

"Angel!" I shouted. I was on my hands and one knee. "Angel!"

The fire was spreading now, and we were in danger.

"Angel!" I could see it in her eyes. She wanted to kill the man. She was going to swing down, like an ax into wood. "Angel!"

Camellia rushed past me and clutched at her. "Angel. Think about Maddie!" she shouted. "She needs you, and you won't do her no good in jail!"

I lunged forward and awkwardly grabbed the end of the bat.

But Angel didn't try another swing. "Where is she?" Angel shouted back.

"Out there with Mama. She needs you."

Angel followed Camellia out. She went straight to Maddie.

SIGMUND BROUWER

I pushed onto one foot and used the bat as a cane. It was barely enough support to allow me to grab Jeremiah's collar with my free hand to try to heave him toward the front door. I would have failed, but Camellia's mother came in shouting for me and helped drag the unconscious giant to the safety of the sidewalk. By then, most of the lower portion of the house was engulfed in flames.

Sirens had begun to scream in the distance.

I found my cell phone and dialed a number. When Jubil answered, I swallowed for air and said, "You're not going to believe this. . . ."

C H A P T E R

28

On Sunday, as the church bells rang across lower Charleston,
I drove to the cemetery where Camellia had told me I would find
Angel. From the road that wound its way among the tall trees and
the headstones, I saw Angel showing Maddie how to lay flowers
on a grave.

Angel had lifted her head as the car approached. I waved and
waited for her to wave back. Things were still unresolved between
us. That conversation we'd had on the front steps just as the fireflies
had begun to glow. The fact that I'd lied to her in the beginning.

I parked. I was driving a rental. With my prosthesis
destroyed, there was no way I could operate a clutch.

Finally, she stepped away from the grave. She took Maddie
by the hand and both of them walked toward me.

I moved awkwardly out of the car and used crutches to
meet them. Until I had my prosthesis replaced, it was the only
way I could get around. A man on a leg and a half.

I pointed to the base of an old oak and Angel nodded.
I leaned my crutches against the tree and sat. Angel sat beside
me and let Maddie explore the grass beside us.

"Hey," I said, "let me tell you a story about cheap people."

"Those two old ladies who reuse their tea bags?" Her arms
were crossed. She leaned on her knees. Looked away from me.
"You told me about that once already."

Despite her body language, I wasn't going to give up that
easily. "Actually, their father and mother. You'd like those two
ladies. Sure, they own a shop on King, but they grew up poor.
That's why they can't change their old habits. Bad as they are,
their parents . . ."

I waited and waited, until she spoke with a degree of impatience. "What about their parents?"

I hid my smile. Finally, some interest. "Believe it or not, the
mother liked to chew tobacco."

"Gross!"

"They lived out of town. It was a long time ago. It was not
a hoity-toity family."

"Hoity-toity?"

"You know, uppity. Thinking they were better than the rest
of the world."

"Oh."

"Anyway, their father liked chewing tobacco, too."

Angel sat up. "Don't try to tell me that when she was
finished chewing a wad, he'd take over and give it another chew.
If you do, I swear I'm going to barf."

"*Vomit* sounds nicer."

"Barf. I'm not hoity-toity like you."

"Either way, you're in luck and you won't have to throw up.

Much as it bothered them that the mother would have to throw out a perfectly good wad when she was done with most of the juice, they didn't chew the same wad twice. It's not like bubble gum. You know, put it under a desk and leave it for someone else later."

"Yuck!" Angel squealed.

This was fun.

"Turns out," I said, "the father decided to switch to smoking a pipe. Wasn't as satisfying to him as chewing and spitting, but with a pipe, why he could take the old chewed-up tobacco, let it dry, and smoke it until there was nothing left."

Maddie came close again, and Angel hugged her to her chest. "I like that story, Nick. But why'd you really come out here?"

"Angel," I said, "anything you might tell me in answer to my questions will stay with me. I promise."

"Well, I ain't promising you those answers."

"Thanks for the encouragement," I said.

"Weren't encouragement."

"I know."

"So ask."

"Grammie Zora got you to hide in the closet and use your camcorder, right? She knew she was going to invite Larrabee over to the house. Otherwise, she would have gone to the Glory Church to face him."

"Yeah," Angel said. "It was Grammie Zora's idea. I told that to your cop friend, Jubil."

"So what took so long?"

"I don't understand."

I hesitated, wanting to frame my questions so they wouldn't

drive Angel away. "Grammie Zora's whole reason for inviting Larrabee was to get it on video that he was the one torturing people. It turned out better than she expected. Shepherd Isaiah admitted enough that the police could have stopped him, just based on the video that you shot from the closet."

"Grammie's smart."

"Angel, they visited your house a couple of months ago. Why didn't Grammie take it to the police the very next day and use the video to stop them then?"

"She was scared, real scared. They said they'd come back and hurt her family. You heard it."

"Then why show it at all? At the church."

"Retha. I had to do it to help her. Even if it meant putting us in danger. I knew how much Retha wanted to be with her baby. 'Cause that's how I feel about Maddie."

"*You* had to do it? Not Grammie?"

Angel set Maddie aside and folded her arms again. "You done with your questions?"

"Sure," I said. "Because I think I got answers."

"I don't want to listen." She stood and reached for Maddie.

"Angel, you got Grammie Zora's house here with no mortgage, and you're smart enough to pay the bills and the taxes as they come in. You got Camellia and her mother right next door to look over you. And you've got Grammie Zora's social security checks coming in that you can cash with the computer guy down the street."

"I ain't listening to you."

But she was, looking across at the gravestone with the fresh flowers she'd just placed. In my mind, I heard something Angel had said fiercely to me more than once: "*All I got is Maddie, and all she's got is me.*"

"That night at the Glory Church, I don't think you showed everything that happened," I said. I lowered my voice to a near whisper. "I think Jeremiah came back because there was more that happened, and he knew you had it on video. I think that's why you were afraid to call the police to stop him, because then they'd ask what he wanted."

No reply.

"Grammie's dead, isn't she, Angel?"

I believed Jubil knew this but didn't want it confirmed. Because if it was, he'd have to do something about it. Leaving it lie meant Angel could stay where she was.

Angel kept staring at the gravestone. She hugged herself and her shoulders began to shake as she cried in silence.

I didn't dare put an arm around her to comfort her. I was not someone she trusted.

"Are you going to tell anyone, Nick?" she asked, sitting down again. "All I've got is Maddie, and all she's got is me. I'm so scared they'll take us away and make us live in different homes."

"I'm not going to tell," I said. "And if you want to talk about it, I'm here to listen."

Which I did.

As she spoke, I couldn't fathom how much courage it had taken for Angel to make her decision to live alone in the world, how she was able to force herself to move forward from the horrible event that had ripped so much love from her life.

✛

Angel was there in the closet with the camcorder, just the way Grammie Zora had arranged it as a trap for Timothy Larrabee.

Angel, like the camcorder, was a witness as Grammie Zora lifted a small pistol from beneath her shawl and pointed it at the belly of Shepherd Isaiah.

"Leave my home now," Grammie Zora commanded. "I have delivered my message. And you will listen."

This is all that Angel had shown at the church. But there was more for her to witness from the closet.

Elder Jeremiah stepped into the small room with the voodoo altar, holding Maddie. "Such a sweet child," he said. "Even if she is black."

Grammie swung the pistol toward him.

"No, old woman. You might harm the baby. Can you live with that?"

Without warning, Elder Jeremiah tossed Maddie the short distance to Grammie Zora. Her first instinct was Maddie's safety, and she lunged for her, dropping the pistol as she caught the baby. Elder Jeremiah calmly stepped forward and kicked the pistol away.

"That problem is solved, brother," he said to Shepherd Isaiah. "Now go on out. I'll take care of the rest of it."

"You can't kill the woman. I've suffered endless hell because I was responsible for another's death."

"Who said anything about killing?" Elder Jeremiah replied. "Now go. And don't ask questions. But make sure this white-haired weasel doesn't leave. He and I are going to have a discussion about his silence, too."

"You ain't going to kill him neither," Shepherd Isaiah said. "I can't abide killing."

"I'll leave the church quietly," Larrabee said. "Give me all my money, and I'll go. Just stop the torture."

"Sure." If Elder Jeremiah was going to lie about Grammie Zora, he'd lie about ending the branding, too. Anything to get them out of the house.

When they left, Elder Jeremiah turned to Grammie Zora, who sat very still with Maddie in her lap. "My brother," Jeremiah began, "he's spent his whole life protecting me. Now it's my turn to help him. I'm sorry it's come down to this."

Grammie Zora knew his intent. There was something about his intense calm. "Don't hurt the baby. She's too young to be any danger to you."

"Fair enough, I won't. As long as you don't fight me on this. When I'm done, I promise I'll lay you in bed, as if it happened in your sleep. That's how the neighbors can find you. The little one won't have to grow up thinking anything but old age took you away from her. "

"If you must, then I wouldn't want anyone to try to stop you. Because then Maddie might get hurt."

"Yes, old woman. I already told you I'd leave the child be."

Elder Jeremiah stepped toward the elderly woman.

Grammie Zora faced death without fear. She didn't resist as he put his massive hand over her nose and mouth and gently pinched off her breathing. Didn't fight as she lost air and finally all consciousness. Because she knew that there was another who needed her last gift of protection. One she loved as much as she loved Maddie.

Grace Louise. Her little angel. Helpless in the closet.

✛

"I had to watch it," Angel said, barely controlling herself. "I couldn't do anything. If I did, then what would happen to

Maddie? I knew I couldn't stop him and Grammie was going to die. But Maddie needed me. Oh, Nick, what could I do? I chose Maddie over Grammie."

She lost control. Violent sobs racked her body. This time I did put my arm around her. I thought of what I'd finally learned about my own mother, who in her final moments had been thinking only of me. I thought of the intense private agony that Angel had endured, believing she'd betrayed her grammie. I thought of her bravery. Again. Of the DVDs of her mother and her grammie she played in the solitude of a pitiful house in a pitiful neighborhood. But because she'd been loved, unlike Timothy in his tragic childhood, this angel had not been broken.

I allowed my own tears as I waited for Angel to stop weeping. It was a long wait. I doubt she'd allowed herself to openly grieve for Grammie Zora until this moment.

"Oh, Nick," she said when she could finally speak, "I miss Grammie. I hope she don't hate me for choosing to save Maddie."

"She told you to," I said quietly. "She wasn't speaking to Jeremiah when she said she didn't want anyone to try to stop him. She was speaking to you. She knew the same thing, Angel. You couldn't stop what he intended to do. And your silence was the only hope for you and Maddie. You have to understand that."

There was another long silence.

"Then maybe Grammie will be proud of me," she said. "Once she was gone, I had to do what I could for Maddie. I knew there'd be enough money every month for us to live here. Much as I hated that man for doing what he did, I told myself I'd have to wait six years to bring what I had on my camcorder to the police."

"Because you'd be eighteen then. Old enough that no one could take Maddie from you."

"But when Maddie got sick and I knew I had to take her to the hospital, I had to find extra money. The painting was the only thing I could think of."

"You'll get it now," I said. An image of Richard Freedman popped into my head. Proud. Black. Who'd likely consider it a privilege to invest wisely on Angel's behalf. "I think I know someone who can help you make it last a long time."

She wiped her face. "That would be good, Nick."

Maddie began to get restless.

"I think I need to take Maddie home and feed her."

"Yeah," I said, filled with sorrow for Angel.

She must have understood the tone in my voice. "I'll be okay," she said. "We can live with Camellia and her family for as long as we need to. My rent money will help them plenty."

"Yeah," I said again. "Want a ride home?"

"We'll be okay. Really. Mama and Grammie Zora, they gave me love all the time. Whenever I want, I can close my eyes and feel what it was like when they hugged me and called me little angel."

So she understood, too. Love was what mattered.

"I know you got to go," she said. She patted my knee. "Don't worry. Me and Maddie, we got each other."

I hobbled back to the rental car on my crutches. I sat behind the steering wheel and looked for Angel. She and Maddie had gone back to Grammie's headstone.

I sat there, with the keys in my palm.

✢

Broken angels. Timothy Larrabee. Retha Herndon. Grace Louise Starr. Even me.

Weren't we all, in some way, broken?

I'd learned that the healing began by reaching for the love of God. Yet I'd learned there was more. That it wasn't about just taking this love. It was about giving it, too. This was the great command of Jesus himself, who gave up his own life and, while broken on the cross, had begged for his persecutors to be forgiven. This was the man I professed to follow. In whose name I wrote out numbers on slips of paper and sent those checks to charitable organizations. What love was there in that, in cold pieces of paper?

And what had I given in my role as a dispassionate observer of life? What had I ever truly committed to? To anyone.

I felt shamed by Angel. She was a thief. A scoundrel. A bold-faced liar. But when Retha had needed her help, Angel had decided to show the world the video footage that would rescue Retha. Despite the risk for Angel that the authorities might find out about Grammie Zora's death.

And Jubil. Who did find out about Angel, as she feared. But chose to risk his career by hiding what he knew.

So where was I in all of this?

⊹

I stepped out of the car, hobbled passed the rows of headstones, waited for Angel to look up from the quiet words she was speaking to her buried grandmother.

I stood there. A man with a recently acquired big empty house and a large inheritance.

"Nick?" she asked.

"You've heard of guardian angels," I said. "What would you think about an angel's guardian?"

She smiled.

Visit us at movingfiction.net

Check out the latest information on your

favorite fiction authors and upcoming new

books! While you're there, don't forget to

register to receive Page Turner's Journal,

our e-newsletter that will keep you up to

date on all of Tyndale's Moving Fiction.

MOVING FICTION...*leading by example*

THE NICK BARRETT MYSTERIES

OUT OF THE SHADOWS

A mysterious note lures Nick Barrett back to Charleston, where he discovers the dangerous secrets of his past.

"A riveting tale of intrigue..." *Publishers Weekly*
ISBN-10: 1-4143-0887-6 Softcover US $12.99
ISBN-13: 978-1-4143-0887-6

CROWN OF THORNS

Nick Barrett returns in another compelling psychological thriller that explores the ultimate mercy—God's grace. Nick is drawn into another mystery as he unearths a secret hidden beneath Charleston's high society.

ISBN-10: 1-4143-0888-4 Softcover US $12.99
ISBN-13: 978-1-4143-0888-3

Coming Winter 2006

THE LIES OF SAINTS

A private investigator friend asks Nick Barrett for help in solving a cold case. Nick's investigation uncovers a century-old conspiracy to expose and punish the secret sins of Charleston's high society. Lives are at stake—including his own.

ISBN-10: 1-4143-0889-2 Softcover US $12.99
ISBN-13: 978-1-4143-0889-0

The Nick Barrett mystery series by best-selling author SIGMUND BROUWER will keep you turning pages.

for more information on other great Tyndale fiction,
visit www.tyndalefiction.com

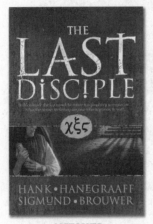

THE WEEPING CHAMBER

by SIGMUND BROUWER

Foreword by HANK HANEGRAAFF

SOFTCOVER ISBN 0-8423-8715-3

The Weeping Chamber transports us into the heart of ancient Jerusalem during the turbulent last days of Christ.

"A breathtaking journey that will lead you to the cross."
- HANK HANEGRAAFF